Michael Dobbs has spent many years at the most senior levels of British politics, advising Mrs Thatcher, Cecil Parkinson and many other leading politicians. He worked as a journalist in the United States throughout the Watergate crisis, and after returning to London in 1975 played major roles in the general elections of 1979 and 1983, and was Chief of Staff at Conservative Party headquarters during the 1987 elections. He has a doctorate in defence studies. He is currently Deputy Chairman of Saatchi & Saatchi and lives in London with his wife and young son.

'Pace and readability . . . a well-written and well-constructed political thriller. Let's hope it is the first of many.' *Sunday Times*

'The exciting new thriller that has Westminster buzzing . . . here is a political-thriller writer with a marvellous inside track knowledge of government. *House of Cards* is fast-moving, revelatory and brilliant.' *Daily Express*

'Watergate set in Westminster . . . *House of Cards* must not be allowed to fall into the hands of impressionable Tory backbenchers.' *Daily Telegraph*

'Whipping up a storm . . . the thinking man's Jeffrey Archer.' *Today*

'Michael Dobbs' first novel makes an appalling tale of skulduggery at Westminster into a tremendously exciting affair . . . he weaves his story convincingly with pace and style.' *Newsline*

For Amanda.
And for William

HOUSE OF CARDS

MICHAEL DOBBS

FONTANA/Collins

First published in Great Britain by
William Collins Sons & Co. Ltd 1989

A continental edition first issued
in Fontana Paperbacks 1989
This edition first issued 1990

Copyright © Michael Dobbs 1989

Printed and bound in Great Britain by
William Collins Sons & Co. Ltd, Glasgow

Part One

THE SHUFFLE

THURSDAY 10TH JUNE

It seemed scarcely a moment since she had closed her eyes, yet already the morning sun was waking her as it crept around the curtain and began to shine on her pillow. She turned over irritably, resenting the unwanted intrusion. The past few weeks had been hard, with days of poorly digested snacks washed down by nights of too little sleep, and her body ached from being stretched too tightly between her editor's deadlines.

She pulled the duvet more closely around her, for even in the glare of the early summer sun she felt a chill. It had been like that ever since she had left Yorkshire almost a year before. She had hoped she could leave the pain behind her but it cast a long, cold shadow which seemed to follow her everywhere, particularly into her bed. She shivered, and buried her face in the lumpy pillow.

She tried to be philosophical. After all, she no longer had any emotional distractions to delay or divert her, just the challenge of discovering whether she really did have what it took to become the best political correspondent in a fiercely masculine world. But it was bloody difficult to be philosophical when your feet were freezing.

Still, she reflected, sex as a single girl had proved to be excellent basic training for politics – the constant danger of being seduced by a smile or a whispered confidence, the unending protestations of loyalty and devotion which covered, just for a while, the bravado, the exaggeration, the tiny deceits which grew and left behind only reproach and eventually bitterness.

And in the last few weeks she had heard more outrageous and empty promises than at any time since – well, since Yorkshire. The painful memories came flooding back and the chill in her bed closed unbearably around her.

With a sigh Mattie Storin threw back the duvet and clambered out of bed.

As the first suggestion of dusk settled across the June skies, four sets of HMI mercury oxide lamps clicked on with a dull thud, illuminating the entire building with 10,000 watts of high intensity power. The brilliant beams of light pierced deep behind the mock Georgian facade, seeking out and attacking those inside. A curtain fluttered at a third floor window as someone took a quick glance at the scene outside before retreating quickly.

The moth also saw the lamps. It was resting in a crevice in the mortar of the building, waiting for the approaching dusk. As the shafts of light began to pierce through its drowsiness, the moth began to tingle with excitement.

The lamps glowed deep and inviting, like nothing it had ever known. It stretched its wings as the light began to warm the early evening air, sending a tremor throughout its entire body. The moth was drawn as if by a magnet and, as it approached, the glow of the lamps became more intense and hypnotic. The moth had never felt like this before. The light was as brilliant as the sun yet much, much more approachable.

Its wings strained still harder in the early evening air,

forcing its body along the golden river of light. It was a source of unimaginable power which seemed to be dragging the willing moth ever deeper into its grasp. Nearer and nearer it flew – until, with one final triumphant thrust, it was there!

There was a bright flash and crackle as the moth's body hit the lens a millisecond before its wings wrapped around the searing glass and vaporised. A charred and blackened carcass fell back from the lamp towards the ground. The night had gained the first of its victims.

A police sergeant cursed as she tripped over one of the heavy cables. The electrician looked the other way. After all, where the hell was he supposed to hide the miles of wiring which now ran around the square. The graceful Wren church of St John peered down darkly in disapproval. You could almost feel it wanting to shake itself free of the growing crowds of technicians and watchers who now clung tenaciously around its footings. The ancient steeple clock had long since stopped at twelve, as if the church was willing time to stand still and trying to hold back the encroachment and pressures of the modern age. But like looting heathens they swarmed over and around it more vigorously with every passing minute.

Above the church's four soaring limestone towers, the dusk was slowly spreading red streaks through the skies over Westminster. Yet the day was far from over, and it would be many hours before the normal gentility of Smith Square crept back over the piles of discarded rubbish and empty bottles.

The few local residents who had remained in the square throughout the devastation of the campaign gave up a silent prayer to St John and his Creator that at last it was almost over. Thank God elections only happen every three or four years.

High above the square, in a portable cabin perched temporarily on the flat roof of party headquarters, the Special

Branch detectives in their election base were taking advantage of the relative lull while the senior politicians were out of London making one last effort in their constituencies. A poker school was in full session in one corner, but the detective inspector had declined to join in. He had better ways of losing his money. All afternoon he had been thinking of the WPC who worked on traffic control at Scotland Yard, all starched efficiency on duty and unrestrained passion off. He hadn't seen his wife since the start of the campaign nearly a month before, but he hadn't seen the WPC either. Now his first free weekend beckoned, and he would have to choose between the open pleasures of his mistress and the increasing suspicions of his wife. He knew that his wife would not believe him if he told her he was on protection duty again this weekend, and he had spent all afternoon trying to decide whether he cared.

He cursed silently to himself as he listened once more to the raised voices inside him, tearing him in different directions as they argued between themselves. It was no damned good; the decisiveness which he had displayed to all of his police promotion boards had simply deserted him. He would have to do what he always did in such situations – let the cards decide.

Ignoring the jibes of the poker school, he took out a pack of cards and slowly began building the base of a house of cards. He had never got above six levels before; if he got up to seven now, he would spend the weekend with the WPC and to hell with the consequences.

He decided to give Fate a helping hand and reinforced the base with a double layer of cards. It was cheating, of course, but wasn't that what it was all about? He lit a cigarette to calm his nerves, but the smoke only got in his eyes, so he decided on a cup of coffee instead. It was a mistake. As the strong dose of caffeine hit his stomach, he felt the little knot give an extra twist of tension and the cards began to tremble in his hand.

Slowly, carefully so as not to disturb the rising construction of cards, he got up from the table and walked to the cabin door, taking in the view as he gulped down the fresh evening air. The roof tops of London were bathed in the red glow of the setting sun, and he imagined himself on some Pacific island, stranded alone with the incandescent WPC and a magical supply of ice cold lager. He felt better now, and with fresh determination returned to the cards.

The cards seemed to rise effortlessly in front of him. He had now reached the sixth level, as high as his card houses had ever gone before, and he started quickly on the seventh level so as not to destroy his rhythm. Two more cards to go – he was nearly there! But as the penultimate card got to within half an inch of the top of the tower, his hand began to shake again. Damn the caffeine!

He cracked his knuckles to relax his fingers, and picked up the card once more. With his left hand clamped firmly around his right wrist for extra support, he guided the card slowly upwards and sighed in relief as he watched it come to rest gently on top of the others. One more to go, but try as hard as he could he was unable to stop the tremble. The tower had become a great phallic symbol, his mind could see nothing but her body, and the harder he tried to control it the more his hand shook. He could no longer feel the card, his fingers had gone numb. He cursed Fate and implored it for just one last favour. He sucked in another lungful of breath, positioned the shaking card a half inch above the tower and, scarcely daring to look, let the card fall. It dropped precisely into its appointed place.

Fate, however, had other ideas. Just as the inspector watched the final card complete his masterpiece, the first cool breeze of evening passed across the top of Smith Square, lightly kissed the tall towers of St John's, and wafted through the door of the cabin which the inspector had left open. It nudged gently into the house of cards, which first trembled, then twisted, and finally crashed to the table top with a roar which cut dead the inspector's

11

inner cry of triumph and echoed inside his head as loudly as if the house had been built of brick and steel.

For several long moments he stared at the ruins of his weekend, trying in desperation to convince himself that he had after all succeeded, if only for an instant, before his house of dreams had crumbled. Perhaps he had, but he knew now he would have to make up his own mind. He felt more miserable than ever.

His private misery and the poker game were cut short by the crackling of the radio in the corner. The Party Chairman was on his way back from visiting the troops at the front line, and soon other senior politicians would be joining him in party headquarters. The work of the long night was about to begin for the Special Branch protection officers. Just time for the inspector's colleagues to lay a few final bets as to which Ministers they would still be protecting next week, and which would by then have been dumped in the great waste bin of history.

The Right Honourable Francis Ewan Urquhart was not enjoying himself. Ministerial office brought many pleasures, but this was not one of them. He was squashed into the corner of a small and stuffy living room pressed hard up against a hideous 1950s standard lamp, which showed every sign of wanting to topple over. Try as he could, he had been unable to escape the devoted attentions of the posse of matrons who doubled as his constituency workers and who now surrounded him, chattering proudly about their canvass returns and pinched shoes. He wondered why they bothered. This was suburban Surrey, where Range Rovers stood in the driveways and only got mud on their tyres when being driven carelessly over the lawns late on a Friday night. They didn't count votes here, they weighed them.

He had never felt at home in his constituency, but then he never felt at home anywhere any more, not even in his native Scotland. As a child he had loved to wander through

12

the bracing, crystal air of the Perthshire moors, accompanying the old gillie on a shoot, lying for hours in the damp peat and sweetly scented bracken waiting for the right buck to appear, just as he had imagined his older brother was waiting even at that same moment for German tanks in the hedgerows outside Dunkirk. But the Scottish moors and ancestral estates had never completely satisfied him and, as his appetite for politics and power grew, so he had come steadily to resent the enforced family responsibilities which had been thrust at him when his brother failed to return.

So amidst much family bitterness he had sold the estates, which could no longer provide him with an adequate lifestyle and would never provide him with a secure majority, and at the age of thirty-nine had exchanged them for the safer political fields of Westminster and Surrey. His aged father, who had expected no more of his only surviving son than that he devote himself to the family duties as he and his own father had done, had never spoken to him again. To have sold his heritage for the whole of Scotland would have been unforgivable, but for Surrey?

Urquhart had never disciplined himself to enjoy the small talk of constituency circles, and his mood had begun to sour as the day drew on. This was the eighteenth committee room he had visited today, and the early morning smile had long since been transfixed into a rigid grimace. It was now only forty minutes before the close of the polling booths, and his shirt was wringing wet under the Savile Row suit. He knew he should have worn one of his older suits: no amount of pressing would get it back into shape again. He was tired, uncomfortable and losing patience.

He spent little time in his constituency nowadays, and the less time he spent the less congenial his demanding constituents seemed. The journey to the leafy suburbs, which had seemed so short and attractive when he had gone for his first adoption meeting, seemed to grow longer

13

as he climbed the political ladder from backbencher through Junior Ministerial jobs and now attending Cabinet as Chief Whip, one of the two dozen most powerful posts in the Government, with its splendid offices at 12 Downing Street just yards from the Prime Minister's own.

Yet his power did not come directly from his public office. The role of Chief Whip does not carry with it full Cabinet rank. Urquhart had no great Department of State or massive civil service machine to command; his was a faceless task, toiling ceaselessly behind the scenes, making no public speeches and giving no television interviews. Less than 1 per cent of the Gallup Poll gave him instant name recognition.

His was a task which had to be pursued out of the limelight for, as Chief Whip, he was responsible for discipline within the Parliamentary Party, for delivering a full turnout on every vote. Which meant he was not only the Minister with the most acute political antennae, knowing all the secrets of Government before almost any of his colleagues, but in order to deliver the vote day after day, night after night, he also needed to know where every one of his Members of Parliament was likely to be found, with whom they were conspiring, with whom they might be sleeping, whether they would be sober enough to vote or had any personal crisis which could disrupt their work and the smooth management of parliamentary business.

And in Westminster, such information is power. More than one of his senior colleagues and many more junior members of the Parliamentary Party owed their continuing position to the ability of the Whips Office to sort out and occasionally cover up their personal problems. And many disaffected backbenchers had found themselves suddenly supporting the Government when reminded of some earlier indiscretion which had been forgiven by the Party and Whips Office, but never forgotten. Scarcely any scandal in Government strikes without the Whips Office

14

knowing about it first, and because they know about it first, many scandals simply never strike – unless the Chief Whip and his ten Junior Whips wish it to.

Urquhart was brought up sharply by one of his ladies whose coyness and discretion had been overcome by the heat and excitement of the day.

'Will you still stand at the next election, Mr Urquhart?' she enquired brashly.

'What do you mean?' he spluttered, taken aback.

'Are you thinking of retiring? You are sixty-one years old now, aren't you? Sixty-five or more at the next election,' she persisted.

He bent his tall and angular figure low in order to look her directly in the face. 'Mrs Bailey, I still have my wits about me and in many societies I would just be entering my political prime,' he responded defensively. 'I still have a lot of work to do and things I want to achieve.'

But deep down he knew she was right. Instead of the strong red hues of his youth, he was now left with but a dirty smear of colour in his thinning hair, which he wore over-long and straggly as if to compensate. His spare frame no longer filled the traditionally cut suits as amply as in earlier years, and his blue eyes had grown colder with the passage of time. While his height and upright bearing presented a distinguished image in the crowded room, those closest to him got no warmth from his carefully rationed smile, which revealed only uneven teeth badly stained by nicotine from his forty-a-day habit. He was not ageing with the elegance or the authority for which he would have wished.

Time was not on his side. Like most of his colleagues he had first entered Parliament harbouring unspoken ambitions to make it all the way to the top, yet during his career he had watched as younger and less gifted men had found more rapid advancement. The bitter experience had tempered his ambition while not being able to extinguish it completely. If not Downing Street, then at least a major

Department of State would allow him to become an acknowledged national leader, repaying his father's scorn with greater prominence than the old man could ever have dreamed of. He still had time to make his mark. He believed in his destiny, but it seemed to be taking an unholy long time to arrive.

Yet now was surely the time. One of the most important responsibilities of a Chief Whip is to advise the Prime Minister on any Ministerial reshuffle – which Ministers should be preferred, which backbenchers deserved elevation, which colleagues were dispensable and should make way. Not all the suggestions were accepted, of course, but the majority usually were. He had given the post-election reshuffle a lot of thought, and he had in his pocket a hand-written note to the Prime Minister covering all his recommendations. They would not only mean a stronger and more effective Government, and God knew they needed that after the last couple of years, but also one in which his close colleagues and allies would be in the strongest positions of influence. And he, of course, would have that prominent position which he had so long deserved. Yes, at last his time had come.

He tapped his pocket to reassure himself that the envelope was still there, just as Mrs Bailey switched her attention to the proposed one-way system for the High Street shopping centre. He raised his eyes in supplication and managed to catch the attention of his wife who was busily engaged in conversation on the far side of the room. One glance told her that his rescue was long overdue, and she hurried to his side.

'Ladies, you will have to excuse us, but we have to go back to the hotel and change before the count. I can't thank you enough for all your help, you know how indispensable you are to Francis.'

Urquhart made quickly for the door, but as he tried to complete his escape he was waved to a halt by his election agent, who was busily scribbling down notes while talking

16

into the telephone.

'Just getting the final canvass returns together,' she explained.

'That could have been done an hour ago,' snapped Urquhart.

The agent blushed. Not for the first time she resented Urquhart's sharp tongue and lack of gratitude, and promised herself that this would be her last election for him. She would swap this safe seat for a marginal seat as soon as she could. The pay would be even poorer and the hours longer, but at least she would be appreciated and not treated as another piece of constituency furniture. Or maybe she would give up politics altogether and go and get a proper job.

'It doesn't look quite as cheerful as last time,' she said. 'Turnout is poor, and a lot of our supporters seem to be simply staying at home. It's very difficult to read, but I suspect the majority will be down. I can't tell how much.'

'Damn them. They deserve a dose of the Opposition for a few years. Maybe that would get them off their complacent rumps.'

'Darling,' his wife soothed as she had done on countless previous occasions, 'that's scarcely generous. With a majority of 22,000 you could allow for just a little dip.'

'Miranda, I'm not feeling generous. I'm feeling hot, tired and I've had as much chatter about doorstep opinion as I can take. For God's sake get me out of here.'

As she turned round to wave thanks and farewell to the packed room, she was just in time to see the standard lamp go crashing to the floor.

The air of controlled chaos which usually filled the editor's office had gone, to be replaced by a sense of panic which was getting out of hand. The first edition had long since gone to press, complete with a bold front page headline proclaiming: 'Home and dry!'

But that had been at 6 p.m., four hours before the polls closed. The editor of the *Daily Telegraph*, like all other editors, had taken his chance on the election result in order to make his first edition of even marginal interest by the time it hit the streets. If he was right, he would be first with the news. If he got it wrong, he would be covered in it and would not be allowed to forget.

This was Greville Preston's first election as an editor. He was not feeling comfortable as he constantly changed the front page and demanded rewrites and updates from his political staff. He had been brought in just a few months earlier by the new owner of Telegraph Newspapers, and he had been given only one instruction: 'Succeed'. Failure was not an option if he wished to continue as editor, and he knew he would not be given a second chance – any more than would his staff. The demands of the accountants for instant financial gratification had required ruthless pruning, and a large number of senior staff had found themselves being 'rationalised' – as the accountants put it – and replaced by less experienced but equally less expensive substitutes. It was great for the bottom line but quite dreadful for morale. The purge left the remaining staff insecure, the loyal readers confused and Preston with a perpetual sense of impending doom, a condition which his proprietor was determined to do nothing to dispel.

Preston's efforts at increasing the circulation by taking the paper down-market had yet to show the promised results, and the smooth and dapper appearance which he effected was spoilt by the beads of perspiration and concern which constantly appeared on his brow and made his heavy rimmed glasses slip down his nose. The carefully manufactured attempt at outward authority had never fully hidden the insecurity within.

He turned away from the bank of television monitors which had been piled up against one wall of his office to face the member of staff who had been giving him such a hard time.

'How the hell do you know it's going wrong?' he shouted.

Mattie Storin did not flinch. At twenty-eight she was the

18

youngest recruit to the paper's political staff, having only recently replaced one of the senior correspondents who had fallen foul of the accountants for his habit of conducting interviews over extended lunches at the Savoy. Yet Mattie had a confidence about her judgement which belied the nine hectic months she had spent in the job. Anyway, she was as tall as Preston, 'and almost as beautiful' as she often quipped at his expense. She did not care for this new style of editor whose job was not so much to produce a prime quality newspaper but foremost to return a good profit. Preston came from the 'management school' of editing, where they teach readership audits and costs per thousand rather than what makes a good story and when to ignore the lawyers' advice; and it stuck in Mattie's gullet. Preston knew it, and resented Mattie and her obvious if raw and unfashioned talent, but he knew in many ways that he needed her more than she needed him. Even in the management school of journalism, a newspaper still requires a sharp journalistic nose to reach its circulation target, as Preston was slowly beginning to discover.

She turned to face him with her hands thrust defensively into the pockets of her fashionably baggy trousers, which in spite of the flowing lines somehow still managed to emphasise her willowy elegance. Mattie Storin very much wanted to succeed as a journalist and to develop the skills which she knew she possessed. But she was also a woman, a very attractive one, and was determined not to sacrifice her identity simply to conform to the typecasting expected of young women working their way up in journalism. She saw no reason why she should attempt either to grow a beard in order to have her talent recognised, or to play the simpering lovely lady to satisfy the chauvinistic demands of her male colleagues, particularly so inadequate an example as Preston.

She began slowly, hoping he would get the full flavour of her logic. 'Every single Government MP I've been able to talk to in the last two hours is downgrading his forecast, and every Opposition spokesman I have talked to is smiling. I've telephoned the returning officer in the Prime Minister's constituency, who says the poll looks as if it's going to be down by 5 per cent. That's scarcely an overwhelming vote of confidence. Something is going on out there. You can feel it. The Government are not yet home and are certainly not dry, and our story is too strong.'

'Crap. Every poll taken during the election suggests a strong Government win, yet you want me to change the front page on the basis of feminine instinct?'

Mattie could sense her editor's nervousness. All editors live on their nerves, but the secret is not to show it. Preston showed it.

'OK,' he demanded, 'they had a majority of 102 at the last election. Tell me what you think it's going to be tomorrow. All the opinion polls are predicting around 70 seats.'

'You trust the polls if you want, Grev,' she warned, 'but I'd rather trust the feel I get out on the streets. There's no enthusiasm amongst Government supporters. They won't turn out and it will drag the majority down.'

'Come on,' he bullied. 'How much?'

She shook her head slowly to emphasise her caution, her short blonde hair brushing around her shoulders. 'A week ago I would have said it would be about 50. Now it could be even less,' she responded.

'Jesus, it can't be less. We've backed those bastards all the way and they've got to deliver.'

And you've got to deliver, too, she mused. She knew that the editor's only firm political view was that his newspaper couldn't afford to be on the losing side. The new cockney proprietor, Benjamin Landless, had told him so and editors didn't argue with Landless. As the country's most recent newspaper magnate constantly reminded his already insecure staff, it was easier to buy ten new editors than one new newspaper, thanks to the Government's competition policy, 'so we don't piss off the Government by supporting the other bloody side'.

He had delivered his growing army of newspapers into the Government camp, and he expected his newspapers to deliver the proper election result. It wasn't reasonable, of course, but Landless had never found that being reasonable helped get the best out of his employees. Over lunch a few weeks earlier the proprietor had explained to Preston that a change of Government could be difficult for Landless, but for Preston such a result would be fatal.

Mattie tried again. She sat herself on the corner of the editor's vast and far too tidy desk and marshalled her case, hoping that for a change he would concentrate on her arguments rather than her legs.

'Look, Grev, forget the opinion polls for a minute. Put it in perspective. When Margaret Thatcher at last decided to retire, they concluded in their wisdom that it was time for a change of style. They wanted a new fashion. Something less abrasive, less domineering; they'd had enough of trial by ordeal and being shown up by a woman.'

You of all people should understand that, she thought.

'So in their wisdom they chose Collingridge, for no better reason than he was confident on TV, smooth with little old ladies and was likely to be uncontroversial.' She shrugged her shoulders dismissively. 'But they've lost their cutting edge. It's rice pudding politics and there's no energy or enthusiasm left. He's campaigned with as much vigour as a Sunday school teacher. Another seven days of listening to him mouthing platitudes and I think even his wife would have voted for the other lot. Anything for a change.'

For the tenth time that evening Mattie wondered if her editor used lacquer to keep his carefully coiffured hair so immaculate. She suspected he had an aerosol and hair-brush in his drawer, and she was certain he used eyebrow tweezers.

'Let's dispense with the analysis and mysticism and stick to hard numbers, shall we?' challenged Preston. 'What's the majority going to be? Are they going to get back in, or not?'

'It would be a rash man who said they wouldn't,' she replied.

'And I have no intention of being rash. Any majority will be good enough for me. In the circumstances it would be quite an achievement. Historic, in fact. Four straight wins, never been done before. So the front page stays.'

Preston quickly brought his instructions to an end by finding solace in his glass of champagne, but Mattie was not to be so easily put off. Her grandfather had been a modern Viking who in the stormy early months of 1941 had sailed across the North Sea in a waterlogged fishing boat to escape from Nazi-occupied Norway and join the RAF. He had handed down to Mattie not only her natural Scandinavian looks but also a strength and independence of spirit which she needed to survive in the masculine worlds of politics and newspapers. Her old editor on the *Yorkshire Post* who had given Mattie her first real job had always encouraged her to fight her own corner. 'You're no good to me, lass, if I end up writing all of your stories for you. Be a seeker, not just another scribbler.' It was an attitude which did not always commend itself to her new masters, but what the hell.

'Just stop for a moment and ask yourself what we could expect from another four years of Collingridge. Maybe he's too nice to be Prime Minister. His manifesto was so light-weight it got blown away in the first week of campaigning. He has developed no new ideas and his only philosophy is to cross his fingers and hope that neither the Russians nor the trade unions break wind too loudly. Is that really what the country wants?'

'Daintily put, as always, Mattie,' he taunted, reverting, as was his custom, to being patronising whenever he was confronted by an argumentative woman. 'But you're wrong,' he continued, sounding none too certain. 'The punters want consolidation, not upheaval. They don't want the toys being thrown out of the pram all the time.' He stabbed his finger in the air to indicate that the discussion was almost over and this was now official company policy. 'So a quiet couple of years will be no bad thing. And Collingridge back in Downing Street will be a great thing!'

'It'll be murder,' she muttered.

It was the Number 88 bus thundering past and rattling the apartment windows which eventually caused Charles Collingridge to wake up. The small one-bedroom flat above the travel agency in Clapham was not what most people would have expected of the Prime Minister's brother, but a messy divorce and an indulgent lifestyle had a nasty habit of making the money disappear much faster than it came in. He lay slumped in the armchair, still in his crumpled suit which had got him through lunch and which still carried some of it on the lapel.

He cursed when he saw the time. He must have been asleep for five hours yet he still felt exhausted. He needed a drink to pick himself up, and he poured himself a large measure of vodka. Not even Smirnoff any more, just the local supermarket brand. Still, it didn't hang on the breath or smell when you spilled it.

He took his glass to the bathroom and soaked in the tub, giving the hot water time to work its wonders on those tired limbs. Nowadays they often seemed to belong to an entirely different person. He must be getting old, he told himself.

He stood in front of the mirror, trying to repair the damage of his latest binge. He saw his father's face, reproachful as ever, urging him on to goals which were always just beyond him, demanding to know why he never managed to do things quite like his elder brother Henry. They both had the same advantages, went to the same school. But somehow Henry always had the edge, and gradually had overshadowed him in his career and his marriage. He did not feel bitter. Or at least he tried not to be. Henry had always been there to help when he needed it, to offer advice and to give him a shoulder to cry on when Mary had left him. Particularly when Mary had left him. But hadn't even she thrown Henry's success in his face? 'You're not up to it. Not up to anything!' And Henry had much less time to worry about other people's problems since he had gone to Downing Street.

As young boys they had shared everything together, as young men they had shared much, even a few girlfriends. But these days there was little room left in Henry's life for his younger brother, and Charles felt angry – not with Henry, but with life. It had not worked out for him, and he did not understand why.

He guided the razor past the old cuts on his baggy face, and began putting the pieces back together. The hair brushed over the balding pate, the fresh shirt and clean tie. He would be ready soon for the election night festivities to which his family links still ensured he was invited. A tea towel over his shoes gave them back a little shine, and he was almost ready. Just time for one more drink.

North of the river, a taxi was stuck in a traffic jam on the outskirts of Soho. It was always a bottleneck, and election night seemed to have brought an additional throng of revellers onto the streets. In the back of the taxi Roger O'Neill drummed his fingers impatiently, watching help-lessly as the bikes and pedestrians flashed past. He did not have much time.

'Get over here quick, Rog,' they had said. 'We can't wait all bleedin' night, not even for you. And we ain't back till Tuesday.'

He neither expected nor received preferential treatment, even as the Party's Director of Publicity and one of its best-known members of staff. But then he doubted whether they voted at all, let alone for the Government. What did politics matter when there was a lot of loose tax-free money to make?

The taxi at last managed to make it across Shaftesbury

Avenue and into Wardour Street, only to be met by another wall of solid traffic. Christ, he would miss them. He flung open the door.

'I'll walk,' he shouted at the driver.

'Sorry, mate. It's not my fault. Costs me a fortune stuck in jams like this,' replied the driver, indicating that O'Neill's impatience should not lead him to forget a tip.

O'Neill jumped out into the road, jammed a note into the driver's hand and dodged another motorcyclist as he made his way past peep shows and Chinese restaurants into a narrow, Dickensian alley piled high with rubbish. He squeezed past the plastic bin liners and cardboard boxes and broke into a run. He was not fit and it hurt, but he did not have far to go. As he reached Dean Street he turned left, and a hundred yards further down ducked into the narrow opening to one of those Soho mews which most people miss as they concentrate on trying either to find the whores or to avoid them. Off the main street, the mews opened out into a small yard, surrounded on all sides by workshops and garages which had been carved out of the old Victorian warehouses. The yard was empty and his footsteps rang out on the cobbles as he hurried towards a small green door set in the far, dark corner of the yard. He stopped only to look around once before entering. He did not knock.

Less than three minutes later he had re-emerged, and without glancing to either side hurried back into the crowds of Dean Street. Whatever he had come for, it clearly was not sex.

Inside party headquarters the atmosphere was strangely quiet. After the weeks of ceaseless activity during the general election campaign, most of the officers and troops had disappeared on election day itself to carry the combat into the far outposts of the constituencies, drumming up the last few and possibly crucial converts for the cause. Most of those who remained were by now taking an early supper at nearby restaurants or clubs, trying to sound confident and relaxed but lapsing repeatedly into insecure discussion of the latest rumours about voter turnout and exit polls. Few of them enjoyed the break, and they soon began drifting back, pushing their way through the ever-growing crowds of spectators and cordons of police. They found great comfort in their overcrowded and cluttered offices which for the last month had become their home, and they settled in for what would seem an interminable wait.

As Big Ben struck 10 o'clock and dusk at last began to take a firm hold, an audible sigh of relief went up from around the building. The polling booths had closed and no further appeal, explanation, attack, insinuation or – more predictably – almighty cock-up could now affect the result. It was over. One or two of them shook each other's hand in silent reassurance and respect for the job done. Just how well done they would shortly discover.

As on so many previous evenings, like a religious ritual they turned their attention to the familiar voice of Sir Alastair Burnet. He appeared for every purpose like a latter-day Gabriel, with his reassuring tones and flowing silver hair which had just enough back lighting to give him a halo effect. For the next few hours God would have to take second place.

'Good evening. The election campaign is now over. Just seconds ago thousands of polling booths across the country closed their doors, and the first result is expected in just forty-five minutes. We shall shortly be going over live for interviews with the Prime Minister, Henry Collingridge, in his Warwickshire constituency, and the Opposition leader in South Wales.

'But first ITN's exclusive exit poll conducted by Harris Research International outside 153 polling booths across the country during today's voting. It gives the following prediction . . .'

The country's most senior newsreader opened a large envelope in front of him, as reverently as if the A4 Manila contained his own death certificate. He extracted a large card from within the envelope, and glanced at it. Not too quickly, not too slowly he raised his eyes once more to the cameras, and the venerable broadcaster held 30 million viewers in the palm of his hand, teasing them gently. He was entitled to his moment. After twenty-eight years and nine general elections as a television broadcaster, he had already announced that this was to be his last.

'ITN's exclusive exit poll forecast – and I emphasise this is a forecast, not a result – is . . .'

He glanced once more at the card, just to check he had not misread it. His professional, emotionless eyes betrayed not a hint of his own views on the matter. From somewhere within Smith Square the sound of a prematurely loosened champagne cork broke the straining silence, but they ignored the cold and sticky froth as it splashed over the desk top.

'. . . that the Government will be re-elected with a majority of 34.'

The building itself seemed to tremble as a roar of triumph mixed with relief came from deep within. It was winning and only winning that mattered to the professionals, not how they played the game or how close the result. Time enough later for sober reflection as to whether they would be deemed to have had a 'good' war or not.

The whoops of joy drowned out the protesting tones of Sir Alastair as he continued to remind his audience that this was a forecast and definitely not a result, and in any event was much closer than the opinion polls had been predicting. The screen briefly divided between mute shots of the party leaders taking in the prediction, Collingridge displaying a thin humourless smile which indicated no pleasure, while the broad grin and shake of his opponent's head left viewers in no doubt that the Opposition had yet to concede. 'Wait and see,' he was mouthing, 'wait and see', but the producer did not wait to see and cut back to Burnet as he proceeded to report on the rest of the election night news.

'Bollocks,' Preston was shouting, his hair falling into his eyes. 'What have they done?' He looked at the ruins of his first edition, and began furiously scribbling on his note pad. 'Government Majority Slashed!' he tried. 'It's Too Close To Call'. 'Collingridge Squeaks In'. They all ended up in the bin.

He looked around desperately for some help and inspiration.

'Let's wait,' Mattie advised. 'It's only thirty minutes to the first result.'

Even without the first result, celebrations were already well under way at the Party's advertising agency. With the confidence that is shown by all positive thinkers, the staff of Merrill Grant & Jones Company PLC had been squashed for nearly three hours in the agency's reception area to witness history in the making projected on two vast TV screens. Not that history would be made for at least another seventeen minutes or so, but like all positive thinkers they prided themselves in being ahead of the game, and the champagne was already flowing to wash down an endless supply of deep pan pizzas and Big Macs. Indeed, the predictions of a drastically reduced majority had only served to spur those present on to greater efforts. Even at this early hour it was clear that two ornamental fig trees which had graced the reception area for several years would not survive the night, and it seemed probable that several young secretaries wouldn't either. Most of the wiser heads were pacing themselves much better, but there seemed to be little reason to exercise excessive restraint. Particularly as the client was setting a fearsome example.

Like so many expatriate Dublin adventurers, Roger O'Neill was renowned for his quick wit, exaggeration and determination to be involved in everything. So many and varied had been his involvements and so wittily had he exaggerated them that no one could be quite certain precisely what he had done before he joined the Party – it was something in public relations or television, they thought, and there was rumour about a problem with the Inland Revenue – but he had been available when the post of Publicity Director had become vacant and he had filled it with great energy, fuelled by a ceaseless supply of Gauloises and vodka-tonics.

As a young man he had shown great promise as a fly-half on the rugby field, but had never fulfilled it, his highly individualistic style making him ill-suited for team games. 'With him on the field,' complained his coach, 'I've got two teams out there, Roger and fourteen other players.'

At the age of forty his unruly shock of dark hair was now perceptibly greying and his muscle tone long since gone, but O'Neill refused stubbornly to acknowledge the evidence of middle age, hiding it beneath a carefully selected wardrobe worn with a deliberate casualness which displayed the designers' labels to their best advantage. His non-conformist approach and the lingering traces of an Irish accent had not always endeared him to the Party's grandees – 'all bullshit and no bottom' one of them had loudly observed – but others were simply overwhelmed by his unusual energy and charm.

And then there was his secretary. Penelope – 'Hi, I'm Penny' – Guy. Five foot ten, an exciting choice of clothes, a devastating figure on which to hang them. And she was black. Not just dusky or dark but a polished hue of black that made her eyes twinkle and her smile fill the entire room. She had a university degree in the History of Art, 120 wpm shorthand, and was ruthlessly efficient and practical. Of course there had been much gossip when she had first arrived with O'Neill, but her sheer efficiency had silenced, if not won over, the Doubting Thomases, of which there were many.

And she was totally discreet. 'I have a private life,' she explained. 'And that's just how it's going to stay.'

Right now at Merrill Grant & Jones – Grunt & Groans as Penny preferred to call them – she was effortlessly providing the centre of attention for several red-blooded media buyers plus the deputy creative director while at the same time carefully ensuring that O'Neill's glass and cigarettes were always available but closely rationed. She didn't want him going over the top tonight of all nights.

He was deep in conversation with the agency's managing director.

'I want you to complete the analysis as soon as possible, Jeremy. It's got to show just how effective our marketing and advertising have been in the election. It needs to be divided into the usual age and social groups so that we can show how we hit our target voters. If we win, I want everyone to know that they owe it to us. If we lose, God help us . . .' He sneezed violently. '. . . I want to be able to show the press that we beat them hands down at communications and it was only the politics which blew it. We shall have to live off this for the next few years, so don't screw it up. You know what we need, and it's got to be ready by Saturday morning at the latest if we're to get it in the Sunday papers as prominently as possible.'

He spoke a little more quietly. 'If you can't get the figures, make the bloody things up. They will all be too exhausted to look at them closely, and if we get in there first and loudest we'll be fine.'

He paused only to blow his nose, which did nothing to ease the other man's visible discomfort.

'And remember that I want you to send the most enormous bunch of flowers around to the PM's wife first thing in the morning. In the shape of a gigantic letter 'C'. She must get them as soon as she wakes up. She'll get into a twist if they don't arrive because I've already told her they are coming. And I want the TV cameras to film them going in and to know who's sent them, so make sure they are bigger and more eye-catching than anything they've ever seen before. Even better, send them round in the back of one of your company vans. That should look good pulled up outside Number Ten.'

The advertising executive was used to his client's breathless monologues by now, and even to some of the extraordinary instructions and accounting procedures issued by O'Neill. But a political party was unlike any other client he had ever encountered, and the last two years working on the account had given him and his youthful agency more than enough publicity to stifle most of the lingering doubts.

Now the election was over, however, and he was waiting nervously for the results, a silent fear struck him as he thought of what would happen if they lost; to have supported the losing side, probably to be made the scapegoat for failure. It had all looked rather different when they had started the work, with the opinion polls predicting a comfortable win. But his confidence had begun to evaporate with the exit polls. In an industry of images, he realised that his business could wither as rapidly as the flowers which O'Neill was making such a fuss about.

He sucked his lip nervously as O'Neill rattled on, until their attention was grabbed by the six-foot image of Sir Alastair, who was now holding his ear with his head cocked to one side. Something was coming through his earpiece.

'And now I believe we are ready for the first result of the evening, which looks likely to be in Torbay once again. Breaking all records. It is just forty-three minutes after the polls have closed, and already the candidates are gathering behind the returning officer and it's time to go over live . . .'

In Torbay Town Hall, amidst the banks of hyacinths and spider plants, rosettes and mayoral regalia, the first result was being announced. The scene resembled more a village pantomime than an election, as the promise of nationwide television coverage had attracted more than the usual number of crank candidates who were now doing their best to capture the moment by waving balloons and brightly coloured hats to attract the cameras' attention.

The Sunshine Candidate, dressed from head to toe in a bright yellow leotard and waving the most enormous plastic sunflower, stood firmly in front of the sober suited Tory, who tried to move to his left to escape from the embarrassment but only succeeded in bumping into the National Front candidate, who was inciting a minor riot in the crowd by displaying a clenched fist and an armful of tattoos. Not quite sure what his candidates manual would prescribe in such circumstances, he reluctantly retreated back behind the sunflower.

Sir Alastair came to his rescue. 'So there we have it from colourful Torbay. The Government hold the first seat of the night but with a reduced majority and a swing against them of, the computer says, nearly 8 per cent. What does that mean, Peter?' asked Burnet, as the screen cut to ITN's tame academic commentator, a bespectacled and rather ragged figure in Oxford tweeds.

'It means the exit poll is just about right, Alastair.'

'Great show, Roger, isn't it? After all, it looks like another majority. I can't tell you how absolutely relieved and delighted I am. Well done indeed,' enthused the chairman of one of Grunt & Groans major clients, thoroughly enjoying what was turning into a fully-fledged victory party irrespective of the fact that the Government had just lost its first two seats of the night. He was standing crushed together along with two other invited clients and the agency's chairman in a corner which gave some slight relief from the pressure of celebration going on all around.

'That's very kind of you, Harold. Yes, I think a 30 or 40-seat majority will be enough. But you must take some of the credit.' O'Neill was gushing. 'I was reminding the Prime Minister just the other day how your support goes way beyond the corporate donation. I remember the speech you gave at the Industrial Society lunch last March. You know, it was extremely good, you really got the message home well. Surely you've had professional training?'

32

Without waiting for an answer, O'Neill rushed on. 'You've pushed home the message about gaining co-operation from all sides by showing leadership from the top and I told Henry – I'm sorry, the PM! – that we need to find more platforms for captains of industry like you to express these views.'

'There was no need for that,' replied the captain without the slightest trace of sincerity. The champagne had already overcome his natural caution and images of ermine and the House of Lords began to materialise in front of his eyes. 'But that was very kind of you. Look, when this is all over perhaps we could have lunch together. Somewhere a little quieter, eh? I have several other ideas on which I would very much welcome your views.'

O'Neill's response was a series of enormous sneezes which bent him almost double, leaving his eyes tearful and rendering any hope of continued conversation impossible.

'Sorry,' he spluttered. 'Hay fever. I always seem to get it early.' As if to emphasise the point he blew his nose forcefully and wiped his eyes.

The TV screen promptly announced the loss of another Government seat, a Junior Minister with responsibility for Transport who had spent the last four years earnestly visiting every motorway crash scene in the country and who had quite convinced himself of the human race's unquenchable capacity for violent self-sacrifice. It did not help him, however, to accept their demand for his own self-sacrifice, and he was finding it very difficult to put on a brave face.

'More bad news for the Government,' commented Burnet, 'and we shall see how the Prime Minister is taking it when we go over live for his result in just a few minutes. In the meantime, what is the computer predicting now?'

He punched a button and turned to look at a large screen behind his shoulder. 'Still around 30 by the look of it.'

A studio discussion then began as to whether a majority of 30 was enough to see a Government through a full term of office, but the discussion was interrupted by more results which now began to flood in. O'Neill excused himself from the group of businessmen and fought his way through a growing and steadily more voluble group of admirers which had gathered around Penny. In spite of their protests he drew her quickly to one side and whispered briefly in her ear, as the ruddy face of Sir Alastair intruded once more into the celebrations to announce that the Prime Minister's own result was just about to be declared.

A respectful if not total silence grew over the revellers, and O'Neill returned to the industrial captains. All eyes were fixed on the screen. No one noticed Penny gathering her bag and slipping quietly out.

The screen announced another Government win, but yet again with a reduced majority. While the commentators analysed and sought to be the first to get in with their view that the Government were indeed having a less than splendid night of it, a loyal roar of approval arose from all the agency staff present, most of whom had by now totally forgotten their own political convictions and were ready to celebrate at the slightest excuse. After all, it was only an election.

The Prime Minister waved back from the screen, his stretched smile indicating that he was taking the result rather more seriously than was his audience. The festive mood began to drown out his speech of thanks to the returning officer and local police, and by the time he had left the platform to begin his long drive back to London two agency art directors were pronouncing the official demise of the battered fig trees.

A shout from across the room reached through to O'Neill's group.

'Mr O'Neill. Mr O'Neill. Telephone for you.' The security guard held the telephone up in the air and pointed dramatically to the mouthpiece.

'Who is it?' mouthed O'Neill back across the room.

'What?' queried the guard, looking nervous.

'Who is it?' he mouthed again.

'Can't hear you,' the guard yelled above the hubbub, gesticulating wildly.

O'Neill cupped his hands around his mouth and once more demanded to know who it was.

'It's the Prime Minister's Office!' screamed the frustrated guard, unable to restrain himself and not quite knowing whether he should be standing to attention.

His words had an immediate effect, and the noise of celebration subsided into an expectant hush. An avenue to the telephone suddenly opened up in front of O'Neill, and he slowly and obediently made his way over to the phone, trying to look modest and matter of fact.

'It's one of his secretaries. She will put you through,' said the guard, obviously grateful to hand over the awesome responsibility.

'Hello. Hello. Yes, this is Roger.' A brief pause. 'Prime Minister! How are you? Many, many congratulations. The result is really very good in the circumstances. A victory is sweet whether you win 5–0 or 5–4 . . . Yes, yes. Oh, that's so kind. I'm at the advertising agency as it happens.'

The room was now so hushed they could almost hear the fig trees crying. 'I think they have performed marvellously, and I certainly couldn't have done it without their support . . . May I tell them that?'

He put his hand over the mouthpiece and turned to the totally enraptured audience. 'The Prime Minister just wants me to thank you all on his behalf for helping run such a fantastic campaign. He says it made all the difference.' He went back to the phone and listened for a few seconds more. 'And he's not going to demand the money back!'

With that the room erupted into a great roar of applause and cheers, and O'Neill held the phone aloft to catch every last sound.

'Yes, Prime Minister. I am totally thrilled and honoured to receive your first telephone call after your own election . . . I look forward to seeing you, too. Yes, I shall be at Smith Square later . . . Of course, of course. I will see you then, and congratulations once again. Good night.'

He replaced the telephone gently in its cradle, and turned to face the whole room. Suddenly his face burst into a broad smile, and as he did so the entire gathering broke out into a series of ringing cheers. They pummelled him forcefully on the back as he tried to shake all their hands at once. He was still trying to force his way back to the beaming captains as, in the next street, Penny carefully put down the car phone and began to adjust her lipstick in the car mirror.

FRIDAY 11TH JUNE

The onlookers in Smith Square had increased dramatically in number as they waited for the Prime Minister's arrival. Midnight had long since tolled but tonight biological clocks would be stretched to the limit. They could see from the TV technicians' monitors that his convoy, escorted by police outriders and pursued by camera cars, had long since left the M1 and was now approaching Marble Arch. It would be less than ten minutes before they arrived, and three youthful cheerleaders were encouraging the crowd to warm up with a mixture of patriotic songs and shouts.

They were having to work harder than at previous elections. While some people were waving enormous Union Jacks, the members of the crowd seemed to be less keen on brandishing the large mounted photographs of Henry Collingridge with which they had been supplied. Several of them were wearing personal radios, and informing those around them of the results. Even the cheerleaders would stop occasionally to discuss the latest information.

They also had competition, because several Opposition supporters had decided to infiltrate the crowd and were now proceeding to wave their own banners and chant their own slogans. Half a dozen policemen moved in to ensure that high spirits on both sides were kept under control, but they did not interfere.

Reports began to circulate that the computers were now forecasting a majority of 28, and two of the cheerleaders broke off to indulge in an earnest discussion as to whether this constituted an adequate working majority. They concluded that it probably was, and returned to their task. But the crowd had turned into an unresponsive audience, the early enthusiasm increasingly deflated with concern, and they decided to save their effort until Henry Collingridge arrived.

Inside the building, Charles Collingridge was getting increasingly drunk. His ruddy and capillaried face was covered in perspiration, and his eyes were liquid and blood-shot.

'A good man, brother Henry. A great Prime Minister,' he was babbling. Those around him who were still listening could detect the alcoholic lisp which had begun to creep into his voice as he repeated the familiar family history. 'I always thought he would have been an even better man-ager of the family business, could have made it one of the country's truly great companies, but he always preferred politics. Mind you, manufacturing bath fittings was never my cup of tea, either, but it kept father happy. Henry could have grown the business, made something of it, I'm sure. Do you know they even import the stuff from Poland nowadays? Or is it Romania . . . ?'

He interrupted his monologue by knocking what was left of his glass of whisky over his already stained trousers and, amidst the fluster of apologies and appeals for help, the Party Chairman Lord Williams took the opportunity to move well out of range. His wise old eyes revealed none of it, but he resented having to extend hospitality to the Prime Minister's brother. Although Charles was not a bad man, he was a weak man who was becoming a bloody nuisance on a regular basis, and the Party's ageing and most senior *apparatchik* liked to run a very tight ship. Yet as experienced as he was, he was only the navigator and knew there was little point in trying to throw the admiral's brother overboard.

He had once raised the problem directly with the Prime Minister of the increasing rumours and the growing num-ber of snide references to his brother in the gossip columns. As one of the few men left who had been a prominent player even in the pre-Thatcher days, he had the seniority and some would argue even the responsibility to do so. But it had been to no avail.

'I spend half my time having to spill blood,' the Prime Minister had pleaded. 'Please don't ask me to spill my own brother's.'

Henry had agreed to ensure that Charles would watch his behaviour, or rather that he would watch Charles's behaviour himself. But he never really had the time, and he knew that Charles would promise anything even while he became increasingly incapable of delivering. He couldn't moralise or be angry, because he knew it was always the other members of the family who suffered most from the pressures of politics. And Williams understood that, too, for hadn't he gone through three marriages since he first entered politics nearly forty years ago?

It was not a matter of lack of love, more a lack of time for loving, with lonely women and neglected families stuck at home and suffering much more from the unkind barbs of politics than the politicians themselves. Politics left a trail of pain and tortured families in its wake, all the more hurtful because it was incidental and unintended. Even the hardened Party Chairman felt a twinge of sorrow as he watched Collingridge stumble from the room. But such feelings were not a sound basis on which to run a Party, and he resolved to have another discussion with the Prime Minister now that the election was over.

Michael Samuel, the Secretary of State for the Environment and one of the newest and certainly most telegenic members of the Cabinet, came over to greet him. He was young enough to be the Chairman's son, and he was something of a protégé for the elderly statesman. He had been given his first major step up the greasy Ministerial pole by Williams when, as a young Member of Parliament, on Williams' recommendation he had been made a Parliamentary Private Secretary, the unpaid skivvy to a senior Minister who is meant to fetch and carry, to do so without complaint and to offer his support without question on any issue – qualities designed to impress Prime Ministers when selecting candidates for promotion. Williams' help had ignited a spectacular rise through Ministerial ranks for Samuel, and the two men remained firm friends.

'Problem, Teddy?' Samuel enquired.

'Michael. A Prime Minister can choose his friends and his Cabinet, but unfortunately not his relatives.'

'Any more than we can select our colleagues.'

Samuel nodded towards Urquhart, who had just entered with his wife after driving up from his constituency. Samuel's glance was cold. He did not care for Urquhart, who had not supported his promotion to Cabinet and who on more than one occasion had been heard to describe Samuel as 'a latter day Disraeli, too good looking and too clever for his own good.'

The veneer over the traditional and still lingering anti-Semitism wore very thin at times, but Williams had offered the brilliant young lawyer good counsel. 'Don't be too intellectual,' Williams had advised, 'and don't look too successful. Don't be too liberal on social matters or too prominent on financial matters. And for God's sake watch your back. Many more politicians have been betrayed by their colleagues than have ever been destroyed by their opponents. Remember it.'

Samuel watched unenthusiastically as Urquhart and his wife were forced by the crush of people towards him. 'Good evening, Francis. Miranda.' Samuel forced his practised smile. 'Congratulations. A 17,000 majority. I know about 600 MPs who are going to be very jealous of you in the morning with a majority like that.'

'Michael! Well, I'm sure you managed to hypnotise the female voters of Surbiton once more. If only you could pick up their husbands' votes as well, you too could have a majority like mine!'

They laughed gently at the banter, accustomed in public to hiding the fact that they did not enjoy each other's company, but there was an embarrassed silence as neither of them could think of a suitable means of disengaging rapidly from the conversation.

They were rescued by Williams, who had just put down the phone. 'Don't let me interrupt, but Henry will be here any minute.'

'I'll come down with you,' volunteered Urquhart immediately.

'And you, Michael?' asked Williams.

'I'll wait here. There will be quite a rush when he arrives. I don't want to get trampled.'

Urquhart wondered whether Samuel was having a gentle dig at him, but chose to ignore it and accompanied Williams down the stairs, which had become crowded with excited office staff as the word had spread of the Prime Minister's imminent arrival. The appearance of the Party Chairman and Chief Whip outside on the pavement galvanised the cheerleaders, who resumed their attempts to raise the spirits of the crowd. An organised cheer went up as the armoured black Daimler with its battalion of escorts swung around the square, to be greeted by the brilliance of the television lights and a thousand flaring flashguns as both professional and amateur cameramen tried to capture the scene.

As the car drew to a halt, Collingridge emerged from the rear seat and turned to wave to the crowd and the cameras. Urquhart tried just a little too hard to get to him to shake his hand, and instead managed to get in the way. He retreated apologetically while on the other side of the car Lord Williams, with the chivalry and familiarity which comes of many years, carefully assisted the Prime Minister's wife out of the car and planted an avuncular kiss on her cheek. A bouquet appeared from somewhere along with two dozen party officials and dignitaries who all wished to get in on the act, and the whole heaving throng somehow managed to squeeze through the swing doors and into the building.

Similar scenes of confusion and congestion were repeated inside as the Prime Minister's party tried to push its way upstairs through the workers, pausing only for a traditional word of thanks to the staff from the stairs, which had to be repeated because of the press photographers had not managed to assemble themselves quickly enough.

Once upstairs in the relative safety of Lord Williams' suite, the signs of strain which had been so well hidden all evening began to appear for the first time on the Prime Minister's face. The television set in the corner was just announcing that the computer was predicting a still lower majority, and Collingridge let out a long, low sigh. His eyes wandered slowly round the room.

'Has Charles been around this evening?' he asked quietly. Charles Collingridge was nowhere to be seen. The Prime Minister's eyes met those of the Chairman.

'I'm sorry,' the older man replied.

Sorry for what?, thought Collingridge. The fact that my brother's a drunk? Sorry that I seem almost to have thrown away our parliamentary majority? Sorry that you will have to carry the can along with me? But anyway, thanks for caring.

He was suddenly feeling desperately tired as the adrenalin ceased to flow. After weeks of being hemmed in on all sides by people and without a single private moment to himself, he felt an overwhelming need to be on his own and he turned away to find somewhere a little quieter and a little more private. Instead he found his way blocked by Urquhart who was standing right by his shoulder. The Chief Whip was thrusting an envelope at him.

'I've been giving some thought to the reshuffle,' he said. 'While this is hardly the time, I know you will be thinking about it over the weekend so I have prepared some suggestions. I know you prefer some positive ideas rather than a blank sheet of paper, so I hope you find this of use.'

Collingridge looked at the envelope and raised his exhausted eyes to Urquhart. 'You're right. This is scarcely the time. Perhaps we should be thinking about securing our majority before we start sacking our colleagues.'

The sarcasm cut deep into Urquhart, deeper than the Prime Minister had intended, and he realised he had gone too far.

'I'm sorry, Francis. I'm afraid I am a little tired. Of course you're quite right to think ahead. Look, I would like you and Teddy to come round on Sunday afternoon to discuss it. Perhaps you would be kind enough to let Teddy have a copy of your letter now, and send one round to me at Downing Street tomorrow – rather, later this morning.'

Urquhart stood rigid with embarrassment at the semi-public rebuke he had received. He realised that he had been all too anxious about the reshuffle, and cursed himself for his folly. His natural assurance seemed to desert him when it came to Collingridge, a grammar school product who in social terms would have had trouble gaining membership of his club. The role reversal in Government unnerved him, unsettled him, and he found himself acting out of character when he was in the other man's presence. He was frustrated with his inadequacy, and quietly loathed Collingridge and all his kind for undermining his position. But now was not the time, and he retreated into affability.

'Of course, Prime Minister. I will let Teddy have a copy straight away.'

'Better copy it yourself. Wouldn't do to have that list getting around here tonight,' smiled Collingridge as he tried to bring Urquhart back into the conspiracy of power which always hovers around Downing Street. 'In any event, I think it's time for me to depart. The BBC will want me bright and sparkling in four hours' time, so I shall wait for the rest of the results in Downing Street.'

He turned to Williams. 'By the way, what is the computer predicting now?'

'It's been stuck on 24 for about half an hour now. I think that's it.' There was no sign of pleasure or sense of victory in his voice. He had just presided over the Party's worst election result in nearly two decades.

'Never mind, Teddy. A majority is a majority. And it will give the Chief Whip something to do instead of sitting idly around with a majority of over a hundred. Eh, Francis?' And with that he strode out of the room, leaving Urquhart clutching his envelope.

With the Prime Minister's departure the crowds both inside and outside the building began perceptibly to melt, and Urquhart made his way to the back of the first floor where he knew the nearest photocopier could be found.

Room 132A was not an office at all, but a windowless closet barely six feet across which was kept for supplies and confidential photocopying. As Urquhart opened the door the smell hit him before he had time to find the light switch. Slumped on the floor by the narrow metal storage shelves was Charles Collingridge, who had soiled his clothes even as he slept. There was no glass or bottle anywhere to be seen, but the smell of whisky was heavy in the air. He had crawled away to find the least embarrassing place to collapse.

Urquhart coughed as his nostrils rebelled at the stench, and he reached for his handkerchief and held it to his face. He stepped over to the body and turned it on its back. A shake of the shoulders did little other than disrupt still further the fitful heavy breathing. A firmer shake gave nothing more, and a gentle slap across the cheeks produced equally little result.

He gazed with disgust at what he saw. Suddenly Urquhart's body stiffened as his contempt mingled with the lingering humiliation he had suffered at the Prime Minister's hands and welded into a craving for revenge. He turned cold and the hairs on the nape of his neck tingled as he stood over the stupefied body. Slowly, powerfully, Urquhart's hand swung down and began to slap Colling-ridge's face and, as his signet ring began to rake across the flesh of the cheeks, the whole head whipped from side to side until blood began to seep from the mouth and the body coughed and retched. Urquhart bent over the other man, staring closely as if to see that the body still breathed. He remained motionless for several minutes, like a cat at its prey, his muscles tense and expression contorted until he straightened with a start, towering over the drunk.

'And your brother's no damned better,' he hissed.

He turned to the photocopier, took the letter out of his pocket, made one copy and left without looking back.

SUNDAY 13TH JUNE

It was the Sunday after the election. At 3.50 p.m. Urquhart's official car turned from Whitehall into Downing Street to be greeted by a policeman's starched salute and a hundred exploding flashguns. The press were gathered behind the barriers which cordoned them off across the road from the world's most famous front door. It stood wide open as the car drew up – like a political black hole, Urquhart thought, into which new Prime Ministers disappeared and rarely if ever emerged without being surrounded and suffocated by the protective hordes of civil servants. Somehow the building seemed to suck all political vitality out of some leaders.

He had made sure to travel on the left-hand side of the car's rear seat that day in order that his exit in front of Number Ten would provide an unimpeded view of himself for the TV and press cameras, and as he climbed out and stretched himself to his full height he was greeted by a chorus of shouted questions from across the road, providing him with a good excuse to walk over for a few quick words amidst the jungle of notepads and microphones. He spotted Charles Goodman, the legendary Press Association figure, firmly planted under his battered trilby and conveniently wedged between ITN and BBC news camera crews.

'Hello, Charles. Did you have any money on the result?' he enquired, but Goodman was already into his first question as his colleagues pressed around him.

'Are you here to advise the Prime Minister with the reshuffle, Mr Urquhart, or has he called you to give you a new job?'

'Well, I'm here to discuss a number of things, but I suppose the reshuffle might come into it,' Urquhart responded coyly.

'It's rumoured that you are expecting a major new post.'

'Can't comment on rumours, Charles, and anyway you know that's one for the PM to decide. I'm here at this stage solely to give him some moral support.'

'You'll be going to advise the PM along with Lord Williams, will you then?'

'Lord Williams, has he arrived yet?' Urquhart tried to hide any suggestion of surprise.

'About 2.30. We were wondering whether someone else was going to turn up.'

Urquhart hoped that they hadn't noticed the steel which he felt entering his eyes as he realised that the Prime Minister and Party Chairman had been working on the reshuffle without him for an hour and a half. 'Then I must go. Can't keep them waiting,' he smiled. He turned smartly and strode back across the road and over the threshold. He was annoyed, and it smothered the sense of excitement which he still felt whenever he passed that way.

The Prime Minister's youthful political secretary was waiting at the end of the corridor which led away from the front door towards the Cabinet Room at the rear of the building. As Urquhart approached, he sensed that the young man was uneasy.

'The PM is expecting you, Chief Whip,' he said quite unnecessarily. 'He's in the study upstairs. I'll let him know you have arrived,' and bounded off up the stairs.

It was a full twelve minutes before he reappeared, leaving Urquhart to stare for the hundredth time at the portraits of previous Prime Ministers which adorned the famous staircase. He could never get over the feeling of how inconsequential so many of the recent holders of the office had been. Uninspiring and unfitted for the task. Times had changed, and for the worse. The likes of Lloyd George and Churchill had been magnificent natural leaders, but one had been promiscuous and the other arrogant and often drunk, and neither would have been tolerated by the modern media in the search for sensationalism. The media's prying and lack of charity had cast a blanket of mediocrity over most holders of the office since the war, stifling individualism and those with real inspiration. Collingridge, chosen largely for his television manner, typified how superficial much of modern politics had become, he thought. He yearned for the grand old days when politicians made their own rules rather than cowering before the rules laid down by the media.

The return of the political secretary interrupted his thoughts. 'Sorry to keep you waiting, Chief Whip. He's ready for you now.'

As Urquhart entered the room traditionally used by modern Prime Ministers as their study he could see that, in spite of efforts to tidy up the desk, there had been much shuffling of paper and scribbling of notes in the previous hour and a half. An empty bottle of claret stared out of the waste paper bin, and plates covered with crumbs and a withered leaf of lettuce lurked on the windowsill. The Party Chairman sat to the right of the Prime Minister's desk, his notes spilled over the green leather top. Beside them stood a large pile of MPs' biographies supplied by party headquarters.

Urquhart brought up a chair and sat in front of the other two, who were silhouetted against the sun as it shone in through the windows overlooking Horse Guards Parade. He squinted into the light, balancing his own folder of notes uneasily on his knee.

Without ceremony, Collingridge got straight down to business. 'Francis, you were kind enough to let me have some thoughts on the reshuffle. I am very grateful; you know how useful such suggestions are in stimulating my own thoughts, and you have obviously put a lot of work into them. Now before we get down to the specific details, I thought it would be sensible just to chat about the broad objectives first. You've suggested – well, what shall I call it? – a rather radical reshuffle with six new members being brought into the Cabinet and some extensive swapping of portfolios amongst the rest. Tell me why you would prefer an extensive reshuffle and what you think it would achieve.'

Urquhart did not care for this. He had expected some inevitable discussion of individual appointments, but he was being asked to justify the strategy behind the reshuffle proposals before he had any chance to sniff out the Prime Minister's own views. He knew that it was not healthy for a Chief Whip to fail to read his Prime Minister's mind correctly, and he wondered whether he was being set up.

As he peered into the sunlight streaming in from behind the Prime Minister, he could read nothing of the expression on Collingridge's face. He desperately wished now that he had not committed all his thoughts to paper instead of talking them through, but it was too late for regrets.

'Of course, they are only suggestions, indications really of what you might be able to do. I thought in general that it might be better to undertake more rather than fewer changes, simply to indicate that you are firmly in charge of the Government and that you are expecting a lot of new ideas and new thinking from your Ministers. And a chance to retire just a few of our older colleagues; regrettable, but necessary if you are to bring in some new blood and bring on those Junior Ministers who have shown most promise.'

Dammit, he thought suddenly, that was a stupid thing to say with that ancient bastard Williams sitting on the PM's right hand. He knew he should have been more careful, and now he had a knot in the pit of his stomach. Collingridge had never seemed to be a Prime Minister with grip, one who enjoyed making decisions, and Urquhart had felt sure that most if not all of his proposals would be favourably received. All of his suggested promotions were men of talent which few would deny. He hoped that even fewer would realise that most were also men who owed him.

Ministers whom he had helped out of trouble, whose weaknesses he knew, whose sins he had covered up and whose wives and electors would never find out.

Williams was staring at him with his old, cunning eyes. Did he know, had he figured it out? The room was silent as the Prime Minister tapped his pencil on the desk, clearly having trouble with the argument Urquhart had put forward.

'We've been in power for longer than any Party since the war, which presents a new challenge. Boredom. We need to ensure we have a fresh image for the Government team,' Urquhart continued. 'We must guard against going stale.'

'That's very interesting, Francis, and I agree with you to a large extent. Teddy and I have been discussing just that sort of problem. We must bring on a new generation of talent, find new impetus by putting new men in new places. And I find many of your suggestions for changes at the lower Ministerial levels below Cabinet very persuasive.'

'But they are not the ones that matter,' Urquhart muttered beneath his breath.

'The trouble is that too much change at the top can be very disruptive. It takes most Cabinet Ministers a year simply to find their feet in a new Department, and a year is a long time to struggle through without being able to show positive signs of progress. Rather than Cabinet changes helping to implement our new programme, Teddy's view is that on balance it would more likely delay the programme.'

What new programme?, Urquhart screamed inside his skull. We deliberately published the most flaccid and uncontroversial manifesto we could get away with! He calmed himself before responding.

'Don't you think by cutting our majority the electorate was telling us of its desire for some degree of change?'

'An interesting point. But as you yourself said, no Government in our lifetimes has been in office as long as we have. Without in any way being complacent, Francis, I don't think we could have rewritten the history books if the voters believed we had run out of steam. On balance, I think it suggests that they are content with what we offer, and there is no great sign of them demanding upheaval or change. There's another vital point,' he continued. 'Just because our majority has been cut, we must avoid giving the impression that we are panicking. That would send entirely the wrong signal to the Party and the country, and could bring about just that demand for change which you are so nervous of. Remember that Macmillan destroyed his own Government by panicking and sacking a third of his Cabinet. "The Night of the Long Knives" they called it, and he was out of office the following year. That was a mistake I am not anxious to repeat. So I'm thinking of a much more controlled approach myself.'

Collingridge slipped a piece of paper across the desk towards Urquhart, who picked it up. On it was printed a list of Cabinet positions, twenty-two in all, with names alongside them.

'As you see, Francis, I am suggesting no Cabinet changes at all. I hope it will be seen as a sign of great determination and strength. We have a job to do, and I think we should show we want to get straight on with it.'

Urquhart quickly replaced the paper onto the desk, anxious that the tremble in his hand might betray his inner feelings.

'If that is what you want, Prime Minister,' he said, slipping into a formal tone. 'I have to say that I am not sure how the Parliamentary Party will react. I've not had sufficient chance to take soundings since the election.'

'I'm sure they will accept it. After all, we are proposing a substantial number of changes below Cabinet level to keep them happy.' There was the slightest pause. 'And of course I assume I have your full support?' he asked quizzically.

There was another pause, slightly longer this time, until Urquhart heard himself responding.

'Of course, Prime Minister.'

His own voice sounded strangely distant. He knew he had no choice: it was either support or suicide through instant resignation. The words of acceptance came out automatically, but without conviction. He felt the Whips Office closing around him like the walls of the condemned cell. Once again Urquhart felt uneasy in Collingridge's presence, not knowing how to read him or how to respond to him. But he could not leave it there. His words faltered as he found his mouth suddenly dry.

'I have to say that I . . . was rather looking for a change myself. A bit of new experience . . . a new challenge.'

'Francis,' the Prime Minister said in his most reassuring manner, 'if I move you, I have to move others. The whole pile of dominoes begins to fall over. And I need you where you are. You are an excellent Chief Whip. You have devoted yourself to burrowing right into the heart and soul of the Parliamentary Party. You know them so well, and we have to face it that with such a small majority there might be one or two sticky patches over the next few years. I need to have a Chief Whip who is strong enough to handle them. I need *you*, Francis. You are so good behind the scenes. We can leave it to others to do the job out front.'

'You appear to have made up your mind,' Urquhart said, hoping that it sounded like a statement of fact rather than the accusation which he felt.

'I have,' replied the Prime Minister. 'And I am deeply grateful that I can rely on your understanding and support.'

Urquhart felt the cell door slam shut. He thanked them, cast a dark eye at the Party Chairman, and took his farewell. Williams hadn't uttered a single word.

He left through the basement of Number Ten which led him past the ruins of the old Tudor tennis court to the Cabinet Office, which faces onto Whitehall. He was well out of sight of the waiting press. He couldn't face them. He had been with the Prime Minister less than half an hour, and he did not trust his face to back up the lies he would have to tell them. He got a security guard at the Cabinet Office to telephone for his car to be brought round.

The battered BMW had been standing outside the house in Cambridge Street, Pimlico for almost a quarter of an hour. Amidst the chaos of discarded newspapers and granary bar wrappers which covered the vacant seats, Mattie Storin sat biting her lip. Ever since the reshuffle announcement from Downing Street late that afternoon, fevered discussions had been undertaken in editorial offices trying to decide whether the Prime Minister had been brilliant and audacious or simply lost his nerve; they needed the views of the men who had helped shape the decisions. Williams had been persuasive and supportive as usual, but Urquhart's phone had only rung and rung.

Without knowing quite why, after work Mattie had decided to drive past Urquhart's London home, just ten minutes away from the House of Commons. She expected to find it dark and empty but instead she discovered that the lights were burning and there were signs of movement around the house, yet still the telephone rang unanswered.

She knew it was not the done thing in Westminster circles for political correspondents to pursue their quarry back to their homes; indeed, it was a practice which was darkly frowned upon not only by politicians but also by other correspondents. The world of Westminster is a club which has many unwritten rules, and those rules are guarded jealously by both politicians and press – particularly the press, the so-called Westminster 'lobby' of correspondents which quietly and privately regulates all media activity in the Palace of Westminster. The lobby system sets the rules of conduct which permit briefings and interviews to take place without their ever being reported, which encourage politicians to be indiscreet and to break confidences without ever being quoted, which allow the press to get round the Official Secrets Act and the oaths of collective Ministerial responsibility without ever giving their sources away. It was the lobby correspondent's passport, without which he – or she – would find all doors closed and all mouths firmly shut.

Mattie gave the inside of her cheek another bite. She was nervous. She did not lightly bend the rules, but why was the bloody man not answering his phone? What on earth was he up to?

A thick Northern voice whispered in her ear, the voice she had so often missed since leaving the *Yorkshire Post* and its old, wise editor. What had he said? 'Rules, my girl, are meant for the guidance of the wise and the emasculation of the foolish. Don't ever tell me you haven't got a good story because of somebody else's sodding rules.'

'OK, OK, you miserable bugger,' Mattie said out loud. She didn't feel good about breaking lobby rules, but she knew she would feel even worse missing a valuable opportunity. She checked her hair in the mirror, running a hand through it to restore some life, and opened the car door wishing that she were somewhere else. Twenty seconds later the house echoed with the heavy thumping of the ornate brass knocker on the front door.

Urquhart was alone, and not expecting visitors. His wife had returned to the country, and the maid didn't work weekends. He opened the door impatiently, and he did not immediately recognise the caller.

'Mr Urquhart, I've been trying to contact you all afternoon. I hope it's not inconvenient but I need some help. Downing Street has announced that there will be no Cabinet changes, and I'd appreciate your help in trying to understand the thinking behind it.'

How do these damned journalists always find where you are? thought Urquhart.

'I'm sorry but I have nothing to say,' he responded and began to close the door. He saw the journalist throw her hands up in exasperation and take a step forward. Surely the silly girl wasn't going to put her foot in the door, it would be too comic for words. But Mattie spoke calmly and quietly.

'Mr Urquhart. That's a great story. But I don't think you mean it.'

Intrigued, Urquhart paused. What on earth did she mean? Mattie saw the hesitation, and threw a little more bait into the water. 'The story would read: "There were signs last night of deep Cabinet divisions over the non-shuffle. The Chief Whip, long believed to have harboured ambitions for a move to a new post, refused to comment on or to defend the Prime Minister's decision." How would you care for that?'

Only now did Urquhart recognise the *Telegraph* correspondent away from her usual surroundings. He knew Mattie Storin only slightly as she was relatively new to the Westminster circuit, but Urquhart had seen her in action often enough to suspect she was no fool. He was therefore astonished that she was now on his doorstep trying to intimidate the Chief Whip.

'You cannot be serious,' Urquhart said slowly.

Mattie broke into a broad smile. 'Actually, no, sir. Although you won't answer your telephone or talk face-to-face, even I wouldn't go that far to get a story. But it does raise some very interesting questions in my mind, and frankly I would prefer to get the truth rather than having to concoct something out of thin air. And that's all you are leaving me at the moment, thin air.'

Urquhart was disarmed by the young journalist's candour. He ought to be furious and on the phone to her editor, demanding an apology for such blatant harassment. But Mattie had already sensed there might be a much deeper story behind the formal announcement from Downing Street. Now she stood in a pool of light at his front door, highlights glinting in her short, blonde hair. What had he got to lose?

'Perhaps you had better come in after all – Miss Storin, isn't it?'

'Please call me Mattie.'

He led the way upstairs to a tasteful, if very traditional, sitting room, covered in oil paintings of horses and country scenes, and crammed with ancient but comfortable furniture. He poured himself a large Scotch and, without asking her, a glass of white wine for his guest before settling into an overstuffed armchair. Mattie sat opposite, nervously perching on the edge of the sofa. She got out a small notebook, but Urquhart waved it away.

'I'm tired, Miss Storin – Mattie. It's been an arduous campaign, and I am not sure I would express myself particularly well. So no notes and no quotations, if you don't mind.' Urquhart knew he had to be careful.

'OK, Mr Urquhart. Let's do this entirely on a lobby basis. I can use what you tell me, but I can't attribute it to you in any way and absolutely no quotations.'

'Precisely.'

He took a cigarette from a silver cigarette box and relaxed back in his chair, inhaling deeply. He did not wait for Mattie's questions before starting his defence.

'So what if I tell you that the Prime Minister sees this as being the best way of getting on with the job? Not letting Ministers get confused with new responsibilities and new civil service teams, but allowing us to continue full steam ahead?'

'I would say, Mr Urquhart, that we would scarcely have to go off the record and on to a lobby basis for that!'

Urquhart chuckled at the young journalist's bluntness. Yes, he would have to be very careful.

'I would also say that the election result showed the need for some new blood and some new thinking,' she continued. 'You lost a lot of seats, and your endorsement by the voters wasn't exactly gushing, was it?'

'Steady on, steady on. We've got a clear majority and won many more seats than the main opposition party. Not too bad after so many years in office . . .' He rehearsed the official creed.

'But not really full of promise for the next election, is it? Even some of your own supporters have described your programme for the next five years as being "more of the same". "Steady as she sinks", I think one of your opponents called it. And you may remember I came to one of your election rallies. You were speaking a great deal about new energy, new ideas and new enterprise. The whole thrust of what you were saying was that there would be change – and some new players.'

She paused, but Urquhart didn't seem keen to respond. 'Your own election address – I have it here . . .' She fished a glossy folded leaflet from a wad of papers which were stuffed into her shoulder bag. Urquhart stared at her intently. 'It speaks about "the exciting years ahead". All this is about as exciting as last week's newspapers.'

'I think that's a little harsh,' protested Urquhart, knowing he should be protesting more. He had no enthusiasm for inventing excuses, and he suspected that it showed.

'Let me ask you bluntly, Mr Urquhart. Do you really think that this is the best the Prime Minister could do?'

Urquhart did not answer directly but raised his glass slowly to his lips, without for a moment taking his eyes off her. They both knew that they were role playing, but neither was yet clear quite how this theatre piece would finish.

Urquhart savoured the fine Islay malt around his tongue, and let it warm him inside before replying. 'Mattie, how on earth do you expect me to reply to a question like that? You know as Chief Whip I am totally loyal to the Prime Minister and his shuffle – or rather non-shuffle.' There was an edge of sarcasm in his voice.

'Yes, but what about Francis Urquhart, a man who is very ambitious for his party and is desperately anxious for its success. Does *he* support it?'

There was no reply.

'Mr Urquhart, in my piece tomorrow I shall faithfully record your public loyalty to the reshuffle and your justification of it. I know you would not wish to see anything appear in the press which even remotely hinted that you were not happy with events. But I remind you we are speaking on lobby terms. I sense that you are not content with what is happening. I want to know. You want to ensure that it doesn't get back to my colleagues, or to your colleagues, or become common Westminster gossip. I give you my word on that. This is just for me, because it might be important in the months ahead. And by the way, no one else knows I came to see you tonight.'

Mattie was offering a deal. In exchange for Urquhart's real views she would ensure that nothing she wrote could ever be traced back to its source.

Urquhart toyed in his mind with a variety of stilettos, wondering which one to throw first. 'Very well, Mattie, let me explain the real story to you. It's really very simple. The Prime Minister has to keep the lid firmly closed on the pressure cooker in order to contain the ambition of some of his colleagues. Those ambitions have grown since the poor election result and, if he were to release the pressure now, there would be the danger of the entire Government getting plastered all over the kitchen ceiling.'

'Are you telling me that there is a lot of rivalry and dissent within the Cabinet?'

'Let me put it this way.' He paused to consider his words carefully before continuing in a slow, deliberate voice. 'Some elements of the Party are deeply distressed. They believed the PM came dangerously close to throwing away the last election, and they don't see him as having the stamina or authority to last all the way through for another four or five years. So they are thinking of what life might be like in another eighteen months or two years, and what position they want to be in if there happened to be a leadership race. The game has suddenly become a very different one since Thursday, and Henry Collingridge is no longer playing with a full team behind him. It could get very unsettling.'

'So why doesn't he get rid of the troublesome ones?'

'Because he can't risk having several former Cabinet Ministers rampaging all over the backbenches when he has got a majority of only 24 which could disappear at the first parliamentary cock-up. He has to keep everything as quiet and as low key as possible. He can't even move the Awkward Brigade to new Cabinet posts because every time you get a new Minister in a new Department they get a rush of enthusiasm and want to make their mark, while you gentlefolk of the press give them a honeymoon period and plenty of personal publicity. Their views suddenly take on a renewed importance for the leader writers, and all of a sudden we find that they are not simply doing their Ministerial jobs but also promoting themselves for a leadership race. The whole of Government business is thrown into chaos because everyone is looking over their shoulders at their colleagues rather than training their sights on the Opposition. Government becomes confused, the Prime Minister becomes even more unpopular – and suddenly we are confronted with a real leadership race.'

'So everyone simply has to remain where they are. Do you think that's a sound strategy?'

He took a deep mouthful of whisky. 'If I were the captain of the *Titanic* and I saw a bloody great iceberg dead ahead, I don't think I would be saying "steady as she goes". I'd want a change of course.'

'Did you tell this to the Prime Minister this afternoon?'

'Mattie, you take me too far!' he chuckled in protest. 'While I respect your professional integrity and I am thoroughly enjoying our conversation, I think I would be offering you too much temptation if I started divulging the details of private discussions. That's a shooting offence!'

Mattie had not moved from the edge of her chair. She understood very clearly the significance of his words, and was determined to gather more. 'Well, let me ask you about Lord Williams. He was with the PM an extraordinarily long time this afternoon if all they were deciding was to do nothing.'

Urquhart had been toying with this specific stiletto for several minutes. Now he threw it with deadly accuracy. 'Have you heard the phrase, "Beware of an old man in a hurry"?'

'You surely can't imagine that he believes he could become Party Leader. Not from the Lords!'

'No, even he's not that egotistical. But he still has a couple of years left, and like so many elder statesmen would like to make sure that the leadership found its way into suitable hands.'

'Whose hands?'

'If not him, then one of his acolytes.'

'Like who?'

'Do you have no thoughts of your own?'

'You mean Michael Samuel.'

Urquhart smiled as he heard the stiletto thud home. 'I think I've said enough. We must call this conversation to a halt.'

Mattie nodded reluctantly, and remained silent, pondering the pieces of the political jigsaw which now lay in front of her. Without further discussion Urquhart guided his guest downstairs, and they were shaking hands by the front door before she spoke again.

'You've been very helpful, Mr Urquhart. But one last question. If there were a leadership election, would you be part of it?'

'Good night, Mattie,' Urquhart said, and closed the front door firmly behind her.

Daily Telegraph. Monday 14th June. Page 1.

In a move which startled most observers, the Prime Minister yesterday announced that there were to be no immediate Cabinet changes following the election. After conferring for several hours with his Party

61

Chairman, Lord Williams, and also with the Chief Whip Francis Urquhart, Mr Collingridge issued a 'steady as she goes' message to his Party.

Downing Street sources said it was intended that the Government would be able to pursue their programme as quickly and as effectively as possible by leaving all Cabinet Ministers in place. However, senior Westminster sources last night expressed astonishment at the decision. It was seen in some quarters as betraying the weakness of the Prime Minister's position after the decimation of his parliamentary majority and criticisms of what was seen as a lacklustre campaign, for which both he and the Party Chairman are being blamed.

There was speculation last night that the Prime Minister was unlikely to fight another election, and that some senior Ministers were already manoeuvring for position in the event of an early leadership contest. One Cabinet Minister compared the Prime Minister to 'the captain of the *Titanic* as it was entering the ice pack'.

The decision not to make any Cabinet changes, the first time since the war that an election has not been followed by some senior reshuffle, was interpreted as being the most effective way for Collingridge to keep the simmering rivalries of some of his Cabinet colleagues under control.

Last night, the Chief Whip defended the decision as being 'the best means of getting on with the job'. However, speculation is already beginning as to who might be the likely contenders in the event of a leadership race.

Lord Williams described any suggestion of an imminent leadership election as 'nonsense'. He said, 'The Prime Minister has gained for the Party an historic fourth election victory, and we are in excellent shape.' However, the position of the Party

Chairman would be crucial during a leadership race, and Williams is known to be very close to Michael Samuel, the Environment Secretary, who could be one of the contenders.

Opposition spokesmen were quick to pounce on what they saw as indecisiveness on the part of the Prime Minister. Claiming that he had been greatly heartened by the gains his Party had made last Thursday, the Opposition Leader said: 'The fires of discontent are glowing within the Government. I don't think Mr Collingridge has the strength or the support to put them out. I am already looking forward to the next election . . .'

TUESDAY 22ND JUNE

Roger O'Neill sat back comfortably in the arms of one of
the large leather armchairs which surround the snooker
tables in the back room at White's Club. When the tables
are not in use, the seats which are spread around the games
room offer a quiet and confidential spot for members to
take their guests. He had been delighted, and not a little
astonished, to receive the invitation from the Chief Whip
to dine at his prestigious club in St James's. Urquhart had
never shown much warmth towards O'Neill in the past,
and O'Neill had been more used to a cold and condescending gaze down Urquhart's aquiline nose, rather like a
well-fed bird eyeing future prey, than an invitation 'to
celebrate the splendid work which you have done for us all
throughout the campaign'.

O'Neill, hypertense as always, had tried to calm his
nerves with a couple of mighty vodka-tonics before he
arrived, but they had not been necessary. Urquhart's cosy
manner, two bottles of Château Talbot '78 and the large
cognacs which Urquhart was even now ordering from the
bar suggested that O'Neill had at last been able to break
through the barriers which some traditionalists within the
party leadership still erected against the likes of O'Neill
and his 'marketing johnnies with their vulgar cars'. Even
as O'Neill derided the traditionalists and their narrow
jealousies, he desperately wanted their acceptance, and
now he felt guilty for having misjudged Urquhart so badly.
He beamed broadly as his host returned from the bar with
two crystal glasses on a silver tray. O'Neill stubbed out his
cigarette in preparation for the Havana which he hoped
would be following.

'Tell me, Roger, what are your plans now the election is over? Are you going to stay on with the Party? We can't afford to lose good men like you.'

O'Neill flashed yet another winning smile and assured his host that he would stay on as long as the Prime Minister wanted him.

'But how can you afford to, Roger? May I be brutally honest with you? I know just how little the Party pays its employees, and money is always so short after an election. It's going to be tough for the next couple of years. Your salary will probably get frozen and your budget cut. Aren't you tempted by some of the more handsome offers you must be getting from outside?'

'Well, it's not always easy, Francis, as you've already guessed. It's not so much the salary, you understand. I work in politics because I'm fascinated by it and love to play a part. But it would be a tragedy if the budget gets cut.'

His smile faded as he contemplated the prospect and began to fidget nervously with his glass. 'We should start working for the next election now, not in three years' time when it may be too late. Particularly with all these rumours flooding around about splits within the Party and who is to blame for the loss of seats. We need some strong and positive publicity, and I need a budget to create it.'

'The Chairman receptive to all this?' Urquhart raised an enquiring eyebrow.

'Are Chairmen ever?'

'Perhaps, Roger, there is something I can do about that. I would like to be able to help you very much, because I think you've done such excellent work. I'll go in to bat with the Chairman about your budget, if you want. But there is something I must ask you first. And I must be blunt.'

The older man's blue eyes looked directly into O'Neill's, taking in their habitual flicker. He paused while O'Neill blew his nose loudly. Another habit, Urquhart knew. He examined O'Neill closely. It was as if there were another life going on within O'Neill which was quite separate from

66

the rest of the world, and which communicated itself only through O'Neill's hyperactive mannerisms and twitching eyes.

'I had a visit the other day from an old colleague I used to know from the days when I held directorships in the City,' Urquhart continued. 'He's one of the financial people at the Party's advertising agency. And he was very troubled. Very discreet, but very troubled. He said you were in the habit of asking them for considerable sums of cash to cover your expenses.'

The twitching stopped for a moment, and Urquhart noticed just how rarely he had ever seen O'Neill stop moving.

'Roger, let me assure you I am not trying to trap you or trick you. This is strictly between us. But if I am to help you, I must be sure of the facts.'

The face and the eyes started up again, and O'Neill's ready laugh made a nervous reappearance. 'Francis, let me assure you that there's nothing wrong at all. It's silly, of course, but I am grateful that you raised it with me. It's simply that there are times when I incur expenses on the publicity side which are easier and more convenient for the agency to meet rather than putting them through the Party machine. Like buying a drink for a journalist or taking a Party contributor out for a meal.'

O'Neill was speeding on with his explanation, which showed signs of having been practised. 'You see, if I pay for them myself I have to claim back from the Party. We have a pretty laborious accounts department which takes its own sweet time paying those invoices – two months or more. Frankly, with the way I get paid, I can't afford it. Yet if I charge them through the agency, I get the money back immediately while they have to put them through their own accounts before invoicing us at headquarters. That takes another month or so, which simply means that the Party gets an even longer holiday on repaying those expenses. It's like an interest-free loan for the Party. And in the meantime I can get on with my job. The amounts are really very small.'

O'Neill reached for his glass.

'Like £22,300 in the last ten months small?'

O'Neill nearly choked. He put his glass down quickly and his face contorted as he struggled simultaneously to gulp down air and blurt out a denial.

'It's nothing like that amount,' he protested. His jaw dropped as he debated what to say next. This explanation he hadn't practised.

Urquhart turned away from him to signal for another two cognacs. His eyes returned calmly to O'Neill, whose twitching now resembled a fly caught in a spider's web. Urquhart spun more silken threads.

'Roger, you have been charging regular expenses to the agency without clearly accounting for those amounts to the tune of precisely £22,300 since the beginning of September last year. What began as relatively small amounts have in recent months grown up to £4,000 a month. You don't get through that many drinks and dinners even during an election campaign.'

'I assure you, Francis, that any expenses I've charged have all been entirely legitimate!' The choking had begun to subside. As the steward placed the fresh drinks on the table, Urquhart moved in to bind his prey with a lethal touch.

'And let me assure you, Roger, that I know precisely what you have been spending the money on,' he said quietly.

He took a sip from his cognac as his victim remained motionless, transfixed. 'Roger, as Chief Whip I have to become familiar with every problem known to man. Do you know, in the last two years I have had to deal with cases of wife beating, adultery, fraud, mental illness. I've even had a case of incest. We didn't let him stand for re-election, of course, but there was nothing to be gained by making a public fuss about such things. That's why you almost never hear about them. Incest I draw the line at but in general we don't moralise, Roger. Every man is allowed one weakness or indulgence – so long as it remains a private one.'

He paused. 'In fact, one of my Junior Whips is a doctor who was appointed specifically to help me spot the signs of strain, and we get quite practised at it. After all, we have well over 300 MPs to look after, all of whom are living on the edge and under immense pressure. You'd be surprised, too, how many cases of drug abuse we get at Westminster. The specialists say there is something like 10 per cent of the population, including MPs, who are physiologically or psychologically vulnerable to chemical addiction of one sort or another. Not their fault, it's something in their makeup, and they have much more trouble than the rest of us in resisting drink, pills and the rest. There's a charming and utterly private drying-out farm just outside Dover where we send them, sometimes for a couple of months. Most of them recover completely and return to a full political life.'

He paused yet again to swill the cognac around his glass and sip it gently, but continued to watch O'Neill closely. The other man did not stir. He sat there as if petrified.

'But it helps to catch them early,' Urquhart continued, 'which is why we are so sensitive to the signs of drug abuse. Like cocaine. It's become a real problem recently. They tell me it's fashionable – whatever that means – and too damned easy to obtain. Do you know it can rot your nasal membranes clean away if you let it? Funny drug. Gives people an instant high and persuades them that their brain and senses can complete five hours' work in just five minutes. Makes a good man brilliant, so they say. Pity it's so addictive.'

There was another pause. 'And expensive.'

Urquhart had not taken his eyes off O'Neill for a second during his narrative, and had witnessed the exquisite agony which had racked O'Neill inside. Any doubt about his diagnosis that he had started with had been brushed aside with the whimpering which began slowly to emerge from the other man. Now his words were tortured and pleading.

'What are you saying? I am not a drug addict. I don't do drugs!'

'No, of course not, Roger.' Urquhart adopted his most reassuring tone. 'But I think you must accept that there are some people who could jump to the most unfortunate conclusions about you. And the Prime Minister, you know, is not a man to take chances. It's not a matter of condemning a man without trial, simply opting for a quiet life without unnecessary risks.'

'The Prime Minister can't believe this!' O'Neill gasped as if he had been butted by a charging bull.

'I'm afraid that the Chairman was a little less than helpful with the PM the other day – he knows nothing, of course, but I don't think the dear Lord Williams is one of your greatest fans. Don't worry, I reassured the Prime Minister about you, and you have nothing to fear. As long as you have my support.'

Urquhart knew full well of the paranoia which dominates the minds of cocaine addicts, and the impact which his totally invented story about the Chairman's disaffection would leave on O'Neill's helter-skelter emotions. He also knew that the paranoia was matched by a lust for notoriety, which O'Neill could only achieve through his political connections and the continued patronage of the Prime Minister, and this he could not bear to lose. 'As long as you have my support,' rang in O'Neill's ears. 'One slip and you are dead,' it was saying. The web around O'Neill was complete, and now Urquhart offered him the way out.

'You see, Roger, I have seen gossip destroy so many men. Gossip founded on no more than circumstantial evidence or even naked jealousy, perhaps, but you know that the corridors around Westminster have been killing fields for less fortunate people than you or me. It would be a tragedy if you were pilloried either because of Lord Williams' hostility towards you or because people misunderstood your arrangement about expenses and your – hay fever.'

'What should I do?' The voice was plaintive.

'Your position is a delicate one, particularly at a time when the political currents within the Government are ebbing and flowing. I would suggest that you trust me. You need a strong supporter in the inner circles of the Party, particularly as the Prime Minister appears to be getting into more difficult waters and will be concentrating on rescuing himself rather than spending his time rescuing others.'

He paused to watch O'Neill writhe in his chair. 'I would suggest the following. I shall tell the agency I have fully established that your expenses are legitimate. I shall ask them to continue with the arrangement, on the basis that we are doing it this way to avoid unhelpful jealousy from some of your colleagues within party headquarters who do not support extensive advertising budgets and who might use your high but perfectly legitimate expenses to attack the whole communications set-up. The agency can regard it as a sensible insurance policy. Also, I shall ensure that the Prime Minister continues to be fully informed of the good work you are doing for the Party. I shall certainly try to persuade him of the need to continue a high level publicity campaign to get him through the difficult months ahead, so that your budget is not cut to shreds by the Chairman.'

'You know I would be most grateful. . .' O'Neill mumbled.

'In return, you will keep me informed of everything that is going on at party headquarters and in particular what the Chairman is up to. He's a very ambitious and dangerous man, you know. Playing his own game while professing loyalty to the Prime Minister. Between us, though, I think we can ensure that no harm is done to the Prime Minister's – or to your – interests. You must be my eyes and ears, Roger, and you will have to let me know immediately of anything you hear of the Chairman's plans. Your future could depend upon it.' He punched home the words to let O'Neill be in no doubt that he meant it.

'We must work together on this. You will have to help me. I know how much you love politics and the Party, and I think the two of us together can help steer the Party through some difficult times ahead.'

'Thank you,' O'Neill whispered.

WEDNESDAY 30TH JUNE

The Strangers Bar in the House of Commons is a small, dark room overlooking the Thames where Members of Parliament may take their 'Stranger' or non-Member guests. As a result it is usually crowded and noisy with rumour and gossip. Tonight was no exception as O'Neill propped up the bar with one elbow and struggled valiantly with the other to avoid knocking the drink out of his host's hand.

'Another one, Steve?' he asked of his immaculately dressed companion.

Stephen Kendrick looked somewhat out of place in his light grey Armani mohair suit, pearl white cuffs and immaculately manicured hands clasped around a glass of Federation bitter, a draught beer for which the bars of the Palace of Westminster afford a warm home.

'Now you know better than me that Strangers can't buy drinks here. And anyway, I've only been here two weeks and I wouldn't want to ruin my career by having anyone see the Prime Minister's pet Irish wolfhound forcing drinks down the Opposition's newest and fastest rising backbencher. Some of my more dogmatic colleagues would treat that as treachery!'

He grinned and winked at the barmaid to attract her attention. Another pint of dark bitter and a double vodkatonic were quick in coming.

'You know, Rog, I'm still pinching myself. I never really expected to get here, and I still can't decide whether it's a dream or just a bloody awful nightmare. When we worked together at the same little PR shop seven years ago, who would have guessed you would now be the chief grunter for the Prime Minister and I would be a humble if wonderfully talented Opposition MP?'

'Certainly not that little blonde telephonist we used to take turns with,' ribbed O'Neill. They both chuckled at the memory of younger and more frivolous days.

'Dear little Annie,' mused Kendrick.

'I thought her name was Jennie,' protested O'Neill.

'Rog, in those days I never remember you being fussy about what they were called.'

The banter finally broke the ice between the two men which had been slowly thawing with the drink. When O'Neill had telephoned the new MP to suggest a drink for old times' sake, they had both found it difficult to revive the easy familiarity which they had known in earlier years. They had been careful, perhaps too careful, to avoid the subject of politics which now dominated both their lives and it had forced their conversation along artificial lines. Now O'Neill decided to take the plunge.

'Steve, I don't mind you buying the drinks all night as far as I'm concerned. The way my masters are going at the moment, I think a saint would be driven to drink.'

Kendrick accepted the opening. 'Your lot do seem to be getting their robes of office in something of a twist. There are all sorts of weird rumours going round this place about how Samuel is furious with Williams for putting his head on the block with the PM, Williams is furious with Collingridge for screwing up the election campaign, and Collingridge is furious with just about everyone.'

'Maybe it's simply that they are all tired after the election and can't wait to get away on holiday,' O'Neill responded. 'Like an irritable family squabbling about how the car is packed before taking a long trip.'

'If you don't mind me saying, old chum, I think your leader is going to have to put an end to all the bickering very quickly, or else he'll go into the Summer Recess with the family looking more like a pack of Westminster alley cats. No Prime Minister can afford to let those sort of rumours run away from him, otherwise they begin to gain a life of their own. They become reality. Still, that's where you and your vast publicity budgets come to the rescue, like the Seventh Cavalry over the hill.'

'More like Custer's last bloody stand,' O'Neill said with some bitterness.

'What's the matter, Rog, Uncle Teddy run off with all your toy soldiers or something?' Kendrick asked with genuine curiosity.

O'Neill emptied his glass and Kendrick ordered another round.

'Between you and me, just as old chums, Steve, he's run off with almost all of them. Hell, we need to find new friends more than ever, but instead of going onto the offensive the Chairman seems content to retreat behind the barricades.'

'Ah, do I detect the cries of a frustrated Publicity Director who has been told to shut up shop for a while?'

O'Neill banged the bar in exasperation. 'I shouldn't tell you this, I suppose, but as it's not going to happen there's no harm. The new hospital expansion programme which we promised at the election giving matching Government funds for any money raised locally. We had a wonderful promotional campaign, all ready to go throughout the summer while all you bastards were off on the Costa del Cuba or wherever it is you go.'

Kendrick held his silence, not responding to the jibe.

'By the time you all came back in October, we would have won the hearts and minds of voters in every marginal seat in the country. We had the campaign all set! Advertising, a party political broadcast, ten million leaflets, direct mail. "Nursing Hospitals Back To Health." It would have made a wonderful build-up to the party conference as "The Party Which Delivers". But . . . he's pulled the plug. Just like that.'

'Why?' asked Kendrick consolingly. 'Money problems after the election?'

'That's the damnable thing about it, Steve. The money's in the budget and the leaflets have already been printed, but he won't even let us deliver them. He just came back from Number Ten this morning and said the thing was off. Then he had the nerve to ask whether the leaflets would be out of date by next year. It's so bloody amateurish!'

He tried to sound morose as he took another large mouthful of spirits, and hoped that he had followed Urquhart's instructions properly, not showing too much disloyalty or too much frankness, just professional pique. He had no idea why Urquhart had told him to concoct an entirely spurious story about a non-existent publicity campaign to pass on in the Strangers Bar. But it seemed a small thing to do for a man on whom he knew he depended.

As he gazed into the bottom of his glass, he saw Kendrick give him a long and deliberate glance. With the air of camaraderie squeezed from his voice, the MP asked 'Why, Rog, why?'

'If only I knew, old chum. Complete bloody mystery to me.'

THURSDAY 1st JULY

The Chamber of the House of Commons is of relatively modern construction, rebuilt following the war after one of the Luftwaffe's bombs had missed the docks and carelessly scored a direct hit on the Mother of Parliaments instead. Yet in spite of its relative youth the Chamber has an atmosphere centuries old. If you sit quietly in the corner of the empty Chamber, the freshness of the leather on the narrow green benches fades and the ghosts of Chatham, Walpole, Fox and Disraeli pace the gangways once again.

It is a place of character rather than convenience. There are seats for only around 400 of the 650 Members, who cannot listen to the rudimentary loudspeakers built into the back of the benches without slumping to one side and giving the appearance of being sound asleep. Which sometimes they are.

The Chamber places Members in face to face confrontation with their antagonists in opposition parties, separated only by the distance of one sword's length, lulling the unwary into complacency and into forgetting that the greatest danger is always but a dagger's length away, on the benches behind.

Least of all can a Prime Minister forget that well over half the members of his own Parliamentary Party usually believe they can do his job far better, with a firmer grip of detail, or diplomacy, or both. Prime Ministers are called to account twice a week when Parliament is sitting through the time honoured institution of Prime Minister's Question Time. In principle it gives Members of Parliament the opportunity to seek information from the leader of Her Majesty's Government; in practice it is an exercise in survival which owes more to the Roman arena of Nero and Claudius than to the ideals of the constitutionalists who developed the system.

The questions from Opposition Members usually do not seek information, they seek to criticise and to inflict damage. The answers rarely seek to give information, but to retaliate. Prime Ministers always have the last word, and it is that which gives them the advantage in combat, like the gladiator allowed the final thrust.

But Prime Ministers also know that they are expected to win, and it is the manner rather than the fact of their victory which will decide the level of vocal support and encouragement from the troops behind. Woe betide the Prime Minister who does not dispatch the Opposition's questions quickly but who allows them to return once again to the attack. The noisy enthusiasm of the Government backbenches can soon turn to sullen resentment and silent condemnation, for a Prime Minister who cannot dominate the floor of the House of Commons soon finds that he can count on the support of few of his colleagues. Then the Prime Minister must watch not only the opposition in front, but also the competition behind.

It was this constant challenge which made Macmillan sometimes sick with tension before Question Time, which caused Wilson to lose sleep and Thatcher to lose her temper. And Henry Collingridge was not quite up to any of their standards.

The day following O'Neill's evening foray into the Strangers Bar had not been going smoothly for the Prime Minister. The Downing Street press secretary had been laid low by his children's chicken pox, so the normal daily press briefing was of inferior quality and, even worse to the impatient Collingridge, was late. So was Cabinet, which had gathered at its accustomed time of 10 a.m. on Thursday to resolve Government policy. It had dragged on, embarrassed and confused by the explanation from the Chancellor of the Exchequer of how the Government's reduced majority had taken the edge off the financial markets, making it impossible in this financial year to implement the hospital expansion programme which they had promised so enthusiastically during the election campaign. The Prime Minister should have kept a grip on the discussion, but it rambled on and ended amidst acrimony.

'A great pity the Chancellor wasn't a little more cautious before allowing us to run off and make rash commitments,' the Education Secretary commented, dripping acid.

The Chancellor muttered defiantly that it wasn't his fault the election results were worse than even the cynical Stock Market had expected, a comment he had instantly regretted making although he knew it was precisely what all his colleagues were thinking. Collingridge had knocked their heads together and instructed the Secretary of State for Health to prepare a suitable explanation for the change of plans, which would be announced in a fortnight's time during the last week before the August recess.

'Let us hope,' said the septuagenarian Lord Chancellor, 'that everybody's minds will by then be on the lighter follies of summer rather than the more depressing follies of their political masters.'

Cabinet overran by twenty-five minutes, which meant that in turn the Prime Minister's briefing meeting with officials for Question Time was also late, and his ill-temper ensured that he took in very little of what they were saying. When he strode into a packed Chamber just before the appointed time of 3.15 p.m., he was not as well armed or as alert as usual.

This did not seem to matter for the first thirteen minutes fifty seconds of combat, as he batted back questions from the Opposition and accepted plaudits from his own party with adequate if not inspired ease. The Speaker of the House, in charge of parliamentary proceedings, decided that with just over a minute left there would be time for just one more quick question to round off the session.

'Stephen Kendrick,' he called across the Chamber to

summon the Member whose question was next on the Order Paper. It was the first occasion on which the new Member had been involved at Question Time, and many older Members were nudging their colleagues to find out who this new man was.

'Number Six, sir.' Kendrick rose briefly to his feet to indicate the question from the Order Paper he wished the Prime Minister to answer: 'To ask the Prime Minister if he will list his official engagements for the day'. It was a hollow question, identical in form to Questions One, Two and Four which had already preceded it, and designed not to elicit information but to hide from the Prime Minister the nature of the following supplementary thrust. Such is the nature of the combat.

The Prime Minister rose ponderously to his feet and glanced at the red briefing folder already open on the Despatch Box in front of him. He read in a monotone.

'I refer the Honourable Member to the reply I gave some moments ago to Questions One, Two and Four.' Since his earlier reply had said no more than that he would spend the day holding meetings with ministerial colleagues and hosting a dinner for the visiting Belgian Prime Minister, no one had yet learned anything of interest about the Prime Minister's activities – which was precisely his intention.

Collingridge resumed his seat, and the Speaker summoned Kendrick once more to place his supplementary question. The gladiatorial courtesies were now over, and battle was about to commence. Kendrick rose to his feet from the rear row of the Opposition benches.

Kendrick was a gambler, a man who had found professional success in an industry which emphasised ostentatious reward, yet who had decided to risk his expense account and sports car by fighting a marginal parliamentary seat. Not that he had really expected or indeed wanted to win; after all, the Government had been sitting on a pretty reasonable majority. Fighting the seat, he reasoned, would give him a platform and a prominence which would help him both socially and professionally, and would certainly give him a higher profile in the public relations trade magazines. 'The man with the social conscience' always made good copy in an aggressively commercial industry, and the ability to be able to drop a name or two usually helped.

His majority of 76, after three recounts, at first had come as an unpleasant shock as suddenly he was forced to contemplate the reduced income and additional hours of a parliamentary career. It would not be much of a career at that, either, since he knew the odds were that after the next election he would probably be looking for a new seat or a new job. In either case he knew that the plodding progress of a loyal and patient backbencher was not for him. He would have to make his mark, and make it quickly.

Kendrick had spent all of the previous evening and much of that morning turning over O'Neill's remarks in his mind. Why cancel a publicity campaign promoting a vote-winning policy which had been sold heavily during the election, when the campaign was all set to go? Whichever way he looked at it, the pieces would only fit together into a pattern suggesting that it was the policy rather than the publicity campaign which was in trouble. But should he enquire or accuse? To question or condemn? Or simply take the course expected of new Members and be completely anodyne? He knew that if he got it wrong, the first and lasting impression he made would be that of the House fool.

His momentary uncertainty caused the general commotion of the House to die away as MPs sensed indecision and surprise. Had the new Member frozen? But Kendrick felt calm and at ease. He remembered his small majority, and he knew he must gamble. What had he got to lose, except his dignity, which in any event was a commodity of little practical value in the modern House of Commons? He took a deep breath.

'Will the Prime Minister explain to the House why he is not implementing the promised hospital expansion programme?'

No criticism. No elaboration. No added phrase or rambling comment which would allow the Prime Minister to dodge or divert the question. Kendrick had thrown his grenade and he knew that if his gamble were wrong the grenade would be picked up by a grateful Prime Minister and thrown directly back to explode in his own lap.

A murmur went up as he resumed his seat. The sport had taken an interesting new turn, and the 300-odd spectators turned as one to look towards Collingridge. He rose aware that there was nothing in his red briefing folder from which to draw inspiration. The whole House could see the broad smile with which Collingridge accepted the challenge; only those sitting very close to him could see the whites of his knuckles as he gripped the Despatch Box.

'I hope that the Honourable Gentleman will be careful to avoid being carried away by the summer silly season, at least before August arrives. As he is a new Member, may I remind him that in the last four years under this Government the health service has enjoyed a substantial real increase in spending of some 6 to 8 per cent?' Collingridge knew he was being inexcusably patronising, but he could not find the right words. 'The health service has gained more than any Government service from our success and continuing determination in defeating inflation, which compares . . .'

'Answer the bloody question,' came the irreverent growl from below the gangway on the Opposition benches, which was immediately echoed by several Members around the interrupter. Kendrick was no longer alone.

'I shall answer the question in my own way and in my own time,' snapped the Prime Minister. 'It is a pathetic sham for the Opposition to whine on about such matters when they know that electors have reached their own conclusions and only recently voted with their feet for this Government. They support us and I can repeat our determination to protect them and their hospital service.'

Increasingly rude shouts of disapproval began to rise from the Opposition benches, most of which would go unrecorded by Hansard but which were clearly audible to the Prime Minister. His own backbenchers began to shift uneasily, uncertain as to why Collingridge did not simply reaffirm often stated party policy.

'The House will be aware that it is not the custom of Governments to discuss the specifics of new spending plans in advance, and we shall make an announcement about our intentions at the appropriate time.'

'You have. You've bloody dropped it, haven't you?' the Honourable and usually disrespectful Member for Newcastle West shouted, so loudly that even Hansard could not claim to have missed it.

The Opposition Front Bench smiled and chuckled, beginning to appreciate that the Prime Minister's increasingly taut smile hid inner turmoil. The Leader of the Opposition, not six feet from where Collingridge stood, turned to his nearest colleague and whispered loudly. 'Do you know I think he's fluffed it. He's running away!'

Opposition Members began taunting him from all around, slapping their thighs and chortling like old hags around a guillotine.

The tension and pain of a thousand such encounters in the House welled up inside Collingridge. He was unprepared for this. He could not bring himself to admit the truth, yet neither could he lie to the House, and he could find no form of words which would tread that delicate line between honesty and outright deceit. As he observed the sneers and smugness on the faces in front of him and listened to their jeers, he remembered all the many lies they had told about him in the past, the cruelty they had shown and the tears they had caused his wife to shed. As he gazed at the sea of waving Order Papers and contorted faces just a few feet in front of him, his patience vanished. He had to bring it to an end, and he no longer cared how. He threw his hands in the air.

'I don't have to take comments like that from a pack of dogs,' he snarled, and sat down.

Even before the shout of triumph and rage had a chance to rise from the Opposition benches, Kendrick was back on his feet.

'On a point of order, Mr Speaker. The Prime Minister's remarks are an absolute disgrace. I asked a perfectly straightforward question about why the Prime Minister had reneged on his election promise to patients and nurses, and all I have got are insults and evasion. While I understand the Prime Minister's reluctance to admit to the House that he has perpetrated a gigantic and disgraceful fraud, is there nothing you can do to protect the right of Members of this House to get a straight answer to a straight question?'

A roar of approval grew from Opposition members as the Speaker struggled to be heard above the commotion. 'The Honourable Member, although he is new, seems already to have developed a sharp eye for parliamentary procedure, in which case he will know that I am no more responsible for the content or tone of the Prime Minister's replies than I am for the questions which are put to him. Next business!'

As the Speaker tried to move matters on, a red-faced Collingridge rose and strode angrily out of the Chamber, gesticulating for the Chief Whip to follow him. The very unparliamentary taunt of 'Coward!' rang after him across the floor. From the Government benches there was an uncertain silence.

'How in Christ's name did he know? How did that son-of-a-bitch know?'

The door had barely closed upon the Prime Minister's office just off the rear of the Chamber when the screaming began. The normally suave exterior of Her Majesty's

First Minister had been drawn back to reveal a wild Warwickshire ferret.

'Francis, it's simply not good enough. It's not bloody good enough I tell you. We get the Chancellor's report in Cabinet Committee yesterday, the full Cabinet discusses it for the first time today, and by this afternoon it's known to every snivelling creep in the Opposition. Less than two dozen Cabinet Ministers knew, only a handful of civil servants knew, but now every single Member of the Opposition knows. Who leaked it, Francis, who? I'm damned if I know, but you're Chief Whip and I want you to find out who the hell it was.'

Urquhart breathed a huge sigh of relief. Until the Prime Minister's outburst he had no idea if the finger of blame was already pointing at him, and the last couple of minutes had been distinctly uncomfortable.

'It simply astonishes me that one of our Cabinet colleagues would want deliberately to leak something like this,' Urquhart began, implicitly ruling out the possibility of a civil service leak and narrowing the circle of suspicion to include each and every one of his Cabinet colleagues.

'They've got us by the balls now, and it's going to hurt. Whoever is responsible has humiliated me, and I want him out, Francis. I want – I insist – that you find the worm. And then I want him fed to the crows.'

'I'm afraid there's been too much bickering amongst our colleagues since the election. Too many of them seem to want someone else's job.'

'I know they all want *my* job, damn them, but who would be so – cretinous . . .' – the words were spat out – 'as to deliberately leak something like that?'

'I can't say for sure, Prime Minister.'

'Can't you even give me an educated guess, for Chrissake?'

'That would not be fair.'

'Life's not fair, Francis. Tell me about it.'

'But . . .'

'No "buts", Francis. If it's happened once it can and almost certainly will happen again. Accuse, imply, whatever you damned well like. There are no minutes being taken here. But I want some names!' Collingridge kicked a chair in frustration.

'If you insist, I'll speculate. But I hope I'll not live to regret anything I'm going to say. I know nothing for sure, you understand . . . let's work from deduction. Given the time scale involved, it seems more likely to have leaked from yesterday's Cabinet Committee rather than from today's full Cabinet. Agreed?'

Collingridge nodded his assent.

'And apart from you and me, who is on that Committee?'

'Chancellor of the Exchequer, Financial Secretary, Health, Education, Environment, Trade and Industry.' The Prime Minister reeled off those Cabinet Ministers who had attended.

Urquhart remained silent, forcing Collingridge to finish off the logic himself. 'Well, the two Treasury Ministers were scarcely likely to leak the fact that they had screwed it up. But Health bitterly opposed it, so Peter McKenzie had a reason to leak it. Harold Earle at Education has always had a loose lip. And Michael Samuel has a habit of enjoying the company of the media rather too much for my liking.'

The shadowy suspicions which lurk in a Prime Minister's mind were being brought into the light, and Urquhart relished the spectacle as he watched the seed of accusation grow alongside Collingridge's insecurity.

'There are other possibilities, but I think them unlikely,' Urquhart joined in. 'As you know Michael is very close to Teddy Williams. They discuss everything together. It could have come out of party headquarters. Not from Teddy, I mean, but one of the officials there. They can be as tight-lipped as drunken Glaswegians on a Friday night.'

Collingridge pondered this possibility for some moments in silence. 'Could it really have been Teddy?' he mused. '*Et tu, Brute!* Could that really be, Francis? He was never my greatest supporter – we're from different generations – but I made him one of the team. Now surely not this?'

Urquhart was delighted at the effect his words were having on his battered leader, who sat grey and tired in his chair, staring ahead, lost in surmise and suspicion.

'Perhaps I have relied on him too much recently. I thought he had no axe to grind, no real ambition in the House of Lords. One of the loyal old guard. Was I wrong, Francis?'

'I simply don't know. You asked me to speculate. I can do no more at this stage.'

'Make sure, Francis. I want him, whoever he is.'

With that the Prime Minister announced open season, and Urquhart felt himself back on the heather moors of his childhood, gun in hand, waiting for the bucks to appear.

FRIDAY 16TH JULY – THURSDAY 22ND JULY

The life of the House of Commons is arduous and little appreciated. Long hours, heavy workloads, too much entertaining and too little respite ensure that the long summer break beckons to all Members like an oasis in a desert. As they approach closer to the oasis during the dog days of July, their thirst and their irritability increase, particularly after the exhaustion of an early summer election campaign.

During the next couple of weeks, Urquhart was prominent in moving steadily around the corridors and bars of the House, trying to bolster morale and calm the doubts of many Government backbenchers about Collingridge's increasingly scratchy performance. Morale is easier to shatter than to rebuild, and some old hands thought that Urquhart was trying perhaps a little too hard, his high profile serving to remind many that the Prime Minister was in especial need of support at a time when he should have been dominating events. But if it were a fault, it was one they recognised as aggressive loyalty in the Chief Whip. In any event, the end of the Session was only a week hence and the grapes of the South of France would soon be washing away much of the parliamentary cares.

It was because of this safety valve of August that Governments have developed the knack of making difficult announcements on the last day of the Session by means of Written Answers published in Hansard, the voluminous official report of parliamentary proceedings. Statements of Government intent can be placed openly and clearly on the public record, but at a time when most Members are packing up their desks rather than poring over the endless pages of Hansard, and when in any event there is little time or opportunity to make a fuss. The truth, the whole truth and nothing but the truth – so long as you read the fine print.

Which is why it was most unfortunate that a photocopy of a draft Written Answer from the Secretary of State for Defence informing the House of substantial cuts in the Territorial Army on the grounds that they were increasingly less relevant in the nuclear era should have been found, a full ten days before it was due to be published, lying under a chair in Annie's Bar where Members and journalists congregate to exchange views and gossip. It was still more unfortunate that it was found by the lobby correspondent of the *Independent*, because everybody liked and respected him, and he knew how to check the story out. When the story was reported as the lead item in the *Independent* four days later at the start of the final full week of the Parliamentary Session, people knew that it was reliable.

Stories of 'cuts' are nothing new for Governments to deal with. If they maintain spending at existing levels while new and inevitably more expensive techniques for performing the task are discovered, they are accused of 'cuts'. If they increase expenditure in vital areas, but not as much as the self-appointed 'experts' require, they are still accused of 'cuts'. If they shift resources from one area to another, once again the accusations of 'cuts' fly. But should they dare make actual 'cuts' in any area other than their own salary levels, retribution is swift.

Retribution on this occasion came from unusual sources. While Territorial Army pay is not large, their numbers are great and they represent important votes to Government Members of Parliament. Moreover, throughout the higher echelons of the Government's constituency parties up and down the country could be found prominent figures with the initials 'TD' after their names – 'Territorial Decoration' – someone who has served in, respects and will defend The Terrors to their last drop of writing ink.

Thus it was that, when the House gathered next to discuss forthcoming Parliamentary Business with the Leader of the House, the air was heavy with the mid-summer heat, made more oppressive by the accusations of betrayal and emotional appeals for a change of course which on this occasion were coming from the Government benches, while the Opposition sat back like enthusiastic and very contented Roman lions watching the Christians do all the work for them.

The Right Honourable Sir Jasper Grainger, OBE, JP, TD, was on his feet. The old man proudly sported a carefully ironed regimental tie along with a heavy three piece tweed suit, refusing to compromise his personal standards in spite of the inadequate air-conditioning. And as the elected Chairman of the Backbench Defence Committee, his words carried enormous weight.

'May I return to the point raised by several of my Honourable Friends about the unnecessary and deeply damaging cuts in our Territorial Army establishment? Will the Leader of the House be in no doubt about the depth of feeling amongst his own supporters on this matter? Have he and the Prime Minister yet fully understood the damage that will be done to the Government's support over the coming months? Will he even now allow the House time to debate and reverse this decision, because I must ask him not to leave his colleagues defenceless to the accusations of bad faith which will follow if this goes through?'

The Leader of the House, Simon Lloyd, straightened and readied himself once again to come to the Despatch Box, which he was beginning to feel should have been con-structed with sandbags. It had been a torrid twenty min-utes of trying to defend the Government's position, and he had grown increasingly tetchy as he found the response he had prepared earlier with the Prime Minister and Defence

Secretary affording increasingly less protection from the grenades being thrown by his own side. He was glad Collingridge and the Defence Secretary were sitting beside him on the Front Bench. Why should he suffer on his own?

'My Right Honourable Friend misses the point. The document which found its way into the newspapers was stolen Government property. These are issues which rise high above the details of the document itself. If there is to be a debate, it should be about such flagrant breaches of honesty. Will he not join me in wholeheartedly condemning the theft of important Government documents as being the major issue at stake here? He must realise that by coming back to the details of expenditure he is as good as condoning the activity of common theft and assisting those who are responsible for it.'

Sir Jasper rose to seek permission to pursue the point and, amidst waving of Order Papers throughout the Chamber, the Speaker consented. The old soldier gathered himself up to his full height, back as straight as a ramrod, moustache bristling and face flushed with genuine anger.

'Does my Right Honourable Friend not realise that it is he who is missing the point,' he thundered, 'that I would rather live alongside a common British thief than a common Russian soldier, which is precisely the fate this policy is threatening us with?'

The uproar which followed took the Speaker a full minute to calm sufficiently for any chance of a response to be heard. During that time, the Leader of the House turned and offered a look of sheer desperation to the Prime Minister and the Defence Secretary, huddled together on the Front Bench. Collingridge muttered briefly in the ear of his colleague, and then gave a curt nod to the Leader of the House.

'Mr Speaker,' the Leader of the House began, and paused to let the clamour subside and to clear his throat, which was by now parched with tension. 'Mr Speaker, I and my Right Honourable Friends have listened carefully to the mood of the House. I have the permission of the Prime Minister and the Secretary of State for Defence to say that, in light of the representations put from all sides today, the Government will look once again at this important matter to see whether any alternative solution can be found.'

He had run up the white flag, and he didn't know whether to feel sick or relieved.

The cries of victory and relief reached far outside the Chamber as the parliamentary correspondents drank in an emotional scene and recorded it in their notebooks. Amidst the hubbub and confusion on all sides, the lonely figure of Henry Collingridge sat small and shrunken, staring straight ahead.

Some minutes later, a breathless Mattie Storin had pushed her way through the crowd of politicians and correspondents who were jostling in the lobby outside the entrance to the Chamber, as Opposition Members claimed victory for themselves while Government supporters with considerably less conviction tried to claim victory for common sense. Few were in any doubt that they had witnessed a Prime Minister on the rack. Above the mêlée Mattie saw the tall figure of Urquhart edging his way around the outside of the crowd, avoiding the questions of several agitated backbenchers. He disappeared through a convenient door, and Mattie pursued him. By the time she had almost caught up with her quarry, Urquhart was striding two at a time up the stairs which led to the upper galleries surrounding the Chamber.

'Mr Urquhart,' she shouted breathlessly after the fleeing Minister, promising herself once again that she would give up late nights and resume jogging. 'I need your view.'

'I'm not sure I have one today, Miss Storin.' Urquhart did not stop.

'Surely we're not back on the "Chief Whip refuses to endorse Prime Minister" game again?'

Urquhart stopped and turned to face the still panting

Mattie. He smiled in amusement at the young correspondent's cheek. 'Yes, Mattie, I suppose you have a right to expect something. Well, what do you think?'

'If the PM had trouble in controlling his Cabinet before this, his task now is going to be – what, a nightmare? Impossible?'

'It is not unusual for Prime Ministers to change their minds. But to be forced to change your mind publicly, simply because you are unable to defend your own decision, is . . .'

Mattie waited in vain for Urquhart to finish, but realised he would not do so. He would not condemn his Prime Minister, not openly on the stairs, but it was clear there would be no justification either. She prompted the Chief Whip yet again. 'Isn't the Government getting accident prone – the second major leak in a matter of weeks? Where are these leaks coming from?'

'As Chief Whip I am responsible only for discipline on the Government backbenches. You can scarcely expect me to play headmaster to my own Cabinet colleagues as well.'

'But if it's coming from Cabinet – who, and why?'

'I simply don't know, Mattie. But doubtless the Prime Minister will instruct me to find out who and why.'

'Formally or informally?'

'I can't comment on that,' muttered Urquhart, and continued up the stairs pursued by Mattie.

'So we have got to the point where the Prime Minister is about to launch an inquiry into which of his own Cabinet colleagues is leaking sensitive information. Is that what you are saying?'

'Oh, Mattie. It seems I have already said too much. You're a damn sight quicker on the uptake than most of your colleagues. It seems to me that your logic rather than my words has led you to your conclusions, eh? And I trust that you will be keeping my name out of this.'

'Usual lobby terms, Mr Urquhart,' she assured him. 'Just let me get this perfectly clear. You are not denying, indeed you are confirming that the Prime Minister will order an investigation into his Cabinet members' conduct?'

'If you keep my name out of it – yes.'

'Jesus, this will set them all flapping,' Mattie gasped. She could already see her front page lead taking shape.

'June 10th does seem a long time ago, doesn't it, Mattie?'

Urquhart continued up the stairs which led to the Strangers Gallery, where members of the public perched on rows of cramped, narrow benches to view the proceedings of the House, usually with a considerable degree of discomfort and a still larger degree of astonishment. He caught the eye of a small and impeccably dressed Indian for whom he had previously obtained a seat in the Gallery, and signalled to him. The man struggled past the outstretched knees of other visitors packed into the benches, and emerged with obvious embarrassment past two extremely buxom middle-aged ladies. Before he had any opportunity to speak Urquhart motioned to him for silence and led him towards the small hallway behind the gallery.

'Mr Urquhart, sir, it has been a most exciting and highly educational ninety minutes. I am deeply indebted to you for assisting me to obtain such a comfortable position.'

Urquhart, who knew that even small Indian gentlemen such as Firdaus Jhabwala found the seats acutely uncomfortable, smiled knowingly. 'I know you are being very polite in not complaining about the discomfort of the seating. I only wish I could have found you some more comfortable position.'

They chatted politely while Jhabwala secured the release of his black hide attaché case from the attendant. When he had arrived he had firmly refused to hand it over until he discovered that his entry to the Gallery would be forbidden unless he lodged it with the security desk.

'I am so glad that we British can still trust ordinary working chaps with our possessions,' he stated very seriously, patting the case for comfort.

95

'Quite,' replied Urquhart, who trusted neither the ordinary working chap nor Jhabwala. Still, he was a constituent who seemed to have various flourishing local businesses, and had provided a £500 donation towards his election campaign expenses and had asked for nothing in return except, shortly afterwards, a personal interview and private meeting in the House of Commons.

'Not in the constituency,' he had explained to Urquhart's secretary on the phone. 'It's a matter of national rather than local attention.'

Urquhart led the way under the great vaulted oak ceiling of Westminster Hall, at which point Jhabwala asked to stand for a while. 'I would be grateful for a silent moment in this great hall in which Charles I was tried and condemned and Winston Churchill lay in state.'

He noticed the condescending smile appearing at the corner of Urquhart's mouth.

'Mr Urquhart. Please do not think me pretentious. My own family associations with British institutions go back nearly 250 years to the days of the Honourable East India Company and Lord Clive, whom my ancestors advised and to whom they loaned considerable funds. Both before and since my family has occupied prestigious positions in the judicial and administrative branches of Indian Government.'

Jhabwala's eyes lowered, and a strong sense of sadness filled his voice. 'But since Independence, Mr Urquhart, that once great subcontinent has slowly crumbled into a new dark age. Muslim has been set against Hindu, worker against employer, pupil against teacher. You may not agree, but the modern Gandhi dynasty is less inspired and far more corrupt than any my family ever served in colonial days. I am a Parsee, a cultural minority which has found little comfort under the new Raj, and the fortunes of my family have declined. So I moved to Great Britain, where my father and grandfather were educated. I can tell you without a trace of insincerity, Mr Urquhart, that I feel more at home and more attached to this country and its culture than ever I could back in modern India. I wake up grateful every day that I can call myself a British citizen and educate my children in British universities.'

Urquhart saw his opportunity to interrupt this impassioned and obviously heartfelt monologue. 'Where are your children educated?'

'I have a son just finishing a law degree at Jesus College, Cambridge, and an elder son who is undertaking an MBA at the Wharton Business School in Philadelphia. It is my earnest hope that my younger son will soon qualify to read medicine at Cambridge.'

They were now walking towards the interview rooms beneath the Great Hall, their shoes clipping across the worn flagstoned floor where Henry VIII had played tennis and which now was splattered with shafts of bright sunlight slanting through the ancient windows. It was a scene centuries old, and the Indian was clearly in great awe.

'And what precisely do you do?' asked Urquhart.

'I, sir, am a trader, not an educated man. I left behind any hope of that during the great turmoil of Indian Independence. I have therefore had to find my way not with my brain but by diligence and hard work. I am happy to say that I have been moderately successful.'

'What sort of trade?'

'I have several business interests, Mr Urquhart. Property. Wholesaling. A little local finance. But I am no narrow minded capitalist. I am well aware of my duty to the community. It is about that I wished to speak with you.'

By now they had arrived at the interview room and at Urquhart's invitation Jhabwala seated himself in one of the green leather chairs, fingering with delight the gold embossed portcullis which embellished the upright back of this and all the other chairs in the room.

'Mr Urquhart. I was not born in this country, and I know that of necessity I must work particularly hard to gain respectability in the community. That is important, not so much for me but for my children. I wish them to have the advantages which my father could not secure for me at a time of civil war. So I try to participate. I assist the local Rotary Club. I help with many local charities. And as you know, I am an ardent supporter of the Prime Minister.'

'I am afraid that you did not see him to best advantage this afternoon.'

'Then I suspect he needs his friends and supporters more than ever.'

There was a short silence. Urquhart struggled to find the meaning and direction behind his guest's remarks, but it eluded him, although meaning and direction he knew there must be. Jhabwala began again, a little more slowly.

'Mr Urquhart. You know that I have great admiration for you. I was happy to assist in a modest way with your election appeal and would be happy to do so again. I am also a fervent admirer of the entire Government. I would wish to help you all.'

'May I know how?'

'I know election campaigns are expensive, and perhaps I could make a small donation to Party coffers. I imagine that funds must be short at times like these.'

'Indeed, indeed,' said Urquhart. 'Could I ask how much you were thinking of giving?'

Jhabwala lifted his case onto the table top, twirled the combination and flipped the two brass catches. The lid sprang open and he slid the black leather case around to Urquhart.

'I would be delighted if the Party could accept £50,000 as a gesture of my support.'

Urquhart resisted the ferocious temptation to pick up one of the bundles of notes and start counting. He noticed that all the wads were of used £20 notes and were tied with rubber bands rather than bank cashiers' wrappers.

'This is ... most generous, Mr Jhabwala.' He found himself using his guest's name for the first time since they had met earlier in the afternoon. 'But it is a little unusual for me to accept such a large donation on behalf of the Party, particularly in cash.'

'You will understand that during the civil war in India my family lost everything. Our house and business were destroyed, and we narrowly escaped with our lives. In 1947 a Muslim mob burned my local bank to the ground – with all its deposits and records. The bank's head office apologised, of course, but without any records could only provide my father with their regrets rather than the funds he had deposited with them. It may seem a little old fashioned of me, but I still prefer to trust cash rather than cashiers.'

The businessman's smile shone reassuringly from beneath his dark features. Urquhart did not trust him or his story.

'I see.' Urquhart took a deep breath. 'May I be blunt, Mr Jhabwala, and ask if there is anything you wish from us in exchange for your support? It is sometimes the case with first-time donors that they believe there is something the Party can do for them, when in reality our powers are very limited . . .'

Jhabwala beamed and shook his head to halt Urquhart's question. 'There is nothing I wish to do other than to be a firm supporter of the Prime Minister and yourself, Mr Urquhart. You will understand as a local MP that my business interests often bring me into friendly contact with local authorities for planning permission or tendering for contracts and so forth. I cannot guarantee that you will never find my name in the local press or that I will not ask at some point to seek your guidance through the maze of local decision makers, but I assure you I am looking for no favours. I want nothing in exchange, other than to request that I and my wife have the honour of meeting with the Prime Minister at some suitable time, particularly if he should ever come to the constituency. It would mean a great deal to my wife, as you will appreciate.'

And the photographs of Jhabwala closeted with the Prime Minister would go down remarkably well in the local and ethnic press, as Urquhart well knew. He didn't care for the hint about local planning or contract decisions, but he was an experienced hand at dealing with such requests when they arose. Urquhart began to relax and to return the Indian's smile.

'I am sure that could be arranged. Perhaps you and your wife would like to attend a reception at Downing Street?'

The Indian was nodding. 'It would be an honour, of course, to be able to have just a few private words with him, simply to express my great personal enthusiasm.'

'That might be possible, too, but you will understand that the Prime Minister himself could not accept the money. It would not be – how should I put it? – delicate for him to be involved with such matters.'

'Of course, of course, Mr Urquhart. Which is why I would be delighted if you would accept the money on his behalf.'

'I'm afraid I can only give you a rudimentary receipt. Perhaps you would prefer to deliver the money directly to the party treasurers.'

Jhabwala threw up his hands in horror. 'Sir, I do not require a receipt from you. You have my fullest trust. It was you as my local Member of Parliament I wished to see, not a party official. I have even taken the liberty of engraving your initials on the hide case, Mr Urquhart, a small gesture which I hope you will accept for all your dutiful work in Surrey.'

You crafty, ingratiating little sod, thought Urquhart, all the while smiling broadly at Jhabwala and wondering how long it would be before he got the first call about planning permission. Perhaps he should have thrown the Indian out, but an idea was already forming in his mind. He reached across the table and shook Jhabwala's hand warmly.

'It has been a great pleasure meeting you at last, Mr Jhabwala.'

*   *   *

The night was hot and humid, even for late July. Mattie had taken a long, cool shower and thrown the windows wide open, but she could get no relief from the still and heavy air. She lay in the darkness upon her bed, feeling her hair stick clammily to the nape of her neck. She could not sleep while the scenes of parliamentary turmoil she had witnessed earlier in the day kept tumbling through her thoughts. But there was something else, too, something not of the mind but in her body that was disturbing her, making her restless.

She lay back on her lonely, cold bed and felt the dampness trickling between her shoulder blades. She could not forget that it was the first time since Yorkshire she had sweated in bed, for any reason . . .

FRIDAY 23RD JULY

The following morning a young black woman walked into a scruffy newsagents just off Praed Street in Paddington and enquired after the cost of accommodation address facilities advertised on the card in the shop window. She explained that she was working in the area and needed a local address to which she could direct her mail. It was a brilliant summer's day in London, but behind the thick shutters and dirty windows the shop was dark and musty. At first the fleshy, balding assistant behind the counter scarcely lifted his eyes from his copy of *Playboy*. This was one of London's notorious red light areas, and young women or seedy men asking to open an accommodation address was one of the less surprising requests he had to deal with. This girl was particularly attractive, though, and he wondered where she did business. His wife was staying with her mother over the weekend, and a little distraction would be better than the long list of household jobs she was threatening to leave behind.

He brushed away the cigarette ash he had spilled over the counter and smiled encouragingly at her. He got no response, however. With scarcely another word, the young woman paid the fee for the minimum three months, carefully put away the receipt which would be needed for identification, and left.

The assistant had time only for one last look at the retreating and beautifully curved backside before he was engaged by the complaints of an old age pensioner who had not yet received her morning newspaper, and he did not see the young woman get into the taxi outside.

'All right, Pen?' asked the man waiting inside.

'No problem, Roger,' his secretary answered. 'But why couldn't he do it himself?'

'Look, I told you that he has some delicate personal problems to sort out and needs some privacy for his mail. Dirty magazines for all I know. So no questions, and not a word to anyone. OK?'

Urquhart had sworn him to secrecy, and he suspected that the Chief Whip would be furious if he discovered that O'Neill had got Penny Guy to carry out his dirty work. But he knew he could trust Penny with such chores. After all, what were secretaries for?

As the taxi drew away, Penny once again remarked to herself how strangely O'Neill was beginning to act nowadays.

The day was growing ever hotter by the time the man in the sports jacket and trilby hat ventured into the North London branch of the Union Bank of Turkey on the Seven Sisters Road. The Cypriot counter clerk often swore that Englishmen only ever had one set of clothes which they wore throughout the winter or summer, irrespective of the temperature. And this one obviously had money since he wanted to open an account. In a slight but perceptible regional accent which the clerk could not quite place, he explained that he lived in Kenya but was visiting the United Kingdom for a few months to develop the holiday business which he ran. He was interested in investing in a hotel which was being built just outside the Turkish resort of Antalya, on the southern Mediterranean coast.

The clerk responded that he did not know Antalya personally, but had heard that it was a beautiful spot, and of course the bank would be delighted to help him in whatever way possible. He offered the prospective customer a simple registration form, requiring details of his name, address, previous banking reference and other details.

Five minutes later, the customer had returned to the clerk's window with the completed form. He apologised for being able to provide a banking reference only from Kenya, but this was his first trip to London in nearly twenty years. The clerk assured the older man that the bank was very accustomed to dealing with overseas enquiries, and the banking reference in Kenya would be no problem.

That's what you think, the other thought. He knew it would take at least four weeks for the reference to be checked, and probably another four before it could be clearly established that the reference was false. By that time the account would have been closed with all bank charges paid, so no one would care or question.

The clerk sought no further verification of any of the other items on the form. 'How would you like to open your account, sir?'

'I would like to make an initial deposit of £50,000 – in cash.'

The man pulled open a brown corduroy holdall and passed the bundles of notes across the counter. He was glad he did not have to count them. It had been years since he had last worn these glasses, and in the meantime he had changed his contact lens prescription twice. His eyes were not focusing properly and they ached, but Urquhart knew that his simple disguise would be more than enough to avoid recognition by any but his closest colleagues. There was after all some benefit in being the most faceless senior member of Her Majesty's Government, he told himself sarcastically. He delighted at long last in being able to take advantage of his enforced anonymity.

The clerk had finished counting the money, with a colleague double checking the total, and was already filling out a receipt. Banks are like plumbers, Urquhart thought, cash in hand and no questions asked.

'Rather than have the cash just sitting idle in a current account, I would like you to purchase some shares for me. Can you arrange that?' he requested.

It took only another five minutes for Urquhart to fill out two further forms placing an order for 20,000 ordinary shares in the Renox Chemical Company PLC, currently trading at just over 240p per share. He was assured that the order would be completed by 4 p.m. that afternoon, at a cost of £49,288 including stamp duties and brokers' fees, leaving him exactly £712 in his new account. Urquhart signed the forms with a flourish and a signature that was illegible.

The clerk smiled as he pushed the receipt across the counter. 'A great pleasure doing business with you, Mr Collingridge.'

MONDAY 26TH JULY –
WEDNESDAY 28TH JULY

Seventy-two hours later MPs gathered in the House to begin the final week of bickering before the summer recess. There were relatively few Members present, as many of their colleagues had tried to take their leave of London early. There had been little attempt to dissuade them, since there was already enough tetchiness around Westminster without piling on needless aggravation. There was very much an end-of-term mood amongst the parliamentarians and little business was done. However, the Hansard record of parliamentary proceedings for that day would be thick, fleshed out with a remarkable number of Written Answers to MPs' questions which the Government were anxious to deal with while attention was diverted elsewhere and before Ministers and their civil servants left for their own recuperation. Ministers from the Department of Health were particularly careful not to be seen around the corridors of Westminster that day, because one of the many Written Answers they had issued concerned the long-awaited postponement of the hospital expansion programme. They did not expect to get much comfort from MPs of any party on that subject.

It was not surprising, therefore, that few noted another announcement from the Department concerning a list of three drugs which the Government, on the advice of their Chief Medical Officer and the Committee on the Safety of Medicines, were now licensing for general use. One of the drugs was Cybernox, a new medication developed by the Renox Chemical Company PLC which had proved startlingly effective in controlling the craving for nicotine when fed in small doses to addicted rats and beagles. The same excellent results had been obtained during extensive test programmes with humans, and now the drug had been approved for general use under doctor's prescription.

The announcement caused a flurry of activity at Renox Chemicals. A press conference for the medical and scientific press was called for the following day, the Marketing Director pressed the button on a pre-planned mail shot to every single general practitioner throughout the country, and the company's broker informed the Stock Exchange of the new licence.

The response was immediate. Shares in the Renox Chemical Company PLC jumped from 244p to 295p. The 20,000 ordinary shares purchased two days before by the Union Bank of Turkey's brokers were now worth exactly £59,000.

Shortly before noon the next day, a telephone call instructed the bank to sell the shares and credit the amount to the appropriate account. The caller also explained that regrettably the hotel venture in Antalya was not proceeding, and the account holder was returning to Kenya. Would the bank be kind enough to close the account, and expect a visit from the account holder later that afternoon?

Just before the bank closed at 3 p.m. the same bespectacled man in the hat and sports jacket walked into the branch on Seven Sisters Road and collected £58,962 which he placed in bundles of £20 notes in the bottom of his brown corduroy bag. He bridled at the £750 in charges which the bank had levied on his short-lived and simple account but, as the deputy manager had suspected, he chose not to make a fuss. He asked for a closing statement to be sent to him at his address in Paddington, and thanked the clerk for his courtesy.

The following morning and less than one week after Firdaus Jhabwala had met with Urquhart, the Chief Whip delivered £50,000 in cash to the party treasurers. Substantial payments in cash were not unique, and the treasurers expressed delight at discovering a new source of funds. Urquhart suggested that the treasurers office make the usual arrangements to ensure that the donor and his wife were invited to a charity reception or two at Downing Street, and asked to be informed when this happened so that he could make a specific arrangement with the Prime Minister's political secretary to ensure that Mr and Mrs Jhabwala had ten minutes alone with the Prime Minister beforehand. One of the party treasurers made a careful note of the donor's address, said that he would write an immediate cryptic letter of thanks, and locked the money in a safe.

Probably uniquely amongst Cabinet Ministers, Urquhart left for holiday that night feeling utterly relaxed.

Part Two

THE CUT

AUGUST

The newspapers during August were dreadful. With politicians and the main political correspondents all away, second string lobby correspondents struggled to fill the vacuum and develop any story they could which would get their by-line on the front page. So they clutched at whispers and rumour. What was on Tuesday only a minor piece of speculation on page five of the *Guardian* had become by Friday a hard news story on the front page of the *Daily Mail*. This was the chance for the junior correspondents to make their mark, and the mark they chose to make was all too frequently on the reputation of Henry Collingridge. Minor backbenchers who were too self-promoting even to take a break during the holiday season were honoured with significant pieces quoting 'senior party spokesmen', putting forward their views as to where the Government was going wrong and how a new sense of direction had to be imposed. Rumours about the Prime Minister's dissatisfaction with and distrust of his Cabinet colleagues abounded, and since there was no one around authoritatively to deny the rumours, the silence was taken as authoritative consent. So the speculation fed on itself and ran riot. The early August rumours about an 'official inquisition' into Cabinet leaks had, by later in the month, grown into predictions that there would after all be a reshuffle in the autumn. The word around Westminster had it that Henry Collingridge's temper was getting increasingly erratic, even though he was in fact enjoying a secluded holiday on a private estate many hundreds of miles away near Cannes.

The Prime Minister's brother also became the subject of a spate of press stories, mostly in the gossip columns, and the Downing Street press office was repeatedly called upon to comment on suggestions that the Prime Minister was bailing out 'dear old Charlie' from the increasingly close attentions of his creditors, including the Inland Revenue. But Downing Street would not comment – it was personal, not official – so the formal 'no comment' which was given to the most fanciful of accusations was recorded in the news coverage, usually in the most damaging light.

As August drew on, with only the lightest of nudges down the telephone from Urquhart, the press tied the Prime Minister ever more closely to his impecunious brother. Not that Charlie was saying anything stupid. He had the common sense to keep well out of the way, but an anonymous telephone call to one of the sensationalist Sunday newspapers enabled them to track him down to a cheap hotel in rural Bordeaux. A reporter was despatched to pour enough wine down him to encourage a few vintage 'Charlie-isms', but instead succeeded only in making Charlie violently sick over the reporter and his notebook before passing out. The reporter promptly paid £50 to a big-busted girl with a low-cut dress to lean over the slumbering form, while a photographer captured the tender moment for posterity and the newspaper's 11 million readers.

'"I'm broke and busted" says Charlie' screamed the headline, while the copy reported for the umpteenth time the fact that the Prime Minister's brother was nearly destitute and cracking under the pressure of a failed marriage and a famous brother. Downing Street's 'absolutely no comment' seemed in the circumstances even more uncaring than usual.

The next weekend the same photograph was run alongside one of the Prime Minister holidaying in considerable comfort in the South of France – to English eyes a mere stone's throw from his ailing brother – and seemingly unwilling to leave his poolside to help. The fact that the same newspaper a week earlier had been reporting how deeply Henry was involved in sorting out Charlie's

114

financial affairs seemed to have been forgotten – until the Downing Street press office called the editor to complain.

'What do you want?' came the reply. 'We give both sides of the story. We backed him warts and all throughout the election campaign. Now it's time to restore the balance a bit.'

Yes, the newspapers during August were dreadful.

SEPTEMBER – OCTOBER

September was even worse. As the new month opened, the Leader of the Opposition announced that he was resigning to make way for 'a stronger arm with which to hold our banner aloft'. He had always been a little too verbose for his own good.

Like most political leaders he was pushed by the younger men around him who had more energy and more ambition, who made their move quietly and secretly almost without his knowing until it was too late and he had announced his intention to resign in an emotional late night interview. For a moment he seemed to have changed his mind under pressure from his still intensely ambitious wife, until he discovered that he could no longer rely on a single vote in his Shadow Cabinet. Yet they were warm in their praise of their fallen leader. As so often happens, the faithful were far more effusively united by his death than by anything he had achieved in office.

The news electrified the media, and Mattie was summoned back from her beach in Zakynthos, much to her silent relief. Eight days of lying in the sun watching couples grow increasingly tender and uninhibited in the Ionian sun had made her feel utterly miserable. She was lonely, very lonely, and the loving couples around her only served to rub the point home. When the telephone call came instructing her to return to cover the breaking story, she packed her bags without complaint and found a seat on the next flight home.

She returned to discover an Opposition Party which had been galvanised. Their seemingly endless internal divisions were now being played down as they stepped up the attack on a lacklustre Government, most of whose members were still away on holiday. The real prospect of power at the next election, even one which was still perhaps four years away, was helping to focus Opposition minds and encourage fraternal thoughts. Better as one of twenty senior Cabinet Ministers in Government than the sole Party Leader in endless Opposition, one explained.

So by the time the new leader was elected just a week before the Party's annual conference in early October, the Opposition had dominated the news for several weeks and the conference turned into a united salute to the new leader. Under an enormous slogan of 'VICTORY', the conference was unrecognisable as the assembly of a party which had lost the election only a few months before.

By contrast, just a week later the representatives gathered for the Government Party's conference in a spirit of trepidation and complaint. The conference centre at Bournemouth could be uplifting if filled with 4,000 enthusiastic supporters, but now its bare brick walls and chromium-plated fitments served only to emphasise the sullenness of those who gathered.

As Publicity Director, it was Roger O'Neill's task to present and package the conference, but as the task of raising spirits became increasingly daunting, so he could be seen talking more and more feverishly to journalists – apologising, justifying, explaining, and blaming. And particularly he blamed Lord Williams. The Chairman had cut the budget, he explained, delayed making decisions, not got a grip on things. There were rumours circulating within party headquarters that he deliberately wanted the conference to be low key because he thought the Prime Minister was likely to get a rough ride from the faithful. 'Party doubts about Collingridge leadership' was the first *Guardian* report to come out of Bournemouth.

In the conference hall, the debates proceeded according to the rigid pre-set schedule. An enormous sign hung above the platform – 'FINDING THE RIGHT WAY'. The speeches struggled to obey its command beneath glaring television lights and an annoying buzz from the hall which the stewards were quite incapable of quelling. On the fringes of the hall the representatives, journalists and politicians gathered in little huddles to exchange views, a regular part of any political gathering, and a fertile breeding ground for idle gossip.

The 'buzz' around the conference was one of discontent. Everywhere they listened, the men from the media were able to hear criticism. Former MPs who had recently lost their seats were critical, but asked not to be quoted for fear of endangering their chances of being selected for safer seats at the next election. Their constituency chairmen showed no such reticence. They had not only lost their MP, but also faced several years of the Opposition Party ruling their local councils, nominating the mayor and committee chairmen, and disposing of the fruits of local office.

There was also growing concern that the parliamentary by-election, due on Thursday, would give a poor result. The Member for Dorset East, Sir Anthony Jenkins, had suffered a stroke four days before the general election. Elected while in intensive care, he had died only three weeks later.

His seat, just a few miles from Bournemouth, was a safe one with a majority of nearly 20,000, so the Prime Minister had decided to hold the by-election during conference week. He had been advised strongly against it, but he argued that on balance it was worth the risk. The conference publicity would provide good campaigning material for the by-election, there would still be a strong sympathy vote for the fallen MP, conference representatives could take a few hours off to undertake some much-needed canvassing, and the Prime Minister would be able to welcome the victorious candidate during his own conference speech – a good publicity stunt.

Now the busloads of conference-goers returning from a morning's canvassing were reporting a lack of sympathy on the doorstep. The seat would be held, of course, it had been in the Party since the War, but the thumping victory which Collingridge had demanded was beginning to look more distant with every day's canvass returns.

It was going to be a difficult week, not quite the victory celebration the party managers had planned.

WEDNESDAY 13TH OCTOBER

A cold wet wind was blowing off the sea when Mattie
Storin was woken by a pounding headache early on
Wednesday morning. As the representative of a major
national newspaper she was one of the fortunate few journalists offered accommodation in the headquarters hotel
where she could mix freely with the key politicians and
party officials. She had mixed a little too freely the previous
evening, and she began her regular morning calisthenics
with heavy limbs and a distinct lack of enthusiasm. Her
whole body shouted at her that this was a rotten way to
cure a hangover, so she quickly changed her mind and
opted for an open window – a move which she immediately
recognised as the second bad decision of the day. The small
hotel was perched high on the cliff tops, ideal for catching
the summer sun but exposed and unprotected on such grey
and swirling autumn mornings. Her overheated hotel
room turned into an icebox in seconds, and Mattie decided
that she would make no more decisions until after a gentle
breakfast.

She heard the scuffling of something being delivered
outside in the corridor and pulled the blanket protectively
around her shoulders, stumping her way across to the door.
Work, in the form of the morning newspapers, was piled
outside on the hallway carpet. She picked them up and
threw them carelessly towards the bed. As they spread
chaotically over the rumpled bedclothes, a sheet of paper
fluttered from between the pages and fell to the floor. With
a tired grunt she bent down to retrieve it, and through
the morning mist which seemed completely to have enveloped her head read the words: 'Opinion Research Survey

121

No. 40, 6 October — SECRET', emblazoned across the top.

She rubbed her eyes to open them properly. They've surely not started giving them away with the *Mirror*, she thought. Mattie knew the Party conducted weekly surveys to track the nationwide movement of public opinion on political issues, but these had a highly restricted distribution to Cabinet Ministers and only a handful of top Party officials. She had been shown copies rarely and only when they had good news to convey which the Party wished to publicise; otherwise they were kept under strictest security. She wondered what good news could possibly have been found in the latest survey, and why it had been delivered wrapped up like fried fish and chips.

The contents of the note made her rub her eyes once more. The Party, which had won the election with 41 per cent of the vote, now had only 31 per cent support, 14 per cent behind the main Opposition Party. Even more damaging were the figures on the Prime Minister's popularity. Less than one in four now preferred him while the new Leader of the Opposition stood at well over 50 per cent. It made Collingridge more disliked than any Prime Minister she could remember.

Mattie squatted on her bed. She no longer needed to ask why she had been sent the information. It was dynamite, and she felt the paper almost burning in her hand. 'Government crashes in opinion polls', it seemed to say as she composed her own introduction. And someone wanted her to throw this explosive news right into the middle of the party conference. It was a deliberate act of sabotage which would be an excellent story – her story, as long as she got it in first.

She grabbed for the telephone. 'Hello, Mrs Preston? It's Mattie Storin. Is Grev there, please?'

There was a short pause before her editor came on the phone, and his husky tones announced that he had just been woken up.

'Who's died?'

'What?'

'Who's bloody died? Why else would you call me at such a bloody stupid time?'

'Oh, nobody. I mean . . . I'm sorry. I forgot what time it was.'

'Shit.'

'Sorry, Grev.'

'Well, something must have happened, for pity's sake.'

'Yes, it came with my morning newspapers.'

'Well, that's a relief. We're now only a day behind the rest.'

'No, Grev. Listen will you? I've got hold of the Party's latest polling figures. They're sensational!'

'How did you get them?'

'They were left outside my door.'

'Gift wrapped, were they?' The editor was clearly having great difficulty controlling his sarcasm.

'But they're really sensational, Grev.'

'And who left them outside the door, Santa Claus?'

'Er, I don't know.' For the first time a hint of doubt crept into the young journalist's voice. She was waking up very rapidly now.

'Well, I don't suppose Henry Collingridge left them there. So who do you think wanted to leak them to you?'

Mattie's silence could not hide her confusion.

'Were you out on the town with any of your colleagues last night?'

'Grev, what the hell's that got to do with it?'

'Have you never heard of being set up by your so-called friends?' The editor sounded almost despairing.

'But how do you know?'

'I don't bloody know. But the point is, Wonder Girl, neither do bloody you!'

There was another embarrassed silence from Mattie

before she decided to have a last, despairing attempt to restore her confidence and persuade her editor. 'Don't you even want to know what they say?'

'No. Not if you don't know where they come from or can't be certain they are not a stupid hoax. And remember, the more sensational they look, the more certain it is that you're being set up.'

The crash of the telephone being slammed down exploded in her ear. It would have hurt even had she not been hung over. What a mug. As her headline dissolved back into the grey morning mists of her mind, her headache returned, more insistent and painful than ever. She needed a cup of black coffee badly.

Twenty minutes later Mattie eased gently down the broad stairs of the hotel and slipped into the breakfast room. It was still early and there was only a handful of early morning enthusiasts yet about. She sat down at a table on her own and prayed she would not be disturbed. She hid herself in a copy of the *Express* and hoped people would conclude that she was working rather than fixing a hangover.

The first cup of coffee made no impact, but the second helped a little. Slowly her headache began to loosen its grip and she began to take some interest in the rest of the world. Perhaps she could even stand an early morning gossip.

She looked around the intimate Victorian room and noted another political correspondent who was deeply engrossed in conversation with a Minister, and would not want to be disturbed. Two other people she thought she recognised but could not be sure. The young man on the next table she did not know and Mattie had just decided to finish a solo breakfast when she noticed the pile of papers and folders on the chair next to her neighbour. The papers and the rather academic scruffiness with which he was dressed suggested that the breakfaster was one of the many party officials Mattie had not yet got to know. The name scribbled on top of the folder was K. J. Spence.

The journalist's professional instincts had by now begun gradually to reassert themselves under the steady bombardment of caffeine, and she reached inside her ever-present shoulder bag for a copy of the internal party telephone list that at some point she had begged or stolen – she couldn't remember which.

'Spence. Kevin. Extension 371. Opinion Research.'

Mattie checked again the name on top of the folder, feeling that mistakes on opinion research had caused her enough trouble already that morning, but there was no confusion. Her editor's sarcasm had already demolished her faith in the leaked poll's statistics but she thought there would be no harm in trying to find out what the real figures were. She caught his eye.

'Kevin Spence, isn't it? From party headquarters? I'm Mattie Storin of the *Telegraph*. I haven't been on the paper long, but one of my jobs is to get to know all the party officials. Can I join you for a cup of coffee?'

Kevin Spence, aged thirty-two but looking older, unmarried and a life-long headquarters bureaucrat with a salary of £10,200 (no perks), nodded obligingly, and they were soon in conversation. Spence was rather shy and deeply flattered to be recognised by someone from a newspaper, and he was soon explaining with enthusiasm and in detail the regular reports he had given during the election on the state of public opinion to the Prime Minister and the Party's War Committee. Yes, he admitted, they did take opinion polls seriously in spite of what they always said on television. He ventured the thought that some even took opinion polls too seriously.

'What do you mean, too seriously? That's your job, isn't it?'

Somewhat donnishly Spence explained the foibles of opinion polling, the margin of error you should always remember, the rogue polls which in spite of all the pollsters' efforts still sneaked through and simply got it wrong.

'Like the one I've just seen,' Mattie remarked with a twinge, still tender from her earlier embarrassment.

'What do you mean?' Spence enquired sharply.

Mattie looked at him and saw that the affable official had now developed a flush which even as she looked was spreading from the collar up to the eyes. The eyes themselves had lost their eagerness. Spence was not a trained politician and was not adept at hiding his feelings, and the confusion was flowing through. Why was he so flustered? Mattie mentally kicked herself. Surely the damned figures couldn't be right after all? The dynamic young reporter of the year had already jumped several somersaults that morning, and feeling rather sour with herself decided that one more leap could scarcely dent her professional pride any further.

'I understand, Kevin, that your latest figures are quite disappointing. In fact, somebody mentioned a figure of 31 per cent.'

Spence, whose cheeks had been getting even redder as Mattie spoke, reached for his tea to give himself time to think, but his hand was trembling.

'And the PM personally is down to 24 per cent,' she ventured. 'I can't remember any Prime Minister being as unpopular as that.'

At this point the tea began to spill from the cup, and Spence returned it quickly to the saucer.

'I don't know what you're talking about,' he muttered, addressing the napkin which he was using to mop up the tea.

'Aren't these your latest figures?' Mattie reached once more inside her bag and pulled out the mysterious sheet of paper which she proceeded to smooth on the table cloth. As she did so, she noticed for the first time the initials KJS typed along the bottom.

Spence reached out and tried to push the paper away

from him, seemingly afraid to get too near to it. 'Where on earth did you get that?' He looked around desperately to see whether anyone had noticed the exchange.

Mattie picked up the piece of paper and began reading it out loud. '"Opinion Research Survey Number 40" – this is yours, isn't it?'

'Yes, but . . . Please, Miss Storin!'

He was not used to dissembling. Spence was clearly deeply upset, and seeing no way of escape decided to throw himself on the mercy of his breakfast companion. In a hushed voice, and still looking nervously around the room, he pleaded with her.

'I'm not supposed to talk to you about any opinion research. It's strictly confidential.'

'But Kevin, it's only one piece of paper.'

'You don't know what it's like. If these figures get out, and I'm the one thought to have given them to you, I'd be out on my ear. Everyone's looking for scapegoats. There are so many rumours flooding around. The PM doesn't trust the Chairman. The Chairman doesn't trust us. Everybody says that heads are going to roll. I like my job, Miss Storin. I can't afford to be blamed for leaking confidential figures to you.'

'I didn't realise morale was so bad.'

Spence looked utterly miserable. 'I've never known it worse. Everyone was exhausted after the election, and there was a lot of bad feeling flying around because the result wasn't as good as we expected. Then all those leaks and reports that the Cabinet were at each other's throats, so instead of a long break during the summer Lord Williams kept us all hard at it. Frankly, all most of us are trying to do is to keep our heads down so that when it hits the fan we get as little of it as possible.'

He looked at Mattie eye-to-eye for the first time. 'Please don't drag me into this.'

'Kevin, you did not leak this report to me and I shall confirm that to anyone who wants to know. But if I'm to help you I shall need a little help myself. This is your latest polling report, right?'

She slipped the paper back across the table. Spence took another anguished look at it and nodded in confirmation.

'They are prepared by you and circulated on a tightly restricted basis?'

Another nod.

'All I need to know from you, Kevin, is who gets them. That can't be a state secret, can it?'

There was no more fight left in Spence. He seemed to hold his breath for a long time before replying.

'Numbered copies are circulated in double-sealed envelopes solely to Cabinet Ministers and five senior headquarters personnel: the Deputy Chairman and four senior directors.'

He tried to moisten his mouth with another drink of tea, but discovered he had already spilt most of it. 'How on earth did you get hold of it?'

'Let's just say someone got a little careless, shall we?'

'Not my office?' he gasped, his insecurity flooding out.

'No, Kevin. You've just given me the names of over two dozen people who receive the figures, and with their secretaries it would bring the possible number of sources to well over fifty.' She gave him one of her most reassuring, warm smiles. 'Don't worry, I won't involve you. But let's keep in touch.'

Mattie left the breakfast room. She should have been feeling elated about the front page story she was now able to write but she was wondering too hard how the devil she was ever going to identify the turncoat.

Room 561 in the hotel could not be described as five star. It was one of the smallest rooms, far away from the main entrance and at the end of the top floor corridor under the eaves. The party hierarchy did not stay here, it was definitely a room for the workers.

128

Penny Guy hadn't heard the steps outside in the corridor before the door burst open. She sat bolt upright in bed, startled and exposing two perfectly formed breasts.

'Shit, Roger, don't you ever bloody knock?' She threw a pillow at the intruder. 'And what the hell are you doing up so early? You don't normally surface until lunchtime.'

She did not bother to cover herself as O'Neill sat down at the end of the bed. There was an ease between them suggesting an absence of any sexual threat which would have startled most people. O'Neill constantly flirted with her, particularly in public, but on the two occasions when Penny had offered, O'Neill had been very affectionate and warm but had complained of being too exhausted. She guessed he had a deep streak of sexual insecurity running through him, which he hid beneath flattery and innuendo. Penny had heard from other women who had spent time with O'Neill that he was frequently too exhausted – attentive, very forward, suggestive, but rarely able to commit himself fully. She was very fond of him, and longed to ease the insecurities out of him with her long, electric fingers, but she knew he would not drop his guard long enough to let her weave her magic. She had worked for O'Neill for nearly three years and had seen him slowly change as he found the pressures of political and public life increasingly infatuating, yet steadily more difficult to cope with.

To those who did not know him well he was extrovert, amusing, full of charm, ideas and energy. But Penny had watched him become increasingly erratic. He rarely came into the office nowadays before noon; he had started making many private phone calls, getting agitated, disappearing suddenly. His constant hay fever and sneezing were unpleasant, but Penny was devoted to him. She did not understand many of the odd ways he had developed – particularly why he would not sleep with her. She had that strange blindness for him which comes with daily familiarity and strong affections. But she knew he depended on her. If he didn't need her in bed, he needed her practically every other moment of his day. It wasn't the same as love, but her warm heart responded anyway. She would do almost anything for him.

'You got up this early just to come and woo me, didn't you? You can't resist me after all,' she teased.

'Shut up, you little tart, and cover up those gorgeous tits. That's not fair.'

Smiling wickedly, she lifted her breasts up towards him, goading him. 'Can't resist them after all. Well, who am I to refuse an order from the boss?'

Playfully she threw the bedclothes off her naked body and moved over on the mattress to make room for him. O'Neill's eyes couldn't help but follow the line of her long legs, and for the first time since Penny had known him he began to blush. She giggled as she noticed him staring hypnotically at her body, and he made a grab for the bedclothes to try and cover her up but instead succeeded only in losing his balance and getting tangled up in her long brown arms. As he lifted his head off the mattress, he found a rigid dark nipple staring at him from less than three inches away, and he had to use all of his strength to tear himself free. He retreated to the other side of the small room, visibly shaking.

'Pen, please! You know I'm not at my best this early in the morning.'

'OK, Roger. Don't worry. I'm not going to rape you.' She was laughing playfully as she pulled the sheets loosely around her. 'But what are you doing up so early?'

'I've just left this incredibly beautiful Brazilian gymnast who has spent all night teaching me a whole series of new exercises. We didn't have any gymnastic rings, so we used the chandelier. OK?'

She shook her head firmly.

'How could one so young and beautiful be so cynical?' he protested. 'All right. I had to make a delivery in the vicinity and I thought I'd come and say good morning.'

He didn't bother to add that Mattie Storin had nearly

130

caught him as he was placing the document amongst the newspapers, and he welcomed the chance to lie low in his secretary's room for a while. He was still elated at the trouble which the leaked poll would cause the Party Chairman, who had been openly hostile to him in the last few weeks. Through his paranoia, worked on by Urquhart, he had failed to notice that the hard-pressed Williams had been short with most of his colleagues as well.

Penny tried to bring him back down to earth. 'Yeah, but next time you come to say good morning, try knocking first. And make it after 8.30.'

'Don't give me a hard time. You know I can't live without you.'

'Enough passion, Roger. What do you want? You have to want something, don't you, even if not my body?'

'Actually, I did come to ask you something. It's a bit delicate really . . .'

'Go ahead, Roger. You can be frank. You've already seen there's no one else in the bed!' She started laughing again.

O'Neill began to recover his salesman's charms, and started upon the story which Urquhart had drummed into him the previous evening.

'Pen, you remember Patrick Woolton, the Foreign Secretary. You typed a couple of his speeches during the election, and he certainly remembers you. He asked after you when I saw him last night and I think he's rather smitten with you. Anyway, he wondered if you would be interested in dinner with him but he didn't want to upset or offend you by asking direct, so I sort of offered to have a quiet word as it might be easier for you to say no to me rather than to him personally, you see.'

'OK, Roger.'

'OK what, Pen?'

'OK. I'll have dinner with him. What's the big deal?'

'Nothing. Except . . . Woolton's got a bit of a reputation with the ladies. He might just want more than – dinner.'

'Roger, every man I've ever been out with since the age of

fourteen has always wanted more than dinner. I can handle it. Might be interesting. He could improve my French!' She burst into fits of giggles once again, and threw her last pillow at him. O'Neill retreated through the door as Penny was looking around for something else to throw.

Five minutes later he was back in his own room and on the phone to Urquhart.

'Delivery made and dinner fixed.'

'Splendid, Roger. You've been most helpful. I hope the Foreign Secretary will be grateful too.'

'But I still don't see how you are going to get him to invite Penny to dinner. What's the point of all this?'

'The point, dear Roger, is that he will not have to invite her to dinner at all. He is coming to my reception this evening. You will bring Penny, who you have established is more than willing to meet and spend some time with him. I shall introduce them over a glass of champagne or two, and see what develops. If I know Patrick Woolton – which as Chief Whip I do – it won't take more than twenty minutes before he's suggesting that they go to his room to discuss – how does *Private Eye* put it – Ugandan affairs?'

'Or French lessons,' muttered O'Neill. 'But I still don't see where that gets us.'

'Whatever happens, Roger, you and I will know about it. And knowledge is always useful.'

'I still don't see how.'

'Trust me, Roger. You must trust me.'

'I do. I have to: I don't really get much choice, do I?'

'That's right, Roger. Now you are beginning to see. Knowledge is power.'

The phone went dead. O'Neill thought he understood but wasn't absolutely sure. He still often struggled to figure out whether he was Urquhart's partner or prisoner, but could never really decide. He rummaged in his bedside cabinet and took out a small carton. He swallowed a couple of sleeping pills and collapsed fully clothed on the bed.

*   *   *

'Patrick. Thanks for the time.'

'You sounded quite serious on the phone. When Chief Whips say they want an urgent private word with you, they usually mean they've got the photographs under lock and key but unfortunately the *News of the World* has got the negatives!'

Urquhart smiled and slipped through the open door into the Foreign Secretary's room. He had not come far, indeed only a few yards from his own bungalow next door in what the local constabulary had named 'Overtime Alley', the row of luxury private bungalows in the grounds of the conference hotel which housed leading Ministers, all of whom had a 24-hour rota of police guards running up huge overtime bills for the hapless local ratepayers.

'Drink?' the genial Lancastrian offered.

'Thanks, Patrick. Scotch.'

The Right Honourable Patrick Woolton, Her Majesty's Principal Secretary for Foreign and Commonwealth Affairs and one of Merseyside's many successful *emigrés*, busied himself at a small drinks cabinet which quite obviously had already been used that afternoon, while Urquhart placed the Ministerial red box he was carrying in the corner of the room beside the four belonging to his overworked host. The brightly coloured leather-clad boxes are provided to all Ministers to house their official papers, speeches and other items which they require to keep secure. Red boxes go wherever Ministers go, even on holiday, and the Foreign Secretary was habitually followed around by a host of the small suitcase-sized containers carrying telexes and despatches, briefing papers and the other paraphernalia of diplomacy. The Chief Whip, with no conference speech to make and no foreign crises to handle, had arrived in Bournemouth with his box filled with three bottles of twelve-year-old malt whisky. Hotel drink prices are always staggering, he explained to his wife, even when you can find the brand you want.

133

He faced Woolton across a paper-strewn coffee table, and dispensed with the small talk.

'Patrick, I need to take your mind. In the strictest confidence. As far as I am concerned, this has to be one of those meetings which never took place.'

'Christ, you do have some photographs!' exclaimed Woolton, now only half joking. His eye for attractive young women was much discussed, but he was usually highly discreet, especially when he travelled abroad. Ten years earlier when he was just starting his Ministerial career, he had spent several painful hours answering questions from the Louisiana State Police about a weekend he had spent in a New Orleans motel with a young American girl who looked twenty, acted as if she were thirty and turned out to be just a few days over sixteen. The incident had been brushed over, but Woolton had never forgotten the tiny difference between a glittering political future and a charge of statutory rape.

'Something which could be rather more serious. I've been picking up some unhealthy vibrations in the last few weeks about Henry. You've sensed some of the irritation with him around the Cabinet table, and the media seem to be falling out of love with him in a very big way. There was no reason to expect an extended honeymoon after the election, but it's in danger of getting out of hand. I have just been approached by two of the most influential grass-roots party members saying that feeling at local level is getting very bad. We lost two more important local council by-elections last week in what should have been very safe seats, and we are going to lose quite a few more in the weeks ahead. Our majority in the Dorset by-election tomorrow is likely to be hit badly. To put no finer point on it, Patrick, the PM's unpopularity is dragging the whole Party down and we would have trouble winning an election for local dogcatcher at the moment. We seem to have blown it rather badly.' Urquhart paused for a sip of whisky.

'The problem is,' he continued, 'there's a view around

134

that this is not just a passing phase. If we are to win yet another election, we will have to show plenty of vigour and life otherwise the electorate will want a change simply out of boredom. Quite a few of our backbenchers in marginal seats are already beginning to get nervous, and with a majority of just 24 we may not have as much time as we would like. A few lost by-elections and we could be forced into an early election.'

He took another sip of whisky, cupping his hands around the tumbler as if to draw reassurance for his difficult task from the warm, peaty liquid.

'I'll come to the point, Patrick. I've been asked as Chief Whip . . .' – notice the formality, nothing personal in this, old chap – '. . . by one or two of our senior colleagues to take some gentle soundings about how deep the problem actually goes. In short, Patrick, and you will appreciate this is *not* easy . . .' – it never is, but it never seems to stop or even slow the inevitable thrust – '. . . I've been asked to find out how much trouble you personally think we are in. Is Henry any longer the right leader for us?' He took a deep draught and settled back in his chair.

The silence settled around the Foreign Secretary, impaling him on the point of the question. It took him more than a minute to respond. A pipe appeared out of his pocket, followed by a tobacco pouch and a box of Swan Vestas. He patiently filled the bowl, tamping down the fresh tobacco with his thumb, and took out a match. The striking of the match seemed very loud in the silence, and Urquhart shifted uneasily in his chair. Smoke began to rise from around Woolton as he drew on the pipe stem, until the sweet smelling tobacco was well alight and his face was almost hidden from view by a clinging blue fog. He waved his hand to disperse it and through the clearing air he looked directly at Urquhart, and chuckled.

'You'll have to forgive me, Francis. Four years in the Foreign Office has not prepared me particularly well for handling direct questions like that. Maybe I'm not used

135

any more to people coming straight to the point. I hope you will forgive me if I struggle a little to match your bluntness.'

This was nonsense, of course. Woolton was renowned for his direct, often combative political style which had found an uneasy home in the Foreign Office. He was simply playing for time, collecting his thoughts.

'Let's try to put aside any subjective views . . .' – he blew another enormous cloud of smoke to hide the patent insincerity of the remark – '. . . and analyse the problem like a civil service position paper.'

Urquhart continued to look strained and nervous, but smiled inwardly. He knew Woolton's personal views, and so he already knew the conclusion at which their hypothetical civil servant was going to arrive.

'First, have we really got a problem? Yes, and it's a serious one. My lads back in Lancashire are hopping mad, we have a couple of local by-elections coming up which we are going to lose, and the polls are looking awful. I think it's right that you should be taking soundings.

'Second, is there a painless solution to the problem? Don't let us forget that Henry has led us successfully through our fourth election victory. He is the leader of the party which the voters supported. So it's not easy so soon after an election to contemplate a radical alteration to either the policies or the personalities with which we were elected.'

Woolton was by now obviously beginning to relish the analysis.

'Think it through. If there were any move to replace him – which is essentially what we are discussing . . .' – Urquhart contrived to look pained at Woolton's bluntness and once more examined the drink in his glass – '. . . it would be highly unsettling for the Party, while the Opposition would be rampant. It would look like a messy palace coup and an act of desperation. What do they say? "Greater love hath no politician than he lay down the life of his friends to save his own'"! We could never make it look like the response of a mature and confident political party, no matter how we tried to dress it up. It would take a new leader at least a year to repair the damage and glue together the cracks. So we should not fool ourselves that replacing Henry represents an easy option.

'Third, when all is said and done, can Henry find the solution to the problem himself? Well, you know my views on that. I stood against him for the leadership when Margaret retired, and I have not changed my mind that his selection was a mistake.'

Urquhart now knew that he had read his man well. While Woolton had never expressed any open dissatisfaction after the waves of the leadership election had settled, public loyalty is rarely more than a necessary cover for private ambition, and the Foreign Secretary had never done more than was strictly necessary to maintain that cover.

Woolton was now refilling their glasses while continuing his analysis. 'Margaret managed an extraordinary balance of personal toughness and sense of direction. She was ruthless when she had to be – and often when she didn't have to be as well. She always seemed to be in such a hurry to get where she was going that she had no time to take prisoners and didn't mind trampling on a few friends either. It didn't matter so much because she led from in front. Yet Henry doesn't have any sense of direction, only a love of office. And without that sense of direction, when he tries to be tough it simply comes across as arrogance and harshness. He tries to mimic Margaret but he hasn't got the balls.

'So there we have it. If we try to get rid of him we're in deep trouble. If we keep him, to use an old Lancashire expression, we're stuffed.'

He returned to his pipe, puffing furiously to rekindle its embers until he disappeared once more behind the haze.

Urquhart hadn't spoken for nearly ten minutes, but now

moved to the edge of his chair once again. 'Yes, I see. But I don't see. What is it you are saying, Patrick?'

Woolton roared with laughter. 'I'm sorry, Francis. Too much bloody diplomatic claptrap. I can't even ask the wife to pass the cornflakes nowadays without confusing her. You want a direct answer? OK. A majority of 24 simply isn't enough, and at the rate we are going we shall get wiped out next time around. We cannot go on as we are.'

'So what is the solution? We have to find one.'

'We wait. We need time, a few months, to prepare the public perception and pressure for the PM to stand down, so that when he does we shall be seen to be responding to a positive public demand rather than indulging in private squabbles. Perceptions are crucial, Francis, and we shall need a little time to get them right.'

And you need a little time to prepare your own pitch for the job, thought Urquhart. You old fraud. You want the job just as badly as ever.

He knew Woolton would need the time to spend as many evenings as possible in the corridors and bars of the House of Commons strengthening relationships with his colleagues, increasing the number of his speaking engagements in the constituencies of influential MPs, broadening his reputation with newspaper editors and columnists, building up his credentials. His official diary would get cleared very rapidly. He would spend less time travelling abroad and much, much more time travelling around Britain making speeches about the challenges facing the country in the year 2000.

'You have a particularly difficult and delicate task, Francis. You are in a central position for judging whether there is any chance of Henry staging some sort of recovery or, failing that, when the time is right to move. Too early and we shall all look like assassins. Too late and the Party will be in pieces. You will have to keep your ear very close to the ground, and decide if and when the time has come to move. I assume you are taking soundings elsewhere?'

Urquhart nodded carefully in silent assent. He's nominated me as Cassius, he thought, put the dagger in my hand and left it to me to nominate the Ides of March. Urquhart was exhilarated to discover that he did not mind the sensation at all.

'Patrick, I'm very grateful that you feel able to be so frank with me. The next few months are going to be difficult for all of us, and if I may I will continue to take your counsel. And you may be sure that not a word of this will pass outside this room.' He rose to finish the meeting.

'My Special Branch team are all going on at me about how walls have ears. I'm damned glad you have the next door bungalow!' Woolton exclaimed, thumping Urquhart playfully between the shoulder blades as his visitor strode over to retrieve his red box.

'I hope you will be joining me there for my reception this evening, Patrick. You won't forget, will you?'

'Course not. Always enjoy your parties. Be rude of me to refuse your champagne!'

'I'll see you in a few hours then,' replied Urquhart, picking up a red box.

As Woolton closed the door behind his visitor, he poured himself another drink. He would skip the afternoon's conference debates and have a bath and a short sleep to prepare himself for the evening's heavy schedule. As he reflected on the conversation he had just had, he began to wonder whether the whisky had dulled his senses. He was trying to remember how Urquhart had voiced his own opposition to Collingridge, but couldn't. 'Crafty sod. Let me do all the talking.'

As he sat there wondering whether he had been just a little too frank with his guest, he totally failed to notice that Urquhart had walked off with the wrong red box.

Mattie had been in high spirits ever since sending through her copy shortly after lunch and had spent much of the afternoon thinking of the new doors which were slowly beginning to open for her. She had just celebrated her first anniversary at the *Telegraph*, and her abilities were getting recognition. Although she was one of the youngest members of staff, her stories had begun to get on the front page on a frequent basis – and they were good stories, too, she knew that. Another year of this sort of progress and she would be ready to make the next step, perhaps move up as an assistant editor or find a role with more room to write serious political analysis and not just daily pot boilers. Mind you, she had no complaints today. It would take an outbreak of war to stop the copy she had just filed from making the splash headline on the front page. It was a strong story about a Government who had lost their way; it was well written and would certainly help to get her noticed by other editors and publishers.

But it was not enough. In spite of it all, she was beginning to realise that something was missing. Even as her career developed, she was gradually discovering an emptiness which hit her every time she left the office and got worse as she walked past her front door into her cold, silent apartment. There was a pit somewhere deep inside her which had begun to ache, an ache she hoped had been left way behind in Yorkshire. Damn men! Why couldn't they leave her alone? But she knew no one else was to blame; her own needs were gnawing away inside her, and they were becoming increasingly difficult to ignore.

Neither could she ignore the urgent message to call her office which she received shortly before 5 o'clock. She had just finished taking tea on the terrace with the Home Secretary, who was anxious to get the *Telegraph* to puff his speech the following day and who in any event wanted an excuse to avoid sitting through another afternoon of his colleagues' speeches. The hotel lobby was crowded as people began to desert the conference hall early in search of refreshment and relaxation, but one of the public telephones was free and she decided to put up with the noise. When she got through, Preston's secretary explained that he was engaged on the phone and connected her with the deputy editor, John Krajewski, a gentle giant of a man she had begun to spend a little time with during the long summer months, spurred on by a shared enjoyment of good wine and the fact that his father, like her grandfather, had been a wartime refugee from Europe. She greeted him warmly, but his response left her feeling like ice.

'Hello, Mattie. Look, let me not cover everything in three feet of bullshit but come straight to the point. We're not – he's not – running your story. I really am sorry.'

There was a stunned silence over the phone as she turned over the words in her own mind to make sure that she had understood correctly.

'What the hell do you mean you're not running it?'

'Just what I say, Mattie.' Krajewski was clearly having grave difficulty with the conversation. 'I'm sorry I can't give you all the details because Grev has been dealing with it personally – I haven't touched it myself – but apparently it's such a hot story that he feels he cannot run it without being absolutely sure of our ground. He says that we have always supported this Government loyally and he's not about to throw editorial policy out of the window on the basis of an anonymous piece of paper. He says we have to be absolutely certain before we move, and we can't be if we don't know where this piece of paper came from.'

'For God's sake, it doesn't matter where the bloody paper came from. Whoever sent it to me wouldn't have done so if he thought his identity was going to be spread all over our news room. All that matters is that it's genuine, and I've confirmed that.'

'Look, I know how you must feel about this, Mattie, and I wish I were a million miles away from this one. Believe me I've argued this one hard and long for you, but Grev is adamant. It's not running.'

Mattie wanted to scream. She suddenly regretted making the call from a crowded lobby, where she could not argue the case for fear that a rival journalist would hear, and neither could she use the sort of language she felt like using with dozens of constituency wives crowding around her.

'Let me talk to Grev.'

'Sorry. I think he's busy on the phone.'

'I'll hold!'

'In fact,' said the deputy editor in a voice heaped with embarrassment, 'I know he's going to be busy for a long time and insisted that I had to be the one to explain it to you. I know he wants to talk to you, Mattie – but tomorrow. There's no point in trying to scream him into submission tonight.'

'So he's not running the story, he hasn't got the balls to tell me why, and he's told you to do his dirty work for him!' Mattie spat out her contempt. 'What sort of newspaper are we running, Johnnie?'

She could hear the deputy editor clearing his throat, unable to find suitable words to respond. Krajewski appreciated just how tearingly frustrated Mattie felt, not only with the story but with Preston's decision to use him as a buffer. He wondered if he should have made more of a fight of it on her behalf, but in recent weeks he had become increasingly distracted by Mattie's obvious if unpromoted sexuality and he was no longer certain just how professionally objective he was.

'Sorry, Mattie.'

'And screw you, Johnnie!' was all she was able to hiss down the line before slamming the phone back into its cradle.

She was consumed with anger, not only with Preston and politics but also with herself for being unable to find a more convincing argument to fight her cause or a more coherent way of expressing it.

Ignoring the tart look flashed at her by the conference steward on the next phone, she stalked across the foyer. 'I need a drink,' she explained loudly to herself and everyone else within earshot, and made straight for the bar.

The steward was just raising the grille over the counter

when Mattie arrived and slapped her bag and a five-pound note down on the bar. As she did so she knocked the arm of another patron who was already lined up at the varnished counter and clearly intent on being served with the first drink of the night.

'Sorry,' apologised Mattie huffily, without sounding entirely as if she meant it. The other drinker turned to face her.

'Young lady, you look as if you need a drink. My doctor tells me there is no such thing as needing a drink, but what does he know? Would you mind if a man old enough to be your father joins you? By the way, the name's Collingridge, Charles Collingridge.'

'So long as we don't talk politics, Mr Collingridge, it will be my pleasure. Allow my editor to buy you a large one!'

The room was spacious, but it had a low ceiling and it was packed with people. The heat from the mass of bodies had combined with the central heating to make the atmosphere distinctly muggy, and many of the guests were quietly cursing the insulation and double glazing which the architects had so carefully installed throughout 'Overtime Alley'. As a consequence the chilled champagne being dispensed by Urquhart's constituency secretary was in great demand, and it was already on its way to being one of his more relaxed conference receptions.

Urquhart, however, was not in a position to circulate and accept his guests' thanks. He was effectively pinned in one corner by the enormous bulk of Benjamin Landless. The newspaper magnate was sweating heavily and he had his jacket off and collar undone, displaying his thick green braces like parachute webbing which were holding up his vast, flowing trousers. Landless refused to take any notice of his discomfort, for his full attention was concentrated on his trapped prey.

'But that's all bloody Horlicks, Frankie, and you know it. I put my whole newspaper chain behind your lot at the last election and I've moved my entire worldwide headquarters to London. I've invested millions in the country. And if you lot don't pull your fingers out, the whole bloody performance is going down the drain at the next election. Those buggers in the Opposition will crucify me if they get in because I've been so good to you, but you lot seem to be falling over yourselves to open the damned door for them.'

He paused to produce a large silk handkerchief from within the folds of his trousers and wipe his brow, while Urquhart goaded him on.

'Surely it's not as bad as that, Ben. All Governments go through sticky patches. We've been through this all before – we'll pull out of it!'

'Horlicks, Horlicks, bloody Horlicks. That's complacent crap, and you know it, Frankie. Haven't you seen your own latest poll? They phoned it through to me earlier this afternoon. You're down another 3 per cent, that's 10 per cent since the election. If you held it today, you'd get thrashed. Bloody annihilated!'

Urquhart relished the thought of the *Telegraph* headline tomorrow, but could not afford to show it. 'Damn. How on earth did you get hold of that? That will really hurt us at the by-election tomorrow.'

'Don't worry. I've told Preston to pull it. It'll leak, of course, and we'll probably get some flak in *Private Eye* about a politically inspired cover-up, but it'll be after the by-election and it will save your conference being turned into a bear pit.' He sighed deeply. 'It's more than you bloody deserve,' he said more quietly, and Urquhart knew he meant it.

'I know the PM will be grateful, Ben,' said Urquhart, feeling sick with disappointment.

'Course he will, but the gratitude of the most unpopular Prime Minister since polls began isn't something you can put in the bank.'

'What do you mean?'

'Political popularity is cash. While you lot are in, I should

144

be able to get on with my business and do what I do best – make money. That's why I've supported you. But as soon as your popularity begins to fade, the whole thing begins to clam up. The Stock Market sinks. People don't want to invest. Unions get bolshy. I can't look ahead. And it's been happening ever since June. The PM couldn't organise a farting contest in a baked bean factory. His unpopularity is dragging the whole Party down, and my business with it. Unless you do something about it, we're all going to disappear down a bloody great hole.'

'Do you really feel like that?'

Landless paused, just to let Urquhart know it wasn't the champagne speaking. 'Passionately,' he growled.

'Then it looks as if we have a problem.'

'You do so long as he goes on like he is.'

'But if he won't change . . .'

'Then get rid of him!'

Urquhart raised his eyebrows sharply, but Landless was not to be deflected. 'Life's too short to spend it propping up losers. I haven't spent the last twenty years working my guts out just to watch your boss piss it all away.'

Urquhart found his arm gripped painfully by his guest's huge fingers. There was real strength behind the enormous girth, and Urquhart began to realise how Landless always seemed to get his way. Those he could not dominate with his wealth or commercial muscle he would trap with his physical strength and sharp tongue. Urquhart had always hated being called Frankie, and this was the only man in the world who insisted on using it. But tonight of all nights he did not think he would object. This was one argument he was going to enjoy losing.

'Let me give you one example, in confidence. OK, Frankie?' He pinned Urquhart still tighter in the corner. 'Very shortly I expect that United Newspapers will be up for sale. If it is, I want to buy it. In fact, I've already had some serious discussions with them. But the lawyers are telling me that I already own one newspaper group and that the Government isn't going to allow me to buy another. I said to them, you are telling me that I can't become the biggest newspaper owner in the country, even if I commit all of the titles to supporting the Government!'

Perspiration was slipping freely from his face, but he ignored it. 'You know what they said, Frankie? It's precisely because I *do* support the Government that I'm in trouble. If I moved to take over United Newspapers the Opposition would kick up the most godawful stink. No one would have the guts to stand up and defend me. The takeover would be referred to the Monopolies and Mergers Commission where it would get bogged down for months with a herd of expensive lawyers stuck in a bloody committee room, with me having to listen to a bunch of closet queen bureaucrats lecturing me on how to run my own business. And whatever arguments I use, in the end the Government will bow to pressure and refuse to allow the deal to go through, because they haven't got the stomach for a public fight.'

He blew cigar smoke in Urquhart's face.

'In other words, Mr Chief Whip, because your Government doesn't have the balls, my company is going to go through the wringer. Because you're buggering up your own business, you're going to bugger up mine as well!'

The point had been forcefully made and the pressure applied. It was not a subtle way to lobby a Minister, but he had always found the direct approach to be far more effective than complicated minuets. Politicians could be bullied like any other men. He paused to refresh himself from his glass, waiting for a reply.

Urquhart framed his response slowly, to emphasise that he too, like Landless, was speaking in earnest.

'That would be a tremendous pity, Ben. You have been a great friend of the Party, and it would be a great shame if we were unable to repay that friendship. I cannot speak for the Prime Minister. In fact, I find myself increasingly unable to speak for him nowadays. But from my point of view, I would do everything I could to support you when you needed it.'

'That's good to know, Frankie. I appreciate it, very much. If only Henry could be so decisive, but I know that's simply not his nature. If it were up to me, he'd be out.'

'But isn't it up to you?'

'Me?'

'You have your newspapers. They are tremendously influential, and you control them. One headline can make news and break politicians. You were saying that the polls show the public's dislike for the PM is undermining the whole Party. It's personal, not political.'

Landless nodded his assent.

'Yet you say you are not going to publish because it will turn the conference into a bear fight. Do you really think you are going to be able to sort this out without one hell of a fight?'

The bullying Landless of a few moments ago had disappeared, to be replaced by a subtle man who understood every nuance of what was being suggested to him.

'I think I see your point, Frankie. And I think we understand each other.'

'I think we do.'

They shook hands. Urquhart almost winced as his hand disappeared inside the vice-like grip of Landless. He knew the other's handshake was distinctly ambiguous – an expression of friendship, by all means, but also a promise to crush anyone who reneged on a deal.

'Then I have some work to do, Frankie. The *Telegraph* first edition is closing in less than thirty minutes and I shall have to make a telephone call.' He grabbed his jacket and draped it over his arm.

'Thanks for the party. It's been most stimulating.'

Urquhart watched silently as the industrialist, damp shirt sticking closely to his broad back, shuffled across the crowded room and disappeared through the door.

*   *   *

Across the other side of the room beyond the dignitaries, journalists and hangers-on who were squashed together, Roger O'Neill was huddled on a small sofa with a young and attractive conference-goer. O'Neill was in an excited and very nervous state. He fidgeted incessantly and his words rattled out at an alarming pace. The young girl from Rotherham had already been overwhelmed with the names O'Neill had skilfully dropped and the passion of his words, and she looked on with wide-eyed astonishment, an innocent bystander in a one-way conversation.

'The Prime Minister's under constant surveillance by our security men. There's always a threat. Irish. Arabs. Black Militants. One of them's trying to get me, too. They've been trying for months, and the Special Branch boys insisted on giving me protection throughout the election. Apparently, they'd found a hit list; if the PM were too well protected they might turn to targets close to the PM like me. So they gave me twenty-four-hour cover. It's not public knowledge, of course, but all the journos know.'

He dragged furiously at a cigarette and started coughing. He took out a soiled handkerchief and blew his nose loudly, inspecting it before returning it to his pocket.

'But why you, Roger?' his companion ventured.

'Soft target. Easy access. High publicity hit,' he rattled. 'If they can't get the PM, they'll go for someone like me.'

He looked around nervously, his eyes fluttering wildly.

'Can you keep a confidence? A real secret?' He took another deep drag. 'They think I've been followed all week. And this morning I found my car had been tampered with, so the Bomb Squad boys went over it with a fine tooth comb. They found the wheel nuts on one of the front wheels had been all but removed. Straight home on the motorway, the wheel comes off at eighty miles an hour and – more work for the road sweepers! They think it was deliberate. The Murder Squad are on their way over to interview me right now.'

'Roger, that's awful,' she gasped.

'Mustn't tell anyone. The SB don't want to frighten them off if there's a chance of catching them unawares.'

'I hadn't realised you were so close to the Prime Minister,' she said with growing awe. 'What a terrible time for . . .' She suddenly gasped. 'Are you all right, Roger? You are looking very upset. Your, your eyes . . .' she stammered.

O'Neill's eyes were flickering wildly, flashing still further lurid hallucinations into his brain. His attention seemed to have strayed elsewhere; he was no longer with her but in some other world, with some other conversation. His eyes wavered back to her, but they were gone again in an instant. They were bloodshot and watering, and were having difficulty in finding something on which to focus. His nose was dribbling like an old man in winter, and he gave it a cursory and unsuccessful wipe with the back of his hand.

As she watched, his face turned to an ashen grey, his body twitched and he stood up sharply. He appeared terrified, as if the walls were falling in on him. She looked round helplessly, unsure what he needed, too embarrassed to make a public scene. She moved to take his arm and support him, but as she did so he turned on her and lost his balance. He grabbed at her to steady himself, caught her blouse and a button popped.

'Get out of my way, get out of my way,' he snarled.

He thrust her violently backwards, and she fell heavily into a table laden with glasses before sprawling back onto the sofa. The crash of glass onto the floor stopped all conversation in the room as everyone looked round. Three more buttons had gone, and her left breast stood exposed amidst the torn silk.

There was absolute silence as O'Neill stumbled towards the door, pushing still more people out of the way as he tumbled into the night. The young girl clutched at her tattered clothing and was fighting back the tears of humiliation as he disappeared. An elderly guest was helping her rearrange herself and shepherding her towards the bath-room and, as the bathroom door shut behind the two women, a ripple of speculation began which quickly grew into a broad sea of gossip, washing backwards and forwards over the gathering. It would go on all evening.

Penny Guy did not join in the gossip. A moment before she had been laughing merrily, thoroughly enjoying the engaging wit and Merseyside charm of Patrick Woolton. Urquhart had introduced them more than an hour earlier, and had ensured that the champagne flowed as easily as their conversation. But the magic had been smashed with the uproar. As Penny had taken in O'Neill's stumbling departure, the sobbing girl's dishevelled clothing and the ensuing speculation and chatter, her face had dissolved into a picture of misery. She fought a losing battle to control the tears which had welled up and spilled down her cheeks and, although Woolton provided a large handker-chief and considerable support, the pain in Penny's face was all too real.

'He really is *kind*. Very considerate,' she explained. 'But sometimes it all seems to get too much for him and he goes a little crazy. It's so out of character.' She pleaded for him, and the tears flowed still faster.

'Penny. I'm so sorry, dear. Look, you need to get out of this party. My bungalow's next door. Let's go and dry you off there, OK?'

She nodded in gratitude, and the couple squeezed their way through the crowd. No one seemed to notice as they eased their way out of the room, except Urquhart. His cold blue eyes followed them through the door where Landless and O'Neill had gone before. This was certainly going to be a party to remember, he told himself.

150

THURSDAY 14TH OCTOBER

'You're not going to make a bloody habit of getting me out of bed every morning, are you?' Even down the telephone line, Preston made it clear that this was an instruction, not a question.

Mattie felt even worse than she had the previous morning after several hours of alcoholic flagellation with Charles Collingridge who was clearly determined to prove his doctor hopelessly wrong. Now she was having great difficulty grasping what on earth was going on.

'Hell, Grev. I go to bed thinking I want to kill you because you won't run the story, and I wake up this morning and find a bastardised version all over the front page with a by-line by someone called "Our Political Staff". Now I *know* I want to kill you, but first I want to find out why you are screwing around with my story. Why did you change your mind? Who's rewritten my story, and who the hell is "Our Political Staff" if it's not me?'

'Steady on, Mattie. Just take a breath and let me explain. If only you had been around when I tried to call you last night and not flashing your eyes at some eligible peer or whatever it is you were doing, then you would have known all about it before it happened.'

Mattie began vaguely to recall the events of last night through the haze, and her pause to persuade her memory to catch up with itself gave Preston time to continue. He began to search for his words carefully.

'As I think Krajewski may have told you, last night some of the editorial staff here didn't believe there was enough substantiation of your piece on the opinion polls for it to run today.'

He heard Mattie snort at the clumsy twisting of the tale, but knew he must press on or he would never get the chance to finish the justification.

'Frankly, I liked the piece and wanted to make it work, but I thought we needed more corroboration before we tore the country's Prime Minister apart on the day of an important by-election. A single anonymous piece of paper wasn't enough.'

'I didn't tear the Prime Minister apart, you did!' Mattie wanted to interject, but Preston rode through her objections.

'So I had a chat with some of my senior contacts in the Party, and late last night we got the corroboration we wanted just before our deadline. The copy needed to be adapted to take account of the new material and I tried to reach you but couldn't, so I rewrote it myself. I refused to let anyone else touch it, your material is too good. So "Our Political Staff" in this instance is me.'

'But that's not the story I sent in. I wrote a piece about a terrible opinion poll and the difficult days the Party was facing. You've turned it into the outright crucifixion of Collingridge. These quotes from "leading party sources", these criticisms and condemnations. Who else do you have working in Bournemouth apart from me?'

'My sources are my own business,' snapped Preston.

'Bullshit, Grev. I'm supposed to be your political correspondent at this bloody conference, you can't keep me in the dark like this. The paper's done a complete somersault over my story and another complete somersault over Collingridge. A few weeks ago he was the saviour of the nation as far as you were concerned, now he's – what does it say? – "a catastrophe threatening to engulf the Government at any moment". I shall be about as popular as a witch's armpit around the conference hall this morning. You've got to tell me what's going on!'

Preston, his carefully prepared explanation already in tatters, retreated into aggression and pomposity.

'As editor I am not in the dubious position of having to justify myself to every cub reporter stuck out in the provinces. You do as you're told, I do as I'm told, and we both get on with the job. All right?'

Mattie was just about to ask him who the hell it was who could tell the editor what to do when she heard the line go dead. She shook her head in amazement and fury. She couldn't and wouldn't take much more of this. Far from having new doors open up to her, she was finding her fingers getting caught as her editor kept slamming the doors shut. And who else had he got ferreting away at the conference?

It was a good thirty minutes later as she was trying to clear her thoughts and calm her temper with yet another cup of coffee in the breakfast room when she saw the vast bulk of Benjamin Landless lumbering across to a window table for a chat with Lord Peterson, the party treasurer. As the proprietor settled his girth into a completely inadequate chair, Mattie wrinkled her nose. She didn't care for what she smelt.

The Prime Minister's political secretary winced. For the third time the press secretary had thrust the morning newspaper across the table at him, for the third time he tried to thrust it away. He knew how St Peter must have felt.

'For God's sake, Grahame.' The press secretary was raising his voice now; the game of ping-pong with the newspaper was irritating him. 'We can't hide every damned copy of the *Telegraph* in Bournemouth. He's got to know, and you've got to show it to him. Now!'

'Why did it have to be today?' he groaned. 'A by-election just down the road, and we've been up all night finishing his speech for tomorrow. Now he'll want to rewrite the whole thing and where are we going to find the time? He'll blow a bloody gasket, and that won't help the by-election or the speech either.'

He slammed his briefcase shut in uncharacteristic frustration. 'All the pressure of the last few weeks, and now this. There just doesn't seem to be any break, does there?'

His companion chose not to answer, preferring to study the view out of the hotel window across the bay. It was raining again.

The political secretary picked up the newspaper, rolled it up tight, and threw it across the room. It landed with a crash in the waste bin, overturning it and strewing the contents across the carpet. The discarded pages of speech draft mixed with cigarette ash and several empty cans of beer and tomato juice.

'I'll tell him after breakfast.'

It was not to be his best decision.

Henry Collingridge was in a good mood and enjoying his eggs. He had finished his conference speech in the early hours of the morning, and had left his staff to tidy it up and have it typed while he went to bed. He had slept soundly if briefly for the first time during conference week.

The end-of-conference speech always hung over his head like a dark cloud. He disliked conferences and the small talk, the week away from home, the over-indulgence around the dinner tables – and the speech. Most of all the speech. Long hours of anguished discussion in a smoke-filled hotel room, breaking off just when progress seemed in sight in order to attend some ball-breaking function or reception, resuming a considerable time later and trying to pick up where they had left off, only more tired and less inspired. If the speech was good, it was only what they expected and required. If it was poor, they still applauded but said the strain of office was beginning to show. Sod's Law.

But it was now almost over, bar the delivery. The Prime Minister was enjoying breakfast with his wife, watched carefully from surrounding tables by his personal Special

Branch detectives. He was discussing the merits of a winter holiday in Antigua or Sri Lanka.

'I would recommend Sri Lanka this year,' he said. 'You can stay on the beach if you want, Sarah, but I would rather like to take a couple of trips into the mountains. They have some ancient Buddhist monasteries and some nearby wildlife reserves which are supposed to be quite spectacular. The Sri Lankan President was describing them to me last year, and they sounded really . . . Darling, you're not listening!'

'Sorry, Henry. I was . . . just looking at that gentleman's newspaper.'

'More interesting than me, is it? What's it got to say, then?'

He began to feel ill at ease, remembering that no one had yet given him his daily press cuttings. Someone would surely have told him had there been anything that important.

Come to think of it, he had never felt comfortable since his staff had persuaded him that he didn't need to spend his time reading the daily newspapers, that an edited summary of press clippings prepared by them would be more efficient. But were they? Civil servants had their own narrow views on what was important for a Prime Minister's day, and he found increasingly that their briefing on party political matters was scant. Particularly when there was bad news, the controversy and the in-fighting, he often had to find out from others, sometimes days or weeks after the event. He began to wonder if eventually he would never find out at all, and some great political crisis would burst upon the Party about which he was kept blissfully unaware. They were trying to protect him, of course, but the cocoon they spun around him would, he feared, eventually stifle him.

He remembered the first time he had stepped inside 10 Downing Street as Prime Minister. He had left the crowds and the television crews outside and, as the great black door closed behind him, he had discovered an extra-ordinary sight.

On one side of the great hallway leading away from the door had gathered some 200 civil servants, *his* civil servants now, who were applauding him loudly – just as they had done Thatcher, Callaghan, Wilson and Heath, and just as they would his successor. On the other side of the hallway facing the host of civil servants stood his political staff, the team of loyal supporters he had hurriedly assembled around him as his campaign to succeed Margaret Thatcher had begun to take off, and whom he had invited to Downing Street to enjoy this historic moment. There were just seven of them, four assistants and three secretaries, dwarfed in their new surroundings.

He told his wife afterwards that it was rather like the Eton Wall Game, with two hugely unequal sides lined up to do battle, with no clear rules and with him cast as both the ball and the prize. He had felt almost relieved when three senior civil servants called an end to the proceedings by physically surrounding him and guiding him off to the Cabinet Room for his first Prime Ministerial briefing. One of the party officials present had described it more as an Assumption, with the Prime Minister disappearing into a different world surrounded by a band of guardian angels – Civil Service, Grade 1, Prime Ministers, for the Protection and Guidance Thereof: Exclusive. His party officials had scarcely seen him for the next six months as they were effectively squeezed out by the official machine, and none of the original band was still left.

Collingridge's attention returned to the newspaper being read at the far-off breakfast table. At such a distance he had great difficulty in bringing it fully into focus, and he fumbled for his glasses, perching them on the end of his nose and trying not to stare too hard. He found his air of studied indifference difficult to maintain as the large head-line print came into focus.

'Poll crisis hits Government', it screamed. 'PM's future

in doubt as personal slump hits party'. 'By-election disaster feared'. And this in what was supposed to be the most loyal of newspapers.

Collingridge threw his napkin down on the table and kicked back his chair. He left the table even as his wife was still discussing the finer advantages of January in Antigua.

It did not improve the Prime Minister's temper when he had to retrieve the copy of the *Telegraph* from among the cigarette ash in the waste bin.

'Over the bloody breakfast table, Grahame. May I, just occasionally, not be the last to know?'

'I am sorry, Prime Minister. We were going to show it to you just as soon as you had finished,' came the meek response.

'It's just not good enough, not good eno ... What the hell's this rubbish?'

He had arrived at the point in the *Telegraph* report when the hard news – if opinion polls can ever be considered to qualify as 'hard' news – had been superseded by sheer speculation and hype.

> The latest slump revealed in the Party's own private opinion polls is bound to put intense pressure on the Prime Minister, whose conference speech tomorrow is awaited anxiously by party representatives in Bournemouth. Rumblings about the style and effectiveness of the Prime Minister's leadership have increased in intensity since the election, when his performance disappointed many of his colleagues.

> These doubts are certain to be fuelled by the latest poll, which gives him the lowest personal rating any Prime Minister has achieved since these polls began nearly forty years ago.

> Last night, a leading Minister commented, 'There is a lack of grip around the Cabinet table and in the House of Commons. The Party is restive. Our

basically excellent position is being undermined by the leader's lack of appeal.'

Harsher views were being expressed in some Government quarters. Senior party sources were speculating that the Party was fast coming to a crossroad. 'We have to decide between making a new start or sliding gently into decline and defeat,' one source said. 'We have had too many unnecessary setbacks since the election. We cannot afford any more.'

A less sanguine view was that Collingridge was 'like a catastrophe threatening to engulf the Government at any moment'.

The result of today's parliamentary by-election in Dorset East, reckoned to be a safe Government seat, is now being seen as crucial to the Prime Minister's future.

Collingridge was by now almost consumed with fury. His face had flushed and he gripped the newspaper like a drowning man, yet his years of experience in the political trenches kept him in control.

'I want to find out who's behind this, Grahame. I want to know who wrote it. Who spoke to them. Who leaked the poll. And for breakfast tomorrow I want their balls on toast!'

'Shall I give Lord Williams a call?' the political secretary offered as a tentative suggestion.

'Lord Williams!' Collingridge exploded. 'It's his bloody poll that's leaked! I don't want apologies, I want answers. Get me the Chief Whip. Find him, and whatever he is doing get him here right now.'

The secretary summoned his courage for the next hurdle. 'Before he arrives, Prime Minister, could I suggest that we have another look at your speech. There may be various things you want to change as a result of the morning press, and we don't have too much time . . .'

'Grahame, the speech stays, just as it is. I'm not ripping

up a perfectly good speech just in order to run in front of a pack of bloody news hounds. That's just what they want, and that is just what will make us most vulnerable. Maybe we can have another look at it later, but what is top priority at the moment is that we stop the leaks right now, otherwise they will turn into a flood. So find Mr Urquhart, and get him here immediately!'

With a look of resignation, the political secretary reached for the phone.

Urquhart was sitting in his bungalow waiting for a telephone call, which came not from the Prime Minister but from the Foreign Secretary. When Woolton got through, much to Urquhart's relief he was chuckling.

'Damned fool. I must put more water in your whisky next time. You walked off with one of my boxes yesterday and left your own behind. I've got your sandwiches and you've got a copy of the latest secret plans to invade Papua New Guinea, or whatever other damn fool thing they are trying to convince me of this week. I suggest we swap before I get arrested for losing confidential Government property. I'll be round in twenty seconds.'

Less than a minute later Urquhart was smiling his way through an apology to his Ministerial colleague, who was still in high spirits as he left, having thanked Urquhart for – as he put it – 'an exceptionally stimulating evening'.

As soon as Woolton had stepped outside, Urquhart's mood changed. His brow furrowed with concern as he locked the door from the inside, testing the handle to make absolutely certain it was closed. He wasted no time in pulling the blinds down over the windows, and only when he was certain that he could not be observed did he place the red box gingerly on the desk.

He examined the box carefully for any signs of tampering, and then selected a key from the large bunch which he produced from his pocket, sliding it carefully into the lock. As the lid came up, it exposed a thick slab of polystyrene packing which entirely filled the box. He extracted the polystyrene and laid it to one side before turning the box on its end. Delicately he eased up the corner of a strip of four-inch surgical tape which had been stuck across most of the side wall of the box, gently peeling it back until it revealed a small recess carved right through the wooden wall until only the rough red leather covering stood between the recess and the outside world.

Externally there was no sign that the leather covered anything other than a solid piece of wood, and he complimented himself that he had not forgotten the art of using a wood chisel which he had learned at school nearly fifty years before. The recess measured no more than two inches square, and snuggling neatly in its middle was a radio transmitter complete with its own miniaturised mercury power pack, compliments of its Japanese manufacturer.

The manager of the security shop just off the Tottenham Court Road which he had visited two weeks earlier had displayed a carefully practised mask of indifference as Urquhart had explained his need to check up on a dishonest employee, yet had shown great enthusiasm in describing the full capabilities of the equipment he could supply. This was one of the simplest yet most sensitive transmitters on the market, he had explained, which was guaranteed to pick up almost any unobstructed sound within a distance of fifty metres and relay it back to the custom-built receiver and voice-activated tape recorder, which he also highly recommended.

'Just make sure the microphone is pointing generally towards the source of the sound, sir, and I guarantee it will sound like a Mahler Symphony.'

Urquhart went over to his wardrobe and from the back pulled out another Ministerial red box. Like all such boxes, this one was secured with a precision-made, high-security tungsten lock for which he alone had the keys. Inside, nestling in another protective wrapping of polystyrene, sat a modified FM portable radio with inbuilt cassette recorder which was tuned to the wavelength of the transmitter. Urquhart noticed with satisfaction that the long-playing tape he had installed was all but exhausted. He had left the radio transmitter in Woolton's room pointing towards the bed.

'I hope it's not simply because he snores,' Urquhart joked with himself. As he did so, the equipment clicked once more into action, ran for ten seconds, and stopped.

He pressed the rewind button and was watching the twin reels spin round when the telephone rang, summoning him to the Prime Minister for yet another 'plumbing lesson', as he called it.

'Never mind, you'll wait,' he whispered, and relocked both boxes before concealing them in the back of his wardrobe. He was reliving the explosion of excitement he had felt when he had set his first rabbit trap on his father's estate with the help of the gillie. They had gone out into the warm evening air to lay the trap together, but Urquhart could not contain his impatience and had returned alone before dawn the following morning, to find the creature swinging helplessly from the snare.

'Got you!' he exclaimed in triumph.

SATURDAY 16TH OCTOBER

It was not just the *Telegraph* which, the day after the Prime Minister's speech, declared it to be a disaster. It was joined in varying degrees by all the other newspapers, several Government backbenchers, and the Leader of the Opposition. Particularly the Leader of the Opposition, whose animated braying appeared for all the world like a hound which had just scented the first sign of real vulnerability in its prey.

The loss of the Dorset East by-election, when the news had burst on the conference in the early hours of Friday morning, had at first numbed the party faithful. It had taken them until breakfast time before they began to vent their frustration and disillusionment, and there had been only one target – Henry Collingridge.

Correspondents in Bournemouth seemed to have been inundated with nameless senior Party officials, each of whom claimed personally to have warned the Prime Minister not to hold the by-election in conference week and who were now absolving themselves of responsibility for the disastrous defeat. In turn, the Prime Minister's office retaliated – unattributably, of course – that the blame was really in the organisational deficiencies of the party headquarters for which, of course, Lord Williams was responsible. The explanation, however, fell on deaf ears. The pack instinct had taken hold of the press as well as the Leader of the Opposition, as the scarcely restrained phrases of one normally pro-Government newspaper indicated.

The Prime Minister yesterday failed to quell growing doubts being expressed within his Party about his leadership with a closing speech to his party conference in Bournemouth which one Cabinet colleague described as 'inept and inappropriate'. Following this week's leaking of disastrous internal opinion polls and the humiliating by-election defeat in one of the Party's safest seats, conference representatives were looking for a realistic acknowledgement of the problems which have caused the collapse of voter support for the Government.

Instead, in the words of one representative, 'we got a stale rehash of an old election speech'.

The open disenchantment with the Prime Minister is no longer being voiced with traditional caution within Government circles, particularly amongst anxious backbenchers with marginal seats. Peter Bearstead, MP for Leicester North, said last night: 'The electorate gave us a warning slap across the knuckles at the election, and we should be responding with fresh initiatives and a much clearer statement of our policies. But all we got was more of the same, clichés and suffocating complacency. It may be time for the Prime Minister to think about handing over.'

In an office tower on the South Bank of the Thames, near the spot where Wat Tyler 600 years before had gathered disenchanted rebels to launch his attempt at overthrowing the Establishment, the editor of *Weekend Watch*, the leading current affairs programme, studied the newspapers and called a hurried conference of all his staff. Twenty minutes later, the programme planned for the following day on racketeering landlords had been shelved and the entire sixty-minute slot had been recast. Bearstead was going to be invited to participate, as were several opinion pollsters and pundits, in a new programme entitled 'Collingridge – Time To Go?'

From his home in the leafy suburbs near Epsom, the

senior manager of market makers Barclays de Zoete Wedd telephoned two colleagues. They agreed to be in the office very early on Monday. 'All this political nonsense is going to upset the markets, and we mustn't be caught holding on to stock when every other bastard is selling.'

The Chief Whip, at his magnificent Palladian country home in the New Forest of Hampshire, received several calls from worried Cabinet colleagues and senior back-benchers, none wishing to make a break from cover but all of them expressing concern. The chairman of the Party's grass-roots executive committee also called him from Yorkshire reporting similar worries. 'I would normally pass these on to the Party Chairman,' the bluff Yorkshire-man explained, 'but with relations between Downing Street and party headquarters so poor, I just don't want to get caught in the middle of that particular battle.'

The defeated candidate in Thursday's by-election was contacted by the *Mail on Sunday* just after a lunch spent drowning his sorrows, and showed no reticence in his broadside against Collingridge. 'He cost me my seat. Can he feel safe in his?'

At Chequers, the Prime Minister's official country residence set amidst rolling lawns and massive security in rural Buckinghamshire, Collingridge just sat, ignoring his official papers and devoid of inspiration. The rock had begun to roll down hill, and he had no idea how to stop it.

When it hit later that afternoon, the news caught almost everyone by surprise. Even Urquhart. He had expected the *Observer* to take at least a couple more weeks checking the bundle of papers and photostats he had sent them and obtaining their lawyers' clearance. Clearly, however, they had felt pressured by the growing political clamour and feared that a competitor might also be on the trail. 'Damned if we don't publish, damned if we do. So let's go!' the editor had shouted at his investigative reporters.

Urquhart was adjusting the triple carburettors on his 1933 Rover Speed Pilot, which he kept for touring around the lanes of the New Forest, when Miranda called from inside the house.

'Francis! Chequers on the phone!' He picked up the extension on the garage wall, wiping his hands carefully on a greasy rag.

'Urquhart here.'

'Chief Whip, please hold on. I have the Prime Minister for you,' a female voice instructed.

The voice which now came on the end of the phone was almost unrecognisable. It had no more vitality than a voice from the grave.

'Francis, I am afraid I have some bad news. The *Observer* have just called up the Downing Street press office to let us know of a story they will be running tomorrow. I can't explain it all, but apparently my brother Charles has been buying shares in companies just before they benefit from Government decisions, and making a killing on them. They say they've got documentary evidence – bank statements, brokers' receipts, the lot. He bought nearly £50,000 worth of Renox, they say, a couple of days before we are supposed to have approved a new drug of theirs for general use, and sold them a day later for a substantial profit. They say he used a false address in Paddington. It's going to be the lead story.'

There was an exhausted pause, as if he no longer had the energy to continue. 'Francis, everyone's going to assume I'm involved with this. What on earth do I do?'

Urquhart settled himself comfortably in the front seat of the car before replying. It was a seat from which he was used to taking risks and making split-second decisions.

'Have you said anything to the *Observer*?'

'No. I don't think they were expecting a comment from me. They were really trying to find Charlie.'

'Where is he?'

'Gone to ground, I hope. I managed to get hold of him. He . . . was drunk. I just told him to take the phone off the hook and not to answer the door.'

Urquhart gripped the steering wheel, staring ahead. He felt strangely detached. He realised for the first time that he had set in motion a machine which was far more powerful than his ability to control it. He had manipulated, analysed and considered, but in spite of weeks of planning he knew that events were no longer under his command. He imagined that he was speeding down a country lane, the Rover ready to respond to his every command as he slammed it through its four gears and accelerated around the curve of the road, knowing now that he was lost in the exhilaration of its speed. He thrilled to its performance and the scent of danger in his nostrils, pressing ever more firmly down on the accelerator, oblivious of what lay around the next blind corner. It was already too late for second thoughts. It was instinct, not intellect, which would take over now.

'Where is he?'

'At home in London.'

'Yes, I know it. You must get someone down there to take care of him. Look, I know it must be painful as he's your brother, but there's a drying-out clinic outside Dover which the Whips Office has used for the occasional back-bencher. Very confidential, very kind. Dr Christian, the head of the clinic, is excellent. I'll give him a call and get him to Charles immediately. You must arrange for someone else from the family to be there, too, in case your brother proves to be difficult. Your wife, Sarah, perhaps? I will find someone from the Whips Office to get there and keep a careful eye on it all. But we must move fast, because in four hours' time when the *Observer* hits the streets your brother's home is going to be besieged by journalists. We have to beat them to the punch. With Charles in his present state there is no knowing what he might say or do.'

'But what do we do then? I can't hide Charlie for ever. He's got to face up to it sooner or later, hasn't he?'

'Is he guilty?'

'I simply don't know,' the words said, but the tone

167

conceded doubt and probable defeat. 'The office checked after they got the phone call. Apparently we did license a new Renox drug a couple of months ago, and their shares jumped sharply. Anyone holding any of their shares would have made a handsome profit. But Charlie hasn't got any money to splash around on shares. And how would he know about Renox?'

Urquhart came back in a tone which did not imply any argument. 'Let's worry about that when we have taken care of him. He must be put away somewhere quiet, somewhere the press can't get to him. He needs help, whether he wants it or not, and you must get some breathing space. You must be very careful how you decide to respond.'

There was a short pause for the words to sink in. 'You cannot afford to get this one wrong.'

Collingridge's wearied assent was mumbled down the phone. His Chief Whip's sudden authoritativeness had stripped away piece by piece both his family pride and the dignity of his office. He had neither the will nor the capacity to argue. He looked through the leaded windows across the fields surrounding Chequers to an ancient beech wood. He tried to draw strength and confidence from the magnificent trees glowing golden in the evening sunshine of autumn. They had always been an inspiration to him, a constant reminder that all problems eventually pass, yet this evening, no matter how he tried, they left him feeling empty and hollow.

'What else do I do?'

'Nothing. Let us see precisely what the *Observer* says, then we shall have a better idea. In the meantime, instruct your press office to say nothing while we sort out your brother.'

'Thank you, Francis. May I call you later when we see what they print? In the meantime, I would be grateful if you would contact Dr Christian. Sarah will be at my brother's home in just under two hours if she leaves right now. I'll instruct her immediately.'

168

Collingridge had adopted a formal tone in an attempt to stifle the tension inside him, but Urquhart could hear the emotion trembling in his voice.

'Don't worry, Henry. Everything will work out. Trust me.'

Charles Collingridge did not object when his sister-in-law let herself into the flat with the spare key. In fact, he was snoring soundly in an armchair, the clutter of an afternoon's heavy indulgence spread around him. He only began to object when Sarah had spent five frustrating minutes trying to shake him awake, and had resorted to ice wrapped in a tea towel. His objections became more vigorous when he began to understand what Sarah was saying, persuading him to 'come away for a few days', but the dialogue became totally incoherent when she began to question him about shares. She could get no sense out of him, and neither could she persuade him to move.

It took the arrival of Dr Christian and a Junior Whip almost an hour later before the situation progressed any further. An overnight bag was rapidly packed, and the three of them bundled the still-protesting brother into the back of Dr Christian's car, which was parked out of sight at the back of the building. Fortunately for them, he had lost the physical coordination to take his objections further.

Unfortunately, however, the whole matter had taken some considerable time, so that when the doctor's Granada swept out from behind the building into the High Street with Sarah and Charles in the back, the whole scene was witnessed by an ITN camera crew, the first to arrive on the scene.

The video tape of a fleeing Charles apparently hiding in the back seat of the car and accompanied by the Prime Minister's wife was played on the late evening news, together with details of the *Observer*'s allegations. The night duty editor at ITN had phoned the managing editor to get approval to play the tape before putting it on air. He

169

wanted his arse covered by senior management on this one. As he had explained, 'Once this gets out, there's no way the Prime Minister can argue he's not involved right up to his neck.'

SUNDAY 17TH OCTOBER

The scenes of the fugitive Charles Collingridge were still being played at midday on Sunday as *Weekend Watch* came on the air. The programme had been thrown together in frantic haste, and there were many untidy ends. The control room reeked of sweat and tension as the programme started. It had not been rehearsed fully, much of it was being done live, and the autocue for the latter stages of the programme was still being typed as the presenter welcomed his viewers.

It had been impossible to find any Minister who would agree to appear on the programme, and one of the invited pundits had not yet arrived. A special overnight opinion poll had been commissioned through Gallup and the polling company's chief executive, Gordon Heald, was presenting the results himself. He had been kicking his computer all morning and was sitting slightly flushed under the hot lights. The computer analysis did nothing to help his sense of ease, for his polling agents had uncovered still further disenchantment with the Prime Minister.

Yes, admitted Heald, it was a significant fall. No, he acknowledged, no Prime Minister had ever won an election after being so low in the polls.

The gloomy prognostications were supported by two senior newspaper commentators and an economist forecasting turmoil in the financial markets in the days ahead, before the presenter switched his attention to Peter Bearstead. Normally the garrulous East Midlands MP would have been videotaped beforehand, but there had been no time for recording. The Honourable and diminutive Member for Leicester North was on live. He was scheduled on

171

the director's log for only two minutes fifty seconds, but the presenter soon discovered that it was the politician who had taken charge of proceedings.

'Yes, Mr Bearstead, but how much trouble do you think the Party is in?'

'That depends.'

'On what?'

'On how long we have to go with the present Prime Minister.'

'So you are standing by your comment of earlier in the week that perhaps the Prime Minister should be considering his position?'

'Not exactly. I'm saying that the Prime Minister should resign. His present unpopularity is destroying the Party, and now he has become enmeshed in what looks like a family scandal. It cannot go on. It must not go on!'

'But do you think that the Prime Minister is likely to resign? After all, there are almost another five years before an election is necessary, and that must leave enormous scope for recovering lost ground.'

'We will not survive another five years with this Prime Minister!' The MP was clearly agitated, rocking back and forth in his studio chair. 'It is time for clear heads, not faint hearts; and I am determined that the Party must come to a decision on the matter. If he does not resign, then I shall stand against him for election as Leader of the Party.'

'You will challenge him for the Party leadership?' the presenter spluttered in surprise. He was nervous, trying to follow the voluble MP while at the same time listening to instructions in his earpiece which were getting rapidly more heated. 'But surely you can't win?'

'Of course I can't win. But it's up to the senior figures within the Party to grasp the initiative and sort the problem out. They are all constantly griping about it, but none of them has the guts to do anything. If they won't take a stand or won't act, then I will. Flush it into the open. We can't let this continue to fester behind closed doors.'

'I want to be absolutely clear about this, Mr Bearstead. You are demanding that the Prime Minister resigns, or else you will stand against him for leadership of the Party . . . ?'

'There has to be a leadership election no later than Christmas: it's Party rules after an election. Instead of a mere formality I shall make it into a real contest where my colleagues will have to make up their minds.'

There was a pained expression on the presenter's face. He was holding his earpiece, through which a shouting match was under way. The director was demanding that the dramatic interview should continue and to hell with the schedule; the editor was shouting that they should get away from it before the bloody fool changed his mind and ruined a sensational story.

'We shall be going for a short commercial break,' announced the presenter.

MONDAY 18TH OCTOBER –
FRIDAY 22ND OCTOBER

Shortly before midnight in London as the Tokyo financial markets opened, sterling began to be marked down heavily. By 9 a.m. and with all the Monday newspapers leading on the public challenge to Collingridge's leadership, the FT All Share Index was down 63 points, and down a further 44 points by 1 p.m. when it became clear that Bearstead intended to proceed. The money men don't like surprises.

The Prime Minister wasn't feeling on top form, either. He hadn't slept and had scarcely talked since Saturday evening. His wife had kept him at Chequers rather than allowing him to return to Downing Street, and had called the doctor. Dr Wynne-Jones, Collingridge's loyal and highly experienced physician, had immediately recognised the signs of strain and had prescribed a sedative and rest. The sedative gave some immediate release in the form of the first lengthy spell of sleep he had had since the start of the party conference a week earlier, but his wife could still detect the tension which fluttered beneath his closed eyelids and which kept his fingers firmly clamped onto the bedclothes.

Late on Monday afternoon when he had come out of his drugged sleep, he instructed the besieged Downing Street press office to make it known that of course he would contest the leadership election and was confident of victory. He was too busy getting on with official Government business to give any interviews, but undoubtedly he would have something to say later in the week. He effected to give a display of total authority and Prime Ministerial stature, but unfortunately no one had yet been able to get any sense out of Charles and there was not a word to be said to refute the allegations of illegal share dealing.

While Downing Street tried to give the impression of business as usual, over at party headquarters Lord Williams ordered additional opinion research to be rushed through. He wanted to know what the country really thought.

The rest of the party machinery moved less quickly. For a further forty-eight hours it was stunned into silence by events which had suddenly sprung off in a totally unexpected direction. The rules for a contested leadership election following a general election were dusted off both in party headquarters and in the media, with many discovering for the first time that the process was under the control of the Chairman of the Parliamentary Party's Backbench Committee, Sir Humphrey Newlands, although the choice of timing was left in the hands of the Party Leader. This proved to be a wise decision since Sir Humphrey, displaying an acutely poor sense of timing, had left the previous weekend for a ten-day holiday on a private island in the West Indies, and was proving extraordinarily difficult to contact. Some speculated that he was deliberately keeping his head low while the awesome but invisible powers of the party hierarchy were mobilised to persuade Bearstead to withdraw. It would be only weeks rather than months, they thought, before Bearstead found himself preoccupied with a senior directorship in industry, in Government as a Junior Minister, or silenced in some other lucrative fashion.

By Wednesday, however, the *Sun* had discovered Sir Humphrey on a silver stretch of beach somewhere near St Lucia along with several friends, including at least three scantily clad young women who were obviously nearly half a century younger than him. It was announced that he would be returning to London as soon as flights could be arranged, for consultation about the election with the Prime Minister.

Collingridge was back in Downing Street, but not in better spirits. Every day brought racy new headlines about turmoil in the Party as newspapers fought to find some new angle on the story. As still further reports began to circulate of growing disaffection between Downing Street and party headquarters, Collingridge began to find himself drifting, cut off from the information and advice which he had previously gained so freely from his wise and wily Party Chairman.

He had no specific reason to distrust Williams, of course, but the constant media discussion of a growing gulf between the two began to make a reality of what previously had been only irresponsible and inventive gossip. Distrust is a matter of mind, not fact, and the press had created strong and virulent perceptions. In the circumstances the ageing and proud Party Chairman felt he couldn't offer advice without being asked, while Collingridge took his silence as probable evidence of disloyalty. Anyway, rationalised Collingridge, party headquarters had let him down badly if not deliberately, and who was responsible for that?

Sarah went for the first visit to Charles, and came back late and very depressed. They were in bed before she could bring herself to talk about it. 'He looks awful, Henry. I never realised quite how ill he was making himself, but it all seems to have caught up with him in a few days. The doctors are still trying to detoxify him, get all the alcohol out of his system. They said he was close to killing himself.' She buried her head in his arms.

'I blame myself. I could have stopped him. If only I hadn't been so preoccupied . . . Did he say anything about the shares?'

'He's scarcely coherent yet; he just kept saying "£50,000? What £50,000?" He swore he'd never been anywhere near a Turkish bank.'

She sat bolt upright in bed, looking deep into her husband's eyes. 'Is he guilty?'

177

'I simply don't know, darling. But what choice do I have? He has to be innocent. If he did buy those shares, then who on earth is going to believe that I didn't tell him to do so. If Charles is guilty, then I shall be judged guilty with him.'

She gripped his arm in alarm.

Collingridge smiled to reassure her. 'Don't worry, my love, I am sure it will never come to that.' But his voice was tired, unconvincing.

'Couldn't you say that Charles was ill, he didn't know what he was doing, he somehow . . . found the information without your knowing . . .' Her voice faded away as she began to realise how transparent the argument was.

He took her gently in his arms, surrounding her with warmth and comfort. He kissed her forehead and felt a warm tear fall on his chest. He knew he was close to tears, too, and felt no shame.

'No, Sarah, I shall not be the one to finish off Charlie. God knows he's been trying hard enough to do that himself, but I am still his brother. On this one we will survive, or sink if we must, as a family. Together.'

Mattie's original intention had been to take the whole week off recovering from the after-effects of the media circus which had spent the best part of six weeks travelling around some of the country's less splendid bars and boarding houses following the various political parties' annual conferences. It was an exhausting schedule, and most of the following weekend she had intended to devote to sampling some exotic Chilean wines and soaking in the bath. But the relaxation she sought proved to be elusive. Her indignation at the way Preston had not only trampled on her story but also abused her sense of journalistic pride seemed to make the wine taste acidic and the bathwater turn cold.

So she tried burning off her anger with strenuous physical work, but after three days of taking it out on the woodwork of her Victorian apartment with sandpaper and paint, she could stand her frustration no longer. On Tuesday morning at 9.30, Mattie was planted firmly in the leather armchair in front of the editor's desk, determined not to move until she had confronted Preston. He would not be able to put the phone down on her this time.

She had been there nearly an hour before his secretary peered apologetically round the door. 'Sorry, Mattie. He's just called in to say he's got an outside appointment. He won't be in until after lunch.'

Mattie felt as if the world was conspiring against her. She wanted to scream or smash something or put chewing gum in his hair brush – anything to get her own back. It was therefore unfortunate timing that John Krajewski decided at that moment to see whether the editor was in his office, only to discover an incandescent Mattie.

'I didn't know you were in!'

'I'm not,' she said between clenched teeth. 'At least, not for much longer.' She stood up to go.

Krajewski was ill at ease and awkward, glancing around the room to make sure they were alone.

'Look, Mattie, I've picked up the phone a dozen times to call you since last week, but . . .'

'But what?' she snapped.

'I was afraid I couldn't find the words to stop you biting my head off,' he said softly.

'Then you were right!' But Mattie's voice had changed, growing gentler as she realised how totally she had lost her sense of humour. It wasn't Johnnie's fault, so why take it out on him, just because he was the only man around to kick? He was worth more than that.

Since his wife had died two years earlier, Krajewski had lost much of his self-confidence, both about women and his professional abilities. He had survived in his demanding job on the strength of his undoubted journalistic talents, but his confidence with women was only slowly returning, penetrating and gradually cracking the shell which his pain had built around him. Many women had tried, attracted by his tall frame, dark hair and deep, sad eyes. But he wanted more than their sympathy, and slowly he had begun to realise that he wanted Mattie. At first he had allowed himself to show no special interest in her, just the respect of a professional colleague which had only slowly developed into something more relaxed during their shared moments in the office and over countless cups of machine coffee. The thrill of the chase was at last beginning to return to his empty life, helping him tolerate the lash of Mattie's tongue. And now he sensed the softening in her mood.

'Mattie, let's talk about it. But not here, not in the office. Over dinner where we can get away from all this.' He made an irritated gesture in the direction of the editor's desk.

'Is this an excuse for a pick up?' The slightest trace of a smile began to appear at the corners of her mouth.

'Do I need an excuse . . . ?'

She grabbed her bag and swung it over her shoulder. 'Eight o'clock,' she instructed, trying in vain to look severe as she walked past him and out of the office.

'I'll be there,' he shouted after her. 'I must be a masochist, but I'll be there.'

And indeed at eight o'clock prompt, he was. They hadn't gone very far, just around the corner from Mattie's flat in Notting Hill to The Ganges, a little Bangladeshi restaurant with a big clay oven and a proprietor who ran an excellent kitchen during the time he allowed himself away from his passionate preoccupation with trying to overthrow the Government back home.

They were waiting for the chicken tikka to arrive when Mattie told him. 'Johnnie, I've been burning up with anger all afternoon. I think I've made a terrible mistake. With all my heart I want to be a journalist, a good journalist. Deep down I always thought I could be a great journalist, but it will never happen working for a man like that. Grev Preston is not what I left everything behind and came to

London for, and I'm not taking any more of his crap. I'm quitting.'

He looked at her sharply and took his time in responding. She was trying to smile defiantly, but he could see the sense of bitter failure tearing at her inside.

'Don't rush it. And don't leave until you have something else to go to. You would regret it if you were out of action right now, just when the political world seems to be falling apart.'

She looked at him quizzically. 'Frankly, Johnnie, you surprise me. That's not the impassioned plea to stay on as part of the team that I was expecting from my deputy editor.'

'I'm not speaking as the deputy editor, Mattie. You mean more to me than that.' There was a short, embarrassed, very English silence which he covered by elaborately breaking a large hunk of nan bread in two. 'I understand why you feel like that. I feel exactly the same way.' There was an edge of bitterness in his words.

'You are thinking of leaving, too?' said Mattie with astonishment.

His eyes were dark and sad once more, but with anger rather than self pity.

'I've been with the paper over eight years. It used to be a quality paper, one I was proud to work for — before the takeover. But what they have done to you, and what they are doing to everyone there, is not my idea of journalism.' He bit into the warm, spicy bread as he considered carefully what he would say next.

'As deputy editor I bear some responsibility for what appears in the paper. Perhaps I shouldn't tell you the story of what happened the other night, but I'm going to because I can't tolerate any more being stuck with the responsibility for the things that are happening now. Mattie, do you want to know what happened to your story?'

There was no need to answer the question. The chicken tikka and vegetable curry had arrived, with the strongly flavoured dishes crowded onto the tiny table, but neither of them showed any interest in the food.

'That night a few of us were standing around in the news room shortly before the first edition deadline. It was a quiet night, not much late breaking news. Then Grev's secretary shouted across the floor that there was a phone call for him and he disappeared to take it in his own office. Ten minutes later he reappeared, very flustered. Someone had really lit a fire under him. "Hold everything," he shouted. "We're going to change the front page." I thought, Jesus, they must have shot the President. He was in a real state, very nervous. Then he asked for your story to be put up on one of the screens. He announced we were going to lead with it, but first we had to beef it up.'

'But the reason he spiked it in the first place was because he said it was too strong!' she protested.

'Of course. But wait, it gets better. So there he was, looking over the shoulder of one of our general reporters who was sitting at the screen, dictating changes directly to him. Twisting it, hyping it, turning everything into a personal attack on the Prime Minister. And you remember the quotations from senior Cabinet sources on which the whole rewrite was based? He made them up, on the spot. Every single one of them. It was fiction from beginning to end. You should have been delighted that your name wasn't on it.'

'But why? Why on earth invent a story like that? Changing the whole editorial stance of the newspaper by dumping Collingridge. What made him change his mind in such a hurry?' She paused for a second, biting her lip with impatience. 'Wait a minute. Who was he talking to on the phone? Who was this so-called source in Bournemouth?' she demanded. 'Of course, I see it now.' She let out a low sigh of understanding. 'Mr Benny Bunter Landless.'

He nodded confirmation.

'So that's why Grev was jumping through the hoops and

screwing around with my story. I should have realised it earlier. The ringmaster was cracking the whip.'

'And that's why I feel I can't go on either, Mattie. We are no longer a newspaper, we're beginning to act as the proprietor's own personal edition of *Pravda*.'

But Mattie's curiosity had already begun to overhaul her own anger and disappointment. There was a story lurking somewhere, and the excitement of the chase began to take a hold on her. 'So Landless has suddenly turned against Collingridge. All his newspapers were craven sycophants during the election, yet now we are running a lynch party. Why, Johnnie, why?'

'That's an excellent question, Mattie, but I don't know the answer. It can't be politics, Landless has never given a damn about that. He has politicians of every party in his pocket. I can only think it's personal in some way.'

'If it's personal it must be business. That's the only thing which really rattles his cage.'

'But I can't figure out why he should have fallen out with Collingridge over business.'

'And I would love to know who he's got on the inside.'

'What do you mean?' asked Krajewski.

'Grev couldn't have concocted that article without the material on the opinion poll. Without my copy on which to work he had nothing, and without the leaked statistics I had nothing either. And at the same time as this occurs, Landless decides to ditch Collingridge. It's too much of a coincidence for that all to have come together by chance.' She banged her hand on the table with a renewed passion. 'But it can't be Landless on his own. There's somebody on the inside of the Party leaking polls and pulling strings.'

'The same person who's supposed to have been leaking all the material since the election?'

'The one the Chief Whip was trying to sort out? That's a fascinating thought. He found nothing definite and before tonight I was never convinced that it was a deliberate campaign of leaks rather than a series of cock-ups . . .'

'But now . . . ?'

'Now I've got just two questions, Johnnie – who, and why?'

The adrenalin was pouring into her veins, replacing her earlier despondency with electric urges which tingled throughout her body and brain. She felt exhilarated. Something had touched her deep down, an almost animal lust to pursue her prey until she had found and trapped it. This is what she had come south for. This made it all worthwhile.

'Johnnie, you sweet man. How wise you are! Something smells and I want to find out what – I knew it when I saw Landless prowling around at Bournemouth. You're right. Now is definitely not the time to throw in the towel and resign. I'm going to get to the bottom of this even if I have to kill someone. Will you help me?'

'If that's what you want – of course.'

'There's another thing I want, Johnnie.' She felt alive, charged with excitement and a feeling burning deep inside her which she thought she had long ago forgotten. 'Let's pass on the bloody biryani and go back to my place. I've got a bottle of vintage Sauterne in the fridge, and I need some company tonight. All night. Would you mind?'

'Mattie, it's been a long time . . .'

'Me, too, Johnnie. Too long.'

The statement – or briefing, in fact, because it was not issued in the form of a quotable press release – was made available on Wednesday and was simple. As the Downing Street press secretary told the gathered lobby correspondents, 'The Prime Minister has never provided his brother with any form of commercially sensitive Government information, and has never discussed any aspect of Renox Chemicals with him. The Prime Minister's brother is extremely ill, and is currently under medical supervision. His doctors have stated that he is not in a fit state to give interviews or answer questions. However, I can assure you that he categorically denies purchasing any Renox shares, having a false address in Paddington, or being involved in this matter in any way whatsoever. That's all I can tell you at the moment.'

'Come on, Freddie,' one of the correspondents carped, 'you can't get away with just that. How on earth do you explain the *Observer* story if the Collingridges are innocent?'

'I can't. Perhaps they were getting confused with another Charles Collingridge, how do I know? But I've known Henry Collingridge for many years, just as you've known me, and all of my experience tells me he is incapable of stooping to such ridiculous and sordid depths. My man is innocent, and you have my word on that!'

He spoke with the vehemence of a professional placing his own reputation on the line along with that of his boss, and the lobby's respect for one of their old time colleagues swung the day for Collingridge – just.

'We're innocent!' bawled the front page of the *Daily Mail* the following day, with most of the other newspapers following on cue. Finding no more incriminating information with which to play, the media and the Party together sat back exhausted, relishing the opportunity to concentrate for just a moment on other disasters.

Urquhart once again had stepped from the Chief Whip's office at Number 12 Downing Street along to Number 10 at the request of Collingridge. 'You're the only smiling face I see at the moment, Francis, and I need you to keep my spirits up!' They were sitting together in the Cabinet Room reviewing the newspapers, with Collingridge at last managing a smile of his own. For the first time in days he felt he could see the mists beginning to clear.

'What do you think, Francis?'

'Perhaps we are through the worst.'

'No, not necessarily. But at least we have a breathing space and I can tell you, I need that more than anything. The pressure . . .' He shook his head slowly. 'Well, you understand, I'm sure.'

Collingridge took a deep breath to summon up fresh resources from within. 'But it is only a breathing space, Francis.' He waved to the empty seats around the Cabinet table. 'I don't know how much firm support I still have amongst colleagues, but I have to give them something to hold on to. I can't afford to run away. I have to show I've nothing to hide, to take the initiative once again.'

'What do you intend to do?'

The Prime Minister sat quietly, beneath the towering oil painting of Robert Walpole, his longest-serving predecessor who had survived countless scandals and crises and whose magnificent portrait had inspired many leaders during times of trial. As Collingridge gazed in contemplation across St James's Park, the sun burst through the grey autumn skies, flooding the room with light. The sound of children playing rose up from the park. Life would go on.

He turned to face Urquhart. 'I have an invitation from *Weekend Watch* to appear this Sunday and put my own case – to restore the balance. I think I must do it – and I think I must do it damned well! They've promised no more than ten minutes on the *Observer* nonsense, the rest on broad policy and our ambitions for the fourth term. What do you think?'

Urquhart chose not to express any opinion. He was more than content to let Collingridge use him as a sounding board while he made up his own mind, bouncing ideas and arguments off him to see how they sounded, letting Urquhart know of every move along the way.

'At times like these, men must make up their own minds.'

'Good!' Collingridge exclaimed with a chuckle. 'I'm glad you think that way. Because I've already accepted.' He took a deep breath and exhaled fiercely through flared nostrils. 'The stakes are high, Francis, and I know there are no easy options. But for once I feel lucky!'

It was Urquhart's turn to gaze out through the window

and think hard. As he did so, the sun disappeared once more behind the clouds, and the rain began to beat down on the pane.

Penny put the call from the Chief Whip through to O'Neill in his office. A few seconds later the door was carefully closed. Penny heard the sound of O'Neill's raised voice some minutes later, but could not decipher what he was shouting about.

When the red light on the extension phone flashed off to indicate the call was finished, there was no sound at all from O'Neill's office. Pressed forward by a mixture of curiosity and concern, she knocked gently on his door, and opened it cautiously. O'Neill was sitting at his desk with his head in his hands. He looked up as he heard Penny come in, and confronted her with wild, staring eyes.

His voice croaked and his speech was disjointed.

'He . . . threatened me, Pen. He said if I don't he would . . . tell everyone. I said I wouldn't but . . . I've got to alter the file . . .'

'What file, Roger? What have you got to do?' She had never seen him like this. 'Can I help?'

'No, Pen, you can't help. Not on this . . . Damned computers!' He seemed to regain a little self-control. 'Penny. I want you to forget all about it. I want you to go home. Have the rest of the day off. I'm . . . going out shortly. Please, don't hang around waiting for me, go home now.'

'But, Roger, I . . .'

'No questions, Pen, no questions. Just leave!'

She gathered her things in tearful confusion as O'Neill slammed his door shut once again and she heard it locking from the inside.

SUNDAY 24TH OCTOBER

Collingridge began to relax as the programme unfolded. He had rehearsed hard for the previous two days, and the questions were much as expected, giving him an excellent opportunity to talk with genuine vigour about the next few years. He had insisted that the questions concerning the *Observer* allegations be kept until the end, partly so that *Weekend Watch* could not renege on its promise to restrict the section to ten minutes, and partly because he wanted to be into his stride and in command before grappling with them. He hoped that after forty-five minutes of him talking about the bright future for the country the questions would look mean and irrelevant.

Sarah was smiling encouragingly from the edge of the studio as they went into the final commercial break. He gave her a thumbs-up sign as the floor manager waved his arms to let them know that they were about to go back on air.

'Mr Collingridge, for the final few minutes of this programme, I would like to turn to the allegations printed in the *Observer* last week about Charles Collingridge and possible improper share dealing.'

Collingridge nodded seriously into the camera to show that he had nothing to fear from such questions.

'I understand that earlier this week Downing Street issued a statement denying any connection of your family with the matter, and suggesting that there may have been a case of mistaken identity. Is that correct?'

'There may have been some confusion with another Charles Collingridge for all I know, but I am really not in a position to explain the extraordinary *Observer* story. All I

189

can tell you is that none of my family have anything whatsoever to do with this matter. You have my word of honour on that.' He spoke the words slowly, leaning forward, looking directly at the presenter to give added dramatic emphasis.

'I understand that your brother denies ever having opened an accommodation address in a Paddington tobacconists.'

'Absolutely,' Collingridge confirmed.

'Prime Minister, earlier this week one of our reporters addressed an envelope to himself, care of Charles Collingridge, at the Paddington address used to open the bank account. He used a vivid red envelope to make sure it stood out clearly. I would like you to look at this video tape which we took at that address yesterday when he went to reclaim it. I apologise for the poor quality, but I am afraid we had to use a concealed camera, as the proprietor of the shop concerned seemed very reluctant to cooperate.'

The presenter swivelled his chair so that he could see the dark and fuzzy but still discernible video which was being projected onto the large screen behind him. Collingridge flashed a concerned look at Sarah, and cautiously swivelled his own chair around. He watched as the reporter approached the counter, pulled out various pieces of plastic and paper from his wallet to identify himself, and explained to the counter assistant that a letter was waiting for him in the care of Charles Collingridge, who used this address for his own post. The assistant, the same overweight and balding man who had served Penny several months before, explained that he could not release letters except to someone who could produce a proper receipt. 'Lots of important letters come here,' he sniffed. 'Can't go handing them out to just anyone.'

'But look, it's there. The red envelope. I can see it from here.'

A little uncertain as to what he should do, the assistant turned and extracted the envelopes from a numbered pigeon hole behind him. There were three of them. He placed the red envelope on the counter in front of the reporter, with the other two envelopes to one side. He was trying to confirm that the name on the envelope, c/o Charles Collingridge, matched that of the reporter's identity cards while the camera zoomed in closely on the other two envelopes. It took a few seconds for the operator to focus the concealed equipment properly, but as he did so, the markings on the envelopes came clearly into view. Both were addressed to Charles Collingridge. One bore the imprint of the Union Bank of Turkey. The other had been sent from the Party's Sales and Literature Office at Smith Square.

The presenter turned once more to confront Collingridge – and there was no doubt left in Collingridge's mind that the triumphant interview had now turned into open confrontation.

'The first envelope would seem to confirm that the address was indeed used to buy and sell shares in the Renox Chemical Company through the Union Bank of Turkey. But we were puzzled about the letter from your own party headquarters. So we called your Sales and Literature Office, pretending to be a supplier with an order from Charles Collingridge but with an indecipherable address.'

Collingridge was just about to shout an angry denunciation of the immoral and underhand methods adopted by the programme when the studio was filled with the recorded sound of the telephone call.

'. . . so could you just confirm what address we should have for Mr Collingridge and then we can get the goods off to him straight away.'

'Just one minute, please,' said an eager young man's voice. 'I'll call it up on the screen.'

There was the sound of a keyboard being tapped. 'Ah, here it is. Charles Collingridge, 216 Praed Street, Paddington, London W2.'

'Thank you very much indeed. You have been most helpful.'

The presenter turned once again to Collingridge. 'Do you wish to comment, Prime Minister?'

He shook his head, uncertain of what to say, or whether he should walk off the set. He was astonished that Charles was registered with the Sales and Literature Office, because he had only ever shown interest in the social side of politics. But he suspected that this was likely to be the least of his surprises.

'Of course, we took seriously your explanation that it might be a case of mistaken identity, of confusion with another Charles Collingridge.'

Collingridge wanted to shout in protest that it was not 'his' explanation, that it was simply an off-hand and speculative remark made without prejudice by his press secretary. But he knew it would be a waste of time, so he remained silent.

'Do you know how many other Charles Collingridges there are listed in the London telephone directory, Prime Minister?'

Collingridge offered no response, but sat there looking grim and ashen faced.

The presenter came to the assistance of his silent guest. 'There are no other Charles Collingridges listed in the London telephone directory. Indeed, sources at British Telecom tell us that there is only one Charles Collingridge listed throughout the United Kingdom. Your brother, Prime Minister.'

Again a pause, inviting a response, but none was offered.

'Since a Mr Charles Collingridge seems to have acted on inside information concerning the Renox Chemical Company and decisions of the Department of Health relating to it, we asked both organisations if they had any knowledge of a Charles Collingridge. Renox tells us that neither they, nor their subsidiaries, have any Collingridge amongst their employees. The Department of Health's press office was rather more cagey, promising to get back to us but never did. However, their trade union office was much more cooperative. They, too, confirmed that there is no Collingridge listed as working at any of the Department's 508 offices throughout the country.'

The presenter shuffled his notes. 'Apparently they did have a Minnie Collingridge who worked at their Coventry office until two years ago, but she went back to Jamaica.'

'They're laughing at me,' screamed Collingridge to himself. 'They have convicted, sentenced and now are executing me!' In the background he could see Sarah, and the tears which were running like rivers of blood down her cheeks.

'Prime Minister. We have almost come to the end of our programme. Is there anything you wish to say?'

Collingridge sat there, staring ahead at Sarah, wanting to run to her and embrace her and lie to her that there was no need for tears, everything would be all right. He was still sitting motionless in his chair a full minute later, as the eerie studio silence was broken by the programme's theme music. While the lights dimmed and the credits rolled, the viewers saw him rise from his seat, walk slowly over to embrace his sobbing wife, and start whispering all those lies.

When they arrived back at Downing Street, Collingridge went straight to the Cabinet Room. He entered almost like a visitor, looking slowly and with a new eye around the room, at its elegant furnishings, fine classical architecture and historic paintings. Yet his gaze kept coming back to the Cabinet table itself, symbol of the uniquely British form of collective Government. He walked slowly around it, trailing his hand on the green baize cloth, stopping at the far end at the seat he had first occupied ten years ago as the Cabinet's most junior member. He raised his eyes to meet those of Robert Walpole, who seemed to be looking directly at him.

'What would you have done, old fellow?' he whispered. 'Fight, I suppose. And if you didn't win that one then fight and fight again. Well, we'll see.'

He reached his own chair and settled slowly into it, feeling physically lost as he sat alone at the middle of the great table. He reached for the single telephone which stood beside his blotter. There was a duty telephonist on call every hour of the day and night.

'Get me the Chancellor of the Exchequer, please.'

It took less than a minute before the receiver buzzed, with the Chancellor on the line.

'Colin, did you see it? How badly will the markets react tomorrow?'

The Chancellor gave an embarrassed but honest opinion.

'Bloody, eh? We shall have to see what can be done about it. We shall be in touch.'

He then spoke to the Foreign Secretary. 'What damage, Patrick?'

Woolton told him bluntly that with the Government's reputation so weak it would now be impossible to achieve the reforms of the Common Market's budgetary system which the United Kingdom Government had long been demanding and which had been made a clear priority during the election. 'A month ago it was there, within our grasp, after all these years. Now we carry about as much political clout around the negotiating table as O'Reilly's donkey. Sorry, Henry, you asked me to be brutally frank.'

Then it was the turn of the Party Chairman. Williams could hear the formal tone being used by Collingridge on the end of the phone, and responded in kind.

'Prime Minister, within the last hour I have had calls from seven of our eleven Regional Party Chairmen. Without exception, I am sorry to say, they think the situation is quite disastrous for the Party. They feel that we are beyond the point of no return.'

'No, Teddy,' contradicted Collingridge. 'They feel that *I* am beyond the point of no return. There's a difference.'

He made one more phone call, to his private secretary asking him to seek an appointment at the Palace around lunchtime the following day. The secretary rang back four minutes later to say Her Majesty looked forward to seeing him at 1 o'clock.

He felt suddenly relieved, as if the tremendous weight had already shifted from his shoulders. He looked up one last time to face Walpole.

'Oh, yes. You would have fought. You would probably have won. But this office has already ruined my brother and now it is ruining me. I will not let it ruin Sarah's happiness, too. If you will excuse me, I had better let her know.'

Walpole's forty-ninth successor as Prime Minister strode towards the Cabinet Room door for almost the last time and, with his hand on the brass handle, turned once more.

'By the way, it already feels better.'

Part Three

THE DEAL

MONDAY 25TH OCTOBER

Shortly before 10 o'clock the following morning, the members of the Cabinet assembled around the Cabinet table. They had been called individually to Downing Street rather than as a formal Cabinet, and most had been surprised to discover their colleagues also gathered. There was an air of expectation and great curiosity, and the conversation around the table while they waited for their Prime Minister was unusually muffled.

As the tones of Big Ben striking the hour reached into the room, the door opened and Collingridge walked in.

'Good morning, gentlemen.' His voice was unusually soft. 'I am grateful to see you all here. I shall not detain you long.'

He took his seat, and extracted a single sheet of paper from the leather bound file he was carrying. He laid it carefully on the table in front of him, and then looked slowly around at his colleagues. There was not a sound to be heard in the room.

'I am sorry I was unable to inform you that this morning's meeting was to be one of the full Cabinet. As you will shortly see, it was necessary to ensure that you could all be assembled without creating undue attention and speculation amongst the press.'

He let out a long sigh, a mixture of pain and relief.

'I am going to read to you a short statement that I shall be issuing later today. At 1 o'clock I shall be going to the Palace to convey the contents to Her Majesty. I must ask all of you, on your oaths of office, not to divulge the contents of this message to anyone before it is officially released. I must ensure Her Majesty hears it from me and not through the press. I would also ask it of each one of you as a personal favour to me.'

He looked slowly around the table to catch the eye of those present, all of whom nodded their assent as he did so. He picked up the sheet of paper and began to read in a slow, matter-of-fact voice. He squeezed out any trace of regret he might have felt.

'Recently there has been a spate of allegations in the media about the business affairs of both me and my family, which shows no sign of abating.

'I have consistently stated, and repeat today, that I have done nothing of which I should be ashamed. I have adhered strictly to the rules and conventions relating to the conduct of the Prime Minister.

'The implied allegation made against me is one of the most serious kind for any holder of public office, that I have used that office and the confidential information available to me from it to enrich my family. I cannot explain the extraordinary circumstances referred to by the media which have given rise to these allegations, and I have asked the Cabinet Secretary to undertake a formal independent investigation into them.

'The nature of these allegations makes it impossible for me to prove my innocence of the charge of misconduct, but I am confident that the official investigation by the Cabinet Secretary will eventually establish the full facts of the matter and my complete exoneration.'

He swallowed hard; his mouth was dry and increasingly he was struggling with some of the words.

'However, this investigation will inevitably take some time to complete, and in the meantime the spread of doubts and insinuations is doing real harm to the normal business of Government, and also to my Party. While the time and attention of the Government should be devoted to implementing the programme on which we were so recently re-elected, this is not proving possible in present circumstances.

'The integrity of the office of Prime Minister has been brought into question, and it is my first duty to protect that office. Therefore, to re-establish and preserve that unquestioned integrity, I have today asked the permission of Her Majesty the Queen to relinquish the office of Prime Minister as soon as a successor can be chosen.'

There was a sharp intake of breath from somewhere around the table, but otherwise there was absolute silence throughout the room. Hearts had momentarily stopped beating.

Collingridge cleared his throat and continued.

'I have devoted my entire adult life to the pursuit of my political ideals, and it goes against every bone in my body to leave office in this fashion. I am not running away from the allegations, but rather ensuring that they may be cleared up as quickly and expeditiously as possible, and striving to bring a little peace back to my family. I believe history will show that I have made the right judgement.'

Collingridge replaced the piece of paper in his folder. 'Gentlemen, thank you,' he said curtly, and in an instant strode out of the door and was gone.

Urquhart sat at the end of the Cabinet table transfixed. As the murmuring and gasps of surprise broke out around him he would not, could not, join in. He gazed for a long time at the Prime Minister's empty chair, exulting in his own immense power.

He had done this. Alone he had destroyed the most influential man in the country, wielding might beyond the dreams of the petty men who sat with him around that table. And he knew he was the only one of them who could truly justify filling that empty seat. The others were pygmies, ants.

He was seized by the same exhilarating perspective which had gripped him forty years earlier when as a raw military recruit he had prepared to make his first parachute jump 2,500 feet above the fields of Lincolnshire. All the instruction in the world could not have prepared him for the chilling excitement as he sat in the open hatchway of a twin engine Islander, his feet dangling in the fierce slipstream, gazing down at the green and yellow landscape far below.

He was attached to a parachute which in turn was fastened to a static line and this, so the instructors had assured him, would guarantee a safe landing. But this was no matter of mere logic. It was an act of faith, of trust in one's destiny, a willingness to accept the danger if that were the only way of finding the fulfilment which every real man sought. Despite the logic of the static line, sometimes even the most courageous of men froze in the open hatchway as his faith deserted him and his self-respect was ripped away in the slipstream. Yet Urquhart had felt omnipotent, God-like, viewing His Kingdom from on high, disdaining the logic and fears which beset the ordinary mortals around him.

As he gazed now at the empty chair, he knew there was no time for doubt. He must have faith in himself and his destiny. He had launched himself and was rushing through the air until he reached that point on the very edge of discovery where he would find what Destiny had decided for him. He gave an inner smile of anticipation, while contriving outwardly to look as shocked as those around him.

Still shivering from the excitement, Urquhart walked the few yards back to the Chief Whip's office in Downing Street. He locked himself in his private room and by 10.20 a.m. he had made two phone calls.

Shortly after 10.30, Roger O'Neill called a meeting of the entire press office at party headquarters.

'I'm afraid I am going to have to ask you to cancel all your lunch arrangements today. I've had the word that shortly after 1 o'clock this afternoon we are to expect a very important statement from Downing Street. It's absolutely confidential, I cannot tell you what it is about, but we have to be ready to handle it. It's a real blockbuster.'

By 11 a.m., five journalists had been contacted by various press officers in party headquarters to apologise for not being able to make lunch. All of them were sworn to secrecy and told with various shades of detail and speculation that 'something big was going on in Downing Street'.

Charles Goodman of the Press Association, using the formidable range of contacts and favours he had built up over the years, quickly discovered that there had been a meeting of all Cabinet Ministers at Downing Street that morning, although the Number Ten press office had nothing to say on the matter. Too many official schedules for 10 a.m. had been hastily altered for anyone to be able to hide the fact. On a hunch he then phoned the Buckingham Palace press office, which also had nothing to say – at least officially. But the deputy press secretary there had worked with Goodman many years before on the *Manchester Evening News*, and confirmed entirely off the record and totally unattributably that Collingridge had asked for an audience at 1 p.m.

By 11.25 a.m. the PA tape was carrying the story of the secret Cabinet meeting and the unscheduled audience expected soon to take place between the Prime Minister and the Queen, an entirely factual report.

By midday IRN local radio was running a sensationalised lead item on their news programmes.

'The news at noon is that Henry Collingridge will soon be on his way for a secret meeting with Her Majesty the Queen. Speculation has exploded in Westminster during the last hour that either he is going to sack several of his leading Ministers and inform the Queen of a major Cabinet reshuffle, or he is going to admit his guilt to recent charges of insider trading with his brother. There are even rumours that she is going to sack him. Whatever the outcome, it seems certain that in just over an hour's time somebody in Government is going to be very unhappy.'

In fact it took less than a couple of minutes to infuriate

Henry Collingridge for, when the Prime Minister looked out of his front window, the other side of the street was obscured in a forest of television cameras around which was camped an army of reporters and press photographers.

He was purple with rage as he slammed the door of his office shut with a noise which echoed along the corridor. Two passing messengers witnessed his fury. 'What was that he was muttering?' asked one.

'Didn't quite get it, Jim. Something about "oaths of office".'

When Collingridge walked out through the front door and into his car at 12.45, he ignored the screams of the press corps from the other side of the road. He drove off into Whitehall, where he was pursued by a camera car which in its eagerness to chase him nearly crashed into the rear of the Prime Minister's police escort. There was another crowd of photographers outside the gates of Buckingham Palace. His attempt at a dignified resignation had turned into a three-ring circus.

As he watched these frenzied scenes on live television, Benjamin Landless, alerted more than two hours earlier by Urquhart, contented himself with a broad smile and a second bottle of champagne.

The Prime Minister had asked not to be disturbed unless it was absolutely necessary. After returning from the Palace, he had retired to the private apartment above Downing Street, wanting to be alone with his wife for a few hours. Somehow, those official papers no longer seemed so pressing.

The private secretary apologised. 'I'm terribly sorry, Prime Minister, but it's Dr Christian. He said it was important.'

The phone buzzed gently as the call was put through.

'Dr Christian. How can I help you? And how is Charles?'

'It's about Charles I'm calling, Mr Collingridge. As we have discussed before, I have been keeping him very isolated and away from the newspapers so that he wasn't disturbed by all the allegations. But we have a problem. Normally we switch his television off and find something to divert him during news programmes, but we weren't expecting the unscheduled programme about your resignation – I'm deeply sorry you've had to resign, by the way, but it's about Charles I am most worried. I have to put his interests first, you understand.'

'I do understand, Dr Christian, and you have your priorities absolutely right.'

'He heard of the allegations about you and himself for the very first time, and how they had helped bring about your resignation. He is deeply upset and disturbed, Mr Collingridge; it's come as a great shock. He believes he is to blame for all that's happened, and I'm afraid is talking about doing harm to himself. I thought we were just on the verge of making real progress in his case, and now I fear this will not only set him right back but in his present delicate emotional state could bring about a real crisis for him. I don't wish to alarm you unduly, but he needs your help. Very badly.'

Sarah saw the look of anguish on her husband's face, and came over to sit beside him and hold his hand. It was trembling.

'Doctor, what can I do? I'll do anything, anything you want.'

'We need to find some way of reassuring him. He's desperately confused.'

There was a pause as Collingridge bit deep into his lip, hoping it would distract from the pain burning inside.

'May I talk to him, doctor?'

There was a wait of several minutes as Charles was brought to the telephone.

'Charlie, how are you old boy?' he said softly.

'Henry, what have I done to you? I've ruined you, destroyed you!' The voice sounded old, touched by hysteria.

'Charlie, Charlie. You've done nothing. It's not you who

has hurt me, you have nothing to feel guilty about.'

'But I've seen it on the television. You going off to the Queen to resign. They said it was because of me and some shares. I don't understand it, Henry, I've screwed it all up. Not only my life, but you and Sarah too. I don't deserve to be your brother. There's no point in anything any more.' There was a huge, gulping sob on the end of the phone.

'Charlie, I want you to listen to me very carefully. Are you listening? It's not you who should be asking for pardon, but me who should be down on my knees begging for forgiveness from you.'

He cut through the protest beginning to emerge from his brother.

'No, listen, Charlie! We've always got through our problems together, as family. Remember when I was running the business – the year we nearly went bust? We were going down, Charlie, and it was my fault. And who brought in that new client, that order which saved us? I know it wasn't the biggest order the company ever had, but it couldn't have come at a more vital time. You saved the company, Charlie, and you saved me. Just like you did when I was a bloody fool and got caught driving over the limit that Christmas. The local police sergeant was a rugger playing friend of *yours*, not mine, and it was you who somehow managed to persuade him to fix the breath test at the station. If I had lost my licence then, I would never have been selected by the constituency for the seat. Don't you see, Charlie, far from ruining it for me, you made it all possible. We've always faced things together, and that's just how it's going to stay.'

'But now I've ruined everything for you, Henry . . .'

'No, it's me that's ruined things. I got too high and bloody mighty, and forgot that the only thing that matters in the end is those you love. You were always around when I needed help, all the time. But I got too busy. When Mary left, I knew how much you were hurting. I should have been there. You needed me, but there always seemed other things to do. I was always going to come and see you tomorrow, or the next day. Always tomorrow, Charlie, always tomorrow.'

The emotion was cracking Collingridge's voice.

'I've had my moment of glory, I've been selfish, I've done the things that *I* wanted to do. While I watched you become an alcoholic and practically kill yourself.'

It was the first time that either of them had spoken that truth. Charles had always been under the weather, or overtired, or suffering from nerves – never uncontrollably, alcoholically drunk. They both knew there were no secrets now, no going back.

'I will walk out of Downing Street and will be able to say good bloody riddance – if only I know I still have my brother. I'm just terrified, Charlie, that it's too late, that I've neglected you too much to be able to ask for your forgiveness, that you've been alone too long for you to want to get better.'

The tears of genuine anguish were flowing down his cheeks. Sarah was hugging him tightly.

'Charlie, without your forgiveness, all this will have been for nothing.'

There was silence from the other end of the phone.

'Say something, Charlie!' he said in desperation.

'I love you, big brother.'

He let out a sigh of release and total joy.

'I love you too, old boy. I'll come and see you tomorrow. We'll both have a lot more time for each other now, eh?'

They were both laughing through the tears, with Sarah joining in. Henry Collingridge hadn't felt so whole for years.

She was sipping a drink, admiring the night view of London from his penthouse apartment when he came up behind her and embraced her warmly.

'Hey, I thought we came here to discuss business,' she said, not resisting.

'There are some things I don't have the words for,' he said, burying his face in her blonde hair and rejoicing at its freshness.

She turned round in his arms to face him and look directly into his eyes.

'You talk too much,' she said, and kissed him passionately. She was glad he had made the first move; she was not competing tonight, she wanted to be free, uncomplicated, just a woman.

She made no sound of protest as he slipped her silk blouse over her shoulders and it fell away, revealing a smooth and unblemished skin which could have been a model's. Her breasts were immaculate, small but very feminine and sensitive. She gasped as his fingers gently ran over her nipples, which responded instantly. She undid her own belt and let her trousers fall straight to the floor, stepping out of them and out of her shoes in one graceful movement. She stood tall and unashamed against the glittering lights of London behind her.

He marvelled for a moment at what he saw. He couldn't remember when he last had felt like this, so excited and so much a man.

'Mattie, you look lovely.'

'I hope you are not just going to look, Johnnie,' she said.

He took her to the fireplace where the flames flickered invitingly, held her close against him and prayed that the moment would last for ever.

When they were spent, for some while they lay silently on the rug, lost in their thoughts and each other's arms. It was Mattie who broke the spell.

'Is it all coincidence, Johnnie?'

'Let's try again and see.'

'Not this, you fool,' she laughed. 'It's time to talk now!'

'Oh, I wondered how long it would take you to get back to that,' he said with an air of resignation. He got them both blankets to wrap themselves in.

'We find a plan, effort, plot – call it what you will –

in which our paper is involved, to chop the legs off Collingridge. For all we know it has been going on for months. Now Collingridge resigns. Is it all part of the same operation?'

'How can it be, Mattie? In the end Collingridge hasn't been forced out by his opponents but by his brother's apparent fiddling of share purchases. You're surely not suggesting all that was part of the plan.'

'You have to admit it's a hell of a coincidence, Johnnie. I've met Charles Collingridge, spent several hours drinking and chatting with him at the party conference, as it happens. He struck me as being a pleasant and straightforward drunk, who certainly didn't seem as if he had two hundred pounds to put together, let alone being able to raise tens of thousands of pounds to start speculating in shares.'

Her face was screwed up in concentration as she grappled with her still confused thoughts. 'It may seem silly, I know he's an alcoholic and they often aren't responsible for their actions, but I don't believe he would have jeopardised his brother's whole career for a few thousand pounds' profit on the Stock Market. And do you really think it's likely that Henry Collingridge, the Prime Minister of this country, was feeding his drunk brother insider share tips to finance his boozing?'

'Is it any more credible to believe there is some form of high-level plot involving senior party figures, the publisher of our newspaper and God knows who else to kill off the Prime Minister? Surely the easiest explanation is the simple one – that Charles Collingridge is a drunk who is not responsible for his actions and who has done something so overwhelmingly stupid that his brother's had to resign.'

'There's only one person who can tell us, I suppose. Charles Collingridge.'

'But he's locked away in some clinic or other, isn't he? I thought his whereabouts were a closely guarded family secret.'

'True, but he's the only one who could help us get to the bottom of this.'

'And how does our Reporter of the Year propose to do that?' he teased.

She was concentrating too intently to rise to the bait. Instead, she sat on the hearth rug wrapped deep in thought and an enormous yellow blanket while he refreshed their drinks. As he returned with two glasses, she spun round to face him.

'When was the last time anyone saw Charles Collingridge?' she demanded.

'Why, er . . . When he was driven away from his home over a week ago.'

'Who was he with?'

'Sarah Collingridge.'

'And . . . ?'

'A driver.'

'Who was the driver, Johnnie?'

'Damned if I know. Never seen him before. Hang on, being a dutiful deputy editor I keep all the nightly news on tape for a fortnight, so I should have it here somewhere.'

He rummaged around by his video player for a few moments before slotting a tape into the chamber and winding it forward. In a few seconds, through the blizzard produced by the fast replay button, appeared the scenes of Charles Collingridge huddled in the back of the fleeing car.

'Go back!' she ordered. 'To the start.'

And there, for less than a second at the front of the report, as the car swept from behind the building into the main road, they could clearly see the face of the driver through the windscreen.

Krajewski punched the freeze frame button. They both sat there entranced, staring at the balding and bespectacled face.

'And who the hell is he?' muttered Krajewski.

'Let's figure out who he's *not*,' said Mattie. 'He's not a

Government driver – it's not a Government car and the drivers pool is very gossipy, so we would have heard something. He's not a political figure or we would have recognised him . . .'

She clapped her hands in inspiration. 'Johnnie, where were they going?'

'Not to Downing Street, not to some hotel or other public place.' He pondered the options. 'To the clinic, I suppose.'

'Precisely! That man is from the clinic. If we can find out who he is, we shall know where Charles is!'

'OK, Clark Kent. Seems fair enough. Look, I can get a hard copy of the face off the video tape and show it around. We could try old Freddie, one of our staff photographers. Not only does he have an excellent memory for faces, he is also an alcoholic who dried out a couple of years ago. He still goes religiously every week to Alcoholics Anonymous, and he might well be able to put us on the right track. There aren't that many treatment centres, we should be able to make some progress – but I still don't accept your conspiracy theory, Mattie. It's still all much more likely to be circumstance and coincidence.'

'You cynical bastard, what do I have to do to convince you?'

'Come here and show me a little more of that feminine intuition of yours,' he growled.

At almost exactly the same time in the private booth of a fashionable and overpriced restaurant in the West End of London, Landless and Urquhart were also locked together, in an embrace of an entirely mercenary kind.

'Interesting times, Frankie, interesting times,' mused Landless.

'In China, I believe, it is a curse to live in interesting times.'

'I'm sure Collingridge agrees!' said Landless, bursting into gruff laughter.

He tapped the ash off his thick Havana cigar and savoured the large cognac before returning to his guest.

'Frankie, I invited you here this evening to ask just one question. I shan't beat around the bush, and I shall thank you to be absolutely blunt with me. Are you going to stand for the leadership?' He glared directly at Urquhart, trying to intimidate him into total frankness.

'I can't tell yet. The situation is very unclear, and I shall have to wait for the dust to settle a little . . .'

'OK, Frankie, let me put it this way. Do you want it? Because if you do, old son, I can be very helpful to you.'

Urquhart returned his host's direct stare, looking deep into the protruding, bloodshot eyes.

'I want it very, very much.'

It was the first time he admitted to anyone other than himself his burning desire to hold the reins of Prime Ministerial power, yet with Landless, who wore his naked ambition on his sleeve, he felt no embarrassment in the confession.

'That's good. Let's start from there. Let me tell you what the *Telegraph* will be running tomorrow. It's an analysis piece by our political correspondent, Mattie Storin. Pretty blonde girl with long legs and big blue eyes – d'you know her, Frankie?'

'Yes,' mused Urquhart. 'Only professionally, of course,' he hastened to add as he saw the fleshy lips of his companion preparing a lewd comment. 'Bright, too. I'm interested to discover how she sees things.'

'Says it is an open race for the leadership, that Collingridge's resignation has come so quickly and unexpectedly that no potential successor has got his public case prepared very well. So almost anything could happen.'

'I believe she is right,' nodded Urquhart. 'Which worries me. The whole election process could be over in less than three weeks, and it's the slick, flashy television performers who will gain the best start. The tide is everything in winning these contests; if it's with you, it will sweep you home; flowing against you, then no matter how good a swimmer you are, you'll still drown.'

'Which slick, flashy television performers in particular?'

'Try Michael Samuel.'

'Mmmm, young, impressive, principled, seems intelligent – not at all to my liking. He wants to interfere in everything, rebuild the world. Got too much of a conscience for my liking, and not enough experience in taking hard, sound decisions.'

'So what do we do?' asked Urquhart.

Landless cupped the crystal goblet in his huge hands, swirled the dark liquor and chuckled quietly.

'Frankie, tides turn. You can be swimming strongly for the shore one minute, and the next be swept out to sea . . .'

He took a huge gulp of cognac, raised his finger to order another round, and settled his bulk as comfortably as he could into his chair before resuming the conversation.

'Frankie, this afternoon I instructed a small and extremely confidential team at the *Telegraph* to start contacting as many of the Government's Members of Parliament as they can get hold of in the next twenty-four hours to ask which way they are going to vote. In the next edition of the *Telegraph*, they will publish the results – which I confidently predict will show Mr Samuel with a small but clear lead over the rest of the field.'

'What?' exclaimed Urquhart in horror. 'How do you know this? The poll hasn't even been finished yet . . .'

'Frankie, I know what the poll is going to say because I am the publisher of the bloody newspaper.'

'You mean you've fixed it? But why are you pushing Samuel?'

'Because although the poll will show a very reasonable level of support for you, at the moment you can't win the contest. You're the Chief Whip, you don't have any great public platform from which to preach, and if it becomes a free-for-all you're going to get trampled in the rush.'

213

Urquhart had to acknowledge the weakness of his position as the faceless man of Government.

'So we push Mr Samuel, get him off to a roaring start, which means instead of a free-for-all we have a target at which everyone is going to shoot. In a couple of weeks' time, he's going to be amazed at the number of bad friends he's got within the Party, all trying to do him down. He'll be on the defensive. Fighting the tide.'

Urquhart was astonished at the clarity of the Landless analysis, and began to understand why the East-Ender had become such a striking success in the business world.

'So where do I come into this great plan?'

'You've got to develop a unique selling proposition for yourself, something which will be attractive to your fellow MPs and set you apart from your rivals.'

'Such as?' asked the bewildered Urquhart.

'Frankie, you become the archetypal compromise candidate. While all those other bastards are shooting and stabbing each other in public, you slip quietly through as the man they all hate least.'

'That's what the Social Democrats used to pin their hopes on. Remember them? And frankly I'm not sure I have much of a reputation as being the obvious compromise candidate.'

'But the Social Democrats didn't have my help or my bunch of newspapers behind them. You will. High risks, I know, Frankie. But then they are high rewards.'

'What do I have to do?'

'To catch the tide, your timing has to be right. Frankly, I would be happier if there were a little time – perhaps a month – between now and when the voting starts to give the other contenders time to tire, for their campaigns to ship a little water and to get everyone bored with the choice of candidates on offer. Then you discover a large press campaign promoting your late and unexpected entry into the race, which brings back an element of excitement and relief. The tide starts running with *you*, Francis.'

Urquhart noted that Landless had called him by his proper name for the first time. The man was absolutely serious about his proposal.

'So you want me to see if I can slow the election procedure down a little.'

'Can you do it?'

'Although Humphrey Newlands runs the election, according to the Party's constitution the timing of the ballot is entirely in the hands of the Prime Minister, and he would do nothing to help Teddy Williams' favoured candidate. So I think there's a damned good chance . . .'

TUESDAY 26TH OCTOBER

'Prime Minister, I haven't had a chance to speak with you since your announcement yesterday. I can't tell you how shocked and – devastated I was.'

'Francis, that's very kind of you. But no sympathy, please. I feel absolutely content with the situation. In any event, I have little time today for second thoughts. Humphrey Newlands is coming in twenty minutes so we can get the leadership election process under way, then I'm off to spend the rest of the day with my brother Charles. It's marvellous to have time for such things!' he exclaimed.

Urquhart was astonished to see he meant every word of it.

'Prime Minister, you don't appear to be in a mood for maudlin sentiments, so I shan't spend any time adding to them. But you must know how deeply saddened I am. As I listened to you yesterday I felt as if I . . . were falling out of the sky, quite literally. But enough. Let's look forward, not back. It seems to me that some of our colleagues have served you rather badly in recent months, not showing the support you deserved. Now while you have already said you will not support any particular candidate in the election, I suspect you have some clear views as to whom you do *not* wish to get his hands on the leadership. As things stand at the moment I have no intention of becoming a candidate myself, so I thought you might like me to keep you informed of what's going on and give you some feedback from the Parliamentary Party on the state of play. I know you are not going to interfere, but perhaps that won't stop you taking a close interest . . .'

They both knew that even a failed Party Leader in his last

days still has enough influence to sway a crucial body of opinion within the Parliamentary Party. It is not only the favours he has accumulated from placemen over time, but also the not inconsiderable matter of his nominations for the Resignation Honours List, which every retiring Prime Minister is allowed to make. For many senior members of the Party, this would be their last chance to rise above the mob of ordinary parliamentarians and achieve the social status to which their wives had so long aspired.

'Francis, that's most understanding.' Collingridge was clearly in a relaxed and very trusting mood. 'You know, the Prime Minister is expected to be aware of everything that's going on but, as I have discovered to my cost, it's so easy to get isolated, to have events just slip past you without making any contact with them. I suspect dear old Sir Humphrey is past giving the best intelligence on the state of parliamentary opinion, so I would very much welcome your advice. As you so delicately put it, I shall certainly take a close interest in the matter of who is to succeed me. So tell me, how do things look?'

'Early days yet, very difficult to tell. I think most of the press are right to suggest it's an open race. But I would expect things to develop quickly once they get going.'

'No front runners yet, then?'

'Well, one perhaps who seems to have something of a head start. Michael Samuel.'

'Michael! Why so?'

'Simply that it's going to be a short and furious race, with little room for developing solid arguments or issues. In those circumstances, the ones who use television well are going to have a strong advantage. And, of course, he's going to have the strong if subtle support of Teddy and party headquarters.'

Collingridge's face clouded. 'Yes. I see what you mean.' He drummed his fingers loudly on the arm of his chair, weighing his words carefully.

'Francis, I shall be absolutely scrupulous in not favouring

218

any candidate in this race. My only concern is to let the Party have a fair and free leadership election so they can make their own choice. But you make it sound as if the election won't be as open as it perhaps should be, with party headquarters playing too influential a role.'

He chose his words carefully, and uttered them slowly and softly. 'I would not welcome that. I don't think Teddy's bunch of merry men has distinguished itself recently. A poor election campaign, then all those infuriating bloody leaks. Now I'm told that the news of my visit to the Palace yesterday also leaked out of the backdoor at Smith Square.'

His tone hardened. 'I can't forgive that, Francis. The Cabinet swore on their oaths of office to keep it confidential, to let me offer my resignation with some dignity instead of being the clown in a damned media circus. I will not stand for it. I will not have party headquarters interfering in this election!'

He leaned towards Urquhart. 'I suspect you have no great love for Teddy Williams, particularly after he did such an effective demolition job on your reshuffle proposals – I'm sure you guessed that at the time.'

Urquhart was glad to have his suspicions confirmed. On Judgement Day it might help to justify a lot of his recent actions.

'So what can I do, Francis, to make sure this election is run properly?'

Urquhart smiled to himself. A 'proper' election was now defined as one in which Michael Samuel felt the full force of the Prime Minister's revenge.

'My interests, like yours, are simply to ensure fair play. I know that neither you nor I wish to interfere in any way – let party democracy have its way, of course. My only concern is that the process is likely to go ahead in such a rush that there will be no proper time for mature reflection or consideration. In the past, leadership elections have taken place only a week to ten days after they were announced – Ted Heath was elected just five days after

Alec Douglas-Home resigned – but on those occasions the resignations were expected. People had time to think, to make a proper and balanced judgement. That won't be the case this time. I'm afraid it will all be over in a breathless rush, and become just another part of the media circus.'

'So?'

'So give them just a little longer to make their choice. Slow the pace down. Enjoy your last few weeks in office, and hand over to a successor who has been chosen by the Party, not the media.'

'What you say makes sense. I've no wish to extend the period of uncertainty while the campaign is fought, but I'm sure an extra week or so could do no great harm.'

He extended his hand towards Urquhart. 'Francis, I'm sorry to cut this short; Humphrey will be waiting outside. I shall have to consult him as Chairman of the Backbench Committee, but the final choice on timing is entirely in my hands. I'm going to think very carefully overnight about what you have said, and let you know in the morning what I decide.'

He led the Chief Whip towards the door. 'I'm so grateful, Francis. It's really comforting to have a source of advice with no axe to grind.'

Daily Telegraph. Wednesday 27th October. Page 1.

Samuel is favoured candidate – takes early lead in party soundings

Michael Samuel, the youthful Environment Secretary, was last night emerging as the early front runner to succeed Henry Collingridge as Party Leader and Prime Minister.

In a poll conducted during the last two days by the *Telegraph* amongst 212 of the 337 Government MPs eligible to vote, 24 per cent nominated him as their first choice in the forthcoming party leadership election, well ahead of other potential candidates.

While Samuel has yet to announce his candidature, he is expected to do so soon. Moreover, he is expected to get the backing of influential party figures such as Lord Williams, the Party Chairman, whose influence as the Party's elder statesman could be crucial.

No other name attracted more than 18 per cent. Five potential candidates obtained between 12 per cent and 18 per cent, including Patrick Woolton the Foreign Secretary, Arnold Dollis the Home Secretary, Harold Earle the Education Secretary, Peter McKenzie the Health Secretary, and Francis Urquhart the Chief Whip.

The inclusion of Urquhart's name in the list at 14 per cent caused something of a surprise last night at Westminster, as he is not even a full member of the Cabinet. As Chief Whip he has a strong base in the Parliamentary Party and could be a strong outside candidate. However, sources close to Urquhart last night emphasised he had made no decision to enter the contest, and he would clarify his position sometime today.'

'Mattie, I think I've got it!'

Krajewski was striding across the room as if he had discovered a blazing fire in his pocket. He was breathless with excitement. As he reached Mattie's desk in the *Telegraph* news room, he pulled a 10×12 colour photograph out of the large manila envelope he was clutching, and threw it on her desk. The face of the driver stared at her, slightly blurred and distorted from the lines of the video screen, but nonetheless clearly recognisable.

'Freddie came up trumps. He took this along to his meeting of AA last night, and the group leader recognised it immediately. It's a Dr Robert Christian, who's a well known authority on the treatment of drug and alcohol addiction. Runs a treatment centre in a large private house near the south coast in Kent. That's where our Charlie is bound to be.' He was flushed with triumph.

'Johnnie, I could kiss you – but not in the office!'

His face contorted into a picture of mock misery.

'And there I was hoping you would want to sleep your way to the top . . .' he said mournfully.

The Prime Minister read all the newspapers that morning. He smiled ruefully as he read the commentaries which a week before had been excoriating him and for the most part were now, in their fickle and inconstant fashion, lauding him for his statesmanlike and responsible action in allowing the Government to make a fresh start – 'although he must still resolve many outstanding personal and family issues to the public's satisfaction', thundered *The Times*. As always, the press had no shame in playing both sides.

He read the *Telegraph* particularly carefully, and twice. Their prompt polling of Government MPs had given them a lead over the other journals, many of which were forced to refer to the poll findings in their later editions. The consensus seemed to be emerging: it was an open race but Samuel was clearly the front runner.

He summoned his political secretary.

'Grahame. I want you to send an instruction to Lord Williams, with a copy to Sir Humphrey Newlands. Party headquarters are to issue a press release at 12.30 this afternoon for the lunchtime news that nominations for election as Leader of the Party will close in three weeks' time, on Thursday November 18, with the first ballot to take place on the following Tuesday November 23. If a second ballot is required it will be held as prescribed by the Party's rules on the following Tuesday, November 30, with any final run-off ballot two days later. Have you got that?'

He noticed his secretary's obvious anguish. It was the first time since his resignation announcement that they had been able to talk.

'That means in exactly six weeks and one day, Grahame,

222

you and I will be out of a job. Don't worry. You've been an excellent aide to me. I haven't always found time as I should to thank you properly in the past, but I want you to know I'm very grateful.'

The aide shuffled with embarrassment.

'You must start thinking about your own future. I'm certain that there are several newly knighted gentlemen in the City or any other part of industry who would be happy to make you a generous offer. Think about it for a few days and let me know what interests you. I still have a few favours to cash in.'

The secretary mumbled his thanks, looking much relieved, and made to depart.

'By the way, Grahame. It's possible that the Party Chairman might seek to get hold of me and encourage me to shorten the period of the election process. I shall not be available, and you are to ensure he realises that these are instructions, not terms for negotiation, and they are to be issued without fail by 12.30.'

There was a short pause.

'Otherwise, tell him, I shall be forced to leak them myself.'

It is often written that time and tide wait for no man. They certainly did not wait that day for Michael Samuel. He had been as openly astounded and as privately elated by Collingridge's bombshell as the rest of his colleagues. His natural enthusiasm had quickly turned to the positive aspect of events, and the opportunities which they afforded him. He recognised that no one started the race as favourite, and that he had as good a chance as any, if he played his cards right.

He had consulted the redoubtable Lord Williams, who agreed on his assessment of his chances. 'Patience, Michael,' he had advised. 'You will almost certainly be the youngest candidate, and they will try to say you are too youthful, too inexperienced and too ambitious. So don't look too much as if you want the job. Show a little restraint, and let them come to you.'

Which was to prove excellent advice, but entirely irrelevant to the circumstances. The media had been having a busy day. No sooner had the *Telegraph* hit the streets promoting Samuel's name than Urquhart appeared in front of television cameras to confirm that he had no intention of standing, because he felt it was in the Party's best interests that the Chief Whip should be entirely impartial in this contest. These two events had the instant effect of getting the media hunt firmly under way for those candidates who would be standing, and promoting a wide degree of praise for Urquhart's unselfishness and loyalty. The release later that morning of the detailed timetable for nomination and election only added fuel to the flames. None of which helped the front runner.

By the time the television cameras had tracked him down to the Intercontinental Hotel off Hyde Park, which he was just about to enter for an early lunch meeting, they were in no mood to accept conditional answers. He couldn't say no, they wouldn't accept maybe, and after some considerable harassment he was forced into making a reluctant announcement that he would indeed be running.

The one o'clock news offered a clear contrast between Urquhart, in a dignified and elder party statesman role declining to run, and the youthful and apparently eager Samuel, holding an impromptu press conference on the street and launching himself as the first official candidate, nearly a month before the first ballot was to be held.

As Urquhart watched the proceedings with considerable satisfaction, the telephone rang. A gruff voice which he recognised instantly as Landless said simply, 'Moses parted the Red Sea. We shall see whether Michael can catch the tide.'

They both laughed before the voice rang off.

SATURDAY 30TH OCTOBER

The following Saturday, Mattie had a clear day. She climbed into her BMW, filled it with petrol, and pointed it in the direction of Dover. Having barged her way through the shopping crowds of Greenwich, she emerged with great relief onto the A2, the old Roman road which for nearly two thousand years had pointed the way from London into the heart of Kent. It took her past the cathedral town of Canterbury, and a few miles beyond she turned off at the picturesque little village of Barham. Her road map was not very helpful in finding the even smaller village of Norbington nearby, but with the help of several locals she found herself some while later outside a large Victorian house, bearing a subdued sign in the shrubbery which announced, 'FELLOWSHIP TREATMENT CENTRE'.

There were several cars in the driveway and the front door was open. She was surprised to see people wandering around with apparent freedom, and no sign of the formidable white-coated nurses she had expected to find patrolling the grounds for potential escapees. She parked her car on the road and walked cautiously up the drive towards the door.

A large, tweed-suited gentleman with a white military moustache approached and her heart sank. This was surely the security patrol, and she had clearly been spotted as an intruder.

'Excuse me, my dear,' he said in a clipped accent as he intercepted her by the front door. 'Have you seen any member of staff about? They like to keep out of the way on family visiting days, but you can never find one when you want them.'

Mattie offered her apologies and smiled warmly in relief. She realised that by good fortune she had struck the best possible day to look around, and could lose herself amidst the other visitors.

She picked up one of the brochures which were piled on the hall table, and found a quiet chair on which to sit while she inspected it. A brief glance at the literature told her that the treatment centre was run on very different lines than she had imagined. No straitjackets, no locks on the doors, just twenty-three well-trained people waiting to give guidance, encouragement and their medical experience to addicts who sought help in an atmosphere resembling more a fashionable country retreat than an institution. Even more encouragingly for Mattie, the brochure had a plan of the thirty-two-bed house, which Mattie used to guide herself around the premises in search of her quarry.

She found him outside on a garden bench, enjoying the view across the valley and the last of the October sun. She wasn't going to enjoy the deception, but that is what she had come for.

'Why, Charles!' she exclaimed. 'What a surprise to find you here.'

He looked at her with a total lack of comprehension.

'I . . . I'm sorry,' he ventured. 'I don't recognise . . .'

'Mattie Storin. Don't you remember? We spent a most enjoyable evening together in Bournemouth a couple of weeks ago.'

'Oh, I'm sorry, Miss Storin. I don't remember. You see, I'm an alcoholic, that's why I'm here, and I'm afraid I was in no condition a few weeks ago to remember very much at all.'

She was taken aback by his frankness, and he smiled serenely.

'Please don't be embarrassed. The biggest single step I've had to make in curing myself of addiction is to admit that I am an addict. I had a million ways of hiding it, particularly from myself, and it was only when I was able to face myself that I began being able to face the outside world again. That's what this treatment centre is all about.'

Mattie suddenly blushed deeply. She realised that she had intruded into the private world of a sick man, and she felt ashamed.

'Charles, if you don't remember who I am, then you will not remember that I am a journalist.'

The smile disappeared, to be replaced by a look of resignation.

'I suppose it had to happen at some time, although Henry was hoping that I could be left alone here quietly . . .'

'Charles, please let me explain. I've not come here to make life difficult for you, and when I leave here your privacy will continue to be respected so far as I am concerned. I think the press owe you that.'

'I think they probably do . . .'

'But I would like your help. Don't say anything for the moment, just let me talk a little.'

He nodded in encouragement.

'Your brother, the Prime Minister, has been forced to resign because of allegations that he helped you to speculate in shares and make a quick profit.'

He started to wave his hand to bring her to a halt but she pressed on.

'Charles, none of those allegations make any sense to me. You and your brother risking the office of Prime Minister for a measly few thousand pounds – it doesn't add up. What's more, I also know that someone has deliberately been trying to undermine your brother for some time by leaking damaging material to the press. But I only have suspicions. I came to see if you could point me towards something more tangible.'

'Miss Storin – Mattie, as we seem to be old friends – I am a drunk. I cannot even remember meeting you. How can I, of all people, be of help? My word carries no weight whatsoever.'

'I'm neither a judge nor a prosecutor, Charles. I'm just

227

trying to piece together a puzzle from a thousand scattered shards.'

He looked far over the hills towards Dover and the Channel beyond, searching in the distance.

'Mattie, I've tried so hard to remember, believe me. The thought that I have disgraced Henry and forced him into resignation is almost more than I can stand. But I know nothing about buying and selling shares, nothing at all. I don't know what the truth is. I can't help you, I'm afraid.'

'Wouldn't you have remembered something about buying the shares, if you had indeed bought them?'

'For the last month I have been a very sick . . .' – he laughed gently – '. . . a very drunk man. There are many things I have absolutely no recollection of.'

'Wouldn't you have remembered where you got the money to buy the shares, or what you did with the proceeds?'

'I admit that it's hugely unlikely I would have had a small fortune lying around without my remembering it or, more likely, spending it on alcohol. I have no idea where the money could have gone. Even I can't drink away £50,000 in just a few weeks.'

'What about the false address in Paddington?'

'A complete mystery. I don't even know where Praed Street in Paddington is when I'm sober, so it is preposterous to suppose I would have found my way there drunk. It's the other side of London from where I live.'

'But you used it – so they say – for your bank and subscription to the Party's literature service.'

Charles Collingridge roared with laughter. 'Mattie, you're beginning to restore my faith in myself. No matter how drunk I was, I cannot conceive I could possibly have shown any interest in the Party's literature service. I object when political propaganda is pushed through my letter box at election time; having to pay for it every month would be an insult!'

'Have you ever contributed to the Party's literature service?'

'Never!'

The sun was setting and a warm, red glow filled the sky, lighting up his face. He seemed visibly to be returning to health, and to be content.

'I can't prove it, but I don't believe I am guilty of the things they say I have done. It would mean a lot to me if you believed that, too.'

'I do, Charles, very much. And I'm going to try to prove it for you.'

She rose to leave.

'I've enjoyed your visit, Mattie. Now that we are such old friends, please come again.'

'I shall. But in the meantime, I've got a lot of digging to do.'

It was late by the time she got back to London that evening. The first editions of the Sunday newspapers were already on the streets. She bought a heavy pile of them and, with magazines and inserts slipping from her laden arms, she threw them on the back seat of her car. It was then she noticed the *Sunday Times* headline.

'Now why is Harold Earle making such a fuss about environmental matters?' she asked herself. The Education Secretary, not a noted Greenpeace lover, had just announced his intention to stand for the leadership and simultaneously had made a speech entitled 'Clean Up Our Country.'

'We have talked and talked endlessly about the problems of our inner cities, while those who live in them have been forced to watch their neighbourhoods continue to decline. In the meantime, the impoverished state of our inner cities has been matched by the deplorable degeneration of far too much of our rural countryside,' the *Sunday Times* reported him as saying. 'For too long we have neglected such issues, to our cost. Recycled expressions of concern are no substitute for positive action, and it is time we backed our fine

229

words with finer deeds. The opinion polls show that the environment is the most important non-economic issue on which the voters say we have failed. After more than twelve years in office, this is unacceptable, and we must wake up to these concerns.'

'Silly me,' said Mattie. 'I'm getting slow in my old age. Can't decipher the code. Which Cabinet Minister is supposed to be responsible for environmental matters, and therefore responsible for this mess?'

The public fight to eliminate Michael Samuel had begun.

WEDNESDAY 3RD NOVEMBER

Mattie tried many times during the following week to get hold of Kevin Spence, but he was never available. In spite of the repeated assurances of his gushingly polite secretary, Mattie knew that he was deliberately avoiding her. He was therefore not at all pleased when, in some desperation, she called very late on Wednesday evening and was put straight through to his extension by the night security guard.

'No, of course I haven't been avoiding you,' he assured her, 'but I have been very busy. Working very late.'

'Kevin, I need your help again.'

'I remember the last time I gave you my help. You said you were going to write a piece on opinion polls and then you wrote a story slandering the Prime Minister. Now he's gone.' He spoke with a quiet sadness. 'He was always very decent to me, very kind, and I think the press have been unspeakably cruel.'

'Kevin, I give you my word that I was not responsible for that story. You may have noticed that my name was not on the article, and I was even more displeased about it than you. It's about Mr Collingridge's resignation that I'm calling. Personally, I don't believe the allegations which are being made against him and his brother. I would like to be able to clear his name.'

'I can't see how I could assist you,' he said in a distrusting tone. 'Anyway, I'm afraid that nobody outside the press office is allowed to have contact with the media during the leadership campaign. Chairman's strictest orders.'

'Kevin, there's a lot at stake here. Not only the leadership of the Party, and whether you are going to win the next

231

election or not, but also whether history is going to regard Henry Collingridge as a crook and a cheat or whether he is going to have a chance to put the record straight. Don't we owe him that?'

He thought about it for a second, and she heard his hostility slowly melting.

'If I could help, what would you want?'

'Very simply, do you understand the computer system at party headquarters?'

'Yes, of course. I use it all the time to help analyse opinion research. I've got a screen in front of me which is linked directly to our main frame.'

'I think your computer system has been tampered with. Will you let me see it?'

'Tampered with? That's impossible. We have the highest security. Nobody from outside can access it.'

'Not outside, Kevin. Inside.'

There was a stunned silence from the other end of the phone.

'I'm working at the House of Commons. I can be with you in less than ten minutes, and I suspect at this time of night the building is very quiet. No one will notice. Kevin, I'm on my way over.'

Before he could mutter a flustered few words of protest, the phone went dead as he held it. Mattie was with him less than seven minutes later.

They sat in his small garret office, dominated by the mountains of files which tumbled over every available flat surface and onto the floor, with their attention fixed rigidly on the glowing green screen in front of them.

'Kevin, Charles Collingridge ordered material from the Party's sales and literature service and asked them to be delivered to an address in Paddington. Right?'

'Correct. I checked it as soon as I heard, but it's there all right. Look.'

He tapped a few characters on the keyboard, and up came the incriminating evidence on the screen. 'Chas Collingridge Esq 216 Praed St Paddington London W2 — 001A/ 01.0091.'

'What do these other hieroglyphics mean?'

'The first set simply means that he subscribes to our comprehensive literature service and the second that his subscription has been fully paid from the beginning of the year. If he wanted to receive only the main publications, or was a member of our specialist book club or one of our other marketing programmes, that would be shown by a different set of reference numbers. Also if he were behind with his subscription payments.'

'And this information is shown on all the monitors throughout the building?'

'Yes. It's not information we regard as particularly confidential.'

'And if you felt like bending the rules a little and wanted to make me a subscriber to your comprehensive literature service, could you do that, enter my details from this terminal?'

'Without making the proper payments through the accounts department, you mean? Why . . . yes.'

Spence was beginning to follow her line of enquiry.

'You think that Charles Collingridge's details were falsely entered from a terminal within this building, Miss Storin? Yes, it could be done. Look.'

Within a few seconds the screen was showing a comprehensive literature subscription in the name of 'M Mouse Esq, 99 Disneyland Miami.'

'But you couldn't get away with backdating it to the beginning of the year because . . . What a stupid fool I am! Of course!' he exploded, and started thrashing away at the keyboard. 'If you really know what you're doing, which very few people in this building do, you can tap into the main frame subdirectory . . .'

His words were almost drowned in the clattering of the keys.

'That gives access to the more restricted financial data.

So I can check the exact date when the account was paid, whether it was paid by cheque or credit card, when the subscription was first started . . .'

The monitor screen started glowing.

'And those financial details can only be entered or altered by accounts department staff with their security passwords.'

He sat back to consider the details on the screen. He tapped a few more characters into the computer, and then turned to Mattie.

'Miss Storin. According to this, Mr Collingridge has never paid for the literature service, this month or any month. His details only appear on the distribution file, not the payment file.'

'Can you tell me when his name first appeared on the distribution file?'

A few more keystrokes.

'Jesus. Exactly two weeks ago today.'

'So someone in this building, not the accounts staff or anyone who understood computers very well, two weeks ago altered the file to include Charles Collingridge's name for the first time.'

'This is terrible, Miss Storin . . .' Spence's face had gone white.

'Kevin, can you by any chance tell me who might have altered the file, or from which terminal it was altered?'

'Sadly, no. It could have been done from any terminal in this building. The computer programme trusts us . . .' He shook his head as if he had totally failed the most crucial test of his life.

'Don't worry, Kevin. We're on the trail. But I must ask you not to utter a word of this to anyone. I want to catch whoever did this, and if he knows we're looking he will cover his trail. Will you help me once more, and keep quiet until I have something more to go on?'

'Who on earth would believe me, anyway?' he murmured.

SUNDAY 7TH NOVEMBER

The newspapers that weekend were irritable. In the convention of leadership elections, candidates were discouraged from outright electioneering or making personal attacks on their rivals; the right leader was supposed somehow still to 'emerge' without any apparent effort on his part from a process of consensus rather than combat. So all the press had been left with for ten days was a series of coded messages which failed to inspire the public or ignite the hoped-for forest of press headlines. The campaign had not so much run out of steam; it had simply never generated any effective heat.

So the press took it out on the candidates – they had no alternative. 'A disappointing and uninspiring campaign so far, still waiting for one of the candidates to breathe life back into the Party and Government', pronounced the *Observer*. 'Irrelevant and irritating', complained the *Sunday Mirror*. Not to be outdone, the *Sun* in characteristic style described it all as 'flatulent, a passing breeze in the night'.

Far from allowing a thorough airing of the issues, as Urquhart had predicted to the Prime Minister, the lengthy campaign was suffering from a severe dose of boredom, as all along he had secretly hoped.

This came as little comfort to Mattie, who was finding her growing conviction that skulduggery was afoot matched only by her inability to find the opportunity to proceed with her investigations. Journalists have to work much harder when there is no news to report, and the flaccid leadership campaign was causing more than a few nightmares amongst the political lobby in their collective efforts to find new angles with which to fill their column inches.

'You have to face it, Mattie, you still don't have a case,' Johnnie told her. 'Fascinating circumstantial evidence about computers, perhaps, but what about the shares, what about the bank account, what about Paddington?'

She unwrapped herself from his arms where she had been dozing for most of Sunday afternoon. The weather was appalling, the scudding grey skies hurling angry bursts of rain against the windows. They hadn't needed much encouragement to decide to spend the whole afternoon in bed.

'Those shares were bought by whoever had the bank account and arranged the false address in Paddington,' Mattie began, marshalling her arguments. 'That's the only conclusion you can reasonably reach. But the trail is very difficult to follow. Apart from telling us that the account was opened for less than a fortnight, the bank will tell us nothing, and have point-blank refused to let us see the signatures on the documents relating to the bank account. And the Paddington tobacconist's is even less helpful. I think all the attention and notoriety has put paid to some of the more profitable sidelines which he seems to have run out of his back room.'

Johnnie was not finished. 'But what is it you are trying to prove? The documentation is scarcely going to tell you any more than you know already. What you need to establish is not so much whether it was Charles Collingridge, but whether it could have been anyone other than him. If it could, along with your computer tampering you might have the beginnings of a circumstantial story.'

She rolled out of his arms to look him directly in the face.

'You still don't believe it was a frame-up, do you?'

'You haven't even yet proved that a crime was committed, let alone having any idea as to who might have done it,' he argued, but his voice softened as he recognised the growing impatience in her eyes. 'You have to be realistic, Mattie. If you are going to launch yourself publicly into this great conspiracy theory, you will have a very sceptical audience who will want more than a few 'maybes'. If you turn out to be wrong, you will do yourself and your career a lot of harm. And should you turn out to be right, you're going to have some very powerful enemies out there, who could do you even more harm. If they can nobble the Prime Minister, what could they do to you?'

He stroked her hair tenderly.

'It's not a matter of whether I believe your theory, Mattie. It's a matter of caring about you, of not wanting you to get caught in something which could be bigger than both of us and could cause you a great deal of pain. Frankly I'm scared you might be taking this one a bit too far. Is it really worth it?'

Instantly he knew he had said something wrong. He didn't know why, but he sensed her body go rigid, unresponsive, enveloped by a cold shell that had suddenly divided the bed in two.

'Hell, Johnnie, I would be even more scared if it turned out to be true and nobody did anything about it,' she snapped. 'And damn it, it was you who encouraged me to go after the story.'

'But that was before . . . well, before you got into my bed and into my life. This isn't just another story for me, Mattie, this is personal. I really care about you.'

'So that's it. Drop the bloody story and concentrate on getting laid. Thanks, but no thanks! I asked you to go to bed with me, Johnnie, not own me.'

She rolled away from him so that he could no longer see her face. She could sense his bewilderment and pain, but how could she tell him. The feeling of panic which had come over her as he confronted her with a choice between her career and his caring. God, it was going to happen all over again.

'Look, Johnnie . . .' She was having tremendous difficulty finding the right words. 'I am fond of you – very fond, you know that. But my career is most important to me. This story is most important to me. I can't let anything else get in its way.' She paused for a painful moment. 'Perhaps we made a mistake.'

'What are you saying? Goodbye? Just like that? You drag me into bed as if I'm the last caveman left on earth for a couple of hot nights and then – bugger off? What is it? Just adding to your collection of notches on the bedpost?'

The sarcasm bit deep and rattled her. 'I needed you, Johnnie. I needed a man, not a lifelong commitment. I needed to feel like a woman again, it had been so long . . .'

'Great. A million pricks out there and you had to pick this one. I didn't realise it was just that, Mattie. I really wish you hadn't bothered,' he said with evident bitterness and anger.

'Johnnie, stop! This isn't right. Don't make me say something I don't mean. I like you, very much. That's the problem.'

'That's a problem? Well, I'm glad you have managed to put it behind you.' He gave a dry, humourless laugh and stared straight at the ceiling.

Mattie buried her head in the pillow. She hadn't intended to hurt him, but how could she make him understand. She hadn't told anyone in London before, but maybe now was the time.

'There was someone else,' she began, her voice faltering. 'In Yorkshire. Someone I was very close to. We had known each other since we were children and everyone assumed that our relationship was . . . sort of permanent. That was the trouble. No one asked me, they just assumed. But I wanted something more, and when he forced me to choose between him and my career, I chose my career. It was the only way for me to live with myself, Johnnie!' she exclaimed, as if fearing that he would neither understand nor accept. His cold expression told her she was right.

'But . . . he went to pieces. There were begging letters, midnight telephone calls. I would see him just standing at

238

the end of my street, waiting for hours, sometimes all through the night.'

She drew a deep breath as if the memory were exhausting her. 'Then, there was a car crash. A long, straight piece of road with no other traffic, and his car hit a tree. They had to cut him out. When I heard, it was as if it were all my fault, as if I had been the one who had crashed the car. I felt so guilty, do you see, yet I felt so angry with myself for feeling that way. I hadn't done anything wrong!'

She desperately wanted to justify herself and convince him that she deserved no blame but tears of anguish and self-recrimination were filling her eyes and starting to roll, one by one, down her cheeks.

'It took every piece of willpower that I had to go to the hospital, and the hours I spent in the waiting room were the loneliest I have ever known. Then the nurse came to tell me that he wouldn't see me. Never wanted to see me again. Left me standing in the middle of that hospital feeling completely and utterly worthless.'

She was struggling hard to keep hold of her emotions now, as the recollections stirred deep within her. 'It was all or nothing for him, Johnnie. I really did care for him, yet all I did was cause him pain and turn his love to hatred. It . . . it nearly killed him. That's why I left Yorkshire, Johnnie, to bury that feeling of worthlessness and guilt through my work. And for what it's worth, I'm beginning to like you too much to risk all that again.'

As she spoke, his eyes once more met hers. The sarcasm and anger had left him as he listened, but there was still a hard, determined edge to his voice when he spoke.

'Believe me, I know what it's like to lose the one you love and have your world pulled apart around you. I know how much pain and loneliness it's possible to feel when it happens. But you weren't driving that car and you can't change the facts simply by running away from them. And that's precisely what you are doing – running away!'

She shook her head in denial but he cut her short. 'When

you came to London, you may have been chasing your future – but you were also hiding from everything which hurt you in the past. Yet it's not going to work, Mattie, don't you see? You can't hide away in journalism – investigating, exposing, pulling people's worlds apart in search of the truth – unless you are willing to face those people afterwards and live with their pain.'

'That's unfair . . .' she protested.

'Is it? I hope so for your sake, because if you can't accept the fact that your work may cause a lot of innocent people great hurt, then you'll never be a good journalist. Look for the truth, Mattie, by all means, but only if you're willing to recognise and share the pain it may cause. If you think it's enough just to float like a butterfly from one story to another, never hanging around long enough to see the damage that your version of the truth might inflict on other people, how the devil can you put any real value on your work? It's your job to criticise self-important politicians, but how dare you criticise the commitment of others if you are afraid to commit yourself? You say you are afraid of commitment. But commitment is what it is all about, Mattie. You can't run away from it for ever!'

But she was already running, sobbing into the bathroom and into her clothes. In a minute she had fled out of the front door, and all he could hear was the echo of her tears.

MONDAY 8TH NOVEMBER –
FRIDAY 12TH NOVEMBER

The criticisms of the weekend press kicked the campaign to life early on Monday morning. Encouraged by the media view that the right contender still had not emerged, two further Cabinet Ministers announced their candidatures – Peter McKenzie, the Secretary of State for Health, and Patrick Woolton, the bluff Foreign Secretary.

Both were reckoned to have a reasonable chance of success. McKenzie had been prominent in selling the popular hospital scheme, and had managed to ensure that blame for its postponement had been heaped entirely on the Treasury and the Prime Minister's Office.

Woolton had been running hard behind the scenes ever since his conversation with Urquhart at the party conference, having lunched almost every editor in Fleet Street in the previous month. By emphasising his Northern origins he was hoping to establish himself as the 'One Nation' candidate in contrast to the strong Home Counties bias of most of the other major contenders – not that this had impressed the Scots, who tended to view the whole affair as if it were an entirely foreign escapade. Woolton had been hoping to delay his formal entry into the race, wishing to see how the various rival campaigns developed, but the weekend press had been like a call to arms and he decided he should delay no longer. He called a press conference at Manchester Airport to make the announcement on what he termed his 'home ground', hoping that no one would notice he had flown up from London in order to be there.

The weekend press also incited into action those candidates who had already declared themselves. It was becoming clear to the likes of Michael Samuel and Harold Earle that their gentlemanly campaigns with their obscure, coded messages were rapidly running into the sand. With the advent of new candidates, their appeals needed to be freshened up and their cutting edges toughened.

Under the pressures of an extended campaign, the candidates were becoming increasingly nervous – so the press at last got what they wanted. When Harold Earle repeated his environmentalist criticisms, but this time choosing to attack the record of Michael Samuel by name, the gloves came off.

Samuel retorted that Earle's conduct was reprehensible and incompatible with his status as a Cabinet colleague, as well as being a rotten example for an Education Secretary to set for young people. In the meantime, Woolton's loose language at Manchester concerning the need to 'restore English values with an English candidate' was vigorously attacked by McKenzie, who was desperately trying to rediscover his lost Gaelic roots and claiming it was an insult to five million Scots. Trying to find a unique line as always, the *Sun* interpreted Woolton's words as a vicious anti-Semitic attack on Samuel, which had Jewish activists swamping the air waves and letter columns with complaints. A rabbi in Samuel's home constituency called on the Race Relations Board to investigate what he called 'the most atrocious outburst by a senior political figure since Mosley'. Woolton was not entirely unhappy with this overreaction; 'for the next two weeks everyone will be looking at the shape of Samuel's ears rather than listening to what he's saying,' he told one close supporter.

By Wednesday afternoon, Urquhart felt the situation had developed sufficiently well for him to issue a public call for 'a return to the standards of personal conduct for which our Party is renowned and without which collective Government becomes impossible'. It was echoed loudly in the editorial columns, even as the front pages were splashing the latest outburst of internecine bickering.

When, therefore, on Friday afternoon Mattie walked in to Preston's office asking him if he wanted a fresh angle on the contest, his response was generally unenthusiastic.

'Christ, I shall be glad when we can get back to real news,' he blustered. 'I'm not sure we can afford to devote any more space than we're already doing to the back-stabbing.'

'This bit of back-stabbing,' she said defiantly, 'is different.'

He was still looking at a mock-up of the following day's front page rather than showing any interest in Mattie, but she was not deterred.

'The leadership election was caused by Collingridge's resignation, which in turn was caused in the end by allegations that he or his brother had been fiddling share deals through a Paddington tobacconist and a Turkish secondary bank. I think we can prove that he was almost certainly set up.'

Preston at last looked up. 'What the hell are you talking about?'

'He was framed, and I think we can prove it.'

Preston could find no words to express his astonishment; his jaw dropped so low that with his large glasses Mattie felt she was talking to a goldfish.

'Here's what we have, Grev.' Patiently she explained how she had checked the computer file at party headquarters and discovered the distribution file had been tampered with.

'It was deliberately altered to ensure that the false address in Paddington could be tied in directly to Charles Collingridge. But anyone could have opened that accommodation address. I don't think Charles Collingridge ever went anywhere near Paddington. Somebody else did it in his name – somebody who was trying to frame him!'

Preston was listening intently now.

'I went to Paddington myself this morning. I opened up an accommodation address at the same tobacconist shop in an entirely fictional name. I then got a taxi to Seven Sisters

Road and the Union Bank of Turkey, where I opened up an account in the same fictional name – not with £50,000 but with just £100. The whole thing took less than three hours from start to finish. So I can now start ordering pornographic magazines, paid for out of the new bank account and delivered to the Paddington address, which could do a lot of damage to the reputation of one completely innocent politician.'

'Er, who?' asked Preston, still having difficulty catching up.

She laughed and threw down a bank book and the tobacconist's receipt onto the editor's desk. He looked at them eagerly.

'The Leader of the Opposition!' he shouted in alarm. 'What the hell have you done?'

'Nothing,' she said with a smile suggesting victory. 'Except to show that Charles Collingridge was almost certainly framed; that he probably never went near the tobacconist shop or the Union Bank of Turkey, and therefore that he could not have bought those shares.'

Preston was holding the documents at arm's length as if they might catch fire.

'Which means that Henry Collingridge did not tell his brother about Renox Chemicals. . .' Her inflexion indicated that there was more.

'And? And?' Preston demanded.

'He didn't have to resign.'

Preston sagged back in his chair. The beads of perspiration had begun to trickle down his brow, plastering his hair to his forehead. He was looking exceedingly uncomfortable. He felt as if he were being torn in two. With one eye he could see the makings of a superb story, which, when promoted vigorously by his advertising agency, could bring with it the substantial boost in circulation he was finding so elusive. Whether the story was accurate or not hardly bothered him; the lawyers could ensure that it libelled no one and it would make a splendid read.

With his other eye, however, he could discern the enormous impact that such a story would make on the leadership race itself, the uncontrollable shock waves which would stretch out and swamp various innocent bystanders—possibly including himself. And Landless had just told him on the telephone that he had other fish to fry. He brushed back the lick of hair which was stuck clammily above his glasses, but it did not seem to help his vision. He could not focus on which decision would be the right one to take, the one which would be acceptable to Landless. He had been instructed that all major pieces affecting the leadership race were to be cleared with Landless before publication, and he had feared being confronted with an unexpected decision like this. He needed to play for time.

'Mattie, I scarcely know what to say. You've obviously been very . . . busy.' His mind was charging through his Thesaurus of flannel, words which were meaningless and noncommittal but which left their audience with an appropriately warm feeling of encouragement. It was a well thumbed volume. But then it hit him, and the book closed shut with a snap.

'You've illustrated very well that it might have been someone else who was charging round London opening accounts in Collingridge's name, but you haven't proved that it wasn't Collingridge himself. Surely that is the easiest explanation to accept?'

'But the computer file, Grev. It was tampered with. And that wouldn't have happened if Charles Collingridge were guilty.'

'Haven't you considered the possibility that the computer file was altered, not to incriminate Collingridge, but by Collingridge or one of his friends to offer him an alibi, to muddy the waters after he had been found out? For all we know it was not the distribution file but the accounts file which was altered, possibly only minutes before you saw it, just to throw you off the trail.'

'But only a handful of people have access to the accounts

file,' Mattie protested with considerable vigour. 'And how could Charles Collingridge have done that? He's been drying out in a treatment centre.'

'But his brother?'

Mattie was incredulous. 'You can't seriously believe that the Prime Minister took the incredible risk of ordering the party headquarters' computer file to be altered just to falsify the evidence – after he had already announced his resignation.'

'Mattie, think back. Watergate. Files were burnt and tapes erased – by the President. During Irangate, incriminating material was shredded and smuggled out of the White House by a secretary in her underwear. Scores of presidential aides and US Cabinet ministers have gone to prison in recent years. And in this country, Jeremy Thorpe was put on trial for attempted murder, John Stonehouse went to gaol after faking his own suicide and Lloyd George sold peerages from Downing Street while he screwed his secretary on the Cabinet table. Things much stranger than fiction have happened in politics.' Preston was warming to his theme now. 'Power is a drug, like a candle to a moth. They are drawn towards it, no matter what the dangers. They would rather risk everything, including their lives and careers, than do without it. So it's still easier to believe that the Collingridges got caught with their hands in the till and are trying to cover up than to accept there was a great conspiracy against the Prime Minister.'

'So you won't run it!' she accused sharply.

'No, I'm not saying that,' Preston continued, smiling in a manner which betrayed not a shred of sympathy. 'I'm saying you haven't yet got enough for the story to stand up. We have to be careful not to make ourselves look ridiculous. You need to do some more work on it.'

He meant it as a dismissal, but Mattie had been at the receiving end of too many of his dismissals. She had spent every waking hour since running out on Johnnie working on this story, chasing the details and trying to drown her private pain, knowing that only by uncovering the truth would she find any release from the emotions which were twisted in a state of perpetual warfare deep inside her. She would not leave it there. She felt like screaming at him, but she was determined not to lose her self-control. She took a deep breath, lowered her eyes for a moment to help herself relax, and was almost smiling when she looked at him once again.

'Grev. Just explain it to me so I can understand. Either somebody set the Collingridges up, or the Prime Minister of this country has established his guilt by falsifying evidence. One way or the other, we have enough to lead the paper for a week.'

'Er, yes. But which is it? We have to be sure. Particularly in the middle of a leadership contest we cannot afford to make a mistake on something so important.'

'Doesn't Collingridge deserve the chance to establish his innocence? Are you telling me that the story has to be left until after the contest has finished – until after the damage has been done?'

Preston had run out of logic. Once again he was discovering that this inexperienced woman, one of his most junior members of staff, was slipping every argument he could throw at her. As she suspected he would, he sought refuge in bluster and bullying.

'Look!' he snapped, pointing an accusatory finger in her direction. 'You burst into my office with a story so fantastic, demanding that I scrap the front page for it . . . But you haven't written any copy yet! How the devil can I tell whether you've got a good story or simply had a good lunch?'

Her blue eyes glinted like polar ice, her mind tumbling with the many slights she wanted to throw back at him. Instead, a frosty calm settled over her.

'You will have your copy in thirty minutes,' she said as she walked out, barely able to resist the temptation to slam the door off its hinges.

It was actually nearer forty minutes when she walked

back in, without knocking, six pages of double-spaced copy clutched in her hand. Without comment she dropped them on the desk, standing directly in front of Preston to make it clear that she would not budge until she had her answer.

He left her standing while slowly he read through the pages, trying to look as if he were struggling with an important decision. But it was a sham. The decision had already been made just a few minutes after Mattie had left his office and seconds after he had managed to reach the newspaper's owner on the phone.

'She's determined, Mr Landless. She knows she's got the makings of a good story and she won't take no for an answer. What the hell do I do?'

'Persuade her she's wrong. Put her on the cookery page. Send her on holiday. Promote her to editor, for all I care. But keep her quiet!'

'It's not that simple. She's not only stubborn as hell, she's one of the best political brains we've got.'

'Preston, you already have the best political brains in the business. Mine! All I am asking you to do is to control your staff. Are you telling me you can't do even that?' Landless asked in a tone full of menace. 'There are scarcely two weeks before the leadership race is over,' he continued. 'There are great things at stake, the whole future of the country, my business – your job. Do whatever you have to do to keep her quiet. Just don't screw up!'

The proprietor's words were still ringing in Preston's ears as he continued to shuffle the pieces of paper, no longer reading them, concentrating instead on what he was about to say. Normally he enjoyed his power as editorial executioner, but he knew she would never fit the typecast role of whimpering victim. He was unsure how he should handle her.

Finally he put Mattie's story down, and pushed himself back into his chair. He felt more comfortable with the support of the chair behind his back.

'We can't run it. It's too risky, and I'm not willing to blow the leadership contest apart on the basis of speculation.'

It was what she had expected all along. She replied in a whisper, but her soft words hit Preston like a boxing glove.

'I will not take no for an answer.'

Dammit. Why didn't she just accept it, shrug it off or just burst into tears like the others? The quiet insolence behind her words and his inability to handle it made him feel nervous. He started to sweat; he knew that she had noticed this sign of tension, and he began to stumble over his carefully prepared words.

'I . . . cannot run the story. I am the editor, and that's my decision.' He wasn't even convincing himself. 'You have to accept it, or . . .'

'Or what, Grev?'

'. . . or realise that you have no future on our political staff.'

'You're firing me?' This did surprise her. How could he afford to let her go, particularly in the middle of the leadership contest?

'No. I'm moving you to women's features, starting right now. Frankly, I don't think you have developed the judgement for our political columns.'

'Who has nobbled you, Grev?'

'What the hell do you mean . . . ?'

'You normally have trouble making up your mind whether you want tea or coffee. Deciding to fire me from this story is somebody else's decision, isn't it?'

'I'm not firing you! You're being transferred . . .'

He was losing control now, eyes bulging in anger and with a complexion which looked as if he had been holding his breath for three minutes.

'Then, dear editor, I have some disappointing news for you. I quit!'

God, he hadn't expected this. He was scrambling now to regain his authority and the initiative. He had to keep her at the *Telegraph*, it was the only way to control her. But what the hell was he to do? He forced a smile, and spread his hands wide in an attempt to imitate a gesture of generosity.

'Look, Mattie. Let's not be hasty. Let's be mature about this – friends! I want you to get wider experience on the paper, you've got talent, even if I think you haven't quite fitted in on the political side. We want to keep you here, so think over the weekend what other part of the paper you might like to work on.' He saw her steely, determined eyes and knew it wasn't working. 'But if you really feel you must go, don't rush into anything. Sort out what you want to do, let me know, we'll try to assist you and give you six months' salary to help you on your way. I don't want any hard feelings. Think about it.'

'I've thought about it. And if you are not printing my story, I'm resigning. Here and now.'

She had never seen him so apoplectic. His words came spitting out. 'In which case I must remind you that your contract of employment stipulates that you must give me three months' notice of departure, and that until that time has elapsed we retain exclusive rights over all your journalistic work. If you insist, we shall rigidly enforce that provision, in the courts if necessary which would ruin your career once and for all. Face it, your copy isn't going to get printed here or anywhere else. Wise up, Mattie, accept the offer. It's the best one you are going to get!'

She knew now what her grandfather must have felt as he set out from his fishing village on the Norwegian fjord, knowing that once he had started he could never turn back even though ahead of him lay enemy patrol boats, mine fields, and nearly a thousand miles of hostile, stormy seas. She would need some of his courage, and his good fortune.

She gathered up the papers on Preston's desk and ripped them slowly in half before letting them flutter back into his lap.

'You can keep the words. But you don't own the truth. I'm not sure you would even recognise it. I still quit.'

This time she slammed the door.

SUNDAY 14TH NOVEMBER –
MONDAY 15TH NOVEMBER

Some two weeks earlier, immediately after the *Telegraph* had published the Landless opinion poll, Urquhart in his capacity as Chief Whip had written to all of his parliamentary colleagues on the weekly Whips' circular which is sent to party MPs.

> During the course of the leadership election, newspapers and opinion pollsters will undoubtedly be trying to obtain your view as to whom you are likely to support. I would encourage you not to cooperate, since at best the results of these surveys can only serve to disrupt the proper conduct of what is supposed to be a confidential ballot, and at worst will be used by the less responsible press to make mischief and subject our affairs to lurid headlines and comment. The best interests of the Party can only be served by discouraging such activity.

The majority of the Parliamentary Party was more than happy to cooperate, although it is a well established fact that at least a third of MPs are constitutionally incapable of keeping anything quiet, even state secrets.

As a result, the two opinion polls which appeared in the Sunday press following Mattie's abrupt departure from Preston's office were profoundly incomplete, leaving the pollsters scratching their heads at the *Telegraph*'s earlier persuasiveness. Less than 40 per cent of the 337 Government MPs who constituted the electorate for the ballot had responded to the polling companies' pestering telephone calls, which gave the impression that the Parliamentary

Party was still a long way from making up its mind. Moreover, the small sample of those who had agreed to respond gave no clear indication as to the likely result. Samuel was ahead, but only narrowly and to a degree which the pollsters emphasised was 'not statistically significant'. Woolton, McKenzie and Earle followed in close order, with the four other declared candidates a little further behind.

The conclusions to be drawn from such insubstantial evidence were flimsy, but made excellent headlines, just four days before the close of nominations.

'Samuel slipping – early lead lost', roared the *Mail on Sunday*, while the *Observer* was scarcely less restrained in declaring 'Party in turmoil as poll reveals great uncertainty'.

The inevitable result was a flurry of editorials hostile to the Party, criticising both the quality of the candidates and their campaigns. 'This country has a right to expect more of the governing Party than the undignified squabbling we have been subjected to in recent days and the lacklustre and uninspired manner in which it is deciding its fate,' the *Sunday Express* intoned. 'We may be witnessing a governing Party which is finally running out of steam, ideas and leadership after too long in power.'

The following day's edition of the *Daily Telegraph* was intended to resolve all that. Just three days before the close of nominations, it put aside convention and for the first time in its history ran its editorial on the front page. Its print run was increased and a copy was hand delivered to the London addresses of all Government MPs. No punches were pulled in its determination to make its views heard throughout the corridors of Westminster.

This paper has consistently supported the Government, not through blind prejudice but because we felt that they served the interests of the nation better than the alternatives. Throughout the Thatcher years our convictions were well supported by the progress which was made in restoring the economy to health and the inroads which began to be made in some of the more pressing social problems.

In recent months we began to feel that Henry Collingridge was not the best leader to write the next chapter, and we supported his decision to resign. However, there is now a grave danger that the lack of judgement being shown by all the present contenders for his job will threaten a return to the bad old ways of weakness and indecisiveness which we hoped had been left behind for good.

Instead of the steadying hand which we need on the tiller in order to consolidate the economic and social advances of recent years, we have so far been offered a choice between youthful inexperience, environmental upheaval and injudicious outbursts bordering on racial intolerance.

This choice is insufficient. The Government and the country need a leader who has maturity, who has a sense of discretion, who has a proven capacity for working with all his colleagues in the Parliamentary Party.

There is at least one senior figure in the Party who not only enjoys all of these attributes, but who in recent weeks has been almost unique in remembering the need to uphold the dignity of Government and who, so rare in present day politics, has shown himself capable of putting aside his own personal ambition for what he perceives as being the wider interests of his Party.

He has announced that it is not his intention to seek election as Leader of the Party, but he still has time to reconsider before nominations close on Thursday. We believe it would be in the best interests of all concerned if the Chief Whip, Francis Urquhart, were to stand and to be elected.

*   *   *

There were forty press, television and radio men waiting outside Urquhart's home in Cambridge Street when he emerged at 8.10 that morning. He had been waiting rather nervously inside, wanting to ensure that the timing of his exit enabled BBC radio's *Today* programme and all breakfast television channels to take it live. Attracted by the scramble of newsmen, a host of passers-by and commuters from nearby Victoria Station had gathered to discover the cause for the commotion, and the live television pictures suggested a crowd showing considerable interest in the man who now emerged onto the doorstep, looking down on the throng.

The shouted questions from the journalists were identical, and he waved a hand to quieten them so that his answer could be heard. The hand also contained a copy of that morning's *Telegraph*, and for a moment it looked as if he were giving a victory salute which only encouraged the scramble still further, but eventually he managed to bring a degree of calm to the proceedings.

'Ladies and Gentlemen, as Chief Whip I would like to think you had gathered here because of your interest in the details of the Government's forthcoming legislative programme, but I suspect you have other things on your mind.'

The gentle quip brought a chuckle from the journalists and put Urquhart firmly in control.

'I have read with considerable surprise and obvious interest this morning's edition of the *Telegraph*.' He held it up again so that the cameras could get a clear shot. 'I am honoured that such a significant and authoritative newspaper should hold a high opinion of my personal capabilities – one which goes far beyond my own judgement of the matter. As you know, I had made it clear that I had no intention of standing, that I thought it was in the Party's best interest that the Chief Whip should stand above this particular contest.'

He cleared his throat. 'Generally that is still my view.

However, the *Telegraph* raises some important points which should be considered carefully. You will forgive me if I don't come to an instant or snap judgement out here on the pavement. I want to spend a little time consulting with a few colleagues to obtain their opinions, and also to have a long and serious discussion with my wife, whose views will be most important of all. I shall then sleep upon it, and let you all know tomorrow what decision I have reached. In the meantime, I hope you will allow me and my family a few hours of peace to think about things. I shall have nothing more to say until tomorrow.'

With one final wave of his hand, still clutching the newspaper and held for many seconds to satisfy the screaming photographers, Urquhart withdrew into his house and shut the door firmly.

By Monday evening, Mattie was beginning to wonder whether she had been too hasty. After storming out of Preston's office she had persuaded herself that she had resolved all her personal and professional problems in one grand gesture – no more Krajewski, certainly no more Preston, just the story to concentrate on. Yet now she was not so sure. She had spent a lonely weekend identifying the newspapers for which she would like to work, but as she did so she quickly realised that none of them had any obvious gaps in their political reporting teams which she could hope to fill. The newspaper world is highly competitive, and although she could offer youthful energy and talent in abundance, she had just thrown away the track record of experience on which most editors hire their staff.

She had made many telephone calls but they had led to few appointments; she began to discover that somebody was spreading a story that she had stormed out in tears when Preston had questioned her judgement, and sensitive feminine outbursts do not generally commend themselves to the heavily male-dominated club of newspaper editors.

It did not help her mood that the Bank of England had pushed up interest rates sharply to protect sterling from speculators while a new Prime Minister was selected, leading the building societies that morning to threaten a rise in the mortgage rate. It made her realise that she would have no apparent means of paying for it. It was difficult enough with a salary. Without one, her affairs could very soon become impossible.

And she was also lonely. Her bed was once more an Arctic outpost fit only for penguins, and gave her no comfort from her other problems.

Yet the story kept taking over and pushing to one side any thoughts of dismay in her mind, while the *Telegraph*'s editorial intervention had given it a totally new twist. Throughout the early evening she had watched the various television news programmes, all of which were dominated by speculation as to whether Urquhart would stand, and informing a generally unaware audience about what a Chief Whip actually does and who Urquhart was.

She needed to talk, and without wishing to question too deeply the conflicting emotions which were tangling in her mind she found herself waiting on a wooden platform which bobbed in the Thames tide alongside Charing Cross pier. Just a few minutes later she could see the approach of the *Telegraph*'s private river taxi which shuttled employees between the newspaper's dockland plant downstream and the rather more central and civilised reaches of the capital.

As she had hoped, Krajewski was on board. He said nothing as he found her standing on the pier, but accepted her silent invitation to walk.

It was a dry and clear November night, so they wrapped up warm and without speaking strolled along the Embankment, tracing the sharp curves of the river bank and with it the floodlit vistas of the Festival Hall and the Houses of Parliament beyond, with the tower of Big Ben looking down from high above. It was some time before he broke the silence. No questions about the other night, he decided. He knew what was foremost in her mind.

'So what do you make of it all?'

She smiled shyly in gratitude for the lifeline, for not demanding an explanation of her motives which she would not – or was it could not? – give.

'It's extraordinary. They're building him up like a Messiah on a white charger galloping to the rescue. Why did Grev do it?'

'I don't know. He just came in late yesterday, not a word to anyone, turned the paper inside out and produced his front page editorial from out of his pocket. No warning, no explanation. Still, seems to have caused quite a story. Perhaps he got it right after all.'

Mattie shook her head. 'It wasn't Grev. He's not capable of making a decision like that. It took balls to position' – she almost used the word 'commit' but stopped herself just in time – 'to position the paper in that way, and it could only have come from one place: the desk of our – your! – beloved proprietor, Mr Landless. Last time he interfered he was dethroning Collingridge, now he's trying to hand the crown to someone else.'

As they traced their way along the winding river bank, they kicked through the windswept piles of leaves and passed by the pale, massive bulk of the Ministry of Defence.

'But why? Why Urquhart?'

'No idea,' Mattie responded. 'Urquhart is very low profile, although he's been in the House for many years. He comes across as being vaguely aristocratic, patrician, old school tie. He's something of a loner, certainly not one of the boys, which means he's got no great fan club but also no one hates him enough to campaign against him as they are doing with Samuel. Nobody knows what his views really are, he's never had to express them as Chief Whip.'

She turned to face him. 'You know, he might just slip

through the middle as the man the others dislike least. Landless could have picked a winner.'

'You think he'll stand, then?'

'Certain of it. He told me way back in June that there was going to be a leadership race, and he flatly refused then to rule himself out. He wants it all right, and he'll stand.'

'That sounds like a great feature – "The Man Who Saw It Coming".'

'If only I had a paper to write it for,' she said with a wistful smile.

He stopped and looked at Mattie, her fair hair glowing in the lights which bounced back from the soft yellow stone of the Houses of Parliament behind her, wondering if he detected a hint of regret in her voice.

'Grev refuses to print your story and then announces the paper's support for Urquhart. Defusing one bomb and then launching another. Isn't that a bit of a coincidence?'

'I've been thinking about that all day,' she said. 'The simple explanations are always the easiest to accept, and the simple fact is that Grev Preston is a pathetic excuse for an editor who is terrified of getting anything wrong. Knowing that Landless was going to throw Urquhart's hat into the ring, he didn't have the nerve to upset his proprietor's plans and I suspect he found my story simply too hot to handle.'

'So you think Landless may be at the bottom of it all?'

'It's possible. He certainly welcomed the leadership contest, but then so did many others. Urquhart told me the weekend after the election of all the internal rivalry and bitterness inside the Government. Whoever is stirring it behind the scenes, we have the entire Cabinet to choose from, as well as Landless. And I am going to find out who.'

'But how, without a newspaper?'

'Preston has been stupid enough to insist that I shall remain employed by the *Telegraph* for another three months. OK. They may not print it, but I'm still a journalist and I can still ask questions. If the truth is half as devious as I suspect it is, the story will still be worth printing in three months' or even three years' time. They can't lock up the truth for ever. I may have lost my job, Johnnie, but I haven't lost my curiosity.'

And what about your commitment? he asked silently.

'And will you be my spy on the inside, keeping an eye on what that bastard Landless is up to?'

He nodded, wondering just how much she was using him.

'Thanks, Johnnie,' she whispered. She squeezed his hand, and disappeared into the night.

TUESDAY 16TH NOVEMBER

The following day's news was still being dominated by intense speculation as to whether Urquhart would run. It was clear that the media had excited itself to the point where they would feel badly let down if he didn't, yet at 3 p.m. he was still keeping his own counsel. By this time, Mattie was feeling irked, not by Urquhart but by O'Neill. She had been waiting in his office with growing impatience for a full half hour.

When she had telephoned party headquarters the previous day wanting to get an official view about computers, literature sales, accounting procedures, Charles Collingridge and all the other things which were bothering her, she discovered that Spence had been absolutely right about the ban on staff contact with the media for the duration of the campaign. She could only deal with the press office, and no press officer seemed capable or willing to talk to her about computers or accounts.

'Sounds as if you are investigating our expenses,' a voice only half-jokingly had said down the telephone.

So she had asked for the Director of Publicity's office, and had been put through to Penny Guy. Mattie asked to come and talk the following morning with O'Neill, whom she had met a couple of times at receptions.

'I'm sorry, Miss Storin, but Mr O'Neill likes to keep his mornings free to clear his paper work and for internal meetings.' It was a lie, and one she was increasingly forced to use as O'Neill's time keeping had become spectacularly erratic. He rarely came into the office before 1 p.m. nowadays. 'How about 2.30 in the afternoon?' she had suggested, playing safe.

She did not comprehend the mind-pulverising effects of cocaine, which kept O'Neill hyperactive and awake well into the small hours, unable to sleep until a cascade of depressant drugs had gradually overwhelmed the cocaine and forced him into an oblivion from which he did not return before midday or later. She did not comprehend this, but she suffered deeply from it nonetheless.

Now she was getting increasingly embarrassed as Mattie sat waiting for O'Neill. He had promised his secretary faithfully he would be on time, but as the wall clock ticked remorselessly on, her ability to invent new excuses disappeared completely. Her faith in O'Neill, with his public bravado and his private remorse, his inexplicable behaviour and his irrational outbursts, was slowly and painfully fading.

She brought Mattie yet another cup of coffee.

'Let me give him a call at home. Perhaps he's had to go back there. Something he forgot, or not feeling too well . . .'

She sat on the corner of his desk, picked up the direct line and punched the numbers. With some embarrassment she greeted Roger on the phone, explaining that Mattie had been waiting for more than half an hour and . . . Her face became gradually more concerned, then anguished and finally horrified before she dropped the phone and fled from the office as if pursued by demons.

Mattie watched these happenings with complete astonishment, rooted to her chair, clutching her saucer, unable to speak or move. As the door banged shut behind the fleeing secretary she rose and moved over to the phone, picking the dangling receiver up from where it was swinging beside the desk and putting it to her ear.

The voice coming out of the phone was unrecognisable as that of O'Neill, or indeed anyone. The words were incoherent, indecipherable, slowed and slurred to the point where it sounded like a doll with the batteries almost dead. There were gasps, moans, long pauses, the sound of tears

262

falling, and of a man falling apart. She replaced the receiver gently in the cradle.

Mattie went in search of the secretary, and found her washing her face in the cloakroom. Her eyes were red and swollen. Mattie put a consoling arm around her shoulders.

'How long has he been like that, Penny?'

'I can't say anything!' she blurted, and started weeping once more.

'Look, Penny, he's obviously in a very bad way. I'm not going to print any of this, for goodness sake. I would like to help.'

The other girl turned towards Mattie, fell into her arms, let the pain and worry of the last few months gush out, and sobbed until there were no more tears left.

When she had recovered sufficiently to escape from the cloakroom, Mattie took her gently by the arm and they went for a walk in nearby Victoria Gardens, where they could refresh themselves in the cold, vigorous air blowing off the Thames and talk without interruption. Penny told her how the Prime Minister's resignation had deeply upset O'Neill, how he had always been a little 'emotionally extravagant', as she put it, and the recent internal party turmoil and Prime Minister's resignation had really brought him close to a breakdown.

'But why, Penny? Surely they weren't that close?'

'He liked to think he was close to the whole Collingridge family. He was always arranging for flowers and special photographs to be sent to Mrs Collingridge, doing little favours whenever he could. He loved it all.'

Mattie shrugged her shoulders, as if she were shrugging off O'Neill's reputation once and for all. 'It's a great pity, of course, that he should be so weak and go to pieces just when the Party needs him most. But we both heard him this afternoon, Penny. Something has really got to Roger, something which is eating away at him from the inside.'

Mattie threw down the challenge. It wasn't fair, of course, but she gambled that Penny would not stand by and see O'Neill accused of weakness. She would loyally try to defend her boss – and would not lie in order to do so.

'I . . . I don't know for sure. But I think he blamed himself so badly over the shares.'

'The shares? You mean the Renox shares?' said Mattie in alarm.

'Charles Collingridge asked him to open the accommodation address because he wanted somewhere for his private mail. Roger and I went to Paddington in a taxi, and he sent me in to do the paper work. I knew he felt uneasy at the time, I think he sensed there was something wrong. And when he realised what it had been used for and how much trouble it had caused, he just began going to pieces.'

'Why did Mr Collingridge ask Roger to open the address and not do it himself?'

'I've no idea, really. Perhaps he felt guilty because of what he was going to use it for. Roger just breezed into the office one day during the summer and said he'd got a favour to do for Charles Collingridge, that it was terribly confidential and I was to breathe a word to no one.'

Her words reminded her that she had broken her promise of silence and more tears began to flow, but Mattie soon reassured her, and they continued their walk.

'So you never saw Charles Collingridge yourself?'

'No. I've never really met him at all. Roger likes to handle all the important people himself, and as far as I'm aware Mr Collingridge has never come into the office.'

'But you are sure it was Charles Collingridge?'

'Of course, Roger said so. And who else could it have been?' The dampness began to appear again at the corner of her eyes. She shivered violently as a burst of cold November air from across the river sent the dead autumnal leaves cascading around them. 'Oh, God, it's all such an awful mess.'

'Penny, relax! It will be all right. Why don't you take a couple of days off and let Roger take care of himself? He can survive without you for a little while. He knows how to use the office computer, doesn't he?'

'He can struggle through on the basics reasonably well if I'm not around, but even he wouldn't pretend he's a keyboard magician. No, I'll be all right.'

So it was O'Neill who had 'struggled through' with the computer file. Another piece fell into place in Mattie's mind. She didn't feel comfortable squeezing information out of a vulnerable and trusting secretary, but there was no alternative.

'Look, how can I put this . . . Roger sounds as if he is very unwell. He's obviously been under a lot of strain, and he might be having a breakdown. Perhaps he's drinking too much. I'm not a doctor, but I do know one who's very good at that sort of thing. If you need any help, please give me a call.'

They had arrived back in Smith Square by now, and prepared to part.

'Mattie, thank you. You've been a great help.'

'No, Penny. I'm the one who is grateful. Take care of yourself.'

Mattie walked the few hundred yards back to the House of Commons, oblivious of the chill and wondering why on earth Roger O'Neill had framed Charles and Henry Collingridge.

TUESDAY 16TH NOVEMBER –
WEDNESDAY 17TH NOVEMBER

Urquhart declared his intention to seek the leadership of the Party at a press conference held in the House of Commons at 5 p.m., timed to catch the early evening TV news and the first editions of the following day's press. The surroundings afforded by the meeting room in the Palace of Westminster, with its noble carved stone fireplace, its dark oak panelling and its traditional atmosphere of authority gave the proceedings a dignity which the announcements of Samuel, Woolton and others had lacked. Urquhart succeeded in establishing the impression of a man who was being dragged reluctantly towards the seat of power, placing his duty to his colleagues and country above his own, modest personal interests.

It was seventeen hours later, on Wednesday morning, that Landless held his own press conference. He sat in one of the palatial reception rooms of the Ritz Hotel at a long table covered with microphones, facing the cameras and questions of the financial press. Alongside him and almost dwarfed by his bulging girth sat Marcus Frobisher, the Chairman of the United Newspapers Group who, although an industrial magnate in his own right, was clearly cast to play a secondary role on this occasion. Behind them for the benefit of the cameras had been erected a vast backdrop with the colourful logo 'TEN' carefully crafted upon it and highlighted with lasers. To one side was a large video screen, on which was playing a corporate video featuring some of the *Telegraph*'s better advertising material interspersed with cuts of Landless being greeted by workers, pulling levers to start the printing presses and generally running his empire in a warm and personal manner. The press conference, for all its immediacy, had clearly been carefully planned.

'Good morning, ladies and gentlemen.'

Landless called the throng to order in a voice which was considerably less cockney than the one he adopted on private occasions. 'Thank you for coming at such short notice. We have invited you here to tell you about one of the most exciting steps forward for the British communications industry since Julius Reuter established his telegraph service in London more than a hundred years ago.'

He shifted one of the microphones a little closer to stop himself craning his neck. 'Today we wish to announce the creation of the largest newspaper group in the United Kingdom, which will provide a platform for making this country once again the worldwide leader in the rapidly expanding industry of providing information services.

'Telegraph Newspapers has made an offer to purchase the full issued share capital of the United Newspapers Group at a price which values them at £1.4 billion, a premium of 40 per cent above the current market price. I am delighted to say that the board of the United Newspapers Group has unanimously accepted the bid, and also agreed the terms for the future management of the combined group. I shall become Chairman and Chief Executive of the new company, and my good friend and former competitor, now colleague . . .' – he stretched a huge paw to grasp the arm of Frobisher, as menacingly as if he were grasping him around the neck – '. . . is to be the President.'

Several nodding heads around the room indicated that they clearly understood which of the men would be in sole charge of the new operation. Frobisher sat there trying hard to put on a good face.

'This is an important step for the British newspaper industry. The combined operation will control more national and major regional titles than any other newspaper group in this country, and the amalgamation of our international subsidiaries will make us the third largest newspaper group in the world. To mark this new departure we are renaming the company, and as you can see, our new corporate title will be Telegraph Express Newspapers Company PLC – TEN.' He at last released his grip on Frobisher and waved at the logo behind.

'Do you like my new corporate design?' he asked jovially. He hoped they did. His daughter's two-woman partnership had been given the contract – its first – for devising the company's new name and corporate design, and he was determined that she be given almost as much attention as himself.

'You will find waiting for you at the door a document which gives the full details of the offer and agreement. So, questions please!'

There was an excited hum from the audience, and a forest of hands shot up to catch his eye.

'I suppose to be fair I ought to take the first question from someone who will not be working for the group,' jested Landless. 'Now, can we find anyone here who won't be part of the new team?' With theatrical exaggeration he shielded his eyes from the bright lights and searched the audience for a suitable victim, and they all laughed at his cheek.

'Mr Landless,' shouted the business editor of the *Sunday Times*. 'The Government have made it very clear in recent years that they feel the British newspaper industry is already concentrated into too few hands, and that they would use their powers under the monopolies and mergers legislation to prevent any further consolidation. How on earth do you expect to get the necessary Government approval for this deal?'

There was a strong murmur of assent to the question from around the room. The Government had made loud if imprecise noises during the election about their commitment to increasing industrial competition.

'An excellent point.' Landless spread his arms wide as if to hug the question to his chest and slowly throttle it to death.

'You are right, the Government will need to take a view on the matter. And I hope they will be sufficiently wise and visionary to realise that the operation we are putting together, far from jeopardising the British newspaper industry, is vital to its continuing success. Newspapers are just part of the worldwide information industry, which is growing and changing every day. You all know that. Five years ago you all worked in Fleet Street with old typewriters and printing presses which should have been scrapped when the Kaiser surrendered. Today the industry is modernised, decentralised, computerised. Yet still it must keep changing. It has more competition, from satellite television, local radio, breakfast TV and the rest.'

'Shame!' cried a voice within the audience, and they laughed nostalgically about the cosy days of Fleet Street and El Vino's wine bar, and the prolonged printers' strikes and disputes which allowed them weeks or even months off to write books or build boats and dream dreams while still on full pay. But they all recognised the inescapable truth in what Landless was saying.

'In ten years' time more and more people will be demanding information twenty-four hours a day, from all parts of the world. Fewer and fewer of them will be getting that information from newspapers which arrive hours after the news has occurred and which covers them in filthy printing ink. If we are to survive in business we must no longer think of ourselves as parochial newspaper men, but as suppliers of information on a worldwide basis. So our new group, "TEN", will not just be a traditional newspaper business but will be grown into the world's leading supplier of information to business and homes around the world, whether they want that information printed, televised, computerised or sung by canaries. And to do that we need the size, the muscle and the resources which only a large group such as "TEN" can provide.'

He gestured generously towards the questioner.

'And as you so rightly point out, we also need the

Government's permission. So the Government have a choice. They can take the narrow view, prohibit the merger and preside over the decline of the British newspaper industry, which will be dead within ten years as the Americans, Japanese and even Australians take over. Or they can be responsible and visionary, and care about the jobs which exist and which can be created in the industry, and think not about narrow British competition but about the much broader international competition which we need to take on and beat if we are to survive. If they do that, they will allow us to build the biggest and finest information service in the world, based right here in Britain.'

A blitz of flash guns greeted him as he sat back in his chair, the carefully rehearsed appeal finished while the journalists who still took shorthand scribbled furiously to catch up with him. The questioner turned to his neighbour.

'What do you think? Will he get away with it?'

'If I know our Ben, he won't be relying just on industrial logic or compelling rhetoric. He will have prepared the ground very carefully beforehand. We'll soon see how many politicians owe him favours.'

The answer seemed to be that many politicians owed Landless, at least on the Government side. With nominations closing the following day and the first ballot due in just a week, few contenders seemed willing to risk antagonising the combined might of the Telegraph and United groups and their substantial number of national newspapers. Within hours the endorsements for Landless grew into a stampede of support amongst contenders as they struggled not to be left behind in finding airtime to praise his 'enlightened and patriotic industrial leadership'. By teatime, Landless was well pleased with his day's work and the careful planning which had gone into it. Once again, it seemed that his sense of timing and understanding of politicians had been just right.

The *Independent* could not resist the temptation to have

a dig at the proceedings. 'The Landless announcement burst like a grenade in the middle of the leadership race – which presumably was his intention. The sight of so many senior politicians falling over themselves to kiss his hand was reminiscent of Tammany Hall at its worst. It is salutary to reflect that these very same politicians, just a few months ago at the time when Landless bought out Telegraph Newspapers, were insisting that he sign a public declaration of non-interference with the editorial policies of his newspapers. Only on the basis of that solemn and binding undertaking did they allow the purchase to proceed. Today, in their craven attempts to placate Landless, they are acting as if they automatically assume that alongside his personal support goes the editorial support of his many newspapers. They seem to prefer to swim with sharks rather than honour their own undertakings.'

Not all the aspirants joined the stampede, however. Samuel was cautious and noncommittal – he had too many knife wounds in his back from the previous weeks to wish to stick his head above the parapet yet again, and he said he wished to consult the workforce of the two groups before reaching his decision. Immediately the union representatives issued their vigorous denunciation of the scheme. They had noted that there were no guarantees about job security in the published document, and they had plenty of experience of Landless's quite ruthless 'industrial rationalisation programmes'. In a careless moment Landless had once joked that he had fired 10,000 people for every million he had made, and he was an exceedingly wealthy man. Samuel realised after his brief consultation with the unions that it would be absurd in the face of their public opposition for him now to endorse the deal, so sought refuge in silence.

Urquhart also stood out from the crowd. Within an hour of the announcement he was on television and radio giving a thoroughly polished and well informed analysis of the global information market and its likely trends, all of which seemed to support the Landless proposal. His technical expertise far outshone his rivals, yet he was cautious.

'While I have the highest respect for Benjamin Landless I think it would be wrong of me to jump to immediate conclusions before I have had an opportunity to consider all the details of the proposal. I think politicians should be careful; it gives politics a bad name if they are perceived as dashing around trying to buy the support of the editorial columns. So to avoid any possible misinterpretation, I shall not be announcing my own views until the leadership contest is over. By which time, of course,' he said modestly, 'they may be of no interest anyway.'

'If only all his colleagues could have taken the dignified and principled stand of the Chief Whip', praised the *Independent*. 'Urquhart is establishing a statesmanlike tone for his campaign which marks him out from the pack and will certainly improve his chances.'

Other editorials echoed the line, not least of all the *Telegraph*.

> We encouraged Francis Urquhart to stand for the leadership because of our respect for his independence of mind and his integrity. We were delighted when he accepted the challenge, and we are still convinced that our recommendation was correct. His refusal to rush to judgement over the Telegraph–United newspaper merger and his determination to consider his views carefully is no less than we would expect from someone with the qualities to lead this country.
>
> We still hope and believe that after due deliberation he will wholeheartedly endorse the merger plans, but our judgement of Urquhart is based on much more than commercial interest. He is the only candidate who so far has demonstrated that he is also a man of principle.

There was the sound around the corridors of Westminster of doors being slammed shut in frustration as ambitious politicians realised that Urquhart had once again stolen a march on them.

'How the heck does that fart-artist do it?' barked Woolton, discarding any vestige of diplomatic restraint.

In a Mayfair penthouse overlooking Hyde Park, Landless and Urquhart smiled serenely and toasted each other's health and good fortune as they reviewed the success of each other's campaign.

'To the next Prime Minister,' saluted Landless.

'And to his impartial endorsement of the merger,' responded his companion.

THURSDAY 18TH NOVEMBER

When nominations closed at noon on Thursday, the only surprise was the last minute withdrawal of Peter Bearstead, who had been the first to announce his intention to stand.

'I've done what I set out to do, which was to get a proper election going,' he announced punchily. 'I'm not going to win and I don't want a consolation prize of a Ministerial job, so now let the others get on with it.'

He immediately signed up with the *Daily Express* to write personal and indiscreet profiles of the candidates for the duration of the campaign.

That left nine declared candidates, an unprecedentedly large field. However, the general view was that only five of them were in with a serious chance – Samuel, Woolton, Earle, McKenzie and Urquhart. With a completed list of contestants, pollsters redoubled their efforts to contact Government MPs and decipher which way the tide was running.

The starter's flag had now officially fallen, and Peter McKenzie was determined to make an immediate showing. The Secretary of State for Health was a frustrated man. Having been in charge of the health service for more than five years, he had hoped as ardently as Urquhart for a new challenge and new responsibility after the June general election. The long years in charge of an unresponsive bureaucracy, watching almost helplessly as the remorselessly expensive progress of medical science grew faster than the taxpayers' ability or willingness to keep pace, had left him deeply scarred. A few years previously he had been regarded as the rising star of the Party, the man who could combine a tough intellectual approach with an obvious deep sense of caring, and many said he would go all the way. But the health service had been utterly unresponsive to his attempts to reform and improve it, and his repeated encounters with picket lines of protesting nurses and ambulance men had left his image as a man of conscience and humanity in tatters. The postponement of his much touted hospital expansion plan had been the last straw. He had become deeply dispirited, and had talked with his wife about quitting politics at the next election if his lot did not improve.

He greeted Collingridge's downfall like a drowning man discovers a life raft. It was the only thing that mattered to him, and drew all his concentration and effort. Of course he had made mistakes during the initial stages of the campaign, as had most of his rivals, but he entered the final five days before the first ballot full of enthusiasm and energy. He had planned from the start to make an impact on Nomination Day itself, determined to get his head above the crowd. So he had asked his staff to find a suitable visit for him to make which would provide some powerful photo-opportunities for the cameramen and a chance to revive his tarnished image as a humane and caring politician.

But no hospitals, he instructed. He had spent the first three years in the Ministry visiting hospitals and trying to learn about patient care, only to be met on bad days by massed picket lines of boisterous nurses complaining about pay and on worse days by violent demonstrations from ancillary staff protesting about 'savage cuts'. Even the doctors seemed to have embraced the philosophy that health budgets were now set by the level of noise rather than the level of need. He almost never got to see the patients, and even when he tried to sneak into a hospital by a side or back entrance, the demonstrators always seemed to know beforehand precisely where he would be, ready to throw their personal and deeply hurtful abuse at him just when the television camera crews had arrived. No Minister had ever found an effective way of dealing with protesting nurses; the public will always side with the angels of mercy, leaving the politician in the role of perpetual villain. So McKenzie had simply stopped visiting hospitals. Rather than running an inevitable and image-denting gauntlet of abuse, he opted out and stuck to safer venues.

Just a couple of hours after nominations closed, the Secretary of State's car was approaching the Humanifit Laboratories just off the M4 where he would spend a couple of hours in front of cameras opening the new factory and examining the wide range of equipment which they manufactured for handicapped people. They had just developed a revolutionary new wheelchair which would operate to the voice commands of paraplegic patients unable to move their limbs. The combination of new British technology and enhanced care for the disabled was just what he had hoped his office would find for him, and he was looking forward to his afternoon and the media coverage it would generate.

McKenzie had been careful, however, not taking the success of the visit for granted. He had been ambushed by protesters too many times to take chances that the television camera crews would bring a demonstration with them in order to enhance the vividness of their pictures. 'One good demo is worth a thousand new factory openings to us,' a friendly television executive had once advised him, and he had taken care to ensure that the media had been informed only three hours before his impending arrival, soon enough to get their camera crews there, but not sufficient time for anyone to arrange a welcoming demonstration. Yes, he thought as the factory came into view, his office had been very efficient and he had been sensibly cautious. It should all work very well.

Unfortunately for McKenzie, his office had been too efficient. Governments need to know where their Ministers and supporters are at all times, in case of emergency or in case of a sudden vote in the House of Commons for which they will need to be called in at short notice. And the office accorded the responsibility for maintaining and updating the information on the whereabouts of Ministers is, of course, that of the Chief Whip. On the previous Friday, following her standing instructions to the letter, McKenzie's diary secretary had sent a full list of his forthcoming week's engagements over to Urquhart's office in 12 Downing Street. Thereafter, one telephone call was all it took.

As they drove the last few hundred yards down the country road to the factory's green-field site, McKenzie combed his hair and prepared himself for the cameras. They drew alongside the red brick wall which curved around the site and, as the Minister in the rear seat made sure his tie was straight, the car swept in through the front gates.

No sooner was it through than the driver jammed on all the brakes, throwing McKenzie against the front seat, spilling papers on the floor and ruining his careful preparations. Before he had a chance to curse the driver and demand an explanation, the cause of the problem immediately confronted and swirled around him. It was a sight beyond his wildest nightmare.

The tiny car park in front of the factory's reception office was jammed with a throng of seething protesters, all dressed in nurse's uniform and hurling abuse, with every angry word and action recorded by three television cameras which had been dutifully summoned by McKenzie's press officer and placed in an ideal viewing position on top of the administration block. No sooner was the official car inside the gates than the crowd surged around, kicking the bodywork and banging placards on the roof. In a couple of seconds the aerial had gone and the windscreen wipers had also been wrenched off. The driver had the sense to press the panic button fitted to all Ministerial cars which automatically closed the windows and locked the doors, but not before someone had managed to spit directly into Mc-

Kenzie's face. Fists and contorted faces were pressed hard up against the glass, all threatening violence on him; the car rocked as the crowd pressed hard against it, until he could see no sky, no trees, no help, nothing but hatred at close distance.

'Get out! Get out!' he screamed, but the driver raised his hands in helplessness. The crowd had surrounded the car, blocking off any hope of retreat.

'Get out!' he continued to scream, overcome by the claustrophobia of the crowd, but to no avail. In desperation the Minister leaned forward and grabbed the automatic gear stick, throwing it into reverse. The car gave a judder and moved back barely a foot before the driver's foot hit the brake, but the closely penned crowd had felt the impact. The protesters quickly withdrew to leave an exit for the car, taking with them a young woman in nurse's uniform who appeared to be in great pain after having been struck by the retreating car. Seeing his opening, the driver smoothly reversed his vehicle out of the gates and onto the road, pulling off a spectacular hand-brake turn to bring the nose of the car round and effect a rapid escape. He sped away leaving large black rubber scars on the road surface. The cameras continued to record every panic-stricken moment.

McKenzie's political career was also left on the road alongside the ugly burnt tyre marks. It did not matter that the woman was not badly injured, or that she was not indeed a nurse at all but a fulltime union convenor and an experienced hand at turning a picket line drama into a newsworthy crisis. No one bothered to enquire. No man who could antagonise so many nurses and act in such a cowardly fashion in seeking to evade their protest could possibly occupy 10 Downing Street. For McKenzie, the tide had turned again and he watched helplessly as his life raft drifted back over the horizon.

FRIDAY 19TH NOVEMBER

It had been a difficult week for Mattie, and a lonely one too, and she was having to work hard to keep her spirits up. While the pace of activity in the leadership race had picked up sharply, she found herself treading water, feeling as if she were being left behind by events. Nothing had come of her few job interviews; it had become clear to her that she had been blacked by all the newspapers in the expanding Landless empire, and none of his remaining competitors seemed particularly keen to antagonise him unnecessarily. And on Friday morning the mortgage rate had gone up.

Even worse, while she had more pieces of the jigsaw, still she could find no pattern in them. And it hurt. Inside her head the few facts she had gathered collided with her own speculative thoughts, but nothing seemed to fit. The collision left a dull, throbbing ache in her temples which had been with her incessantly for days. So she had hauled her running gear out of the wardrobe and was soon pounding her way around the leaf-covered tracks and pathways of Holland Park, hoping that the much needed physical exercise would purge both body and mind. But the throbbing in her head only combined with the new and growing pains in her lungs and legs to make it all hurt even more. She was running out of ideas, stamina and time. The first ballot was just four days away.

In the fading evening light she ran along the sweeping avenue of chestnut trees which towered magnificent and leafless above her like a living tunnel inhabited by half-seen, ghostly apparitions; down Lime Tree Walk where in daylight the squirrels and sparrows were as tame as house pets; past the red bricked ruins of old Holland House, burned to the ground half a century before along with its books, beauty and secrets, leaving just its brooding memories of

281

past glories. In the days before what was left of Elizabethan London had grown into a voracious urban sprawl, Holland House had been the country seat of Charles James Fox, the legendary 18th century radical who had spent a lifetime pursuing revolutionary causes and who had used his ancestral home to gather all his conspiratorial colleagues and plot the downfall of the Prime Minister. It had always been in vain. Yet who had succeeded now where he had failed?

She went over the ground again, the field of battle on which Collingridge had fallen. It had started with the general election campaign which had gone badly wrong, with Collingridge and Williams left to blame each other and argue whose fault it all was.

Then came the fiasco of the hospital scheme, courtesy of Stephen Kendrick. There were no leads on the leak of Territorial Army cuts to the *Independent;* the document had been discovered floating around Annie's Bar, and they could scarcely blame Annie . . . The opinion poll, too, had been leaked – just another part of Collingridge's death by a thousand cuts – but she had no idea whom to thank for that. O'Neill, she knew, was involved in the extraordinary episode of share purchases through the Paddington address, and Landless had taken a sudden and uncharacteristic interest in high politics, with motive unclear.

That was it. That was all she had. So where did she go from here? As she climbed up the slope towards the highest part of the wooded park, she pounded away at the alternatives.

'Collingridge isn't giving interviews. Williams will only talk through his press office. O'Neill doesn't seem capable of answering questions, and Landless wouldn't stop for me on a pedestrian crossing. Which leaves only you, Mr Kendrick!'

With one final spurt she reached the top of the hill and began stretching out on the long downhill slope which led towards her home. Now she felt better. She had got her second wind.

SATURDAY 20TH NOVEMBER

It had not been too bad a week for Harold Earle. The media had nominated him as one of the five candidates most likely to succeed; he had watched Samuel's bandwagon fail to roll and McKenzie's become derailed. And in spite of the Chief Whip's creditable showing, Earle could not believe that Urquhart would succeed because he had no senior Cabinet experience of running any great Department of State, and at the end of the day experience really counted for the top job. Particularly experience like Earle's.

He had started his climb many years before as the Prime Minister's Parliamentary Private Secretary, a post in which he joked that he held more power than anyone below Chancellor. His promotion to the Cabinet had been rapid, and he had held several important portfolios, including, for the last two years under Collingridge, responsibility for the Government's extensive school reforms as Secretary of State for Education. Unlike some of his predecessors, he had managed to find common ground with the teaching profession, although some accused him of being unable to take really tough decisions and being a conciliator.

But didn't the Party in its present mood need a touch of conciliation? The infighting around Collingridge had left its scars, and the growing abrasiveness of the campaign was only rubbing salt in the wounds. In particular, Woolton's attempt to shed his diplomatic veneer and rekindle memories of his early rough and tumble North Country political style was antagonising some of the more traditional spirits in the Party. Perhaps the time was exactly right for Earle.

On Saturday, he planned a rally amongst the party faithful in his constituency to wave the flag. A brightly decked
hall packed with supporters whom he could greet on first-
name terms – in front of the cameras, of course – seemed
an ideal location for a major pronouncement on schools
policy. He and his officials had been working on it for some
time, and with just a little hurrying forward they would
have it ready for announcement on Saturday – a
Government-sponsored plan offering school leavers who
could not find a job not only a guaranteed place on a
training course, but now the opportunity to complete that
training in another Common Market country, providing
practical skills and language training as well.

Earle was confident it would be well received. The
speech would glow with rapture about the new horizons
and job opportunities which would open up for young
people, and the mortal blow he was delivering to the British
businessman's traditionally apathetic approach to dealing
with foreign customers in their own language.

And then the *coup de grâce.* He had got the Common
Market bureaucrats in Brussels to agree to pay for the
whole thing. He could already feel the tumultuous applause washing over him, carrying him on to Downing
Street.

There was a large crowd of cheering supporters outside
the Essex village hall to greet him when he arrived at
midday. They were waving little Union Jacks and old
election posters which had been brought out to give the
occasion all the atmosphere of the campaign trail. The
village band struck up as he came through the doors at the
rear of the hall, proceeding down the aisle shaking hands on
all sides. The local mayor led him up onto the low wooden
platform as the cameramen and lighting crews scurried
around to find the best angle. He gazed out over the crowd,
shielding his eyes from the lights, waving to their applause
even as the mayor tried to introduce him. He felt as if he
was on the brink of the greatest personal triumph of his life.

Then he saw him. Standing in the front row, squashed between the other cheering supporters, waving and applauding with the rest of them. Simon. The one person in the world he had hoped he would never see or hear from again. He remembered how they had first met – how could he ever forget? It was in the railway carriage as Earle had been coming back from the late night rally in the North West. They had been alone, Earle had been drunk, and Simon had been very, very friendly. And handsome. As the train thundered through the night they had entered a different, dark world cut off from the bright lights and responsibilities they had just left, and Earle had discovered himself committing an act which would have made him liable to a prison sentence several years before, and which was still only legal between consenting adults in private. And a British Rail carriage twenty minutes out of Birmingham is not the most private of locations.

Earle had staggered out of the carriage at Euston, thrust two £20 notes into Simon's hand, and spent the night at his club. He couldn't face going back to the home he shared with his ailing mother.

He hadn't seen Simon for another six months, but suddenly he had turned up in the Central Lobby of the Houses of Parliament asking the police attendants if he could see him. When the Minister arrived the youth didn't make a fuss, explaining how he had recognised Earle from the recent party political broadcast, asking for the money in a very delicate and gentle fashion. Earle had paid him some 'expenses' for his trip to London, but on Simon's second visit a few weeks later he knew there would be no respite. He had instructed Simon to wait, and had sought sanctuary in the corner of the Chamber. He spent ten minutes looking over the scene which he had grown to love so dearly, knowing that the youth outside threatened everything he had.

He could find no answer himself, so he had gone straight along to the Chief Whip's Office and spilled the lot. There was a youth sitting in the Central Lobby blackmailing him for a brief and stupid fling they had had many months before, he had confessed. He was finished.

Never mind, don't worry, he had been assured. Worse things had happened on the retreat from Dunkirk. Point him out and leave it all to the Chief Whip.

Urquhart had been as good as his word. He had introduced himself to the boy, and assured him that if he were not off the premises in five minutes the police would be called and he would be arrested for blackmail. The boy was further assured that in such cases the arrest and subsequent trial were held with little publicity, no one would discover the name of the Member concerned, and few people would even hear how long he had been sent down for. Little more pressure was needed to persuade the youth he had made a terrible mistake and should depart as quickly as possible, but Urquhart had taken the precaution of taking down the details from Simon's driving licence, just in case he were to continue to cause trouble and needed to be tracked down.

And now he was back there, in the front row, ready to make unknown demands about which Earle's fevered imagination could only torment itself. The torment went on throughout the speech, which ended as a considerable disappointment to his followers. The content was there, printed in large type on his small pages of recycled paper, but the fire was gone. The faithful had come to listen to him, not his officials' tired prose, yet he seemed to be elsewhere even as he was delivering the lines.

They still clapped and applauded enthusiastically when he was finished, but it didn't help. The mayor had almost to drag him into the pit of the hall to satisfy the clamour of the crowd for one last handshake and the chance personally to wish their favourite son well. As they shouted at him and kissed his cheeks and pummelled him on the back, he was drawn ever closer to the youthful eyes staring benevolently at him, as if he were being dragged towards the gates of Hell itself.

But Simon caused no scene, did nothing but shake his hand warmly and smile prettily, one hand toying nervously with the gold medallion which swung ostentatiously around his neck. Then he was gone, just another face left behind in the crowd, and Earle was in his car speeding back towards London and safety.

When he arrived back at home, two men were standing outside in the cold street waiting for him.

'Evening, Mr Earle. Simmonds and Peters from the *Mirror*. Interesting rally you had. We've got the press handout, the words, but we need a bit of colour for our readers. Like how the audience reacted. Got anything to say about your audience, Mr Earle?'

He rushed inside without saying anything, slamming the door behind him. He watched through a curtained window as they shrugged their shoulders and retreated to the estate car parked on the other side of the street. They pulled out a book and a thermos flask, and settled in for the long night ahead.

SUNDAY 21ST NOVEMBER

They were still there the following morning just after dawn when Earle looked out. One was asleep, napping under a trilby hat pulled down over his eyes. The other was reading the Sunday newspapers, which bore little resemblance to the previous week's editions. A leadership campaign which then had been dead in the water had now, with Urquhart's intervention and McKenzie's catastrophe, sprung to life. And the pollsters were beginning to wear down the MPs' resistance to their probing.

'All square!' declared the *Observer*, announcing that the 60 per cent of the Parliamentary Party they had managed to cajole into giving a view were now evenly split between the three leading candidates – Samuel, Earle and Woolton, with Urquhart close behind and McKenzie now clearly out of it. The small lead to which Samuel had previously clung had entirely disappeared.

But the news gave no joy to Earle. He had spent a ruinous and totally sleepless night, pacing the floors but being able to find no solace. Everywhere he had looked for comfort, he could see only Simon's face. The presence of the two journalists had kept nagging at him. How much did they know? Why were they squatting on his doorstep? The long wait through the night until the first fingers of dawn spread cold and grey in the November sky had drained him of hope and resistance. He had to know for certain.

Peters nudged Simmonds awake as the unshaven figure of Earle, his silk dressing gown dragged tightly around him, appeared at the front door of the house and made towards them.

'Works like a dream every time,' Peters said. 'They

simply can't resist trying to investigate, like a mouse after cheese. Let's see what he has to say for himself, Alf – and turn that bloody tape machine on.'

'Good morning, Mr Earle,' Peters. shouted as Earle approached. 'Don't stand out there in the cold, sit inside. Care for a cup of coffee?'

'What do you want? Why are you spying on me?'

'Spying, Mr Earle? Don't be silly, we're just looking for a bit of colour. You're a leading candidate in an important election campaign. Seen the newspapers yet? People are bound to take more interest in you – about your hobbies, what you do, who your friends are.'

'I have nothing to say!'

'Could we interview your wife, perhaps?' asked Simmonds. 'Silly me, you're not married, of course, are you Mr Earle?'

'What are you implying?' Earle demanded in a contorted, high pitched voice.

'My goodness me nothing at all, sir. By the way, have you seen the photos of your rally yesterday? They're very good, really clear. We're thinking of using one on our front page tomorrow. Here, have a look.'

A hand thrust a large glossy photograph out of the window and waved it under Earle's nose. He grabbed it, and gasped. It clearly showed him gripping the hand and look-ing straight into the eyes of a smiling Simon. The details were awesomely clear, perhaps too clear. It almost looked as if some hidden hand had added a trace of eyeliner around Simon's large eyes, and his fleshy, petulant lips appeared to have been made darker, more prominent. As his manicured fingers played with the gold medallion around his neck, he looked very, very effeminate.

'Know him well, do you, sir?'

Earle threw the photograph back through the car window.

'What are you trying to do? I deny everything. I shall report your harassment to your editor!'

Earle rushed back towards his front door.

'Editor, sir? Why, bless me, it was him what sent us,' Simmonds shouted at the Minister's retreating back.

As the door slammed shut behind the fleeing figure, Peters turned to his colleague. 'There goes one very worried man, Alf.'

They settled back to their newspapers.

MONDAY 22ND NOVEMBER

Kendrick had accepted Mattie's request for a chat with alacrity. He wasn't sure he had been so keen simply because as an Opposition backbencher he was flattered to be in demand, or simply because his eyes flared and his knees tingled every time he saw her. In any event, it didn't really matter to Kendrick what his real motives were, he was delighted to meet with her. He was making their tea himself in his single room office in Norman Shaw North, the red brick building made famous in countless ageing black and white films as New Scotland Yard, the head-quarters of the Metropolitan Police. The forces of law and order had long since moved to a more modern and efficient base in Victoria Street, but the parliamentary authorities had been delighted to snap up the vacant, albeit dilapidated, space just across the road from the Houses of Parliament to provide much needed additional working room for the horrendously overcrowded Members of Parliament.

As he gazed out over the Thames towards the South Bank arts complex, Kendrick poured tea and opened his heart.

'I have to say I never really expected all this,' he said. 'But I've grown to like it very much indeed.'

'You've also managed to make your mark very quickly,' Mattie smiled her most winning of smiles and recrossed her legs. She had been careful to discard her favoured trousers for a fashionable blouse and skirt which showed off her legs and slender ankles to their best effect. She needed some information, and would buy it with a little flirting if needs be.

'I'm doing a feature piece on the decline and fall of the Prime Minister, trying to get behind the basic news stories and talk to those who played a part in it, whether they had intended to or not. It won't be an unsympathetic piece, I'm not trying to moralise or lay blame. I'm trying rather to offer an insight into how Parliament works and how politics can be so full of surprises. And when it comes to surprises, yours was one of the biggest.'

Kendrick chuckled. 'I'm still amazed at how my parliamentary reputation was built on such a – well, what would you call it? Stroke of luck? Throw of the dice? Guess work?'

'Are you saying you didn't actually know that the hospital scheme had been shelved, that you were guessing?'

'Put it this way. I wasn't absolutely certain. I took a risk.'

'So what did you know?'

'Well, Mattie, I've never really told the full story before to anyone . . .' He glanced down to where Mattie was rubbing her ankles, as if to relieve sore shins. 'But I suppose there's no harm in telling you a little of the background.'

He pondered a second to decide how far he should go. 'I discovered that the Government – or rather their party headquarters – had planned a massive publicity campaign to promote the new plan for expanding hospitals. They had worked hard at it, spent a lot of money on the preparations, yet at the last minute they cancelled the whole thing. Just pulled the plug on it. I thought about this for a long while, and the only explanation I could reach was that they were actually pulling the plug, not just on the publicity campaign but on the policy itself. So I challenged the Prime Minister – and he fell for it! I couldn't have been more surprised myself.'

'I don't remember any discussion at the time about a publicity campaign. It must have been kept very quiet.'

'Of course, they wanted to keep the element of surprise. I believe all the planning of it was highly confidential.'

'You obviously have excellent confidential sources.'

'Yes. And they are staying confidential, even from you, I'm afraid!'

Mattie knew that she would need to offer much more than a flashing pair of ankles to get that sort of information out of him, and she was unwilling to pay so high a price.

'Of course, Stephen. I know how valuable sources are. But can you give me a little guidance? The leak could only have come from one of two sources, Party or Government, yes . . . ?'

He nodded.

'And there has been a tremendous amount of publicity about the rift between party headquarters and Downing Street in recent months. Particularly as it was to be a party publicity drive, it would be logical to suspect that the information came out of party headquarters.'

She raised an enquiring eyebrow, and puckered her lips.

'You're very good, very good, Mattie. But you didn't get that from me, OK? And I'm not saying any more about my source. You're too hot by half!'

He was beginning to chuckle merrily when Mattie played her own hunch.

'No need to worry. I want to write a feature piece, not conduct an inquisition. Roger's secret is safe with me.'

Kendrick spat out the mouthful of tea he was trying to drink and started choking.

'I never . . . said anything about . . . Roger!' he spluttered. But he knew he had betrayed his familiarity with O'Neill, and the calm face he was trying to restore simply eluded him. He decided to surrender.

'Jesus. How did you know? Look, Mattie. Big favour time. I didn't say anything about Roger. We're old friends and I don't want to land him in any sort of hot water. He's got enough at Smith Square as it is, eh?'

Mattie laughed loudly, teasing the politician for his discomfort.

'Your sordid secret is safe with me,' she assured him. 'But when you have risen to become a senior member of Government some time in the future, perhaps even Prime Minister, I hope you will remember you owe me!'

They both laughed loudly at the banter but, inside, Mattie's stomach churned. Another piece of the jigsaw had just fallen into place.

They were there at lunchtime and still there in the evening, just reading, picking their teeth, and watching. Like avenging angels they had waited for Earle in their sordid little car from over forty-eight hours, witnessing every flicker of the curtain, photographing everyone who called including the postman and the milkman.

'What do they want with me?' he screamed to himself inside his head. 'Why are they persecuting me like this?'

He had no one to turn to, no one with whom to share his misery and offer consolation. He was a lonely figure, a sincere and even devout man who had made one mistake, and he knew sooner or later he must pay for it. His mother had always drilled into him the need to pay for one's sins or be consumed by hell fire, and he felt the flames licking at him now with growing ferocity.

He had been home half an hour on Monday evening when they knocked on the door.

'Sorry to bother you, Mr Earle. Simmonds and Peters again. Just a quick question our editor wanted us to ask. How long have you known him?'

Into his face was thrust another photograph, still of Simon, but this time taken not at a public rally but in a photographer's studio, and dressed from head to foot in black leather slashed by zip fasteners. The jacket was open to the waist, exposing a slender, tapering body, while from his right hand there trailed a long bullwhip.

'Go away. Go away. Please – go away!' he screamed, so loudly that neighbours came to the window to investigate.

'If it's inconvenient, we'll come back some other time, sir.'

Silently they filed back to their car, and resumed the watch.

TUESDAY 23RD NOVEMBER

They were still there the following morning. After yet another sleepless night, Earle knew he had no emotional resources left. With red eyes and husky voice, he sat weeping gently in an armchair in the study. He had worked so hard, deserved so much, yet it had all come to this. He had tried so desperately to deserve his mother's love and commendation, to achieve something with which to illuminate her final years, but once again he had failed her, as she always said he would.

He knew he must finish it. There was no point in going on. He no longer believed in himself, and knew he had forfeited the right to have others believe in him. Through misty eyes he reached down into the drawer of his desk, and fumbled as he took out his private phone book. He punched the numbers on the phone as if they were nails being driven through his soul. He fought hard to control his voice throughout the brief conversation, but then it was finished, and he could weep again.

The news that Earle had pulled out of the race left everyone aghast as it flashed round Westminster later on Tuesday morning. It had happened so unexpectedly that there was no time to alter the printed ballot papers except with an ignominious scratching through of the name with a biro. Sir Humphrey was not best pleased that his carefully laid preparations should have been thrown into chaos at the last minute, and had some rough words to use for anyone who was willing to listen. But on the stroke of ten Committee Room Number 14, which had been set aside in the House of Commons for the ballot, opened its doors and the first of the 335 Government MPs who were going to vote began to file through. There would be two prominent absentees – the Prime Minister, who had announced he would not vote, and Harold Earle.

Mattie had intended to spend the whole day at the House of Commons chatting to MPs and gauging their sentiment. Most appeared to think that Earle's withdrawal would tend to help Samuel as much as anyone: 'the conciliators tend to stick with the conscience merchants,' one old buffer had explained, 'so Earle's supporters will drift towards young Disraeli. They haven't got the sense to make any more positive decision.' Behind the scenes and in private conversations with colleagues who could be trusted, the campaign was taking a more unpleasant personal edge.

She was in the press gallery cafeteria drinking coffee with other correspondents when the tannoy system announced there was a telephone call for her. She took it at the nearest extension. The sense of shock which hit her when she heard the voice was even greater than the news of Earle's withdrawal.

'Hello, Mattie. I understand you were looking for me last week. Sorry you missed me, I was out of the office. Touch of gastric 'flu. Do you still want to get together?'

Roger O'Neill sounded so friendly and enthusiastic that she had trouble connecting it with the voice she had heard a few days earlier. Could it really have been O'Neill she had listened to drivelling down the phone? She remembered the reports about his outrageous performance at Urquhart's reception in Bournemouth, and realised the man must be riding an emotional helter skelter, careering between highs and lows like a demented circus ride.

'If you are still interested, perhaps you would like to come across to Smith Square later today,' he offered.

He showed no signs of the verbal bruising he had received from Urquhart, which had been particularly merciless. Urquhart had telephoned to instruct O'Neill to make the appropriate arrangements for Simon to attend Earle's weekend meeting, and to ensure that the *Mirror* was anonymously informed of the connections between the two men. Instead he had discovered that O'Neill was sliding steadily into his cocaine-induced oblivion and losing touch with events outside his increasingly narrow, kaleidoscopic world. There had been a confrontation. Urquhart could not afford to lose O'Neill's services inside party headquarters, or have loose ends unravelling at this point.

'One week, Roger, one more week and you can take a break, forget about all of this for a while if you want, and come back to that knighthood you've always wanted. Yes, Roger, with a "K" they will never be able to look down their noses at you again. And I can arrange everything for you. But you let me down now, you lose control and I will make sure you regret it for the rest of your life. Damn you, get a grip on yourself. You've got nothing to fear. Just hold on for a few more days!'

O'Neill wasn't absolutely sure what Urquhart was going on about; to be sure he had been a little unwell but his befuddled brain still refused to accept there was a major problem which he couldn't handle. Why fill one's life with doubts, especially about oneself? He could cope with it, particularly with a little help . . . Still, a few days more to realise all his ambitions, to get the public recognition he deserved, to wipe the condescending smiles off their faces, would be worth a little extra effort.

He had got back into the office to be told that Mattie had been looking for him, that she was asking questions about the Paddington accommodation address.

'Don't worry, Pen. I'll deal with it.' He fell back on the swaggering confidence of years of salesmanship, of persuading people to buy ideas and arguments, not because they were all particularly good but because his audiences found themselves captivated by his energy and enthusiasm. In a world full of cynicism, they wanted to put their trust in a man who seemed to believe so passionately in what he was offering.

When Mattie arrived in his office after lunch, he was bright, alert, those strange eyes of his still amazingly animated but seeming very anxious to help.

'Just a stomach upset,' he explained. 'Sorry I had to stand you up.'

Mattie acknowledged that his smile was full of charm; it was difficult not to want to believe him.

'I understand you were asking about Mr Collingridge's accommodation address?'

'Sounds as if you are admitting that it *was* Charles Collingridge's address?' she enquired.

'Well, if you want something on the record, you know I have to say that Mr Collingridge's personal affairs are his own, and no one here is going to comment one way or the other on any speculation.' He trotted out the Downing Street line with accomplished ease. 'But may I talk to you off the record, not for reporting?'

He made strong eye contact with her as if to establish his sincerity, rising from behind his desk to come and sit alongside Mattie in one of the informal chairs which littered his office.

'Even off the record, Mattie, there's a limit to how much I can say, but you know how unwell Charles has been. He's not been fully responsible for his actions, and it would be a terrible pity if we were to go out of our way to punish him still further. His life is in ruins. Whatever he has done wrong, hasn't he suffered enough already?'

Mattie felt angry as she watched the loading of guilt onto the shoulders of the absent Charles. The whole world is to blame, Roger, except for you.

'Are you denying that Charles Collingridge himself asked you to open that address?'

'So long as this is not for reporting but for your background information, I'm not going to deny it, but what good will it do anyone to re-open such old wounds? Give him a chance to rebuild his life,' he pleaded.

'OK, Roger. I see no point in trying to subject him to

further harassment. So let me turn to a different point. There have been lots of accusations about how party headquarters has been very careless in allowing damaging material to leak out in recent months. The Prime Minister is supposed to blame Smith Square very directly for much of his troubles.'

'I doubt whether that is fair, but it is no secret that relations between him and the Party Chairman have been very strained.'

'Strained enough for that opinion poll we published during party conference week to have been leaked deliberately from party headquarters?'

Mattie had to look very hard to detect the faint glimmer of surprise behind his flashing eyes before he sped into his explanation.

'I think that assumption is very difficult to justify. There are only – what, five people in this building who are circulated with copies of that material apart from the Party Chairman. I'm one of those five, and I can tell you how seriously we take the confidentiality of such material.' He lit a Gauloise. Time to think. 'But it also gets sent to every Cabinet Minister, all twenty-two of them, either at the House of Commons where it would be opened by one of those gossipy secretaries, or to their Departments where it would be opened by a civil servant, many of whom have no love for this Government. Any leak is much more likely to have come from there.'

'But the papers were leaked at the headquarters hotel in Bournemouth. House of Commons secretaries or unfriendly civil servants don't go to the party conference or roam around the headquarters hotel.'

'Who knows, Mattie. It's still much more likely to have come from a source like that. Can you imagine Lord Williams scurrying around on his hands and knees outside hotel room doors?'

He laughed loudly to show how ridiculous it was, and Mattie joined in, realising that O'Neill had just admitted he knew the manner in which the opinion poll had been handed over, and he could only have known that for one reason. His overconfidence was tightening the noose around his neck even as he laughed.

'Let me turn to another leak then, on the hospital expansion scheme. Now I am told that party headquarters was planning a major publicity drive during last summer, which had to be scrapped because of the change of plan.'

'Really? Who on earth told you that?' asked O'Neill, knowing full well that it could only have been Kendrick, probably egged on by his weakness for a pretty woman. 'Never mind, I know you won't reveal your sources. But they sound exaggerated to me. The Publicity Department here is always ready to sell Government policy, and had the scheme gone ahead then certainly we would have wanted to help promote it, but we had no specific campaign in mind.'

'I was told you had to scrap a campaign which had been carefully planned and which was ready to go.'

The limp ash from his cigarette gave up its struggle to defy the laws of gravity and cascaded like an avalanche down his tie, but O'Neill ignored it. He was concentrating hard now.

'You've been misinformed. Sounds to me like someone wanting to dig up the story again and trying to show the Party in much greater confusion than it actually was. Your source sounds a bit dubious to me. Are you sure he's in a position to know all the facts, or has he got his own angle to sell?'

With a broad grin, O'Neill tried to smother Kendrick as a reliable source, and the smile which Mattie returned betrayed none of her own wonderment at his impromptu yet superbly crafted explanations. But she was asking far too many leading questions, and even a polished performer such as O'Neill was beginning to feel distinctly uncomfortable. He felt a gut-wrenching need for greater stimulation and support than his Gauloise could give him, no matter what Urquhart had said.

'Mattie, I'm afraid I've got a busy day, and I have to make sure we are ready to handle the result of the ballot later this evening. Could we finish it here?'

'Thanks for your time, Roger. I have found it immensely helpful in clearing up a few things.'

'Any time I can help,' he said as he guided her towards the door. As they did so, they passed by the computer terminal stationed in the corner of his crowded office. She bent down to inspect it more closely.

'I'm an absolute moron with these things,' she commented, turning to look straight into his flickering eyes. 'I'm impressed to see your Party is well ahead of the others in using new technology. Are all the terminals in this building linked through the central computer?'

'I. . . believe so,' he said, pressing her more firmly towards the door.

'I never knew you had such high-tech skills, Roger,' she complimented.

'Oh, I don't,' he said in a surprisingly defensive mood. 'We all get put through a training course, but I'm not even sure how to switch the wretched things on, actually. Never use it myself.' His smile had tightened, and his eyes were flickering ever more violently. He propelled Mattie through the door with some force, and bade her a hasty farewell.

At 5 p.m. the doors to the Commons Committee Room were ceremoniously shut to bar any further attempts to lodge votes in the leadership election. The gesture was an empty one, because the last of the 335 votes had been cast ten minutes earlier. Behind the doors gathered Sir Humphrey and his small team of scrutineers, happy that the day had gone smoothly in spite of the appalling start given to their preparations by Earle. A bottle of whisky did the rounds while they fortified themselves for the count. In different rooms around the Palace of Westminster, the candidates waited in various states of excitement for the summons which would tell them that the counting had finished and the result was ready to be announced.

Big Ben had struck the quarter after six before the eight candidates received the call, and at half past the hour more than 120 active supporters and interested MPs accompanied them as the Committee Room doors swung open to allow them back in. There was much good humour mixed with the tension as they filed in and stood around in loose groups, with substantial sums being wagered as Members made last-minute calculations as to the likely result and gambled their judgement against the inconclusive opinion polls which had been filling the press. Outside the room, excluded from what was technically a private party meeting, the men from the media did their own speculating and made their own odds.

Sir Humphrey was enjoying his little moment of history. He was in the twilight of his career, long since past his parliamentary heyday, and even the little misunderstanding over his holiday in the West Indies had helped bring him greater recognition and attention around the Westminster circuit than he had enjoyed for many years. Who knows, if he handled this correctly, his secret longing for a seat in the House of Lords might yet be fulfilled. He sat on the raised dais of the Committee Room, flanked by his lieutenants, and called the meeting to order.

'Since there has been such an unprecedentedly large number of names on the ballot paper, I propose to read the results out in alphabetical order.'

This was unwelcome news for David Adams, the former Leader of the House who had been banished to discontented exile on the backbenches by Collingridge's first reshuffle. Having spent the last two years criticising all the major economic decisions which he had supported whilst in Government, he had hoped for a good showing in order to establish his claim for a return to Cabinet. He stood there stoically, hiding his grief as Newlands announced he had received only twelve votes. He was left to wonder what had happened to all those firm promises of support he had received while Sir Humphrey continued with his roll call. None of the next four names, including McKenzie's, could muster the support of more than twenty of their colleagues with Paul Goddard, the maverick Catholic who had stood on the single issue of banning all forms of legalised abortion, receiving only three. He shook his head defiantly; his rewards were not to be of the earthly kind.

Sir Humphrey had only three more names to announce – Samuel, Urquhart and Woolton – and a total of 281 votes to distribute. The level of tension soared as those present recalled that a minimum of 169 votes was required for success on the first ballot. A couple of huge side bets were instantly concluded in one corner as two Honourable Members wagered that there would, after all, be a result on the first round.

'The Right Honourable Michael Samuel,' intoned the chairman, '99 votes.'

In the dead silence of the Committee Room, the sound of a tug blowing its klaxon three times as it passed on its way up the Thames could be clearly heard. A ripple of amusement covered the tension, and Samuel muttered that it was a pity tug masters didn't have a vote. He was clearly disappointed to be such a long way from the necessary winning total, particularly after Earle's withdrawal.

'The Right Honourable Francis Urquhart – 91 votes.'

Two of the gamblers in the corner looked crestfallen as they calculated the final figure.

'The Right Honourable Patrick Woolton – 91 votes.'

There was general commotion as the tension ebbed, congratulations and condolences were exchanged, and one Member leaned around the door to give the highlights to the anxious press.

'Accordingly,' Sir Humphrey continued, 'no candidate has been elected and there will be a second round of balloting a week today. I would remind everyone that those wishing to offer themselves as candidates for the second

305

ballot must resubmit their nominations to me by Thursday. I declare this meeting closed!'

Urquhart was giving some celebratory drinks to colleagues in his room. It was one of the finest offices available to a Member, located on the premises rather than in one of the various annexes spotted around the periphery of the Palace of Westminster, large and airy with a gracious bow window offering a fine view across the river to the Archbishop of Canterbury's ancient Gothic home at Lambeth Palace. The room was now crowded with several dozen Members, all offering their best wishes for the Chief Whip's success. Wryly he noted that it was the first time during the campaign that he had seen some of these faces, but he did not mind. Votes were votes, wherever they came from.

'Quite splendid, Francis. Absolutely excellent result. Do you think you can go on to win?' enquired one of his senior parliamentary colleagues.

'I believe so,' Urquhart responded with quiet confidence. 'I suspect I have as good a chance as anyone.'

'I think you're right, you know,' his colleague said. 'Young Samuel may be ahead, but his campaign is going backwards. It's between the experienced heads of you and Patrick now. And, Francis, I want you to know that you have my wholehearted support.'

Which, of course, you will want me to remember when I have my hands on all that Prime Ministerial patronage, he thought to himself while he offered his gratitude and a fresh drink to his guest.

New faces were still pouring into the room as word spread that the Chief Whip was entertaining. Urquhart's secretary was pouring a large whisky for Stephen Dunway, the most ambitious of the new intake of MPs who had already that evening made brief but prominent appearances at both Samuel's and Woolton's receptions on the basis that you can never be too sure. The secretary excused herself to answer the telephone, which had been ringing all evening with calls of congratulations and press enquiries.

'It's for you,' she whispered gently into Urquhart's ear. 'Roger O'Neill.'

'Tell him I'm busy and that I will call him later,' he instructed.

'He called earlier and sounds very anxious. Asked me to tell you it was "very bloody hot", to quote his exact words,' she said primly.

With an impatient curse he withdrew from his guests and sought shelter in the corner of the bay window from the noise of celebration.

'Roger,' he spoke sharply into the phone. 'Is this really necessary? I've got a room full of people.'

'She's on to us, Francis. That bloody bitch – she knows, I'm sure. She knows it's me and she'll be on to you next, the cow. I haven't told her a thing but she's got hold of it and God knows how but . . .'

'Roger! Pull yourself together!' snapped Urquhart. O'Neill was gabbling and the conversation was running away like a driverless express. It was clear he had been unable to stick to Urquhart's orders, and was not fully in control.

There was a moment of silence and Urquhart tried to re-establish his authority. 'Tell me slowly and clearly what all this is about.'

Immediately the gabbling began again, and Urquhart was forced to listen, trying to make some sort of sense of the garbled mixture of words, splutters and sneezes.

'She came over to see me, the cow from the press lobby. I don't know how, Francis, it's not me and I told her nothing. I fobbed her off – think she went away happy. But somehow she had got onto it. Everything, Francis. The Paddington address; the computer; she even suspects that someone from headquarters leaked the opinion poll I put under her door. And that bastard Kendrick must have told her about the hospital campaign you told me to concoct. Jesus,

Francis. I mean, what if she doesn't believe me and decides to print something?'

'Hold your tongue for a second,' he seethed down the phone, anxious that none of his guests should overhear him. 'Just tell me this. Who came to see you from the lobby?'

'Storin. Mattie Storin. And she said . . .'

'Did she have any firm evidence?' Urquhart interrupted. 'Or is she just guessing?'

O'Neill paused for the briefest of moments to consider the question.

'Nothing firm, I think. Just guesswork. Except . . .'

'Except what?'

'She's been told I opened the Paddington address.'

'How on earth did she find that out?' Urquhart's fury poured like molten lava down the phone.

'My secretary told her, but there is no need to worry because she thinks I did it for Collingridge.'

'Your secretary knew?'

'I . . . took her with me. I thought she would be more inconspicuous and she's utterly trustworthy. You know that.'

'Roger I could happily . . .'

'Look, it's me who's done all your dirty jobs for you, taken all the risks. You've got nothing to worry about while I'm in it up to my neck if this breaks. I need help, Francis. I'm scared! I've done too many things for you which I shouldn't have touched, but I didn't ask questions and just did what you said. You've got to get me out of this, I can't take much more and I *won't* take much more. You've got to protect me, Francis. Do you hear? You've got to help me!' O'Neill broke down into uncontrollable sobbing.

'Roger, calm yourself,' he said quietly into the receiver. 'She has absolutely no proof and you have nothing to fear. We are in this *together*, you understand? And we shall get through it together, to Downing Street. I shan't let you down. Look, I want you to do two things. I want you to keep remembering that knighthood. It's just a few days away now, Roger.'

A stumbling expression of gratitude came spluttering down the phone.

'And in the meantime, Roger – for God's sake keep well away from Mattie Storin!'

After he had put the phone down Urquhart sat there for a moment, letting his emotions wash over him. From behind him came the hubbub of the powerful men who would project him into 10 Downing Street, fulfilling the dream which had burned inside him all these years. To the front he gazed across the centuries old view of the river which had inspired generations of great national leaders whose ranks he was now surely to join. And he had just put the phone down on the only man who could ruin it all for him.

Trying to sort out the implications of the leadership ballot had left Mattie feeling drained. She needed to assess opinions as they were being formed and while the excitement of the race still gripped the participants, rather than waiting until the morning by which time they would simply be reiterating the noncommittal party line. Even the powerful elder statesmen of the Party would be caught up with the passion of the moment and find themselves offering delphic but expressive signs. Around Westminster a raised eyebrow or a knowing wink can speak as loudly to some ears as a sentence of political death, and it was vital that she knew in which direction the tumbrils were headed.

There was also the complicated election procedure to fathom. The Party's balloting rules made sense to nobody other than those who had devised them; they prescribed that the first ballot should now be set aside and new nominations made. It was even permissible, although not likely, that individuals who had not even stood in the original ballot could now enter the race for the first time. If from the confusion no victor emerged with more than half the votes, a third and final round of voting would be held between the leading three candidates, with the winner being selected by a system of proportional representation which the Government would rather die than allow to be used at a general election. It was clearly a case of one rule for the Party, an entirely different rule for the public. It was all enough to make for furrowed brows and wearied pens amongst the parliamentary correspondents that evening.

She had called Krajewski. It had been more than a week since they had seen or talked to each other, and in spite of herself she felt an inner desire to be with him. She seemed to be surrounded on all sides by doubts and unresolved questions, and she was finding it difficult on her own to pierce through the confusion. She hated to admit it, but she needed to share.

Krajewski was unsure how to respond to the call. He had spent the week debating whether she was important to him or simply using him, or both. When she had asked to see him he had offered a lavish dinner at the Ritz, which he instantly knew was a mistake. She wasn't in a mood for romance, with or without violins. Instead they had settled for a drink at the Reform Club in Pall Mall, where Johnnie was a member. She had walked the half mile from the press gallery in the House of Commons, only to discover that he was exercising the privileges of a deputy editor and was late. Or was this simply his way of expressing frustration with her? She waited in the club's vaulted reception area with its magnificent columns and smoke-laden atmosphere. It was a time capsule, which Gladstone could have re-entered to find scarcely a single significant change since he had enjoyed its hospitality a century earlier. She always felt it was ironic that this great bastion of Liberalism and Reform had taken 150 years to accept women and she had often twisted the noses of its members about their sexual chauvinism until one had reminded her that there never had been a female editor of the *Telegraph*.

When Johnnie arrived they took their drinks and sat

amongst the shadows of the upper gallery in the deep, cracked leather chairs which were so easy to relax in and so difficult to leave. As Mattie drank in the cloistered atmosphere and thick veneer of generations long departed, she desperately wanted to give herself over to the tired will of the flesh and float gently into oblivion. In those chairs, she felt as if she could sleep for a year and wake to find herself transported back several lifetimes. Yet the nagging in her head allowed her no relief.

'What is it?' he asked, although he didn't need to. One glance had been enough to reveal that she was tired, anxious, quite lacking in her usual spark.

'The usual,' she responded grimly. 'Lots of questions, too few answers, and the pieces I do have don't make sense. Somehow I know it has to be tied in with the leadership election, but I simply don't know how.'

'Tell me about it.'

She brought him up to date, how she could with more or less certainty hang most of the identifiable bits of the puzzle around O'Neill's neck.

'He almost certainly leaked the poll to me, he as good as admits he opened the accommodation address in Paddington, he caused the hospitals fiasco by leaking the promotional plans to Kendrick, and I'm sure he altered the headquarters' computer file to incriminate Charles Collingridge. Which means he's mixed up in some way with the share purchase and the bank account as well. But why?'

'To get rid of Collingridge,' prompted Krajewski.

'But what good does that do him? He's not going to take over the Party. What motive does he have for undermining Collingridge?'

He offered no suggestion, but gazed along the gallery at the grand oil portraits of Victorian statesmen to whom conspiracy and cunning had come as second nature, wondering what they would have thought. Mattie could not share his wry amusement.

'He must be acting together with someone else who does

have something to gain – someone more important, more powerful, who could benefit from the change of leadership. There has to be another figure in there somewhere, pulling O'Neill's strings.'

'So you are looking for a mystery man with the means and the motive. Well, he has to be in a position to control O'Neill, and have access to sensitive political information. It would also help if he had been engaged in a much publicised and bitter battle with the Prime Minister. Surely you don't have to look too far for candidates.'

'Give me one.'

He took a deep breath and savoured the dark, conspiratorial atmosphere of the evening air.

'It's easy. Teddy Williams.'

It was late that evening when Urquhart returned to his room in the Commons. The celebrations and congratulations had followed him all the way from his office to the Harcourt Room beneath the House of Lords where he had dined, being interrupted frequently by colleagues eager to shake him by the hand and wish him well. He had proceeded on to the Members' Smoking Room, a private place much loved by MPs who gather there away from the prying eyes of the press not so much to smoke as to exchange views and gossip and to twist a few arms. The Whips know the Smoking Room well, and Urquhart had used his hour there to good effect before once more climbing the twisting stairs to his office.

His secretary had emptied the ashtrays, cleared the glasses and straightened the cushions, and his room was once again quiet and welcoming. He closed the door behind him, locking it carefully. He crossed to the four-drawer filing cabinet with its stout security bar and combination lock which the Government provide for all Ministers to secure their confidential papers while out of their departmental offices. He twirled the combination four times, until there was a gentle click and the security bar fell away into his hands. He removed it and bent down to open the bottom drawer.

The drawer creaked as it came open. It was stuffed full of files and papers, each one with the name of a different MP on it, each one containing the personal and incriminating material he had carefully winnowed out of the safe in the Whips Office where all the best kept parliamentary secrets are stored to await Judgement Day, or some other parliamentary emergency. It had taken him nearly three years to amass this material, and he knew it was more valuable than a drawer crammed full with gold bars.

He knelt down and sorted carefully through the files. He quickly found what he was looking for, a padded envelope, already addressed and sealed. After extracting it he closed the drawer and secured the filing cabinet, testing as he always did to make sure the lock and security bar had caught properly.

It was nearly midnight as he drove out of the entrance gates to the House of Commons, a police officer stopping the late night traffic around Parliament Square to enable him to ease out into the busy road and speed on his way. However, he did not head the car in the direction of his Pimlico home. He first drove to one of the twenty-four-hour motorcycle messenger services which flourish amongst the seedier basements of Soho, where he dropped the envelope off and paid in cash for delivery early the following morning. It would have been easier to post it in the House of Commons, where they have one of the most efficient post offices in the country. But he did not want a House of Commons postmark on this envelope.

WEDNESDAY 24TH NOVEMBER

The letters and newspapers arrived almost simultaneously with a dull thud on Woolton's Chelsea doormat early the following morning. Hearing the clatter, he came downstairs and gathered them up, spreading the newspapers out on the kitchen table while he left the post on a small bench in the hallway for his wife. He received over 300 letters a week from his constituents and other correspondents, and he had long since given up trying to read them all. So he left them for his wife, who was also his constituency secretary and for whom he got a generous secretarial allowance from the parliamentary authorities to supplement his Cabinet Minister's stipend.

The newspapers were dominated by news and analysis of the leadership election. The headlines all seemed to have been written by moonlighting journalists from the *Sporting Life*, and phrases such as 'Neck And Neck', 'Three Horse Race' or 'Photo Finish' dominated the front pages. Inside, the more sanguine commentaries explained that it was difficult to predict which of the three leading contenders was now better placed, while most concluded that, in spite of his first place, Samuel was probably the most disappointed of the contestants since he had failed to live up to his early promise.

'The Party is now presented with a clear choice,' intoned the *Guardian*.

Michael Samuel is by far the most popular and polished of the three, with a clear record of being able to combine a political career with the retention of a well defined social conscience. The fact that he has been attacked by some elements of the Party as being 'too liberal by half' is a badge he should wear with considerable pride. He would undoubtedly provide a firm lead for the Party and would continue to confront the leading social issues head on – a laudable characteristic which has, however, not always commended itself to his colleagues.

Patrick Woolton is an altogether different politician. Immensely proud of his Northern origins, he poses as a man who could unite the two halves of the country. Whether his robust style of politics could unite the two halves of his own Party is altogether more debatable. He plays his politics as if he were still hooking for his old rugby league club, although his recent experience at the Foreign Office has done much to knock some of the sharper edges off his style. Unlike Samuel he would not attempt to lead the Party in any particular philosophical direction, setting great store on a pragmatic approach. But robustness combined with pragmatism has occasionally been an unhappy combination. The Leader of the Opposition has described him as a man wandering the streets of Westminster in search of a fight for any available reason.

Francis Urquhart is more difficult to assess. The least experienced and least well known of the three, nevertheless his performance in the first round ballot was truly remarkable, far outstripping many of his better fancied senior colleagues. Three reasons seem to explain his success. First, as Chief Whip he knows the Parliamentary Party extremely well, and they him. Since it is his colleagues in the Parliamentary Party and not the electorate at large who will decide this election, his low public profile is less of a disadvantage than many perhaps assumed.

Second, he has conducted his campaign in a dignified style which sets him apart from the verbal fisticuffs and misfortunes of the other contenders. What is known of his politics suggests he holds firm to the traditionalist line, somewhat patrician and authoritarian perhaps, but sufficiently ill-defined for him not to have antagonised either wing of the Party.

Finally, perhaps his greatest asset is that he is neither of the other two. Many MPs have certainly supported him in the first round rather than commit themselves to one of the better fancied but more contentious candidates. He is the obvious choice for those who wish to sit on the fence. But it is that which could ultimately derail his campaign, because as the pressure for a clear decision forces Government MPs off the fence, Urquhart is the candidate who could suffer most.

So the choice is clear. Those who wish to air their social consciences will support Samuel. Those who thirst for blood-and-thunder politics will support Woolton. Those who cannot make up their minds have an obvious choice in Urquhart. Whichever way they decide, they will inevitably deserve what they get.

Woolton chuckled as he munched his breakfast toast. He knew it was most unlikely at the end of the day that his colleagues would support a call to conscience – it was so difficult to explain in the pub or over the garden fence, and popular politics shouldn't be too complicated. If Urquhart's support was going to be squeezed, he decided, then the majority of switchers would come to him, and the bleeding hearts could go hang. Margaret Thatcher had shown how it could be done, and she was a woman. Take away her feminine shrillness and the dogmatic inflexibility, he mused, and you had the ideal political leader – Patrick Woolton.

As his wife replenished his tea he debated with himself whether he should rile another prominent rabbi in the next few days just to remind his colleagues of the Jewish issue. He decided against it; it wasn't necessary, the Party's old guard would see to that without his interfering.

'Darling, I have this feeling it is going to be an excellent day,' he proclaimed as he kissed his wife goodbye at their doorstep. A couple of photographers were outside on the pavement, and they asked him to repeat the kiss before he was allowed to get into his official car and drive off for a day's campaigning in the House.

His wife went through her daily routine of clearing the breakfast table before settling down to handle the correspondence. The volume had increased dramatically in the last few years, she noted with a sigh of resignation. Gone were the days when there was any hope of a personal answer to them all; it was now up to the word processor and its carefully programmed series of standard responses. She wondered whether anybody really noticed or cared that most of her husband's constituency letters were written by computer and signed by a little autograph machine he had brought back from the States on a recent trip. The majority of the letters were from lobby groups, professional critics or downright political opponents who weren't the least bit interested in the content of the replies. But they all needed answering nonetheless, she told herself as she began the monotonous daily task of opening the thick bundle of envelopes. She would never risk losing her husband a single vote by failing to offer some form of reply even to the most abusive of letters.

She left the padded brown envelope until last. It had clearly been hand-delivered and was firmly stapled down, and she had to struggle to extract the infuriating metal clips before getting at the contents. As she pulled out the last tenacious staple, a cassette tape fell out into her lap. There was nothing else in the envelope, no letter, no compliments slip, no label on the tape to indicate where it had come from or what it contained.

'Fools. How on earth do they expect me to reply to that!'

She put the tape to one side before switching on the word processor.

It took her three hours of solid work to go through the letters, persuade the word processor to churn out a reply which had some chance of persuading the recipient that they were receiving personalised attention, watch them being signed by machine, then fold and seal them. The tape she left on the desk. Her mouth was gummed up from licking too many envelopes, and she needed a cup of coffee. The silly tape could wait.

It was very much later that evening when she remembered the cassette. Woolton had come back from a hectic day canvassing at the House, and was feeling tired as the adrenalin of the first ballot began to wear off. He had heeded the advice of his close colleagues not to overdo the canvassing, and to get a couple of good nights' rest. He was planning later in the week to make three major speeches, and he would need to conserve his energy.

He was sitting in his favourite armchair sketching out some preliminary speech notes when his wife remembered the tape on the desk.

'By the way, darling, a tape cassette was dropped off for you today without any form of identification. Do you know what it is? A recording of last weekend's speech or a tape of a recent interview, perhaps?'

'Haven't a clue. Pour me another drink and let's listen to it.' He waved broadly in the direction of the stereo unit.

His wife, dutiful as ever, did as he bade. He was just savouring his freshened gin and tonic when the tape deck ate up the last segment of blank tape and with a burst of red light the playback meter on the equipment began to show that the tape heads were reading something. There was a series of low hisses and crackles, it was clearly not a professional recording, and she turned the volume up.

The sound of a girl's laughter filled the room, followed by her low, deep gasp. The noise hypnotised the Wooltons, rooting them to the spot. For several minutes, the speakers

319

gave out the sound of a series of shorter, higher breaths as the unmistakable sounds of sex were accompanied by the rhythmic banging of a bedhead against a wall. The tape left little to the imagination. The woman's sighs became shorter and more shrill, as the two bodies climbed ever higher, pausing occasionally for breath before pressing on remorselessly until with a shrieking crescendo they had burst through to reach the summit of their mountain. They shared gasps of pleasure and satisfaction before descending gently together, accompanied once more by the sound of the woman's laughter mixed with the deep bass chuckling of her companion.

The laughter stopped for an instant, until the turning tape found the next distinctive sound.

'That was great, Patrick. Can we do it again?' The woman's voice laughed.

'Not if you're going to wake up the whole of bloody Bournemouth!' the unmistakable Lancashire accent said.

Neither Woolton nor his wife had moved since the tape had begun, but now she stepped slowly across the room and switched it off. A soft, gentle tear fell down one cheek as she turned to look at her husband. He could not return her gaze.

'What can I say? I'm sorry, love,' he whispered. 'I'll not lie and tell you it's bogus. But I am sorry, truly. I never meant to hurt you.'

She made no reply. The look of reproach and sorrow on her face cut into him far more deeply than any angry words could have done.

'What do you want me to do?' he asked gently.

She turned on him with real anger flaring in her eyes. 'Pat, I've turned many a blind eye over the last twenty-three years, and I'm not so much of a silly little housewife to think this is the only time. You could at least have had the decency to keep it away from me and not rub my face in it. You owed me that.'

He hung his head, and she let her words sink deep into

him before she continued. 'But one thing my pride will not tolerate is having a little tart like that trying to break up my marriage and make a fool of me. I'll not stand for it. Find out whatever the blackmailing little whore wants, buy her off or go to the police if necessary, but get rid of her. And get rid of this!' She flung the tape at him. 'It doesn't belong in my house. And neither will you if I have to listen to that filth again!'

He looked at her with tears in his own eyes now. 'I'll sort it out first thing in the morning. You'll hear no more about it.'

THURSDAY 25TH NOVEMBER

Penny cast an unwelcoming frown in the direction of the steel grey November sky, and stepped carefully onto the pavement from the Earl's Court mansion block in which she lived. The weather men had been talking for days about the possibility of a sudden cold snap, and now it had arrived with a vengeance. As she tried to pick her way over frozen puddles, she regretted her decision to wear high heels instead of boots. She was moving slowly along the edge of the pavement when a car door swung open in front of her, blocking her path.

She bent low to tell the driver to be more bloody careful when she saw Woolton at the wheel. She beamed at him but he did not return her warmth. He was looking straight ahead, not at her as she obeyed his clipped instruction and slipped into the passenger seat.

'What is it you want?' he demanded in a voice which was as frozen as the morning air.

'What are you offering,' she smiled, but there was an edge of uncertainty creeping in as she began to discern the ice in his words. She had never seen him so soulless.

He turned to look at her for the first time. He cursed quietly at his folly when he saw how attractive she still seemed to him.

'Did you have to send that tape to me at home? It was a particularly cruel thing to do, because my wife heard it. It was also extremely stupid, because it means she knows about it and so you can't blackmail me. No newspaper or radio station will touch it, the potential libel damages will frighten them off, so there's not much use you can make of it.'

He hoped she would be too stupid to see how much damage the tape could do to him in the wrong hands, and his bluff seemed to have worked as he watched the sparkle drain out of her eyes and the lustre fade from her cheeks.

'Patrick, what on earth are you talking about?'

'The tape you sent me, you silly trollop. Don't go bloody coy on me!'

'I sent you no tape. I haven't the slightest idea what you are talking about.'

The unexpected assault on her feelings and the unfathomable questions he was throwing at her had come as a considerable shock, and she began to sob and gasp for breath. He grabbed her arm ferociously and tears of real pain began to flow.

'The tape! The tape! You sent me the tape!'

'What tape, Patrick? Why are you hurting me . . . ?'

The trickle had become a flood and now a torrent and, as the outside world began to disappear behind misted windows, he began to realise he had misunderstood. He began to spit out his words, staccato-like, so there could be no doubt about their seriousness.

'Look at me and tell me you did not send me a tape of us in Bournemouth.'

'No. No. I sent no tape. I don't know . . .' She suddenly gasped and stopped crying, his words at last piercing through her confusion. 'There's a tape of us in Bournemouth? God, Patrick, that's horrid. But who?'

Her bottom lip quivered in surprise and horror. He released her arm, and his head sank slowly onto the steering wheel.

'Yesterday a cassette tape arrived at my home address. The tape was of us in bed at the party conference.'

'And you thought that I had sent it and was trying to blackmail you? Why, you miserable bastard!'

'I . . . I didn't know what to think. I hoped it was you, Penny.'

'Why? Why me?' she shouted in disgust.

He took his head off the wheel to look once more at her. He had suddenly aged, his skin stretched like old parchment across his cheeks, his eyes red and tired.

'I hoped it was you, Penny, because if it's not you then I haven't the faintest idea who did manage to record us. And it can be no coincidence that it has arrived now, so many weeks after it was made. It means they're not trying to blackmail me for money, but over the leadership race.'

His voice faded to a whisper. 'As far as next Tuesday goes, I'm dead.'

Woolton spent the rest of the morning trying to think constructively. He had no doubt it was the leadership race which had caused the sudden appearance of the tape; a blackmailer simply wanting money would have had no reason to wait so long before striking. It was the leadership and its power, not money, they were interested in, and he knew their price would be too high. He suspected it was the Russians, who would not be as understanding as the New Orleans police. No, he could not stand.

Faced with such a problem, some might have decided to fade gently from the scene and pray that their quiet retirement would not be disturbed. That was not Woolton's style. He would rather go down fighting, and try to salvage whatever he could from the wreckage of his dreams.

He was in a determined mood by the time the press conference he had called gathered shortly after lunch. With no time to make more formal arrangements he had summoned the media to meet him on the other side of the river directly opposite the Houses of Parliament and under the shade of St Thomas's Hospital, where the Thames and the tower of Big Ben would provide a suitably dramatic backdrop. As soon as the cameramen were ready, he began.

'Good afternoon. I've got a short statement to make, and I'm sorry that I will not have time afterwards for questions. But I hope you will not be disappointed.

'Following the ballot on Tuesday, it seems as if only

325

three candidates have any realistic chance of success. Indeed, I understand that all the other candidates have already announced that they do not intend to stand in the second round next week. So, as you gentlemen have put it, this is a three-horse race.

'Of course, I'm delighted and honoured to be one of those three, but three can be an unlucky number. There are not three real alternatives in this election, only two. Either the Party can stick to the practical approach to politics which has proved so successful and kept us in power for over a decade. Or it can develop a new raft of policies, sometimes called conscience politics, which will get Government much more deeply involved – some would say entrapped – in trying to sort out the everyday problems of individual people and families.'

There was a stir amongst the reporters at this sharp public acknowledgement of the division between the two wings of the Party which politicians habitually denied existed.

'I don't believe that a new emphasis on conscience politics would be appropriate – indeed, I think that however well intentioned that emphasis may be, it would in reality be a disaster for the Party and the country. I think that is also the view of the clear majority within the Party.

'Yet paradoxically that is just the way we could end up drifting if that majority support for a pragmatic approach to politics is divided between two candidates, Mr Urquhart and myself. I am a practical man. I don't deal in personalities but in hard-nosed politics. Because of that I believe it would be wrong for my personal ambitions to stand in the way of achieving those policies in which I believe.'

The cold air was condensing his breath and setting fire to his words.

'So I have decided to ensure that the support for those general policies is not divided. I am withdrawing from the race. I shall be casting my own personal vote for Francis

Urquhart, who I sincerely hope will be our next Prime Minister. I have nothing more to say.'

His last words were almost lost in the clatter of a hundred camera shutters, which continued to click as they captured the sight of Woolton striding so fast up the riverside steps towards his waiting car that he was almost running. A few gave chase, but were unable to catch him before he reached the car and was driven off across Westminster Bridge in the direction of the Foreign Office. The rest simply stood in a state of considerable bewilderment, trying to ensure that they had not only accurately recorded but also understood what Woolton had said. He had given them no time for questions, no opportunity to develop theories or surmise any hidden meaning behind his words. They had only what he had given them, and they would have to report it straight – which is precisely what Woolton intended.

His wife was no less confused when he returned home later that evening and they watched his dramatic announcement lead off the *Nine O'Clock News.*

'I understand why you had to back out, Patrick, and I suppose that ought to be punishment enough. I shall go on supporting you, as I always have. But why did you decide to support Urquhart, for Heaven's sake? I never knew you were that close.'

'That superior bugger? I'm not close to him. Don't even like him!'

'Then why?'

'Because I'm fifty-five and Michael Samuel is forty-eight, which means that he could be in Downing Street for twenty years until I'm dead and buried as a politician. Francis Urquhart is sixty-two, and is likely to be in office for no more than five years. So with Urquhart, there's a chance that there will be another leadership race before I retire. In the meantime, if I can find out who is behind that tape, or they fall under a bus or get driven over by a Ministerial limousine, then I'm in with a second chance.'

His pipe was hurling thick blue smoke into the air as he worked on his logic.

'In any event, I had nothing to gain from remaining neutral. Samuel would never have tolerated me in his Cabinet. So instead I've handed the election to Urquhart on a plate, and he will have to show some public gratitude for that.'

He smiled at his wife for the first time since they had heard the tape. 'How do you fancy being the Chancellor of the Exchequer's wife for the next couple of years?'

FRIDAY 26TH NOVEMBER

The following morning's weather was still well below freezing, but a new front had passed over London bringing with it crystal blue skies to replace the leaden cloud cover of the previous day. As Urquhart looked out from his Commons office across the Thames, the riverscape glowed brightly in the clear winter sunshine like a brilliant symbol of what lay ahead for him. As he gazed at the press reports of Woolton's endorsement, he felt invulnerable, almost home.

Then the door burst open. It was O'Neill. Even before Urquhart could demand to know what on earth he thought he was doing, the babbling commenced. The words were fired like bullets in a battle, being hurled at Urquhart as if to overwhelm and force his submission.

'They know, Francis. They've discovered that the file is missing. The locks were bent and one of the secretaries noticed and the Chairman's called us all in. I'm sure he suspects me. What are we going to do? What are we going to *do*?'

Urquhart was shaking him to stop the incomprehensible gabble, and he was surprised at how much physical force was needed before the man was brought under some sort of control.

'Roger, for God's sake shut up!' He pushed him bodily into a chair and the shock caused O'Neill to pause for breath. 'Now slowly, Roger. What are you trying to say?'

'The files. The confidential party files on Samuel you asked me to send to the Sunday newspapers.' He was panting for breath from physical and nervous exhaustion. 'Well, I was able to use my pass key to get into the basement storage room without any trouble, but the files are all in locked cabinets. I had to force the lock, Francis. I'm sorry but I had no choice. Not very much but it bent a little. There's so much dust and cobwebs around that it looked as if no one had been in there since the Boer War, but yesterday some bitch of a secretary decided to go in there and noticed the bent lock. Now they've gone through the whole lot and discovered that Samuel's file is missing.'

'You sent them the original file? You didn't just copy the interesting bits as I told you?'

'Francis, the file was very thick, it would have taken hours to copy. I didn't know which bits they would be most interested in, so – I sent them the lot. It could have been years before anyone noticed the file was missing, and then they would have thought it was simply misplaced.'

'You bloody fool, you . . .'

'Francis, don't shout at me!' O'Neill screamed. 'It's me who's taken all the risks, not you. The Chairman's personally interrogating everyone with a pass key and there are only nine of us. He's asked to see me this afternoon. I'm sure he suspects me. And I'm not going to take the blame all on my own. Why should I? I only did what you told me . . . Francis, I can't go on lying. I simply can't stand it any more. I'll go to pieces!'

Urquhart froze as he realised the truth behind O'Neill's desperate words. This quivering man in front of him had no resistance or judgement left; he was beginning to crumble and flake like some old, brittle newspaper. The eyes were flickering furiously once more as the words tumbled out, and Urquhart realised that not even for a week, not even for *this* week, could O'Neill control himself. He was on the very edge. The slightest wind could send him hurtling down towards destruction. And he would take Urquhart with him.

'Roger, you are over-anxious. You have nothing to fear, no one can prove anything and you must remember that I'm on your side. You are not alone in this. Look, don't go

330

back to the office, call in sick and go home. The Chairman can wait till Monday. And tomorrow I would like you to come and be my house guest in Hampshire. Come for lunch and stay overnight while we talk the whole thing through – together, just the two of us.'

O'Neill gripped Urquhart's hand in delight and relief, like a cripple clinging to his crutch.

'But don't tell anyone that you are coming to visit me. It would be very embarrassing if the press were to find out that a senior party official is my house guest just before the final leadership ballot – it wouldn't look right for either of us – so this must be strictly between the two of us. Not even your secretary must know.'

O'Neill tried to mutter a word of thanks but was cut short by three enormous sneezes which had Urquhart reeling in disgust. O'Neill didn't seem to notice as he wiped his face and smiled with the new found eagerness of a spaniel.

'I'll be there, Francis. I'll be there.'

SATURDAY 27TH NOVEMBER

Urquhart got up before dawn. He hadn't slept, but was not in the least tired. He knew this was to be a very special day. Well before the early light of morning was breaking above the New Forest moors, he dressed in his favourite hunting jacket, pulled on his boots and strode out into the freezing morning air along the bridle path which led across Emery Down towards Lyndhurst. The ground mist clung closely to the hedgerows, discouraging the birds and damping down all sound. It pressed around him like a cocoon and he was utterly alone, a man on an empty planet who must make his own decisions and decide his own fate.

He had walked nearly three miles before he began a long, slow climb up the southern face of a hill, and slowly the fog began to clear as the rising sun cut through the damp air. He had just emerged from a bank of swirling mist when he saw the stag across the patch of sun-cleared hillside, browsing amongst the damp gorse. He slipped gently behind a low bush, waiting, like a hunter for his prey. But he was not a complete hunter. He had never hunted a man. He had been too young for Hitler, too busy at university for Korea, too late for Suez. He had never known what it was like to exchange another man's life for his own, to condemn someone before they had the chance to do the same to you.

He wondered how his brother had died. He imagined him in a shallow dugout underneath a Dunkirk hedgerow, waiting for the barrel of the first German tank to appear over the brow of the hill. As he lay there ready to kill, to destroy as many other lives as possible, had he felt exhilarated like some savage animal by the chance to shed

333

blood? Had he been immobilised by terror, a man turned rabbit by panic in spite of his training and sense of duty? Or had he felt a calming certainty about the need for self-preservation which had overcome all apprehension and a lifetime of Sunday School morality – just as Urquhart felt now?

The stag edged closer towards him as it continued to browse, oblivious of his presence. Suddenly, Urquhart stood bolt upright, not twenty yards in front of the deer which froze in confusion. Neither breathed as they stood in confrontation, until Urquhart let forth a peal of almighty laughter, racking his body with the sound which bounced off the surrounding banks of mist. The stag, sensing that it should already have been dead, leapt to one side and in an instant was gone.

Urquhart spent all morning walking through the woodlands and across the downs, not returning home until almost noon. When he did so, he walked straight into his study without changing, and picked up the phone.

He first called the editors of the four leading Sunday newspapers. He discovered that two of them were writing editorials supporting him, one was supporting Samuel and the other was noncommittal. However, all four were confident in varying degrees that he had a clear advantage, a conclusion confirmed by the *Observer*'s pollsters who by now had succeeded in contacting a substantial majority of the Parliamentary Party. The survey predicted that Urquhart would win comfortably with 60 per cent of the vote.

'It seems it would take an earthquake to stop you winning now, Francis,' the editor had said.

He then called a Kent number, and asked to be put through to Dr Christian.

'Good afternoon, Chief Whip. Nice of you to take time out of your weekend to enquire about Charles. He is progressing very well indeed, I'm delighted to say. His brother the Prime Minister is down here almost every

334

other day to see him, and it's been like a tonic to both of them.'

'There's something else I wanted to ask you, doctor. I need your advice. We have a Member of Parliament who has a real problem. He's a cocaine addict, and recently his behaviour has deteriorated rapidly. His physical mannerisms – the nasal problems, exaggerated eye movements – have become much worse. His speech varies between a chaotic cavalry charge and a slow, incomprehensible drool. He has become very agitated and disturbed and has caused several public scenes. He has grown utterly paranoid, making wild accusations and threats. The man is clearly very ill, and I am trying to persuade him to take treatment but, as you keep telling me, addicts are often the last people to face up to their problems.

'In the meantime, he occupies a very sensitive position of considerable trust. It could inflict untold damage if he were to break that trust and be indiscreet. The question I have for you, doctor, is to what extent a man in that situation is able to keep his word and any sense of perspective. Is there any chance we can trust him?'

'You sound as if you have a very sick man on your hands, Mr Urquhart. By the time he is unable to keep his behaviour private but makes a public exhibition of himself on a regular basis, showing those sort of physical symptoms, then he is in the final stages of collapse. He is probably taking the drug several times every day, which means he's not only unable to do his work but – much more seriously from your point of view – has lost all self restraint. The habit is very expensive and he will do anything to continue his supply of drugs. Lie, steal, cheat, sometimes kill. He will sell anything he can lay his hands on in exchange for drugs, which includes any information he may have. He will also be getting very paranoid, and if you try to persuade him too hard to seek treatment against his will, he may turn on you as a vicious enemy and do anything to destroy you. I have seen it tear husbands from their wives and mothers from their children. They are driven by a need which stretches far beyond all others.'

'He's already threatened to break the deepest confidences. Are you saying he might be serious about that?'

'Deadly serious.'

'Then we have a problem.'

'A very considerable one, by the sounds of it. I'm sorry. Please let me know if I can help.'

'You already have, doctor. Thank you.'

Urquhart was still sitting in his study when he heard O'Neill's car draw up in the driveway outside.

As the Irishman stepped into the hallway, Urquhart could not help but note that the man who now stood in front of him was almost unrecognisable as the man he had taken to dinner in his club less than six months before. The casual elegance which O'Neill used to effect had now turned into outright scruffiness. His hair was unkempt, the clothes were badly creased as if he had found them at the bottom of a laundry bag, the tie hung loosely round the unbuttoned and crumpled collar. Trying to look at O'Neill as if meeting him for the first time, Urquhart was shocked. The gradual decline over several months had become part of O'Neill's pattern for those colleagues who saw him frequently, and had largely hidden the true extent to which he had deteriorated. The once suave and fashionable communicator now looked like a common tramp. And those deep, twinkling eyes, the features which women had found so captivating and clients so enthusing, had sunk without trace, to be replaced by two wild, staring orbs which flashed around the room in constant pursuit of something they could never find. This was a man possessed.

Urquhart led O'Neill to one of the second floor guest rooms, saying little as they wound their way through the mansion's long corridors while O'Neill babbled away about whatever came into his mind. Increasingly in recent days his conversation had turned to others and their opinion of him; in O'Neill's mind the whole world seemed slowly and unjustly to be turning on him, betraying him. His Chairman, his Prime Minister, his secretary now. Even his local policeman seemingly patrolled the street for no other purpose than to spy on O'Neill, waiting to pounce on him.

O'Neill threw his overnight bag carelessly on the bed, showing little interest in the room and its fine views across the New Forest scenery. They returned the way they had come down two flights of stairs until Urquhart led him through the heavy oak doors into his book-lined study. He suggested O'Neill help himself to a drink, and watched with clinical concentration as O'Neill filled the entire tumbler with whisky and began draining it. Soon the alcohol had begun to do battle with the cocaine, and the raging in O'Neill's eyes became just a touch less frenetic even as his tongue became thicker and his conversation began increasingly to lose its coherence. Depressant fought stimulant inside him, never achieving peace or balance, always leaving him on the point of toppling backwards or forwards into the abyss.

'Roger,' began Urquhart, 'it looks as if we shall be in Downing Street by the end of the week. I've been doing some thinking about what I shall need, and I thought we might talk about what you wanted.'

O'Neill took another gulp before answering.

'Francis, I'm bowled over that you should be thinking of me. You're going to be a class act as Prime Minister, really you are. As it happens, I've also been giving some thought to it all, and I was wondering whether you could use someone like me in Downing Street – you know, as a special adviser or even your press spokesman. You're going to need a lot of help and we seem to have worked so well together that I thought . . .'

Urquhart waved his hand for silence. 'Roger, there are scores of civil servants to take on those responsibilities, people who are already doing that work. What I need is someone like you in charge of the political propaganda, who can supplement the civil service properly and can be trusted to avoid all those mistakes which the party organisation has been making in recent months. I would very much like you to stay at party headquarters – under a new Chairman, of course.'

A look of concern furrowed O'Neill's brow. The same meaningless job, watching from the sidelines as the civil service ran the show, as aloof as he thought they were incompetent? What the devil was in it for him?

'But to do something like that effectively, Francis, I shall need support, some special status. I . . . thought we had mentioned a knighthood.'

'Yes, indeed, Roger. That would be no more than you deserve. You've been absolutely indispensable to me, and you must understand how grateful I am. But I've been making enquiries. That sort of honour may not be possible, at least in the short term. There are so many who are already in line to be honoured when a Prime Minister retires and a new Government comes in, and as you know there is a limit on the number of honours even a Prime Minister can hand out. I'm afraid it could take a while . . .'

Urquhart was determined to test O'Neill, to bully him, disappoint him, torment him, subject him to all the pressures he would inevitably come under in the course of the next few months, trying to see how far O'Neill could be pushed before reaching the limit. He had not a moment longer to wait as the Irishman hit his limit and burst through it with volcanic passion.

'Francis, you promised! That was part of the deal! You gave your word, and now you're telling me it's not on. No job. No knighthood. Not now, not soon, not ever! You've got what you wanted and now you think you can get rid of me. Well, think again! I've lied, I've cheated, I've forged and I've stolen for you. Now you treat me just like all the rest. I'm not going to have people laughing at me behind my back any more and looking down their noses as if I were some smelly Irish peasant. I deserve that knighthood and I demand it!'

The tumbler was emptied and O'Neill, shaking with emotion, refilled it from the decanter, spilling the malt whisky as it flowed over the edge of the glass. He slurped a huge mouthful down before resuming his avalanche of anger.

'We've been through this all together, as a team. Everything I've done has been for you, and you wouldn't have been able to get into Downing Street without me. We succeed together – or we fail together. If I'm going to end up on the compost heap, Francis, I'm damned if I'm going to be there alone. You can't afford to let me tell what I know. You owe me!'

The words had been spoken, the threat made. Urquhart had offered O'Neill a gauntlet of provocation, which almost without pause had been picked up and slapped back into Urquhart's face. It was clear it was no longer a matter of whether O'Neill would lose control, but how quickly, and it had taken no time at all.

There was no point in continuing to test him, and Urquhart brought it to a rapid conclusion with a broad smile and shake of the head.

'Roger, my dear friend. You misunderstand me entirely. I am only saying that it will be difficult this time around, in the New Year's Honours List. But there's another one in the Spring, for the Queen's Birthday. Just a few weeks away, really. I'm only asking you to wait until then. And if you want a job in Downing Street, then we shall find one. We work as a team, you and I. You have deserved it, and on my word of honour I will not forget what I owe you.'

O'Neill could not respond above a murmur. His passion had been spent, the alcohol burrowing its way into his nervous system, his emotions torn asunder and now pasted back together. He sat there drained, ashen, exhausted.

'Look, have a sleep before lunch. We can sort out precisely what you want later,' suggested Urquhart.

Without another word, O'Neill slumped in his chair and closed his eyes. Within seconds his breathing had slowed as he found sleep, but his fingers kept twitching with little spasms of energy as his eyes flickered beneath their lids in constant turmoil. Wherever O'Neill's mind was wandering, it had not found peace.

Urquhart sat looking at the shrunken figure. O'Neill was drooling, with mucus dripping from his nose. It was a sight which would have left some men feeling pity, but Urquhart felt a chilling emptiness. As a youth he had wandered the moors and hills on his family's estates with a labrador which had earned his tolerance through years of faithful service as a gun dog and constant companion. Yet the dog had grown old and less capable, and one day the gillie had come and explained with great sorrow that the dog had suffered a stroke, and must be put down. Urquhart had visited the dog in the stable where it slept, and was greeted with the pitiful sight of an animal which had lost control of itself. The rear legs were paralysed, it had fouled itself and its nose and mouth, like O'Neill's, were dribbling uncontrollably. It was as much as it could do to raise a whimper of greeting as the tail swung laboriously back and forth. There was a tear in the old gillie's eye as he fondled its ear to bring it some comfort.

'There'll be no more chasing o' rabbits for you, old fella,' he had whispered.

Urquhart had dispatched the animal with a single blow of his rifle butt, instructing the gillie to bury the body well away from the house. As he stared now at O'Neill, he remembered the dog, and wondered why some men deserved less pity than dumb animals.

He left O'Neill in the library, and made his way quietly towards the kitchen. Under the sink he found a pair of rubber kitchen gloves, and stuffed them along with a teaspoon into his pocket before proceeding through the back door towards the outhouses which served as garage, workshop and storage. The old wooden door groaned open on its rusty hinges as he entered the potting shed, and the mustiness hit him immediately. He used this place rarely, but he knew precisely what he was looking for. High on the far wall stood an ancient, battered kitchen cupboard which had been thrown out of the old scullery many years before, and which now served as a home for half-used tins of paint, stray cans of oil and a vigorous army of woodworm. The door opened with a protesting creak, and he immediately found the tightly sealed can. He put on the rubber gloves before taking it from its shelf and walking back towards the house, holding the can well away from him as if he were carrying a flaming torch.

Once back in the house, he made his way quietly upstairs after checking that O'Neill was still soundly asleep. As soon as he had reached the guest room, he entered and turned the key in the door, securing it behind him. He was relieved to discover that O'Neill had not locked his overnight case, and taking great care not to leave any signs of interference he began methodically to search through its contents. He found what he was looking for in the toilet bag, crammed alongside the toothpaste and shaving gear. It was a tin of men's talcum powder, the head of which came away from the shoulders when he gave it a slight wrench. Inside there was no talcum powder but a small self-sealing polythene bag, with the equivalent of a tablespoon full of white powder nestling in one corner.

He took the bag over to the polished mahogany writing desk which stood by the window, and extracted three large sheets of blue writing paper from the drawer before slowly pouring the contents of the bag into a small mound on top of one of the blue sheets. Gingerly he opened the tin he had brought from the potting shed and out of it spooned another similarly sized pile of white powder onto a second sheet. Using the flat end of the spoon as a spatula he proceeded with the greatest care to divide both mounds of white powder into two equal halves, scraping one half of each onto the third page of writing paper. With relief he could see that they were of an almost identical colour and consistency, the white grains standing out against the smooth blue background, and he mixed the two halves quickly together to hide the fact that they had ever been anything but one and the same. He made a single crease along the middle of the paper, and prepared to pour the mixture back into the polythene bag.

At that moment it hit him. The conviction which had filled his veins turned to burning acid, the certainty which had guided his hand suddenly deserted him, and the composure in which he took so much pride vanished. His will had become a battleground. The morality and restraint which the system had tried to beat into him from birth screamed at him to stop, to change his mind, even now to turn back, while his guts told him that morality was weakness. What mattered was reality. And the reality was that he was about to become the most powerful man in the country – so long as his nerve held.

It was clarity of purpose which he needed now, which the Government needed. All too often Administrations had been brought to their knees as leaders listened to the siren voices, confronting the harsh realities of power only to withdraw into weakness and compromise. Didn't they say that once they were elected, all politicians were the same? Most politicians *were* the same – weak, irresolute, insignificant characters, who fouled the nest and got in the way of those who had the resolve to move forward.

Great men had an inner strength, and he was furious with himself now for having doubts. Whether they wished to recognise it or not, all politicians played with other men's lives, and all lives had a price – not just in war, but in placing limits on the care of the sick and the elderly, in setting punishment for crime, in sending men down coal mines or out to the angry fishing grounds of the Arctic Circle. The national interest required sacrifice from many, and often of the few.

He looked out at the mists which still clung tenaciously

to the tree tops of the New Forest, blotting out the horizon and transporting his thoughts. He felt as Caesar must have done when faced with the Rubicon, uncertain of what lay on the opposite shore, knowing that he could never retrace his footsteps. Few men were favoured enough to take control of the great decisions of life; most simply suffered the consequences of decisions taken by others. He thought of his brother in the hedgerows of Dunkirk, a pawn like a million others in the games of the great. Urquhart could be one of the great, *should* be one of them, and O'Neill was as insignificant a pawn as he could imagine.

Once more he picked up the paper with its load of white powder. His hand was still trembling, but less than before. He was glad he was not looking down the sights of a shotgun at some deer; he would have missed. Or building a house of cards. The powder slipped unprotesting into the polythene bag, which he then quickly resealed. It looked as if it had never been touched.

Five minutes later he had flushed all the remaining powder down the toilet, following that with the torn-up pieces of writing paper. The writing table was carefully wiped with a damp rag and polished with a towel to hide any trace that he had sat there, and he replaced the polythene bag in the talcum tin, the tin in the toilet bag and the bag back where he had found it. He was absolutely satisfied that O'Neill would never know his case had been tampered with.

He returned to the bathroom where he ran the taps at full flow. He washed the spoon meticulously and as the gushing water swirled down the drain, he poured the remaining contents of the tin into the water and watched it disappear.

Finally, he left the house once more by the kitchen door, walking across the carefully manicured lawns to a far corner behind the weeping willow tree, where his gardener always had a small pile of garden rubbish ready to burn. It was soon ablaze, with the empty tin and rubber gloves buried deep in its midst. When he was satisfied the fire was burning thoroughly, he returned to the house, poured himself a large whisky which he swallowed as greedily as O'Neill, and at last relaxed.

It was done.

O'Neill had been asleep for three hours when he was roused by someone shaking him fiercely by the shoulder. Slowly he focused his eyes, and saw Urquhart leaning over him, instructing him to wake up.

'Roger. There's had to be a change of plan. I've just had a call from the BBC asking if they can send a film crew over here to shoot some domestic footage for their news coverage on Tuesday. Samuel has apparently already agreed, so I felt I had little choice but to say yes. They will be here in about an hour and will be staying all afternoon. It's just what we didn't want. If they find you here it will start all sorts of speculation about how party headquarters is interfering in the leadership race. We must avoid any confusion at this late stage. I'm sorry. I think it best that you leave right away.'

O'Neill was still trying to find second gear on his tongue as Urquhart poured some coffee past it, explaining once again how sorry he was about the weekend but how glad he was they had cleared up any confusion between them.

'Remember, Roger. A knighthood next Whitsun, and we can sort out the job you want next week. I'm so happy you were able to come. I really am so grateful,' Urquhart was saying as he tipped O'Neill into his car.

He watched as O'Neill's car edged its way carefully and with practised caution down the driveway and out through the gates.

'Goodbye, Roger,' he whispered.

SUNDAY 28TH NOVEMBER

True to the information their editors had given him the previous day, the quality Sunday newspapers made good reading for the Chief Whip and his supporters.

'Urquhart ahead', announced the *Sunday Times*, adding the endorsement of its editorial columns to boost the Chief Whip's campaign still further. Both the *Sunday Telegraph* and the *Express* openly backed Urquhart, while the *Mail on Sunday* tried uncomfortably to straddle the fence. Only the *Observer* gave editorial backing to Samuel, but even this was deeply qualified by its front page report of Urquhart's clear lead in the opinion polls.

It took one of the more scurrilous Sunday papers to give the campaign a real shake. 'Samuel was a commie!' it screamed over half its front page, declaring it had discovered that Samuel had been an active left-winger while at university. Indeed, when contacted by a friendly sounding reporter from the newspaper who said he was 'doing a feature on the early days' of both Samuel and Urquhart and had discovered some youthful indulgence in radical politics, Samuel had rather reluctantly admitted to a passing involvement in many different university clubs, saying that until the age of twenty he had been a sympathiser with a number of fashionable causes which, thirty years later, seemed naive and misplaced.

'But we have documentary evidence to suggest that they included CND and gay rights, Mr Samuel,' the reporter pressed.

'Not that old nonsense again,' responded Samuel testily. He thought he had finished with those wild charges twenty years ago when he had first stood for Parliament. An opponent had sent a letter of accusation to party head-quarters; the allegations had been fully investigated by the Party's Standing Committee on Candidates and he had been given a clean bill of health. But here they were again, risen from the dead after all these years, just a few days before the final ballot.

'I did all the things that an eighteen-year-old college student in those days did. I went on two CND marches, and was even persuaded to take out a regular subscription to a student newspaper which I later found was run by the gay rights movement.' He tried to raise a chuckle at the memory, determined not to give any impression that he had something to hide.

'I was also quite a strong supporter of the anti-apartheid movement, and to this day I actively oppose apartheid, although I intensely dislike the violent methods used by some of the self-proclaimed leaders of the movement,' he had told the journalist. 'Regrets? No, I have no real regrets about those early involvements; they weren't so much youthful mistakes as an excellent testing ground for the opinions I now hold. I know how foolish CND is – I've been there!'

Samuel could scarcely believe the manner in which his remarks had been interpreted in the newspaper. It was ludicrous to suggest he had ever been a Communist; he wondered for a moment whether it was actually libellous. Yet underneath the headline, the article got even worse.

'I marched for the Russians', admitted Samuel last night, recalling those days of the 1960s when ban-the-bomb marches frequently ended in violence and disruption.

He also acknowledged that he had been a financial supporter of homosexual rights groups, making regular monthly payments to the Cambridge Gay Charter Movement which was amongst the earliest organisations pushing for a change in the laws on homosexuality.

Samuel's early left-wing involvement has long been a source of concern to party leaders. In 1970 when the twenty-seven-year-old Samuel applied to party headquarters to fight as an official party candidate in the general election of that year, the Party Chairman wrote to demand an explanation of 'the frequency with which your name was associated at university with causes which have no sympathy for our Party'.

He seemed to satisfy the Party then, and won his way into the House of Commons at that election. However, last night Samuel was still defiant about those early involvements.

'I have no regrets', he said, acknowledging that he still sympathised strongly with some of those left-wing movements he used to support.

For the rest of the day there was fluster and commotion amongst the political reporters and in the Samuel household. Nobody really believed that he was a closet Communist; it was another of those silly, sensationalist pieces intended to raise circulation rather than the public's consciousness, but it had to be checked out, causing confusion and disruption at a time when Samuel was trying desperately to reassure his supporters and refocus attention on the serious issues of the campaign.

By midday Lord Williams had issued a stinging denunciation of the newspaper for using confidential documents which had been stolen from a security cabinet by forcing the lock. The newspaper immediately responded that, while the Party itself seemed to be unforgivably incompetent with safeguarding their confidential material, the newspaper was happy to fulfil its public obligations and return the folder on Samuel to its rightful owners at party headquarters – which they did later that day in time to catch the television news and give the story yet another lease of life.

Most observers, after discussing the story at some length, dismissed it as a passing misfortune for Samuel brought about by the typical incompetence of party headquarters. But Samuel's campaign had run into a lot of misfortune since it began. It was not reassuring for someone who claimed to be on top of events, and it was definitely not the way to spend the final weekend of the leadership race.

The phone call upset Krajewski. He had been trying hard to keep a grip on his wayward emotions about Mattie, being alternately eaten away by frustration at her inconsistency and consumed with hunger for her body. He was also discovering that he simply downright missed her, and only occasionally did he succeed in forcing his thoughts about her to the back of his mind. When one of his colleagues telephoned to say that he had met Mattie and that she looked tired and unwell, he hadn't needed a second to realise how concerned he still was.

She had agreed to see him, but rejected his suggestion that he should come straight round. She didn't want him to see the apartment this way, with the dirty plates, the empty cartons which seemed to infest every available table top, and the worn clothes which had simply been dumped in the corner. The last few days had been hell. Unable to sleep, her mind and her emotions snarled up in one immense knot, her bed like a slab of ice, she was no longer sure which way to turn. The walls closed in around her, squeezing out her ability to think straight or feel anything other than growing depression.

So when Krajewski called she had shown little enthusiasm even though she knew she needed support from someone. Reluctantly she had been cajoled into meeting him at the coffee shop on the eastern edge of the Serpentine, the winding duck-strewn lake which dominates the centre of Hyde Park. He cursed as he hurried towards it. The bitter November wind was raising foam-topped waves as it sliced across the water, and as he approached the empty, lifeless coffee shop he realised that it must have closed for the winter. He found the small, forlorn figure of Mattie sheltering under the eaves, wrapped in a thin anorak which suddenly seemed too large for her. She appeared to have shrunk since they had last met. There were uncharacteristic dark rings under her eyes, and the vitality which normally lit her face was missing. She looked awful.

'What a bloody silly place for us to meet,' he apologised.

'Don't worry, Johnnie. I guess I needed the fresh air.'

He wanted to put his arms around her and squeeze the chill out of her bones, but instead he tried to smile cheerfully.

'What's new with Britain's top female journalist?' he enquired. Immediately he wanted to bite his tongue off. He hadn't intended sarcasm, not at all, but it was a clumsy choice of words. She shivered before she replied.

'Perhaps you're right to laugh. A few days ago I thought I had the world at my feet.'

'And now?'

'Now it's all gone wrong. The job . . . The story . . .' – a slight pause – '. . . You. I thought I could do it all on my own. I was wrong. Sorry.'

This was a new Mattie, all full of self-doubt and insecurity. He didn't know what to say, so said nothing.

'When I was a young girl my grandfather used to take me out onto the Yorkshire dales. He said it was a lot like parts of Norway. The weather could get bitter and inhospitable up there but I never had any fears. Grandpa was always there with a helping hand and a smile. He always carried a flask of hot soup and I never felt better or warmer than when I was out with him, no matter how hard it blew. Then one day I thought I was grown up, didn't need Grandpa any more, so I slipped away on my own. I left the track and the ground started getting softer. Soon I was sinking up to my ankles and then slipping deeper and deeper.' She was shivering again. 'I couldn't get out. The more I struggled the deeper I became stuck. I thought I would never get out. It was the first time in my life that I had known what real fear was. But then Grandpa found me and plucked me out, and hugged me while I cried and dried my tears and made everything better.' Johnnie noted how frail and vulnerable she looked now inside the voluminous folds of her anorak, as if she was reliving the experience all over again.

'It's just like that now, Johnnie. I'm desperately trying to find some firm ground, something I can stand on and believe in, both about the story and in my own life. But I'm just sinking deeper and deeper, Grandpa's no longer around and I'm afraid. Do you understand? I feel as if I shall never step on solid ground again.'

'But haven't you seen the Sunday newspapers?' he encouraged. 'Someone filched Samuel's personal papers. Another bombshell hits the leadership race from party headquarters. Even more evidence pointing directly at Teddy Williams. Isn't that firm ground?'

She shook her head sadly. 'If only it were that simple.'

'I don't understand,' he said. 'We've got the deliberate theft of personal files. We've got the tampering with the central computer file – that's deliberate too. We've had the leaking of all sorts of damaging material out of party headquarters to you, to Kendrick, seemingly to anyone who was passing in the neighbourhood. We've got party officials opening accommodation addresses in false names, and politicians' corpses lying around like hedgehogs on a motorway. What more do you need? And it all leads back to party headquarters – which must mean Williams. He can't make Prime Minister himself, so he's making sure he controls whoever does.'

'You're missing the point, Johnnie. Why on earth should Williams need to steal his own documents? He could simply have copied the vital information without breaking in and stealing the whole bloody file. And he doesn't need to force locks – he's got all the keys. He is supposed to be

Samuel's strongest ally, yet Samuel's campaign has been pedalling backwards ever since the election began.'

Her eyes were burning with disappointment. 'Can you really imagine an elder statesman like Williams framing the Prime Minister for fraud? Or leaking so much material from party headquarters that it has made him look like a doddering imbecile? No, Johnnie. It's not Williams.'

'Then who the hell is it? Samuel? Urquhart? Some other Cabinet Minister? Landless?'

'I don't know,' she cried. 'That's why I feel as if I am drowning! The more I struggle, the deeper I get stuck. Professionally. Emotionally. It's like a great quagmire sucking me under. I'm just not sure about anything any more.'

'I'd like to help you, Mattie. Please don't turn me away.'

'Like Grandpa, you're always there when I need you. Thanks, Johnnie. But I've got to find my own path now or I never will. There's all this confusion inside me; I've got to sort these things out for myself.'

'I can wait,' he said gently.

'But I can't. I've got only two more days to come up with the answer and only one strong lead – Roger O'Neill.'

MONDAY 29TH NOVEMBER

The janitor found the body just after he had clocked on at 4.30 on Monday morning. He was beginning his morning duties at the Rownhams motorway service area just outside Southampton on the M27, starting with cleaning out the toilets, when he discovered that one of the cubicle doors would not open. He was nearing his sixty-eighth birthday, and he cursed as he lowered his old bones gently onto their hands and knees so that he could peer under the door. He had great difficulty getting all the way down, but he didn't need to. He saw the two shoes quite clearly, and that was enough to satisfy his curiosity. There was a man in there, and whether he was drunk, diseased or dying meant nothing to him except that it was going to put him way behind his cleaning schedule, and he cursed again as he staggered off to call his supervisor.

The supervisor was in no better temper when he arrived, and used a screwdriver to open the lock from the outside. But the man's knees were wedged firmly up against the door, and push as hard as they might the two of them could not force it open more than a few inches. The supervisor put his hand around the door, trying to shift the man's knees, but instead grabbed a dangling hand which was as cold as ice. He recoiled in horror and gave a wail of anguish, insisting on washing his hands meticulously before he stumbled off to call the police and an ambulance.

The police arrived shortly after 5 a.m. and, with rather more experience in such matters than the janitor and supervisor, had the cubicle door lifted off its hinges in seconds.

O'Neill's body was sitting there, fully clothed and

slumped against the wall. His face, drained of all colour, was stretched into a leering death mask exposing his teeth and with his eyes staring wide open. In his lap they found two halves of an empty tin of talc, and on the floor beside him they discovered a small polythene bag containing a few grains of white powder and a briefcase stuffed with political pamphlets. They found other small white granules of powder still clinging to the leather cover of the briefcase, which had clearly been placed on O'Neill's lap to provide a flat surface. From one clenched fist they managed to prise a twisted £20 note which had been fashioned into a tube before being crumpled by O'Neill's death fit. His other arm was stretched aloft over his head, as if the grinning corpse was giving one final, hideous salute of farewell.

'Another junkie taking his last fix,' muttered the police sergeant, who had seen more than a few such sights in his time. 'It's more usual to find them with a needle up their arm,' he explained to his young colleague who lacked the relevant experience. 'But this one looks as if he was doing cocaine, and either it was too much for his heart or he's got hold of some adulterated stuff. There's quite a lot of drug pushing goes on around these motorway service stations, and the junkies never know what they're buying from whom. You often get impure drugs being peddled, either diluted with anything from castor sugar to baking powder, or mixed with something rather more lethal. The pushers will sell anything for money and the junkies will pay anything for a fix, whatever it is. This is just one of the unlucky ones.'

He started rummaging through O'Neill's pockets for clues to his identity. 'Funny way the body and face have contorted, though. Well, we can let the police surgeon and the coroner's office sort that one out. Let's get on with it, laddie, and call the ruddy photographers to record this sordid little scene. No use us standing here guessing about . . . Mr Roger O'Neill,' he announced as he found a wallet bearing a few credit cards. 'Wonder who he is?'

'There's a car outside in the car park, been here all night by the looks of it,' volunteered the janitor. 'Probably his.'

'Well, let's take the details and check it out then,' instructed the sergeant.

It was 7.20 by the time the coroner's representative had authorised the removal of the body. The sergeant was making sure the junior officer had finished with the required procedures and the ambulancemen were man-handling the rigid, contorted body out from its seat and onto their stretcher when the call came over the radio.

'Sod it,' the sergeant told the radio controller. 'That'll set the cat amongst the pigeons. I'd better make double sure we've done everything this end before we have CID inspectors, superintendents and chief constables floating in for a look.'

He turned to the fresh-faced constable. 'Got yourself a prize one there, you have. Seems the car is registered to the Government's party headquarters, and our Mr Roger O'Neill is – rather was – a senior party official with his fingers in Downing Street and everywhere else, no doubt. Better make sure you write a full report, lad, or we'll both be for the high jump.'

It had been another sleepless night. Her physical reserves of stamina had just about run out and she was on the point of surrendering to her growing mood of depression when the phone call threw her the lifeline she needed. It was Johnnie, calling from the *Telegraph* news room.

'How's this for another one of your coincidences?' he enquired. 'Just come over on the tape. It seems the South-ampton police found your Roger O'Neill dead in a public lavatory just a few hours ago.'

'Tell me this is simply your tasteless way of saying good morning,' she said without humour.

'Sorry. It's for real. I've already sent a reporter down to the scene, but it appears the local police have called in the Drug Squad. Seems he may have overdosed.'

355

Mattie gasped as one of the pieces fell into place with a noise like a coffin lid slamming closed.

'So that was it. An addict. No wonder he was all over the place . . .' As she spoke she nudged in her excitement the large stack of dirty crockery which had built up beside the kitchen telephone, sending them crashing to the floor.

'Mattie, what on earth . . .'

'Don't you see, Johnnie. He was the key man, the only man we knew for certain was involved in all the dirty tricks. Our Number One lead has just very conveniently disappeared from the scene, the day before they elect a new Prime Minister, leaving us with a big fat zero. Don't you see, Johnnie.'

'What?'

'There's not a moment to waste!' she gasped, as he heard the phone go dead.

Mattie almost didn't find Penny Guy. She had rung the bell of the mansion block continuously for several minutes, and was just about to give up when the latch was released by the electronic buzzer and the door swung open. The door to Penny's flat on the first floor was also ajar, and Mattie walked in. She found Penny sitting quietly on the sofa, curtains drawn, staring at nothing.

Mattie did not speak, but sat down beside her and held her. Slowly Penny's fingers tightened around Mattie's hand, acknowledging her presence, begging her to stay.

'He didn't deserve to die,' Penny said in a hushed, faltering voice. 'He was a weak man, but not an evil one. He was very kind.'

'What was he doing in Southampton?'

'He was spending the weekend with someone. Wouldn't say who. It was one of his silly secrets.'

'Any idea who?'

Penny shook her head with painful slowness.

'Do you know why he died?' Mattie asked.

Penny turned to face her with round, dark eyes which

had a faraway look and from which the shock had squeezed any trace of emotion.

'You're not interested in him, are you? Only in his death.' It was not an accusation, simply a statement of fact.

'I'm sorry he died, Penny. I'm also sorry because I think Roger will be blamed for a lot of bad things that have happened recently. And I don't think he's the one who should be blamed.'

Penny blinked for the first time, as if the question had at last disturbed the emptiness which had taken hold of her.

'Why would they . . . blame Roger?' The words were formed slowly, as if half of her were elsewhere, in a world where O'Neill was still alive and where Penny could still save him.

'Because he's a victim who has been set up to take the blame. Someone has been using Roger, has been twisting him and bending him in a dirty little political game – until Roger snapped.'

Penny considered this for several long moments. 'He's not the only one,' she said.

'What do you mean?'

'Patrick. Patrick was sent a tape, of him with me. He thought I'd done it.'

'Patrick who, Penny?'

'Woolton. He thought I had made the tape of us in bed together to blackmail him. But it was someone else. It wasn't me.'

'So that's why he quit,' exclaimed Mattie. 'Who could have made the tape, Penny?'

'Don't know. Almost anybody at the party conference I suppose. Anyone in Bournemouth, anyone at the hotel.'

'But Penny, I don't understand! Who could have blackmailed Patrick Woolton? Who could have known you were sleeping with him?'

'Roger knew. But Roger would never . . .'

'Don't you see, Penny. Someone was blackmailing Roger, too. Someone who must have known he was on

357

drugs. Someone who forced him to leak opinion polls and alter computer files. Someone who . . .'

'Killed him!' The words unlocked the misery which Penny had been trying to hide since they had telephoned her earlier that morning. But now the barriers burst and tears were flooding from her eyes, forced out by the cries of anguish which racked her body. Further discussion with her was clearly impossible, and Mattie helped the sobbing girl into bed, making her as comfortable as she could. She stayed with her until the tears had emptied her soul and she was fast asleep.

Mattie walked down the street in confusion. The first snow of winter was beginning to fall gently around her, but she did not notice it. She was lost in her own misery of doubt. All the firm evidence she had led back to O'Neill. Now he was dead and the door at which she had been pushing, behind which she knew she would find the answer, had suddenly slammed shut on her. It was not the first time that the frustrated ambition of men had led to blackmail and violence – the appeal of political power had fascinated, seduced and corrupted men and women throughout the ages – but none had daubed blood on the door of 10 Downing Street. Until now. It had to be washed clean. She had a day to do it – and no idea where to go next.

'Come on, come on, come on, come on!' she shouted, beating her hands on the desk in frustration. As the day had turned to evening and she had tossed the facts around fruitlessly in her mind she had become more tense, unable to find any new direction. The clock had ticked remorselessly on, and she found her mind crossing the same old ground, travelling up the same blind alleys and discovering the same dead ends. The harder she tried, the more elusive any new insight became. Perhaps a change of scene might fire her imagination. So she had gone for a walk, driven around, taken a bath and was now sitting at home, crying for enlightenment. But it was to no avail. Her inspiration and intuition had failed her as the sleepless nights took their toll, and the one man who could answer all her burning questions was dead, taking his secrets with him. She buried her head in her hands, reduced to praying for a miracle in a world which God seemed to have deserted.

Something sparked. Later she could never recall what aroused it, but among the dying embers of her confidence a small flame began to glow and lick itself back to life. Perhaps it was not all over yet.

Two hours later Krajewski arrived clutching a large box of hot pizza. He had telephoned but got no answer. He was concerned, and was attempting to hide his concern beneath the pepperoni and extra cheese. He found Mattie sitting on the floor in the dark, huddled in the corner with her knees drawn up under her chin, clenching her arms around her tightly. She had been crying.

He said nothing but knelt beside her, and this time she allowed him to hug the tears away. It was some time before she could say anything.

'Johnnie, you told me that if I couldn't offer commitment I could never make it as a journalist, that I would be no better than a butterfly. I realise now that you were right. Until today I was simply chasing a story – oh, a big one, for sure, but what really mattered was ending up with my name at the top of the page one lead. Like a film – rooting out the wrongdoers from their hiding places, never giving a damn about the cost. I've been acting a role, the intrepid journalist struggling to unravel the lies in the face of overwhelming odds. But it's no longer a game, Johnnie . . .'

She looked into his eyes, and he saw that her tears were not tears of fear or pain, but tears of release, as if she had at last struggled from the clutches of the bog onto solid ground.

'All I wanted was a story, a great one. I threw away my job and I even trampled over your feelings just in case you got

359

in the way. Now I would give anything for the whole story to disappear, but it's too late.'

She gripped his hand, needing someone now. 'You see, Johnnie, none of it was coincidence. Woolton was deliberately blackmailed out of the leadership race. Somebody got rid of him, just as they got rid of Collingridge, of McKenzie, of Earle. And of O'Neill.'

'Do you realise what you're saying?'

'O'Neill's death was suicide or murder. And how many people have you ever heard of committing suicide in a public lavatory!'

'Mattie, this isn't the KGB we are dealing with.'

'As far as O'Neill is concerned, it may just as well have been.'

'Jesus!'

'Johnnie, there is someone out there who will stop at nothing to fix the election of the man who in a few hours' time will become the most powerful individual in the country.'

'That's terrifying. But who . . . ?'

She pounded the floor in anger.

'That's the bloody trouble. I don't know! I've been sitting here in the dark knowing that there is a man, a name, some clue which will reveal it all, but I just can't find it. Everything leads back to O'Neill, and now he's gone . . .'

'You are certain that it couldn't have been O'Neill, perhaps, who got so deeply involved . . . got scared. Lost control and killed himself?'

'No! Of course it wasn't O'Neill. It couldn't have been . . .'

The flame spluttered once more, warming her, its heat dispelling a little more of the mists of confusion which clung to her mind.

'Johnnie, while O'Neill played his part with most and possibly all of the leaks, he couldn't have done it by himself. Some of those leaks were from Government, not from the Party. Highly confidential information which

360

would not have been available to all members of the Cabinet, let alone a party official.'

She took a deep breath, as deep as if it were the first breath of fresh air she had taken in days.

'Do you see what that means, Johnnie. There must be a common link. There must be, if only we could find it . . .'

'Mattie, we can't give up now. There has to be a way. Look, have you got a list of Cabinet Ministers?'

'In the drawer of my work table.'

He leapt to his feet and scrabbled about in the drawer before coming up with the list. With a broad sweep of his arm he cleared all the papers, books and assorted debris off the top of her large work table, exposing its smooth, laminated white work surface. The whiteness of the desk was like an open page waiting to be filled. He grabbed an artist's pen and began scrawling down on the laminate all the twenty-two names from the sheet.

'OK. Who could have been responsible for the leaks? Come on, Mattie. Think!' The fire had caught inside him now.

Mattie did not move. She was frozen in the corner, all her last reserves of energy concentrated on sorting out the jumble in her mind.

'There were at least three leaks which had to come from inside the Cabinet,' she said at last. 'There were the Territorial Army cuts, the cancellation of the hospital expansion scheme, and the Renox drug approval. O'Neill would never have known about those first-hand. But who in Government would have?'

Slowly, she began reciting the Cabinet members who would have had early knowledge of the decisions. As she did so, Krajewski feverishly began ticking off the names on his list.

Who was on the Cabinet Committee which dealt with major military matters and would have made the decision on the TA cuts? Concentrate, Mattie, even though every part of your mind wants to go to sleep. Slowly the thoughts began to focus and take form. The Defence Secretary, the Financial Secretary, the Chancellor possibly, and of course the Prime Minister. Damn it, who else? Right, the Employment Secretary and the Foreign Secretary, too.

Then the hospital scheme which would have been considered by another Committee including the Health Secretary and the Treasury Ministers, the Trade and Industry Secretary, Education Secretary and Environment Secretary also. She prayed she hadn't missed any names. The membership and even existence of these committees were supposed to be a state secret, which meant the information was never formally published and was left to become yet another part of the Westminster system of lobby gossip. But the system was so effective she felt sure she had missed no names.

Was she getting closer? The Renox drug approval – damn, that wouldn't have been considered by any Cabinet Committee; it was a Department of Health decision and known solely to the Health Secretary and his Ministers. And of course the Prime Minister would have been informed in advance, but who else?

She leapt up to join Krajewski, who was staring at his handiwork.

'We seem to have screwed up rather badly, I'm afraid,' he muttered quietly.

She looked at the list. There was only one name with three ticks beside it, one man with access to all three bits of leaked information, one man whom her detective work could pronounce guilty. And that was the victim himself – the Prime Minister, Henry Collingridge! Her efforts had left them with the most absurd conclusion of all. The little flame of hope gave one last splutter and prepared to die.

She stood there staring. Something was wrong.

'Johnnie, this list of names. Why isn't Urquhart on it?'

She snorted in ridicule at herself as she provided her own answer. 'Because I'm a silly bitch and forgot that the Chief Whip is not technically a full member of Cabinet and so doesn't appear on my Cabinet list. But it makes no difference. He's not on the Defence Committee, nor could he have known about Renox.'

But she stopped with a gasp. The flame had suddenly sprung into life once again and was burning at her from deep inside.

'But of course . . . He's not formally a member, but if I remember correctly he does sit in on the committee which dealt with the hospital programme. He wouldn't have attended the defence committee, yet as he is responsible for parliamentary discipline they would have been sure to consult him well in advance about a decision which was going to cause uproar on the backbenches.'

'But he couldn't have known about Renox,' interjected Krajewski.

She was gripping his arm so tightly now that the nails were digging into the flesh.

'Johnnie, every Government Department has a Junior Whip attached to it, one of Urquhart's men, to make sure there is proper liaison about Government business. Every week most Secretaries of State hold a business meeting amongst their departmental Ministers to discuss the activities of the week ahead, and the Junior Whip usually attends. He then goes back and reports to the Chief Whip to ensure that Ministers don't trip over each other's feet. It *is* possible, Johnnie. Urquhart could have known . . .'

'But what about the rest of it. How would he have known about O'Neill's drug taking? Or Woolton's sex life? Or any of the other pieces?'

'Because he's Chief Whip. It's his job to know about those things. He had the means, and hell did he have a motive. From nowhere to Prime Minister in a couple of months! How on earth did we miss it?'

'But it's all still circumstantial, Mattie. You don't have a single shred of proof.'

'Then let's see if we can get it!'

She grabbed the phone and began punching a number.

'Penny? It's Mattie Storin. I'm sorry it's so late, but I need some answers. It's very important. I think I know who got Roger into all the trouble. Where did you meet Patrick Woolton?'

'At the Bournemouth party conference,' a sad voice replied.

'But in what circumstances? Please try to remember. Who introduced you?'

'Roger said he wanted to meet me, and took me along to a party to introduce us.'

'Where was the party?'

'At Mr Urquhart's. He had the bungalow right next door to Patrick's, and it was he who actually took me over to say hello to Patrick.'

'Did Roger know Francis Urquhart particularly well?'

'No, not really. At least not until recently. As far as I know they had scarcely spoken to each other before the election, but they have talked with each other a couple of times on the phone since then, and they met for dinner. I don't think even now they are – were – very close, though. Last time they spoke Roger was upset. Something about a computer file which got Roger very angry.'

At last the pieces began to fit.

'One more question, Penny. I presume Francis Urquhart has a country residence as well as his house in Pimlico. Do you happen to know where that is?'

'No, I don't I'm afraid. I've only got a list of Cabinet weekend telephone numbers which I keep for Roger.'

'Can I have the Urquhart number?'

'I can't, Mattie, they are absolutely confidential. You must remember there have been terrorist attacks at Ministers' homes, and it would be totally wrong for me to give them out to the press, even to you. I am sorry, Mattie, truly.'

'Can you tell me the area in which he lives? Not the address, just the town or even the county?'

'I don't know it. I've only got the telephone number.'

'Give me the dialling code, then. Just the dialling code,' she pleaded.

There was the sound of a slight shuffling of paper at the other end of the phone.

'Mattie, I'm not sure why you want it, but it is to help Roger, isn't it?'

'I promise you, Penny.'

'042128.'

'Thanks. You won't regret it.'

Mattie flicked the receiver and got a new line. She punched the area code into the telephone, followed by a random set of numbers. A connection was made, and a phone started ringing at the other end.

'Lyndhurst 37428,' a drowsy voice announced.

'Good evening. I'm sorry to bother you so late. Is that Lyndhurst, Surrey, 37428?'

'No. It's Lyndhurst in Hampshire 37428. And it's very late for you to be telephoning wrong numbers!' an irritated voice snapped before the phone was disconnected.

The fire inside Mattie was roaring brightly now as she threw herself across the room towards her bookcase, where she ripped a road atlas from its place. She scrabbled through the maps until she found the South Coast section, jabbed a finger at the page and whooped with triumph.

'It's him, Johnnie. It's him!'

He looked over her shoulder at where the finger was placed. It was pointing directly at the Rownhams service area on the M27 where O'Neill had died. It was the first service station on the motorway back to London from Lyndhurst. O'Neill had died less than eight miles from Urquhart's country home.

TUESDAY 30TH NOVEMBER

The morning newspapers fell onto the doormats of a million homes like a death knell for Samuel's candidacy. One by one, editor by editor, they began to line up behind Urquhart. It was not surprising to the Chief Whip that all the newspapers in the Telegraph and United Newspapers groups came to the same conclusion – some with more enthusiasm than others, to be sure, but to the same conclusion nonetheless – but it was of even greater satisfaction that many of the others had also decided to throw their weight behind him. Editorial offices tend to provide little comfort for politicians who trail their consciences; and some still remembered how badly their papers had got their fingers burnt with Neville Chamberlain's pious bits of paper. Others had reached the same cynical conclusion as Woolton about the drawbacks of creating another 'era' so soon after Thatcher which, with Samuel's youth, could last another fifteen years or more. Phrases such as 'experience', 'maturity' and 'balance' were peppered freely around the columns. Still others wanted simply to play safe, wishing to swim with the tide which was flooding strongly in Urquhart's favour.

Only two newspapers stood out amongst the quality press, the *Guardian* for its habit of deliberately swimming against the tide, requiring it to support Samuel, and the *Independent* which stood proud and isolated like a rock withstanding the battering of storms and tide, refusing to endorse either.

The mood was reflected in the two camps, with Urquhart's supporters finding it difficult to hide their air of quiet confidence, and Samuel's finding it impossible in private to disguise their sense of looming disappointment.

As the tall doors of Committee Room 14 swung open at 10 a.m. to accept the first batch of MPs waiting outside to vote, neither Sir Humphrey nor others present expected any disappointments.

In best traditional style it would be an orderly and gentlemanly ballot; the loser would be gracious and the winner even more so. The covering of snow which was beginning steadily to blanket Westminster gave the proceedings a surrealistic calm. It would be Christmas soon, it reminded them, and the lights had already long been switched on in Oxford Street. Time soon for the winter break, for family reunions and peace on earth. The long period of indecision would be over in a few hours and ordinary folk could return to their normal lives. In public there would be handshakes and congratulations all the way round when the result was announced, even as in private the victors planned their recriminations and the losers plotted their revenge.

When Mattie walked towards the office of Benjamin Landless just off Charterhouse Square, the snow was several inches thick. Outside the capital the snow had settled much more deeply, making travel difficult and persuading many commuters simply to stay at home. The streets of the City of London were strangely quiet in their white cocoon as the falling flakes muffled all sound and the few cars crept quietly about their business. She felt unreal, as if she were on a film set acting out a role, hoping she would wake up in the morning and discover that the script had been changed. Even now she was tempted to turn around and forget all about it, to let others concern themselves about the great affairs of state while she concentrated on paying her mortgage and whether she could afford a holiday next year.

Then a flurry of snow blew into her face, blinding her and transporting her back many years before she was born to an isolated Norwegian fjord and her grandfather setting off in a leaking fishing boat to risk his life on the tides of war. He could have collaborated, turned a blind eye, left it to others to sort out the world while he got on with his own life. But something had driven him on, just as she was being driven now.

When at first she had realised the necessity of confronting Landless, she had discovered all the many reasons why it would be futile – she wouldn't even get to see him; if she did he would ruthlessly ensure that she would never work as a journalist again, and she wouldn't be the first such victim. She had seen him bully and intimidate so many, how could she expect to succeed where so many other more experienced and powerful hands had failed? She had to confront him yet she desperately needed his help. And how was she supposed to squeeze support from a man who instinctively would prefer to throttle her with his own huge hands?

It was only when she realised that she had run out of time and alternatives that she summoned up the courage to unravel her excuses and deal with them one by one. Her first problem was access to the heavily protected businessman. He may depict himself as a man of the people, but he took elaborate and expensive precautions to ensure that he did not have to rub shoulders with them.

So she had phoned the writer of the *Telegraph*'s diary column, the keeper of society's gossip and scandal. Had Landless recently had any close female friends, women of whom he was known to be particularly fond? Fine! A lady twenty years younger than him, now safely ensconced in Wiltshire with a new husband and brood, but known to have been the favoured recipient of a large measure of the magnate's hugely expensive overtime. Mrs Susannah Richards. Yes, she hoped that would do nicely.

But nothing seemed easy as she walked along the strange, empty streets. She arrived at her destination and shook the snow from her boots and hair. She was surprised to see how small were the offices from which Landless ran his many empires, and how opulently the East-Ender had learned to live. The place reeked of British tradition. The small foyer and reception area was cloaked almost entirely in English carved oak panelling, on which were hung several fine oil paintings of old London scenes and a vast portrait of the Queen. The carpeting was thick, the electronics sophisticated and the commissionaire very ex-military.

'Can I help you, Miss?' he asked from beneath his pencil-line moustache.

'My name is Mrs Susannah Richards. I am a personal friend of Mr Landless, you understand,' she explained with a hint of intrigue, 'and I was passing in the vicinity. He's not expecting me, but could you see if he has five minutes free? I have an important personal message for him.'

The commissionaire was all discretion and efficiency – it was so rare that one of the boss's 'personal friends' came to the office, and he was eager to make a good impression. He relayed the message to Landless's secretary precisely and with just the right degree of enthusiasm. No doubt the secretary passed on the message in similar fashion, for within a few seconds Mattie was being ushered into the lift with instructions to proceed to the top floor.

As she stood in the doorway of the penthouse suite, Landless was seated behind his desk in the middle of a vast office which had been designed to accommodate his own huge bulk. She had time to take in none of the detail before an animal growl of rage began erupting from his throat.

'You miserable bloody cow . . .'

She had to cut him short. Before he had time to make up his mind, let alone utter the angry words of dismissal, she had to take control. It was her only slender chance.

'It's your takeover of United.'

'The takeover? What about it?' he shouted, betraying only the slightest edge of interest.

'It's finished.'

'What on earth do you mean?' he snarled, but a little less loudly this time.

She stood there, silent, challenging him to decide whether his curiosity would overcome his anger. It took a moment before she knew she had won the first round. With a snort, he waved a fleshy hand in the direction of a chair. It was a good six inches lower than his own, down onto which he could glower from beneath his huge, eruptive eyebrows and stare its occupant into submission. She moved slowly into the room, but away from the chair. She wasn't going to give him the advantage of physically intimidating her on the low, uncomfortable perch. Anyway, she felt better moving around.

'You've backed the wrong horse. Francis Urquhart has cheated and lied his way to the party leadership, and possibly much worse. By the time that all gets out, his endorsement of the takeover won't be worth a bean.'

'But he hasn't endorsed the takeover. He said he wouldn't decide until after the leadership election.'

'But you and I know that is only part of the deal you did with him – the support of your newspapers in return for his approval of the takeover after he had won.'

'What the hell are you talking about? You listen to me, you little bitch . . .'

'No, Mr Landless. It's you who's going to have to listen to me!' She was smiling now, trying to display the quiet confidence of a poker player intent on persuading her opponent that the cards she held were of much higher value than his own. She had no proof, of course, only the coincidence of timing to suggest a deal had been done, but now she understood about Urquhart it was the only scenario which made sense. Anyway, she had to keep raising the stakes, she had to force him to show his hand.

'You see, you are not the first proprietor to put puppets into their newspapers as editors, but you made a great mistake when you chose Greville Preston. The man is so weak that every time you pulled the strings he started jerking around totally out of control. He couldn't possibly pretend that he was his own boss. So when you, Mr Landless, decided to go gunning for Henry Collingridge at the party conference, there was no chance that Preston could pretend it was his own decision or hide the fact that he was acting under your direct instructions. And when *you*, Mr Landless, decided to propel Francis Urquhart into the leadership race at the last, dramatic minute through the editorial columns of the *Telegraph*, there was no chance that Preston could justify it to the staff. He had to slip it into the edition on a Sunday evening without any consultation, skulking around his own newspaper like a thief in the night. You see, he's very good at doing what he's told, but he simply doesn't understand half the time why he's been told to do it. If you like to put it that way, Mr Landless, in spite of all his university education you're too good for him.'

Landless did not respond to the backhanded compliment. His fleshy features were set uncharacteristically rigid.

'You made Urquhart's candidacy. Put quite simply – as I am sure you have put it to him yourself – he could not be on the point of becoming Prime Minister without your help. And for that you would have got something in return – his agreement to turn the Government's competition policy on its head and to endorse your takeover of United Newspapers.'

At last Landless came to life, calling her bluff.

'What proof do you have of this extraordinary tale, Miss Storin?'

'That's the beauty of it. I don't need proof. I need just enough to stir up the most awful public row and you will find the politicians deserting your camp and heading for the hills, no matter what they have been saying during the leadership contest. You will find yourself without a single friend.'

'But according to your weird and wonderful hypothesis,

Francis Urquhart is my friend, and he will be in 10 Downing Street,' Landless smiled mockingly.

'But not for long, Mr Landless, not for long. I'm afraid you know less about him than you think. Did you know, when you instructed Preston to use the opinion poll to undermine the Prime Minister, that it was Urquhart who had leaked it in the first place? He set you up.'

There was a sufficient look of surprise on Landless's face to let Mattie know that she was right and he resented being used like that.

'But all politicians leak,' Landless responded. 'It's not criminal, certainly not enough to throw him out of Downing Street.'

'No, but insider share dealing, fraud, blackmail and theft are!' She delighted in the look of concern spreading across his fat jowls.

'I can show beyond a reasonable doubt that it was Urquhart who set up Charles Collingridge by buying Renox shares in his name in a deliberate and very successful attempt to implicate the Prime Minister. That Urquhart blackmailed Patrick Woolton into standing down by bugging his room at Bournemouth. And ordered the theft of confidential personal files on Michael Samuel from party headquarters.' She was bluffing on the Samuel file, she had no proof only inner certainty, but she knew her bluff would not be called from the way in which Landless had by now lost his air of confidence. Yet he was one of nature's fighters. He hadn't given in yet.

'What makes you think anyone is going to believe you? By tonight Francis Urquhart will be Prime Minister, and who do you think is going to want to see the Prime Minister and the country dragged down by a political scandal of that sort? I think you underestimate the Establishment and its powers of self-protection, Miss Storin. If the Prime Minister is dragged down, confidence in the whole system suffers. It's not justice which wins, but the radicals and the revolutionaries. Not even the Opposition would welcome that. So you'll find it damned difficult to get any newspaper to print your allegations, and next to impossible to get a law officer to proceed on them.'

He was beginning to relish his own argument now, regaining his confidence.

'Why, it took them seven years before they were forced to indict Jeremy Thorpe who was only Leader of the Liberal Party, not even the Prime Minister. And he was arrested for attempted murder, which makes your charges of petty theft and blackmail look really rather pathetic. You don't even have a body on which to build your case!'

'Oh, but I do, Mr Landless,' she said softly. 'I believe he killed Roger O'Neill to silence him, and although I'm not sure I can prove it yet, I can raise such a storm as will blow down the shutters of Downing Street and will quite overwhelm your little business venture. Someone in the Thorpe case shot a dog. Here we are talking about murder. Do you really think your Establishment is going to keep quiet about that?'

Landless levered his great girth out of his chair and walked across to the large picture window. From it he could see the chimneys, steeples and hideous tower blocks of Bethnal Green less than two miles away where he had been born and where in the slums of his childhood he had learnt all he needed to know about survival. He had never wanted to move far away from the area even with all his wealth; his roots were there, and if he screwed it all up that was where he knew he would have to return.

When he turned around to face her once more, she thought she could detect the signs of defeat etched deep into his features.

'What are you going to do, Miss Storin?'

'I am too late to stop Urquhart getting elected. But I intend to make sure he stays in office for as short a time as possible. And for that I want your help.'

'My help! I . . . I don't understand. You accuse me of causing all this bleedin' chaos and then you ask for my help. Christ all bloody Mighty!' he spluttered in broadest cockney, his defences in tatters.

'Let me explain. You may be a rogue, Mr Landless, and you may run a rotten newspaper, but I suspect that deep down you care for the idea of a man like Urquhart running this country as little as I do. You have worked very hard to develop the reputation of a working class patriot. Corny to some people, perhaps, but I suspect you mean it – and if I'm right, you would never dream of conspiring to put a murderer in Downing Street.'

She paused but he said nothing.

'In any event, I think I can persuade you to help on straightforward commercial grounds. Whatever happens, your takeover of United Newspapers is dead. You can either watch it be swept away in the storm which will undoubtedly engulf Urquhart, which means the Establishment will turn on you and you will never be able to raise money in the City of London for a business deal ever again – or you can kill it yourself, help me nail Urquhart, save your business and become the hero of the hour.'

'Why should I trust you?'

'Because I need you.'

'Need me?' his jowls fluttered in surprise.

'I need you to be a good newspaper man and publish the full story. If it's published with the backing of the *Telegraph* rather than dribbling out over the next few months in bits and pieces, nobody can ignore it. I will give you an exclusive which will blow your patriotic socks off. And once I've done that, I am scarcely going to be able to turn on you.'

'And if I say no?'

'Then I shall find an army of Opposition backbenchers who would like nothing more than to take all the ammunition I can provide them with, stand up in the House of Commons where they are protected from the laws of slander, and make accusations against both you and Urquhart which will bring you crashing down together.'

All her cards were on the table now. The game was nearly over. Had he any cards left up his sleeve?

'Urquhart will fall, Mr Landless, one way or the other. The only thing you have to decide is whether you fall with him or help me push him . . .'

It was early afternoon before Mattie returned to Westminster. The snow had stopped falling and the skies were clearing, leaving the capital looking like a scene from a traditional Christmas card. The Houses of Parliament looked particularly resplendent, like some wondrous Christmas cake covered in brilliant white icing beneath a crystal blue sky. Opposite in the churchyard of St Margaret's, nestling under the wing of the great medieval Abbey, carol singers brought an air of tranquillity and Victorian charm to the passers-by, wishing goodwill to all men.

Celebrations were already under way in various parts of the House of Commons. One of Mattie's colleagues in the press gallery rushed over to explain.

'About 80 per cent of Government MPs have already voted. They think Urquhart's home and dry. It looks like a landslide.'

Big Ben tolled; to Mattie it had a new and awesome ring. She felt as if an icicle had dislodged itself from the Palace walls and pierced straight into her heart. But she had to press on.

Urquhart was not in his room, nor in any of the bars or restaurants in the Palace of Westminster. She asked in vain around the corridors after him and was just about to conclude that he had left the premises entirely, for lunch or interviews, when one of the Palace policemen told her that he had seen Urquhart not ten minutes earlier headed in the direction of the roof garden. She had no idea that any roof garden existed, or even where it was.

'Yes, miss. Not many people do know about our roof garden, and those that do like to keep quiet about it in case everybody rushes up there and spoils the charm. It's directly above the House of Commons, all around the great central skylights which light up the Chamber itself. It's a flat roof terrace, and we've put some tables and chairs up there so that in summer the staff can enjoy the sunshine, take some sandwiches and a flask of coffee. Not many Members know about it and even fewer ever go up there, but I've seen Mr Urquhart up there a couple of times before. Likes the view, I imagine. But it'll be damned cold and lonely today, if you don't mind my saying so.'

She followed his directions, up the stairs past the Strangers Gallery and up again until she had passed the panelled dressing room reserved for the Palace doorkeepers. Then she saw a fire door which was slightly ajar. As she stepped through it she emerged onto the roof, and drew in her breath sharply. The view was magnificent. Right in front of her, towering into the cloudless sky, made brilliant in the sunshine and snow, was the tower of Big Ben, closer than she had ever seen it before. Every little detail of the beautifully crafted stone stood out with stunning clarity, and she could see the tremor of the great clock hands as the ancient but splendid mechanism pursued its remorseless course.

To the left she could see the great tiled roof of Westminster Hall, the oldest part of the Palace, which had survived the assault of fire, war, bomb and revolution and which had witnessed so much human achievement and misery. To her right she could see the River Thames, ebbing and flowing in its own irresistible fashion even as the tides of history swept capriciously along its banks. And in front of her she could see fresh footsteps in the snow.

He was there, standing by the balustrade at the far end of the terrace, looking out beyond the rooftops of Whitehall, north to where he knew the moors of his childhood still beckoned. He had never seen the view like this before, blanketed in snow. The sky was as clear as the air in the

377

Scottish valleys he had deserted; the rooftops carpeted in white he imagined to be the rolling moors on which he had spent so many enthralling hours hunting with the gillie; the steeples became the copses of spruce in which they had hidden while they watched the progress of the deer. On a day such as this, he felt as if he could see right to the heart of his old Perthshire home, and beyond even to the heart of eternity. It was all his now.

He could see the white stone walls of the Home Office, behind which lay Buckingham Palace where, later that evening, he would be driven in triumph. There stood the Foreign Office, and next to it the Treasury at the entrance to Whitehall which he would shortly command more effectively than any hereditary king. Before him were spread the great offices of state which he would soon dispense and dominate in a way which would at last lay to rest his father's haunting accusations and recompense for all the bitterness and loneliness to which he had so long condemned himself.

He was startled as he realised that someone was at his elbow.

'Miss Storin!' he exclaimed. 'This is a surprise. I didn't think anyone would find me here – but you seem to have a habit of tracking me down. What is it this time – another exclusive interview?'

'I hope it will be very exclusive, Mr Urquhart.'

'You know, I remember you were right in on the start. You were the first person ever to ask if I were going to stand for the leadership.'

'Perhaps it is appropriate that I should also be in on the end . . .'

'What do you mean?'

The time had come.

'Perhaps you should read this. It's the Press Association copy I have just taken from the printer.'

She pulled out of her shoulder bag a short piece of news agency copy which she handed to him.

In a surprise development, Mr Benjamin Landless has announced that he has withdrawn his takeover offer for the United Newspapers Group.

In a brief statement, Landless indicated that he had been approached by senior political figures asking for editorial and financial support in exchange for their approval of the merger.

'In such circumstances,' he said, 'I think it to be in the national interest that the deal be suspended. I do not wish the reputation of my company in any way to be impugned by the reprehensible and possibly corrupt activity which has begun to infect this transaction.'

Landless announced that he hoped to be able to release further details after he had consulted with his lawyers.

'I don't understand. What does this mean?' asked Urquhart in a calm voice. But Mattie noticed that he had crumpled the news release up in his clenched fist.

'It means, Mr Urquhart, that I know the full story. Now so does Benjamin Landless. And in a few days so will every newspaper reader in the country.'

A frown crossed his brow. There was no anger or anguish in his face yet, like a soldier who had been shot but whose nervous system had still to allow the pain to prize away the blanket of numbness which the shock had wrapped about him. But Mattie could have no mercy. She reached into her shoulder bag yet again, extracting a small tape recorder, and pressed a button. The tape which Landless had given Mattie began to turn and in the quiet, snow-clad air they could hear very distinctly the voices of the newspaper proprietor and the Chief Whip as they conspired together. The conversation was unambiguous, the recording of remarkable clarity and the contents unmistakably criminal as the two plotted to exchange editorial endorsement for political endorsement.

Mattie pressed another button, and the voices stopped.

'I don't know whether you make a habit of taping all your colleagues' bedrooms, or just Patrick Woolton's, but I can assure you that Benjamin Landless tapes all of his telephone conversations,' she said.

Urquhart's face had frozen in the winter's air. He was beginning to feel the pain now.

'Tell me, Mr Urquhart. I know you blackmailed Roger O'Neill into opening the false address in Paddington for Charles Collingridge, but when the police investigate will they find his or your signature on the bank account?'

There was silence.

'Come now, as soon as I go to the authorities you will have to tell them everything, so why not tell me first?'

More silence.

'I know you and O'Neill between you leaked opinion polls and the news about the Territorial Army cuts. I know you also got him to enter a false computer file on Charles Collingridge into the Party's central computer – he didn't care for that, did he? I suspect he was even less excited about stealing the Party's confidential files on Michael Samuel. But one thing I'm not sure about. Was it you or Roger who concocted that silly tale about the cancelled publicity campaign on the hospital expansion scheme to feed to Stephen Kendrick?'

At last Urquhart managed to speak. He was breathing deeply, trying to hide the tension inside.

'You have a vivid imagination.'

'Oh, if only I did, Mr Urquhart, I would have caught you much earlier. No, it's not imagination which is going to expose you. It's this tape,' she said, patting the recorder she held in her hand. 'And the report which Mr Landless is going to publish at great length in the *Telegraph*.'

Now Urquhart visibly flinched.

'But Landless wouldn't . . . couldn't!'

'Oh, you don't think Mr Landless is going to take any of the blame, do you? No. He's going to make you the fall guy, Mr Urquhart. Don't you realise? They are never going to let you be Prime Minister. I will write it, he will publish it, and you will never get to Downing Street.'

He shook his head in disbelief. A thin, cruel smile began to cross his lips. He couldn't tell whether it was the freezing weather or the frost he felt inside him, but he had that cold, tingling sensation up his spine once more. His breathing was steadier now, his hunter's instincts restoring his sense of physical control.

'I don't suppose you would be willing to . . . ?' He let out a low, chilling laugh. 'No, of course not. Silly of me. You seem to have thought of almost everything, Miss Storin.'

'Not quite everything. How did you kill Roger O'Neill?'

So she had that, too. The frost finally gripped his heart. His ice-blue hunter's eyes did not flicker. His body was motionless, tense, ready for action. At last he knew how his brother had felt, yet this was no iron-clad enemy which confronted him but a stupid, vulnerable, defenceless young woman. Only one of them could survive, and it must be him!

His voice was soft, almost a whisper, melting into the snow around them. 'Rat poison. It was so simple. I mixed it with his cocaine.' His piercing eyes were fixed on Mattie; she was no longer hunter, but prey. 'He was so weak, he deserved to die.'

'No one deserves to die, Mr Urquhart.'

But he was no longer listening. He was hunting, in a game of life or death whose rules allowed no respect for moral clichés. When he gazed down the gun sights at a deer he did not debate whether the deer deserved to die, nature decreed that some must die in order for others to survive and triumph. No one, particularly now, was going to deprive him of his triumph.

With surprising energy for a man of his age, he picked up one of the heavy wooden chairs from the terrace and held it aloft, poised to strike down at her head. But she did not cower as he had expected. She stood her ground, defiant in front of him, even as she tried to comprehend her own danger.

'In cold blood, Mr Urquhart? Face to face, in cold blood?'

This was like no prey he had ever hunted. Here, face to face, not a thousand impersonal yards away down a rifle sight but staring right back into his eyes! As her words pierced home, the moment was broken. The look of doubt crept into his eyes, and in a single bound his stag and his courage had disappeared. He gave a whimper as the chair dropped from his hands and the awful truth of his own cowardice dawned upon him. He had faced his challenge, a fight to the death, confronted the truth, and had failed. He sank to his knees in the deep snow.

'You can't prove a thing. It's your word against mine,' he whispered.

Mattie said nothing at first, but pressed the rewind button on her recorder. As the tape spun round, she looked down upon Urquhart, who was shivering violently.

'Your final mistake, Mr Urquhart. You thought I switched it off.' She punched yet another button. As she did so, the clearly recorded words of their conversation filled the air, damning him in every syllable, the proof which would condemn him.

As she walked slowly away, leaving him wretched in the snow, the silence in his head was filled with the ghostly, mocking laughter of his father.

The setting sun pierced through the frosty sky. As it did so, it glanced off the snow-covered tower of Big Ben and cascaded into a thousand tiny streams of light, blinding the American tourist who was trying to capture the scene on video.

He was quite clear later in his description of what had happened.

'The Parliament building had suddenly become like a

great torch, set alight by the sun. It was really a beautiful sight, as if the whole building were ablaze. And then from way up under Big Ben, something seemed to fall. As if a moth had flown into the heart of an immense candle, and its blackened and charred body was falling all the way to the ground. It's difficult to believe it was a man, one of your politicians. What did you say his name was?'

She was tired, desperately tired, yet she felt an unaccustomed peace. The struggle with her memories was over, the pain purged. She could stop running now.

He sensed the change and could see it reflected in her exhausted but triumphant eyes. 'You know,' he mused, 'I think you might make a halfway decent journalist after all.'

'Johnnie, I think you may just be right,' she said softly. 'Let's go home.'

Fontana Paperbacks: Fiction

Fontana is a leading paperback publisher of fiction.
Below are some recent titles.

- ☐ THE SCROLL OF BENEVOLENCE John Trenhaile £3.99
- ☐ A CANDLE FOR JUDAS David Fraser £3.50
- ☐ THE FIREMAN Stephen Leather £2.99
- ☐ BLACKLIST Andrew Taylor £3.50
- ☐ SACRIFICIAL GROUND Thomas H. Cook £3.50
- ☐ THE GREEN REAPERS R. W. Jones £3.99
- ☐ THE BLIND KNIGHT Gail van Asten £2.99
- ☐ GLITTERSPIKE HALL Mike Jefferies £6.99

You can buy Fontana paperbacks at your local bookshop or
newsagent. Or you can order them from Fontana Paperbacks,
Cash Sales Department, Box 29, Douglas, Isle of Man. Please
send a cheque, postal or money order (not currency) worth the
purchase price plus 22p per book for postage (maximum postage
required is £3.00 for orders within the UK).

NAME (Block letters)_____

ADDRESS_____

_____